I0552892

CONTENTS

To Gus

For bringing to life the Isle of Skye and the Philadelphia, in all of their dieselpunk, Art Deco greatness.

Voyage of the Skye

Book Two in the Isle of Skye Series

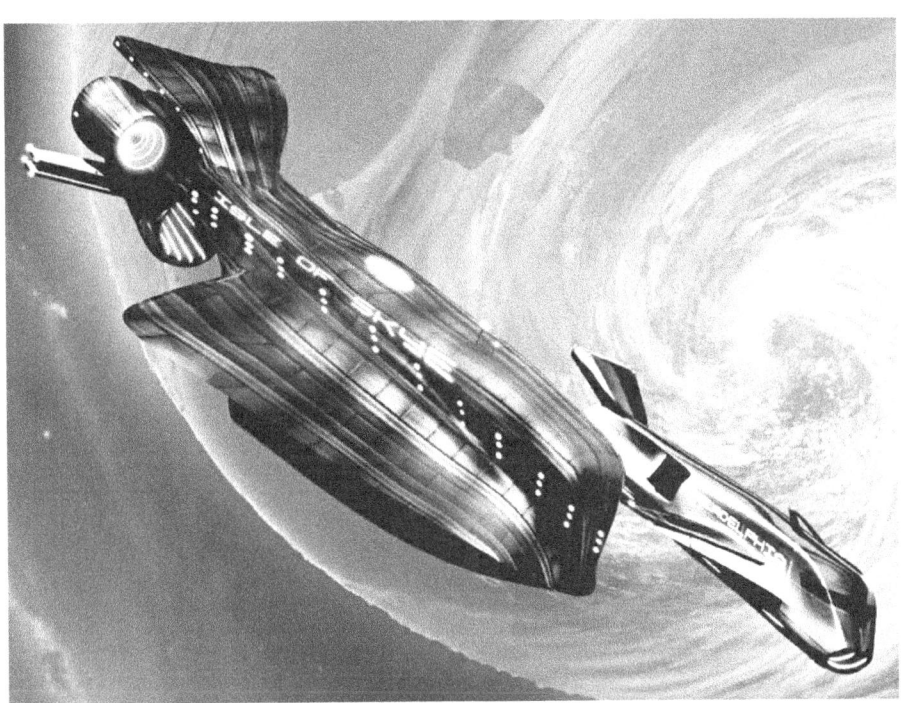

This is a work of fiction. Names, characters, businesses, places, events, locales, and incidents are either the products of the author's imagination or used in a fictitious manner. Any resemblance to actual persons, living or dead, or actual events is purely coincidental.

ISBN: 979-8-9897322-2-7

Cover art, *Isle of Skye* design, and *Philadelphia* design by Gus Amaral (instagram: @mr.goose_art)

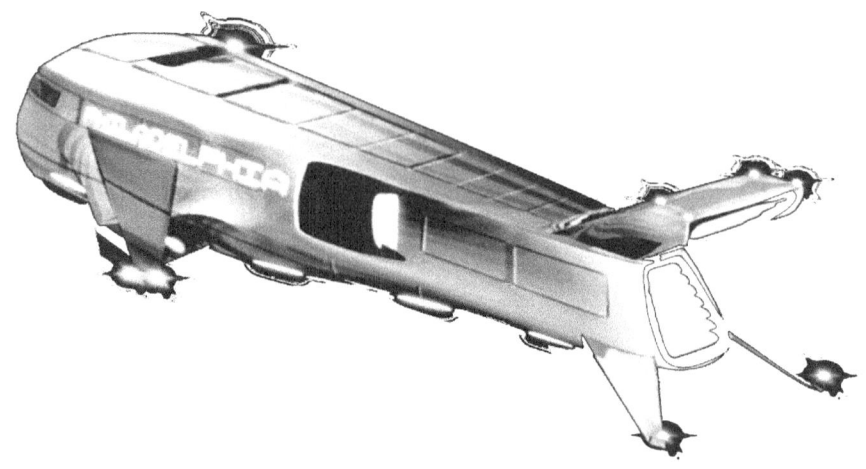

1. FROSTBITE I

Dax promises ribeyes, Philly Cheesesteak swats Jason, Gideon shoots his revolver, Kiwi cracks her whip, and Noora does not have a Merry Christmas.

Dax strolled into the mess hall, enjoying the Christmas lights and the makeshift, welded-together Christmas tree that Kiwi had made in her spare time. A few presents were under it.

He went to pour himself some coffee, just as Kiwi stumbled in, rubbing her eyes and wearing a tank top, shorts, and a floppy Santa hat.

"Jesus Christ, Dax," she said. "You sure you're plowing the right hole? I swear I heard Noora screaming through the bulkheads last night."

"Merry Christmas," Dax said, knowing that was Kiwi's way of saying she was happy for him.

"Merry Christmas, you fucking animal," she said, yawning, and pouring herself some coffee.

"By the way, you're looking cut," Dax said, pointing to her arms.

"Oh thank you!" Kiwi squealed. "Yeah, I've been working out with Noora since we left the solar system. She's showing me how to get all buff."

"So what do you got for me on the ship's systems?" Dax asked.

Kiwi huffed. "Can I have, like, three seconds to drink my coffee first?"

Dax mentally counted three seconds, then said, "All right, so what do you got for me?"

Kiwi huffed again, pulled out her phone, and queued up the *Skye's* systems report. "Ah shit, looks like the gravity field is acting up in the main corridors, and the Liminal's targeting system shorted out again."

Dax sighed. "Well, Merry Fucking Christmas, indeed," he said.

Noora entered the mess, a light bounce in her step. She came up to Dax, put an arm around him, pecked his head with a kiss, and said, "Hey."

"Hey," Dax returned, warmly.

Kiwi smiled to herself, happy to see the two of them together.

Jason dragged himself into the mess.

"Oh look," Kiwi said. "It's fuckboy."

"The one and only," Jason said, pouring himself some coffee, then sitting down with Dax, Kiwi, and Noora.

Gideon made his way into the mess. "Good morning everyone, and Merry Christmas."

"Merry Christmas," Jason said, holding up his coffee again.

"Merry Christmas!" Noora said.

Philly Cheesesteak sauntered into the mess from an air vent, and chirped, "*Br-r-r-reh!*" before going up to Jason and swatting his leg.

"Hey, watch it!" Jason said.

"How are systems this morning?" Gideon asked.

"Gravity's acting up in the main corridors, and the targeting system for the Liminal has shorted out again," Dax said.

"Again?" Gideon said. "Well get at it when you're done here. Make sure it's working properly when we come out of vector space."

Dax frowned, curious at Gideon's priorities. "You, uh, you expecting trouble in Lacaille?"

Gideon gave a vague response. "More like I wanna make sure we're good on all fronts."

"Hey," Kiwi said. "Since everyone's here, we should do Christmas." She got up and fetched the few presents under the spot-welded tree. Hers were the only ones.

She gave a small package to Noora, a bottle-sized package to Dax and Gideon, and a three-foot-long, rod-sized package to Jason.

Dax and Gideon opened theirs. "Oh, thanks," Dax said. "Been wondering where you hide your stash of Twin Diesel bourbon."

"I mean I usually go for Scotch, but thank you, Kiwi," Gideon said.

"Well I would've gotten you some Scotch but you didn't exactly give us enough notice when we left Earth, now did you," Kiwi said.

Noora opened her present. "Oh my gahd, are these .45-70s?" she asked, holding a pack of cartridges.

"Yes!" Kiwi confirmed. "I printed a bunch in the armory. I know your powered lever-action rifle is your favorite."

Jason opened his present. "A steel rod?" he asked.

"Yes," Kiwi confirmed. "So you can finally go fuck yourself."

"You've been telling me to go fuck myself for the last five weeks."

"Exactly! And now you can!" Kiwi looked over to the metal Christmas tree, noting there were no other presents underneath it. "Well, Merry Christmas, everyone."

"Well, actually," Noora said. "It's not much, but I have a bottle of Finnish mead I was gonna break out for dinner tonight."

"Yeah," Dax said. "And I'm making ribeyes tonight, so that's my gift to everyone."

"And, actually," Jason said, tapping at his phone. "Here's my Christmas present to you guys. The entire Ralston database as of when we left the solar system five weeks ago."

Everyone else opened their phones, their jaws going wide. They couldn't believe Jason had stolen his previous employer's entire database.

"Holy shit."

"Holy shit."

"Holy shet!"

"Goddamn," Gideon said, looking at his phone. "Just like that, huh?"

Jason shrugged his shoulders. "They fired me. They blacklisted me. Fuck em. Merry Christmas."

"Are you—" Dax started, "holy shit, man. You could spend years going through this."

"That you could," Jason confirmed.

"How did you get your hands on this?" Dax asked.

Jason winked. "Can't give away all my secrets."

Kiwi punched away at her phone, looking up any info they had on the *Isle of Skye*. "Pfff," she blurted. "Well, they're not up to date. They think we're a crew of four."

"Makes sense," Gideon said. "Jason only just joined us before we took off, and I haven't added him to the crew manifest."

Jason had a confused scowl. "Oh. Okay?"

"Don't take it personally," Gideon said. "Noora was with us for a while before she officially joined."

Noora nodded. "It's true. It wasn't until after I—" she said, cutting herself off and looking down in shame. "It wasn't until after I shot off your engine that I became part of the crew."

"Oh," Jason said, confused again. "I thought that was you," he said, pointing to Kiwi.

"I mean," Kiwi said. "I *did* tell her to shoot."

"By the way," Noora said. "Did, like, anyone die when that happened?"

"You mean anyone on the *Sentinel*?" Jason asked. "No. A lot of bruised egos, but no deaths."

Noora sighed in relief. "Oh thank god. That's always bugged me, like, I always hoped I hadn't killed anyone."

"Well, Gideon," Kiwi said. "Did you get us anything for Christmas?"

"As a matter of fact," Gideon said, making a series of taps on his phone. Everyone else's phones chirped a notification. "Don't spend it all in one place."

"Oh damn, thanks, man," Dax said.

"Oh shit, thank you, Gideon," Noora said.

"Where the fuck are we supposed to spend this out here?" Kiwi asked. "Do small, backwater colonies take digital space currency?"

"You're welcome, Kiwi," Gideon said. "And the answer is yes, assuming they want to trade with anyone like us coming from the solar system."

Jason, confused yet again, said, "I thought I wasn't getting a paycheck."

"Not a paycheck, a Christmas bonus," Gideon said. "And, uh, thank you for Ralston's database. Imagine I'll lose myself in that for hours."

"Well," Jason said. "Thank you very much."

"Right then," Gideon said. "Not to break the mood, but Dax and Kiwi, get on our systems' issues, Noora and Jason, help them out where you can, and Philly Cheesesteak, be a nice boy today and maybe Dax will give you some ribeye tonight."

Philly Cheesesteak licked his mouth.

Gideon, Noora, and Jason were on the bridge. Dax and Kiwi were at the opposite end of the ship in engineering.

Philly Cheesesteak was lurking somewhere in the vents.

"Dax, Kiwi," Gideon said. "You two ready to cut the vector drive?"

"*Yeah,*" Dax answered. "*Looking to cut it in 30 seconds. Noora, that look good to you?*"

"Roger that, Dax," Noora said from her station.

"Hey Dax," Gideon said.

"*Yeah?*"

"How come I can start the vector drive but I can't shut it off?"

"*Because you need me and Kiwi to make sure everything shuts down properly.*"

"You can't just rig up an off switch for that?"

"No, because—oh shit, coming out of vector space in three, two —"

A gentle lurch went through the *Isle of Skye*, then all was normal. The low-frequency humming that echoed through the ship during vector space was gone.

"Noora, how we looking?" Gideon asked.

"We're, um," Noora said, checking her monitor.

Jason also checked his monitor and said, "Goddamn."

"Um, yeah, what he said," Noora said. "We're right on target, looks like just a few hours from Lacaille 9352-C."

"Goddamn," Gideon echoed.

"That's what you call a Finnish snipe from 11-light years away, baby!" Kiwi said over the intercom.

"Yeah," Dax said. *"That's, uh, that's insane we're so close."*

Noora smiled, trying not to let her accuracy go to her head.

Gideon tapped at his monitor, reorienting the *Skye* to come into an orbit around the third planet of Lacaille 9352, when Dax shouted over the intercom.

"Whoah whoah whoah! SLOWLY! Remember, we're flying extra heavy. You reorient the ship too quickly and we'll shear apart!"

"Right," Gideon said. "Sorry about that." He adjusted the *Skye's* heading accordingly, making his maneuvers as slow as possible. He then opened up communications and said, "Lacaille 9352-C, this is the *Isle of Skye*. We've just come out of vector space and are approaching orbit. Requesting communications at your convenience, over."

Gideon knew not to expect an immediate response. He set his message on repeat every 10-minutes, then pinged engineering. "Dax, Kiwi, how we looking on our trajectory?"

"Good," Dax responded. *"Just keep it as gentle as possible and we'll be fine."*

"All right," Gideon said. "Now we just wait for a response."

"Still nothing, huh?" Gideon asked as they entered orbit of

the ice planet Lacaille 9352-C.

"Yeah, still nothing," Jason confirmed.

Gideon exhaled, not liking the situation. They had been broadcasting his message on all frequencies for a few hours. They should've heard something by now.

He was about to cease the repeating message when Noora exclaimed, "Oh shet! Oh shet oh shet! Gideon, someone's locking onto us."

"Pinpoint them, now!" he shouted, tapping an evasive maneuver into his monitor.

"*Hey!*" Dax screamed over the intercom. "*Careful! We can't maneuver that fast! You're gonna rip us—*"

A deep, metallic groan came from the starboard side of the *Skye*.

"The hell was that?" Jason exclaimed.

"*A bulkhead just buckled in starboard aft,*" Kiwi chimed in. "*Might have a hull breach!*"

"*Suit up and go check it out,*" Dax told her. "*Gideon, we're losing gravity field integrity as well! Ease up now or we'll fly apart!*"

Gideon cut his maneuvering and let the *Skye* drift. "Noora, what do you have for me?"

"I've gottem," Noora said. "Got a projectile incoming. Might be a torpedo, or missile."

"Target it with the Liminal and fire," Gideon said.

Noora queued up the Liminal's targeting system, honed in on the projectile, and clicked to fire.

Nothing happened.

"Oh, fuck, *fuck!*" Noora shouted.

"What's wrong?"

"The targeting system is fried again! I can't get a shot!"

"Dax!" Gideon screamed. "You told me you'd fixed the targeting system!"

"*I fucking did!*" Dax screamed back. "*We got two reactors on this ship and more energy pumping through it than should be allowed! Random systems have been giving us shit this whole trip!*"

"Noora," Gideon said. "How long till the projectile gets to

us?"

"About 10-seconds."

"Everyone!" Gideon shouted over the intercom. "Brace for impact!"

10-seconds came. There was no explosion, but systems surged all over the bridge, also in engineering.

An EMP charge. Whoever was firing on them was trying to capture the ship.

"Jason, Noora, what can you see?" Gideon asked.

"Nothing, my monitor shorted out," Jason said.

"Mine, too."

"Dax, you there!" Gideon shouted.

The intercom was a scrambled, electronic mess. "*krZZZZZ—ngines are gone! Comm and naviga—krRRRRRRRRRR—*"

Gideon cut the intercom, getting the gist of it. His own monitor worked, but he couldn't maneuver the ship and had no engine thrust.

"All right," he said to Jason and Noora. "We're adrift and disabled, and we can't escape. The three of us are going to the armory to grab our weapons of choice, because we're about to be boarded."

Jason nodded, understanding the situation.

Noora gasped. "Oh my gahd, really?"

"Yes, really, come on."

Gideon tried to ring up Dax on the intercom again. "Dax, you there? Can you hear me?"

Garbled static came through, but then Dax's voice rang clear. "*Yeah! Can hear you! How are you up there?*"

"We're fine. How's engineering? Anything you can do?"

"*Nothing I can do quickly. Engines are down, navigation's down. Can restart them, but we can't escape whoever's firing at us.*"

"Got it. The three of us are headed for the armory. We're about to be boarded. Kiwi, you there? How's the bulkhead?"

"*Hey! It's uh, it's not pretty, but at least the hull's not breached, and did you just say we're about to be fucking boarded!*" Kiwi replied.

"Yes. Both of you meet us at the docking port. Dax, you want your kinetic fists?"

"*Please and thank you.*"

"Kiwi, you probably want your whip?"

"*Goddamn right, I'm gonna split every one of those fuckers open! Who's boarding us anyway?*"

"No idea."

Noora realized she was shaking when she reached for her powered lever-action rifle. She gripped the stock tightly, trying to make her jitters go away, only to realize her jaw was shaking as well.

She clenched her teeth, and didn't notice when Jason took Gideon aside, saying, "Hey, can I talk to you for a minute?"

Noora went through the muscle-memory ritual of making sure the rifle was clear, racking the lever several times and checking the receiver. She thumbed the power option OFF, not wanting to blast a hole through the hull. The rifle trembled through her hands.

She gripped as hard as she could, clenched her eyes shut, and didn't notice Gideon saying, "Okay, do it," slapping Jason on the shoulder, and Jason leaving the armory.

She pulled a fistful of .45-70 cartridges that Kiwi had made for her. Her hands wouldn't stop shaking, and the first cartridge she tried to slide into the magazine fumbled out of her fingers and clanked to the floor.

"Goddamnit!" she exclaimed. She clenched her eyes shut again, trying to get a grip. The top sniper in her class who could hit any target and blend into any terrain, and who had never seen combat, was about to fight for survival.

She felt Gideon's hand on her shoulder. "Hey, first time in a fight like this?"

Noora nodded spastically. She started loading the magazine with cartridges. "First time in a fight of any kind, actually."

"Here's what'll happen," Gideon said, checking and loading his Remy-Larsson twin barrel revolver. "We don't know who's coming or how many of them. You're gonna have to shoot people, and you can't hesitate. Your nerves will make you fail to your worst day of training, so keep that in mind."

Noora managed a quick smile. "Glad my worst day of training generally goes well." She finished loading the magazine and racked the lever. She grabbed a couple handfuls of .45-70s and stuffed them in her pockets. "I'll grab Dax's kinetic fists."

"And I got Kiwi's whip."

"You gottem on camera?" Gideon asked over a private channel to Jason.

"*Yeah, got the external camera feeds on my phone. Looks like a standard boarding party boat. Maybe 10 or 12 guys. Docking now.*"

Gideon heard the metallic clank-and-lock echo through the hull as the boarding boat docked. He was right outside the entrance of the docking bay.

As were Dax, Kiwi, and Noora.

With all the cargo stacked in the main corridors, there were plenty of places to hide.

"*They're entering the ship,*" Jason said over the private channel. "*I was right, looks about 10 guys. Got AK-style rifles. Don't even know how to hold them properly. They move like amateurs, not anyone with any training.*"

Gideon smiled. This should be easy.

"*Got four of them lining up at the corridor exit, the other six are staying behind as backup,*" Jason said.

Gideon gave a hand signal to Dax, Kiwi, and Noora, indicating four men were coming into the corridor.

The door opened, and the quartet came through. Gideon mentally noted how scrawny they were, and how they all wore the same dull-gray uniform. That and Jason had been right; they held their rifles awkwardly at the hip, as if it was their first time holding one. No trigger discipline, no understanding of the weapon at all.

Gideon gave a silent signal, and in the space of one second, Dax delivered a right hook with his kinetic fists, Kiwi cracked her whip, Noora fired her rifle, and Gideon fired his revolver.

Dax's victim slumped, his head slamming against the floor, out cold.

Kiwi's victim screamed through a hand covering his mouth and nose, blood pouring out of it.

Noora's victim was against the wall, his rifle on the ground, holding what remained of his right shoulder.

Gideon's victim was dead on the floor.

"*Take cover!*" Jason tried to warn. "*They're throwing a flashbang into the corridor!*"

But Gideon didn't hear him, his ears still adjusting from the gunfire.

The door opened again, and out flew a device. The door sealed immediately, right as the concussive flashbang went off.

The *Isle of Skye* crew all went unconscious.

It wasn't long before Gideon, Dax, Kiwi, and Noora all woke up to ringing ears, splitting headaches, their legs tied up, and their hands bound behind their backs.

"And you're sure it's just the four of them?" a voice asked.

"Yeah," someone confirmed. "Only four people listed on the crew manifest."

"Damn. This is a huge ship for four people," the first voice said. "And speaking of, look who's waking up."

As the *Skye* crew woke up and took in their surroundings. They saw the first voice, the seeming leader of the group, in the same gray uniform as everyone else, another person to his side that he had been talking with, and four others attending to the four that had first stormed the corridor.

"I take it you're Gideon," the leader said.

Gideon nodded. "And I take it you're a sack of shit."

The boarding party leader scoffed.

"Hey," Kiwi said to her victim across the corridor, still holding his mouth and still bleeding. "How you like your new cleft palate, sweetheart?"

The man attending him turned to Kiwi. "His mouth and nose are split open, and his four front teeth are gone."

"Happy to do the same to you, sweetie," Kiwi taunted.

"Shut the fuck up, Kiwi," Gideon said.

The leader looked at her. "So that would make you Kiwi." He looked to Dax, who stared back at him. "And you must be Dax." He looked to Noora, who kept her eyes on the floor, trying to hide a panic attack. "And that makes you Noora."

He checked a tablet he was holding and said, "Yup, that's all four of them."

"Throw em out the airlock?" asked the man attending to the corpse.

"Why?" the leader asked. "Four perfectly healthy people here. Send them down to the surface and put them to work."

The man next to the leader directed the four others to grab each of the *Skye's* crew.

"And bring the four of them as well," the leader said, indicating the four casualties. "Nothing we can do for them here. Make sure you bind up these guys together so they can't move, then three of you take the dropship to the surface, the rest come back here and we'll take stock of the ship."

The men did as they were told.

The dropship landed on the frozen wasteland of Lacaille 9352-C. One of the men on guard duty fitted each of the *Skye's* crew with a long, transparent tube connected to a palm-sized device.

"When we exit the ship, breathe in through the tube, then

exhale normally," he said. "If you breathe in through your nose too much, you'll pass out."

"What, you're too cheap for masks?" Dax asked.

"Don't need 'em," the man said. "Bite down on the tube to keep it in your mouth." He lined the crew up into the airlock, rifle aimed towards them, and opened the hatch.

Deep cold stabbed at the crew, who only had the thin clothes they typically wore on the *Skye*.

"Jesus *fucking* Christ!" Gideon exclaimed.

"Wooh!" Kiwi shouted. "Like a nice Wisconsin winter! Noora, is this what Finland's like at Christmas?"

Noora gave a brief smile, shivered, and said, "Worst Christmas of my life." She had finally calmed down somewhat.

"Don't forget to breathe through the tube, or you'll be dead before we get inside!" the guard shouted through the wind and snow. It was a hundred-yard walk to get to the metallic, pipe-lined entry.

Kiwi shouldered up to Gideon. "They really don't know about fuckboy?"

"No, they don't," Gideon confirmed.

Kiwi took a deep breath through her tube. "Well, we're about to see if he's really on our side."

Jason was still hiding in the labyrinth of air vents.

Philly Cheesesteak had found him. He was looking down different angles of the vents, whiskers flared, rotating his ears, still stressed from the noise of the fighting.

Jason tapped his phone. He was able to confirm the dropship had departed and that the crew of the *Skye* were on board. Whoever had captured them had been stupid enough not to search them and confiscate their phones.

He also knew from the camera feeds that at least four of the boarding party were out of commission and on their way back to the surface with them. They would need at least one person to pilot and a couple others to guard the crew.

That left only three on the *Isle of Skye*.

"All right," he said to the cat. "I don't like you, and you sure as hell don't like me. But we got some work to do."

"*Mr-r-reh*," Philly Cheesesteak chirped.

"Let's get out of these vents, first," he said.

Philly Cheesesteak led the way.

2. FROSTBITE II

Gideon gets a rifle stock to the face, Kiwi gets a rifle stock to the face, Dax gets several rifle stocks to the face, Noora doesn't get a rifle stock to the face, and Jason collaborates with Philly Cheesesteak.

"So," a charismatic voice said from behind the desk. He wore the same, dull-gray uniform as everyone else. "Who do we have here?"

"We have a—" Gideon said, before receiving a rifle stock to the face.

"He wasn't asking you," the large guard said.

"Have they been searched?" the charismatic voice asked.

The large guard shrugged.

"Well do it."

The rest of the guards patted down the crew of the *Skye*, confiscating their phones.

"So," the charismatic voice repeated. "Who do we have?"

"We've got all four crew members of the *Isle of Skye*," another guard said.

"All four, huh?" the charismatic leader asked. "The *Isle of Skye*. Interesting name. Why is it called that?"

"It's where I'm from," Gideon said, spitting at the feet of the guard who hit him.

The guard hit him again.

"What do each of you do?" the leader asked.

"I tell the rest of them what to do," Gideon said, before receiving another rifle stock and falling down. He spat blood on the floor.

"Hey, sweetcakes," Dax said to the guard. "Why don't you pick on someone who can kick your ass."

Dax also got a rifle stock to the face. His forehead split open.

"That tickles," Dax said. "Try again."

The heavy guard tried to smack Dax again, but Dax dodged and gave him a knee to the liver. Two other guards were on him in an instant. He got a shot to the back of the head and his right kidney. He groaned as if it was all a minor inconvenience.

"Hey," Kiwi said. "He has a point. Why don't you fucking pricks pick on me, someone who can *actually* kick your ass."

Kiwi got a shot to her upper-left cheek. She fell to the floor, growling like a tiger.

Noora took a sharp inhale. Her body seized up, afraid of what would happen to her if she said a word.

The leader behind the desk took interest in her. "You seem to be the smart one," he said, noticing how terrified she was compared to Gideon, Dax, and Kiwi. "And look at you. Strong and fit. Have the exercise Foreman work with her. Have her lead the exercise routine." The leader looked at his tablet, then looked at the *Skye's* crew. "Now," he said casually. "What do I do with the rest of you?"

"You should let me fuck up the rest of your girlfriends, here," Dax said.

The leader gave an eye signal to the large guard. Dax got another rifle stock to the face, and a couple more to the body.

Noora couldn't watch. She shivered and started crying.

"So tell me again," the leader said, not even looking at the *Skye's* crew. "What do each of you do?"

"I drink," Kiwi said. "And I fix things."

"I drink more," Dax said. "And I engineer things."

"And I'm the captain," Gideon said. "And I tell them when to do those things."

The leader had a purposeful, pensive moment. Then said, "Assign the 'captain' to mining. Assign the small one to tech duty. And assign the big one to engineering, tech, and mining."

"Assign me 15 more things," Dax said. "Then it'll be fair."

Dax got another rifle stock to the face. Noora winced. She wished Dax would shut up so they'd stop beating him.

The leader motioned to the large guard. "You, keep an eye on him. I feel like he's going to need some discipline."

The large guard grabbed Dax's collar and pulled him up.

"Well," the leader said. "Let's pull together an assembly. Have the four of them on stage, bound of course, and seated so that everyone can see them."

Jason couldn't believe his luck.

Whoever had captured the *Skye* hadn't bothered encrypting their transmissions. They figured there was no one else listening. The few left from the boarding party were communicating with whatever ship they'd come from. Jason, secured and locked away in his room, tuned in with his phone.

"*Yes, we know the ship is adrift,*" someone from the boarding party said. "*The EMP charge we hit them with blew out navigation.*"

"*Well we can't dock so long as you're adrift,*" someone from their ship said. "*So get navigation up again and make it so the ship isn't tumbling anymore.*"

"*Why are we even trying to dock with it? Why not just land the thing and take its cargo that way?*"

"*Unless you know how to land a ship that size, that's not happening.*"

"*Just fly one of those crew up here and have them do it.*"

"*Yeah, real smart. Give them back control of the ship.*"

Jason tapped his phone. He could access every function of the ship through it. Navigation was indeed still down. He rebooted it, then locked out the controls. To the boarding party, it would still look like it was out. So long as the *Skye* kept its gentle tumble, their main ship couldn't dock.

Philly Cheesesteak chirped. *"Br-r-reh?"* he asked.

"Yeah, I'm thinking," Jason said. There were only three from the original boarding party left, and they still didn't know he even existed. He thought about cutting oxygen to the ship and sealing himself and Philly Phil in an airtight room, but it would take a week or more for the boarding party to breathe through the remaining oxygen before they started to asphyxiate.

He couldn't risk taking on all three of them at once. Besides, at least two of them still had rifles. He'd need to take them out quietly, one-by-one, so that even their main ship didn't know. To them, it would just seem like the boarding party's communications were down.

He thought about trying to get to the armory to grab a weapon, but dismissed the idea. If he wanted to keep quiet, he couldn't risk firing a single shot.

He looked around his room, trying to think of something, when his eyes fell on exactly what he needed.

He grabbed the steel pipe Kiwi had given him for Christmas. "All right," he said to Philly Cheesesteak. "Here's what we're gonna do."

Gideon, Dax, Kiwi, and Noora all had their hands bound behind their backs. They were sitting in chairs on a makeshift stage with uncomfortable lights shining on them. To their left, at a podium, giving a speech, was the presumed leader of whatever was going on here on Lacaille 9352-C.

"...and we TRIED to negotiate with them, PEACEFULLY, in our mutual best interest! And what did they do? They ATTACKED our ship! They killed FOUR of our comrades!..."

Gideon noted how charismatic he sounded. He also noted

how the leader and his personal guard all seemed well-fed, and how scrawny and gaunt the sea of dull-gray faces watching them looked.

"...and are we angry? YES! But we are also merciful..."

Listening to the speech, Gideon was surprised Kiwi hadn't shouted an interruption. She was next to him, and was looking around the room, trying to observe what she could.

"...they begged, BEGGED us to spare their lives! And because we are merciful, we told them we would gladly accept the four of them for the four lives they stole from us!..."

Dax was in between Kiwi and Noora. His face was swollen and bleeding, and he could barely see, but he wasn't worried about himself. Noora was an absolute mess, shaking in fear. He tried to lean in to her as much as he could, given that they were tied up.

"Hey," he said. "You need to know this. Gideon's already thinking of how to get out of here. So is Kiwi, and so am I. You think about that, too. Focus on it. Make it the only thing you care about."

A guard with a rifle came up to the *Skye's* quartet and motioned for them to stand up. They did.

"...Now, do you accept your new brothers and sisters!"

The crowd raised their right fist in unison and said, "YES!"

"YES!" the leader echoed. Then he pointed at the *Skye* crew and directed his speech at them. "Know this! We are merciful, but we are just! We have accepted you as our own, but if ANY of you betray us, all four of you will be cast out into the cold!"

The crowd cheered.

The leader motioned to one of the guards, said a few things to him, and left the stage. The guard, along with a half dozen more, went up to the *Skye* crew and separated them.

"All right, where we going, lovelies?" Gideon said.

"D—Dax!" Noora shouted as she was hauled away.

"Remember what I told you!" he said back, before a guard poked his ribs with a rifle. "Careful," he winced. "That tickles."

"I know I'm small, but you guys can be rough with me,"

Kiwi said.

The boarding party trio were in the cargo hold of the *Isle of Skye*, trying to take stock of everything.

"Look at this," the smallest member said. "They've got 10-tons just of whey protein."

The larger one whistled. "You know how long that'll last us?"

"Won't last us at all if we can't straighten this ship out," the leader said. "Both of you, come with me to the bridge. Let's see if we can get navigation rebooted."

The trio left the cargo hold and turned to head to the bridge.

Just as a distinct meow echoed from the corridor behind them.

The three of them scowled at each other. "There's a cat onboard?" the larger one said.

"Why would they have a cat?" the smaller one asked.

"*Myeh-br-r-reh!*" they heard again, followed by a feline flash darting out from a cargo pallet and running towards engineering.

The large one racked his rifle and followed.

"Where you going?" the leader asked.

"You don't need me on the bridge. I don't know how to fly," the large one said.

"Well don't shoot anything vital," the leader said. "And remember, the intercom's down and I got the only radio, so don't take too long."

The leader and the shorter one made their way to the bridge.

The larger one went for engineering.

Along the way he kept hearing the cat. A couple times he even caught a glimpse, but it was too fast for him to get a shot.

Stupid little thing. It was just gonna cause trouble. Best to get rid of it.

The door to engineering was open, and he heard the cat's trill echoing from it.

He stepped inside, rifle ready.

But looking around made him realize he couldn't fire a single shot. No telling what any of the equipment and machinery did, or what would happen if a bullet struck it.

He put the rifle down against the wall, just as the cat pranced in front of him, gave him a taunting look, then bolted deeper into engineering.

"Get over here, you little shit," he said.

The cat went into hiding behind a plasma junction. He tried to reach for it, only to receive a steel crack to his skull. He fell, not unconscious, but too stunned to do anything but squirm on the deck plate. Two more cracks to the head put him under.

"You all right?" Jason asked.

"*Br-r-reh*," Philly Cheesesteak chirped, coming out from the plasma junction.

Jason took a number of deep breaths, trying to calm his nerves. He checked the camera feed on his phone. The other two from the boarding party were still on the bridge.

He looked down at the larger one, his face and skull a bloody mess. If he wasn't already dead, he would be when his brain swelled. Jason would have to kill the other two as well. There was no choice.

"All right," he said to Philly Cheesesteak, grabbing the man by the legs. "I'm gonna toss him out the airlock. They'll see on the bridge that the airlock in engineering was activated. Hopefully just one of them comes down to check it out. And if not, well, now I got a rifle."

"*Mr-r-r-reh*," Philly Cheesesteak said, trotting over to guard the entrance.

Gideon, clad in his new dull-gray uniform and layered with

a jacket too thin for the cold, stood in the middle of a group. They were at the airlock that led into the mine. Even here there were several of the propaganda signs he'd seen.

PRIVATE PROPERTY IS A PRIVILEGE.

DO NOT KEEP WHAT YOU DO NOT NEED.

TELL YOUR FOREMAN IF YOU SUSPECT A COMRADE OF HOARDING.

Dax was also in the group, but separated from Gideon.

"Hey," a young man next to Gideon said. "Are you really from off-world?"

"Yeah," Gideon nodded. "Sorry if we killed any friends of yours."

The young man shook his head. "If they had rifles, then they were Foremen. Only Foremen are allowed rifles, and no one's their friend."

"Well then, apology rescinded," Gideon said.

"Why'd you come here?"

"We came here on a trade mission. Didn't realize we'd fall into a commie hell hole."

"It wasn't always this way," the young man said.

A man with a rifle entered the airlock, flanked by the large guard that always followed Dax.

"You'll have to tell me about it later," Gideon said. "What's your name?"

"Andreja."

"I'm Gideon."

"Attention everyone!" the man with the rifle said. "I am your Foreman for today. I see we have a couple of newcomers, so listen closely. That palm-sized device on your person is your rebreather. It breaks down the atmospheric CO_2 into breathable oxygen. Breathe in through that tube, then exhale normally. Make sure the indicator is green. If it goes red, notify me or a comrade immediately, because you will only have a few minutes before you pass out."

The airlock opened.

It was almost the end of her shift, and Kiwi was exhausted. Everything in this colony was broken or in various states of disrepair. That and she was one of a few actually working. Most of the other technicians pretended to work just to look busy. Maybe they didn't even know what they were doing in the first place.

She went up to one of the techs she'd met, one who was actually trying. "It's Natalia, right?"

The timid, mousey worker nodded.

"Natalia, can you please tell me where you guys keep the liquor?"

Natalia only frowned.

"You know," Kiwi said. "Beer, wine, alcohol, booze?"

"Oh," Natalia said. "We, um, we don't get to have that."

Kiwi raised an eyebrow. "So someone *does* have it, then?"

Natalia nodded. "But I heard only Foremen are allowed to have any."

"Is that so?"

Kiwi found the man with the rifle that had been watching them all day. An entire escape plan came to her in an instant. She slinked up to the Foreman in her sexy, cat-like walk, and began working her magic.

"You told me earlier that it wasn't always like this," Gideon said over a ration of gruel.

Andreja nodded, trying to be discreet. He looked around to make sure the Foreman wasn't nearby, then kept his eyes on his own plate and talked. "It wasn't that much better before, but it can't get any worse than it is now."

"What happened?"

"Colony's been in bad shape for a while," Andreja said. "A couple years ago a lot of us were complaining to our leadership.

Our equipment breaks down too fast, we can't make food fast enough, we can't terraform the planet. They didn't know what the hell they were doing. But then Marko Begovic steps up, our current leader, and you've seen him. He talks and people just listen. He starts riling everyone up, blaming leadership for everything, accusing them of hoarding resources and exploiting the rest of us. He got enough of a following to take over the colony."

Gideon forgot about his gruel. "What did leadership do?"

"Some of them were smart. They could tell Marko had riled up a mob that would kill them, so they took the *Morena*, that's our vector drive ship, back to Earth's system to hire some mercenaries."

Gideon nodded, remembering Jason's report.

"But it takes seven weeks to get to Earth, at least on the ship we have," Andreja continued. "They couldn't even hire the mercenaries they wanted, so they bought a bunch of cheap munitions and returned. The problem is that in the time it takes to get there and back, Marko had reorganized everything. We were all on his side. Then our former leaders return, rifles in hand, and Marko calls an assembly to greet them."

Andreja paused for a spoonful of gruel, then continued.

"He didn't even try to keep them out. He let them right in, and they had rifles, but there were only a dozen of them. He invited them up on stage, said if they wanted to shoot him, they'd have to shoot everyone else. We all cheered him on. Leaders gave up, just like that. Then he gave them a chance to join the rest of us. A couple of them refused, and he sent them out to the cold without a rebreather. The rest joined, but they all disappeared within a couple weeks."

"What happened after that?" Gideon asked.

"This happened," Andreja said, motioning around with his spoon. "Marko already had his close inner circle of zealots. Took all the rifles for themselves, gave them to anyone who showed enough loyalty. They all became 'Foremen' making sure the rest of us did what we were told. Problem is we mistook Marko's charisma for competence. As bad as things were, it all got worse. Everyone pretended to keep going along, but everyone lost motivation to do anything. We lost everything we owned 'for the good of the colony,' and things keep getting worse, all while he calls these massive assemblies to tell us how great everything is."

"Sounds like everyone's unhappy to say the least," Gideon said. "How come no one's tried anything?"

Andreja looked at Gideon as though he were crazy. "Because they have rifles."

Gideon nodded. "And I can tell you none of them have held a rifle in their lives and don't know how to use them."

"Still, they gottem."

"And there's a lot more of you than there are of them," Gideon said, a plan starting to take shape in his head. He would just need a way to coordinate with the rest of the *Skye's* crew. "Thanks for that, Andreja."

Noora stood stiff as a rock in front of her Foreman, scared of even breathing without permission. They were in a large exercise room. She was only wearing her sports bra and underwear, and felt exposed and vulnerable.

The Foreman, also a woman, looked her over, as if Noora were some specimen. "You," she said with a terse sting. "You have an incredible physique. How do you do this?"

"I—I—," Noora stuttered.

"Surely you can speak?" the Foreman said.

"I—I just, a lot of weights and protein," Noora said.

"Hmph," the Foreman scoffed. "You will lead our exercise groups. Everyone in the colony is required to do one 30-minute exercise session per day, and you will lead each session starting tomorrow. You will wear what you're wearing now. People need to see your physique and need to know that they can achieve this."

"B—but—"

"But nothing," the Foreman said. "You will do this starting tomorrow. For now, you will report back to your room."

"Y—yes, yes ma'am."

"*Comrade*," the Foreman corrected her.

"Y—Yes, comrade." Noora put on her standard-issue, dull-gray uniform, made her way to her assigned room, which was shared with several other women, and threw herself onto an empty bed.

She was humiliated, frightened, and too mentally paralyzed to do anything. She curled into a protective ball, thinking of the shame she'd feel leading exercise classes while just in her underwear.

She was also depressed. She had never killed anyone, and found out at the assembly that the boarding party member she'd shot had died. She didn't think his wound had been mortal, but she remembered that most of his shoulder had been destroyed. He could have easily bled out or died of sepsis.

She thought of her family back home in Finland, and how she wished she were back in her own bed now, but as soon as she had that thought, it repulsed her. She loved her family, but the *Skye's* crew needed her.

She wondered what was happening to her crewmates. She thought of the beatings they all took. Dax, especially.

Then she thought of how he kept inviting each hit, as though he had wanted to show them that he didn't care. She managed a quick smile to herself. It was a quality in him she liked.

She thought of Gideon doing the same, giving lip that would only earn him a beating. Then there was Kiwi, who gave lip all the time.

Noora realized the subtle message her crewmates had been sending to their captors.

Fuck you, I'm getting the hell out of here.

She remembered Dax's words, how he, Gideon, and Kiwi were already thinking of how to escape, and that she needed to do the same.

But what could she do? A sniper without a rifle or a blind, and a cosplayer without a costume, trapped on a glacier in the side of a mountain on a planet with an unbreathable atmosphere, separated from her ship. It was hopeless.

But Dax's words stuck with her, and her crewmates' attitudes inspired her.

Noora understood that they would never let each other down, and that her hopeless attitude wasn't helping.

Then she asked herself, *What would Kiwi do?*, and immediately knew the answer.

Kiwi wouldn't hesitate to do whatever the hell she needed to, and wouldn't give a flying fuck about the consequences.

Noora decided she would do the same.

Okay, she asked herself. *What can I do?*

I can shoot. I can cosplay. I can hide.

Her body relaxed as she reframed her talent stack.

I can shoot better than anyone here. None of them even know how to hold a rifle. I know how to make a costume, which means I can disguise myself. I can hide for hours, perfectly still, if needed.

She thought of the metallic, prefab corridors of the colony, how she could get the materials she needed to blend into all of it, and how she could make a run for the dropship.

A plan started to take shape in her mind. She fell asleep, thinking of Dax's protective arms around her.

Dax fell onto a bed in his assigned room, not caring how much noise he made. He was exhausted, having worked three consecutive shifts in mining, engineering, and tech.

He was also starving. The gruel they served at the colony didn't nourish him enough for the amount of work he did. No wonder everyone looked so scrawny.

He wondered how his crewmates were doing. He knew Kiwi and Gideon were making the best of their situations, but worried about Noora. She hadn't handled their capture as well as the rest of them.

Anger swelled in him as he thought about how he couldn't protect her.

He focused his anger on the guard that was always tailing him, thinking about ways to take him out, but he was too tired to come up with a plan.

He drifted off to sleep, thinking of his arms around Noora.

"The hell?" the boarding party leader said, seeing a notice on his display.

"What's wrong?" the smaller one asked.

"The airlock in engineering has been activated."

"He's probably just throwing the cat off the ship."

"Yeah, well go back there and make sure he's not destroying the place," the leader said.

The smaller one got up and made the long trek to engineering.

The leader kept trying to reboot navigation, only to see nothing. He had no idea what was wrong. Even after an EMP discharge, he should've been able to reboot everything by now.

20 minutes came and went, and still nothing.

He was about to head back to engineering himself, when the door to the bridge opened. "Well it took you long enough," he said, getting up and turning around. "No! *NO NO NO—*"

The leader fell with two shots to the chest.

Jason finally had control of the *Isle of Skye*.

3. FROSTBITE III

Kiwi has a plan, Dax has a plan, Noora cosplays as a wall, Gideon teaches the cardinal rules of gun safety, and Jason goes to bed.

Gideon sat in the leader's office, flanked by three guards. He understood why this was the man in charge. Just sitting at his desk, he exuded confidence, conviction, and cold intelligence.

"Your crew's done well their first day," he said. His tone was fatherly. Gideon was almost grateful.

"You're welcome," Gideon said. "Now kindly give me my ship back."

The leader gave a condescending smile. "*Your* ship? The *Isle of Skye* now belongs to the People of Lacaille. In case you haven't seen the signs, private property is a privilege. A ship in the hands of one person?" He shook his head. "Out of the question."

"What deal did you make back on Earth?" Gideon asked. "You knew we were coming. You heard us when we arrived. You ambushed us and captured our ship."

"What do you mean?" the leader said, again with the condescending smile. "The official story is that we tried to negotiate with you, and you attacked us. We prevailed, and you begged for your lives, which we mercifully granted." He leaned forward, his demeanor threatening. "And if you spread rumors that contradict that, you and the rest of your crew will be thrown out in the cold without a rebreather." He opened up his tablet and viewed some notes. "Looks like your muscle girl is performing well as the exercise instructor."

"You make her do it in her underwear," Gideon said. "Didn't realize you were both commies and pervs."

"The People need to see her physique," the leader said, convinced of his own words. "Otherwise how can they be inspired? They need to know that they can look like her, that they can be her if they exercise like they're supposed to." He looked back at his tablet. "And that tiny tech is doing well, too. The one with the dark hair."

"Kiwi," Gideon said.

The leader nodded without looking at Gideon. "She's repairing everything. Mining equipment, ventilation, anything we have. I thought she was spicier when I first saw her, but she's fallen in line without any sass."

"She knows her place," Gideon lied.

"But that tall one, your engineer, has me the most surprised," the leader said. "I thought he would be the most trouble, but he's working non-stop."

"That's because you're working him 18-hours straight," Gideon said.

"Someone that skilled needs to make their contribution."

"All to eat the same gruel as everyone else," Gideon said. "Well, *almost* everyone else. You and a few others seem to be well-fed. You keep all the best recycled protein for yourselves?"

"Opinions like that are best kept to yourself," the leader warned.

Gideon said nothing and just held the leader's gaze.

"You know," the leader said. "All of this civil conversation we're having, and you haven't even asked me my name."

Gideon already knew his name, but didn't want to give him the dignity. "Lemme guess," he said. "You go by Supreme Leader, or Prime Father Figure of Lacaille, or some shit like that."

The leader gave him a sharp look.

Gideon was tired of the conversation. "May I head to my room now?"

With a glance, the leader told the guards to remove Gideon from his office.

On the way to his room, Gideon was thinking about his escape plan, but he still had no way of coordinating with the *Skye's* crew. He wondered what the rest of them were up to.

Kiwi already had her Foreman wrapped around her finger, but tonight she played at sulking and being uninterested.

"What's wrong?" he asked her, putting a hand on her back.

"Oh, it's nothing," she said. "It's just, I'm so bored."

"We can, I don't know, play a card game, or something? I can get us more wine if you want?"

"I mean, the wine would be great," Kiwi said, even though what passed for wine in this colony tasted like astringent. Still, it was alcohol. "It's just, I just wish I had my phone."

The Foreman scoffed. "I can't get you your phone."

"Well I don't understand what the problem is," Kiwi whined. "It's not like I can call anyone. I just wanna play games and read my comics and watch my favorite anime. That's all it's good for."

The Foreman tried to rub her back. "Well, I can get us more wine, but the phone is—"

"No, it's okay," Kiwi said, turning passive aggressive and refusing his touch. "You can't get my phone for me. I understand. It's just, whatever." She got up from the bed and sat sulking in the opposite corner of the room.

The Foreman sighed. He got up. "Look, give me, like, 10 minutes. I'll be back." He left the room.

Kiwi grinned. This was too easy.

10 minutes later the Foreman returned. He presented a growler. "I got us more wine, and," he said, procuring a small lock box. "I got you your phone."

"Oh my god you're the best!" Kiwi squealed, jumping into him and holding tightly.

"Well, more accurately," the Foreman said, proud of himself. "I brought all four of those phones. I didn't know which one was yours." He opened the lockbox. Kiwi grabbed hers. The Foreman put the lockbox down, leaving it open.

She kept up the act. "You are seriously, literally the best! Oh my god, we're gonna watch *Tenjou Rayden* together, it's gonna be so much fun! Do you even know what anime is out here?"

"I, uh, no," the Foreman said. "But let's watch it. Here, lemme pour some wine."

Kiwi opened her phone while the Foreman was busy. She immediately texted Jason. So long as the *Skye* was on this side of the planet, he'd receive it.

Fuckboy. Please tell me you're alive and in control of the ship.

10 seconds later, she received a reply.

I'm alive and in control of the ship.

Jason was barely in control of the ship.

The original boarding party was dead, but he had to keep up appearances that that wasn't the case. He let the *Skye* continue its slow, lazy tumble, enough to keep anyone from docking.

Most anyone.

A regular vessel wouldn't be able to, but a small boarding party boat could match the *Skye's* tumble and then dock.

He had the radio from the original boarding party leader. It chirped a communication.

"Boarding party, have you gotten navigation fixed yet? You're still tumbling."

Jason opened a channel, but just sent scrambled garbage.

"Say again, boarding party? You've completely broken up."

Jason repeated the garbled static, hoping it would stall them, just as Philly Cheesesteak tapped his leg.

"Mr-r-reh!" he said.

"Not now!" Jason said.

"All right, boarding party, we're only getting static from you. Assuming it's a communication failure. Sending another boarding party your way with a fresh radio."

Jason sighed. He'd need to think of something fast.

Philly Cheesesteak tapped Jason again. *"Mr-r-rAOW!"* he said.

"NOT NOW!" Jason shouted. "They're about to fucking

board us again! What the hell do you want that's so important?!"

Philly Cheesesteak tapped Jason's leg, then touched his own mouth.

Jason rolled his eyes. "You want *food?*"

"*Myeah*," Philly Cheesesteak confirmed.

"Fine!" he got up and headed for the mess hall, Philly Cheesesteak trotting right behind him, just as his phone chirped a notification.

It was a text from Kiwi.

Fuckboy. Please tell me you're alive and in control of the ship.

He never thought he would be relieved to hear from her. He texted back.

I'm alive and in control of the ship.

"*Mr-r-r-yah?*" Philly Cheesesteak asked.

"That was Kiwi," he said, realizing he should text her a follow up.

Text you later. In some shit right now.

Same, she texted back.

"*Myeh-br-r-yeh?*" Philly Cheesesteak asked.

But Jason was too distracted to answer. He had maybe 20 minutes before the next boarding party arrived. He needed to make sure they didn't get on board.

More importantly, he needed to feed the fucking cat.

Noora stood in front of the exercise group, clad only in her sports bra and underwear, her carved physique on full display. She saw Kiwi in the crowd, smiling at her, which gave her confidence.

Dax was also there. He gave her a wink.

"Notice!" Noora's Foreman announced. "Look at your instructor's physique. She can look like this following our exercises! Why can't you! Everyone give your best effort!"

Noora led the class, making sure to smile and only give positive energy despite the humiliation she felt. She fell into a fun rhythm, running through a series of pushups, situps, squats, and other bodyweight exercises.

After 30 minutes, the class ended. She was quick to don her dull-gray uniform, glad to not be exposed in her underwear anymore.

A number of people came up to her, grateful for her class.

"Thank you, comrade," a young woman said. "It was a wonderful session."

"Thank you, comrade," a young girl said to her. "You're so strong."

Noora felt delighted at everyone's positive feedback, and didn't notice Kiwi going up to Dax and passing him something.

Kiwi eventually came up to Noora and said, "Thank you, comrade," while slipping something into her pocket. Kiwi winked and left the exercise room.

Noora casually touched her pocket, recognizing the size and weight of her own phone. She went up to a wall and leaned against it as everyone left the room. She kept her arms crossed, hands away from her pocket, not wanting to draw attention to it.

"A good exercise session," her Foreman said.

"Thank you," Noora said.

"Keep up the energy for the next session."

Noora nodded. "Of course, comrade."

It was 10 minutes before the start of Dax's mining shift. Today, rather than the mines, they were going outside to rig some blasting charges further along the side of the mountain.

He looked around for Gideon, finding him at a workbench, getting his toolset ready. Dax went up to him, discreetly placing Gideon's phone on the bench. "Comrade," he said.

Gideon masked his surprise, casually taking his phone and putting it in his pocket. "Comrade," he said back. "Anything you, uh, wanna tell me?"

"Jason's got the ship, that's all I know," Dax said quietly.

Someone behind Dax shoved his shoulder. "Hey, fix this," the large guard said, tossing his rebreather on the workbench. "Thing keeps acting up on me."

Dax nodded, not giving any attitude. Gideon moved away as Dax got to work.

The indicator on the rebreather was red. Dax opened the compartment to see what was wrong with it, when an escape plan shot through his brain.

No, he thought. *Not yet. Be patient.*

He gave the rebreather a temporary fix. The indicator flashed green, and he handed it back to the guard.

Jason was about to lose the ship.

A new boarding party wasn't far away. With the *Skye* still in its gentle tumble, a boarding boat could dock, but it was risky. If they were sloppy, they'd pop off the *Skye* in explosive decompression. He needed to make that happen, and to make it look like an accident.

He ran to the armory, looking for anything he could blow up.

He spotted a case of grenades. Crude and risky, but he didn't have time to be picky. He checked the video feed on his phone. The boarding boat was about 100-feet away from the *Isle of Skye*. He grabbed a few grenades and ran for the docking port, getting there just as the boarding boat was about to dock.

He pulled the pin on a grenade as the boat locked in place, rolled it towards the docking door, ran like hell to the main corridor and sealed the door behind him.

A second later, a muffled blast rocked the *Skye* as the docking bay decompressed and the boarding boat tumbled off into space.

Klaxons and emergency lights went off all over the ship. Jason kept them on while he opened up the radio to the ship that had been trying to capture the *Skye*. He kept it mostly a garbled mess, but let in enough key words so they'd get the point.

"kRRRRRZZZZZZZ—ing boat gone!—you not to dock!"

"*Boarding party, say again! What the hell happened?*"

"—ing bay's destroyed! Boarding boat fucked up— kRRRZZZZ—told you not to dock!"

Between the static and the klaxons, they couldn't tell Jason wasn't the boarding party leader.

"*Your communication's been garbled for a while! We couldn't hear you!*"

Jason turned the static all the way up, then cut the radio.

The docking bay was destroyed, but it had worked.

He opened his phone to shut off the alarms and emergency lights, then made his way back to the bridge.

He needed to check on Kiwi and the rest of the crew and see how he could get them the hell off the planet.

––––––––––––––––––––––––––––––––––

Kiwi pretended to play on her phone while in her Foreman's room, but in reality she was texting everybody.

Hey gang. Does everyone have their phone?

Got mine. Noora, you there? You all right? Dax texted back.

I'm here, I'm fine, Noora wrote.

Same, Gideon wrote. *We're getting out of here tomorrow. What are all of you thinking?*

I got a plan, Dax wrote. *Tomorrow morning Gideon and I are back outside on the mountain. Kiwi, Noora, can you both get outside tomorrow morning?*

I'll find a way, Kiwi wrote.

I can do it, Noora wrote. *What time?*

We leave the airlock at 0800 hours. You'll need to be outside within five minutes after that. We're taking the dropship out of here.

Gideon, Kiwi wrote. *I got an idea. Leave your tools behind. I'll use that as an excuse to bring them outside to you.*

Got it, Gideon wrote. *Noora, you sure you're all right to get outside tomorrow morning?*

I'll be there, Noora wrote. She wrote again, forgetting she was on group text. *I love you, Dax.*

I love you, too, Noora, Dax wrote, not caring that everyone would see it.

Jason snapped awake, Philly Cheesesteak tapping his face.

"*Meh?*" he asked.

Jason rubbed his face. He had been awake since the *Isle of Skye* was first boarded, he was sleep-deprived, and had passed out on the bridge.

"Shit, have we been boarded?" he asked, checking everything he could.

"*Mr-rowh,*" Philly Cheesesteak answered.

Nothing was attached to the *Skye*, and all camera feeds were empty. That and he was still alive on the bridge.

He searched for the ship that had been trying to board them, and found it a few kilometers above and aft. He didn't know why he hadn't bothered checking the ship until now. It just hadn't been a priority.

He zoomed in with a camera. The ship looked familiar. He checked his phone to see a flurry of messages from the *Skye's* crew. He put them aside while he called up data on Lacaille.

Of course. It was the *Morena*, the vector drive ship the colony had.

He went back to the messages from the *Skye's* crew. They were from a few hours ago. He messaged them back.

Sorry. Fell asleep. Still have the ship. If you're able to take the dropship, message the Morena on an open channel on your way up. Tell them you heard they're having trouble boarding the Skye, and that you'll take care of it. They still don't know I have the ship.

At least he hoped they didn't know. He opened up a channel to them, keeping it a static, garbled mess.

"krZZZZZZZ—ing in, can youKRZZZZZZZ—"

A bored voice from the *Morena* answered. "*Say again,*

boarding party. Your communication is still garbled. Any progress on restoring navigation yet?"

"krZZZ—vigation almost restorKRZZZZ—ould have in a couple hou—kRZZZ—"

"Uh, confirm that, boarding party, you'll have navigation restored in a couple of hours?"

"RRRRRR—ooking like yeah, maybe two or three—kZRRRRRR—"

Jason closed the channel. He thought about firing on the Morena, but whoever was on the surface would find out and put the colony on lockdown.

That, and he still couldn't fix the Liminal's targeting system. Even if he could fix it, the Morena would detect the target lock and alert the surface immediately.

Philly Cheesesteak tapped him again.

"What, you need more food?"

"Myeah," Philly Cheesesteak confirmed.

"Fine. I need about a pint of coffee anyway," he said, heading for the mess hall.

Dax got another heavy push to his shoulder.

"Hey!" the large guard shouted, tossing his rebreather onto the workbench, its indicator showing red. "This is acting up again. Fix it right this time or I'll fix your face."

Dax nodded. He took the rebreather, opened its casing, and started his escape plan.

He rewired the indicator to permanently read green, then he disconnected the power to the CO_2-to-O_2 converter. The rebreather still showed green but would feed the guard no oxygen.

He handed it back to the large guard, who said, "This goes red again, you're gonna get it."

Dax gave a well-acted, defeated nod. He lined up for the airlock alongside Gideon, who had conveniently forgotten his tools. Andreja stood by them as well, along with about a dozen other men.

Dax nodded to Gideon, who knew it was time.

Once the airlock opened, they would have two or three minutes before the large guard passed out. Then they would have to take care of the Foreman quickly, before he radioed for help.

The airlock opened.

The Exercise Foreman was in the exercise room by 07:45, as she was every morning. But she was surprised. Noora, the new exercise leader, was nowhere to be seen.

This was odd, as Noora was always neurotic about being on time and doing as she was told.

She looked around the exercise room not seeing anything, even in the dimly lit corner where the lights had given out months ago. Every prefab panel was in place, where it should be.

She did notice a uniform on the floor. Noora had probably already been by, then left for some reason, probably to use a restroom.

The Foreman left.

In the dimly lit corner of the exercise room, one of the panels separated itself from the wall, walked up to the uniform and put it on.

Kiwi acted the part. She noticed Gideon's tools, grabbed them, grabbed herself a rebreather, and went up to her Foreman. "Hey, that idiot forgot his fucking tools," she said, putting on a parka. "I'm gonna bring them out to him, back in 10 minutes."

Her Foreman didn't question her. He brought her to the airlock and told the airlock controller to let her through, then he radioed the Mining Foreman to let him know.

Kiwi entered the airlock, saying, "So fucking annoying," to

herself, but loud enough for everyone else to hear her. It sealed behind her and the airlock cycle began. She smiled, knowing she was never stepping back inside that colony again.

She bit down on the tubing to her rebreather as the door to the outside opened.

Noora knew that acting the part was at least as important as the disguise.

She walked with a different gait, a different stride in her arms, a different sway in her shoulders.

She also wore a cap, kept her gaze to the floor, had smudged her face with oil, and had stained her hair with black grease. No one recognized her.

Not even when she walked right by the Exercise Foreman, who was on her way back to the exercise room.

Noora knew she didn't have much time to escape before her Foreman notified somebody, but luckily the airlock to the airfield wasn't far.

That, and it wasn't guarded. No workers had any reason to use that airlock, no one could go outside without a rebreather, and the Foremen took it for granted that no one would bother using this airlock. And they were right. No one knew how to pilot anything, and the only thing in the snowy airfield was the *Skye's* dropship.

Which Noora could command from her phone. She didn't know how to pilot it from her phone, but she could do simple commands. She waited until she was in the airlock before pulling out her phone and opening the dropship's commands.

As the airlock started cycling, she called up the command to open the dropship's door. She just had one small problem.

She had no rebreather, and it was 100-yards to the dropship.

She hyperventilated on purpose, drawing as much oxygen into her blood as she could. She filled her lungs to a final, painful capacity as the outer door opened.

Phone in hand, she ran for the dropship.

The snow dragged her progress, but she kept pace, slowly exhaling along the way. She tapped the command on her phone to open the dropship's airlock. As she made it to the airlock, she instinctively started gasping for air.

But the air she breathed lacked oxygen, and she knew she didn't have long before she passed out. She cycled the airlock and opened up a text to everyone, quickly typing, *On dropship can't fly.*

She felt light-headed as the airlock cycled shut.

She stumbled into a wall panel, fell to the floor, and passed out.

"Yeah, okay, got it!" the Foreman shouted into his radio. He quickly found Gideon and pointed his finger. "You! You forgot your tools! Wait here, someone's coming out to deliver them!"

Dax noticed the large guard stumble a bit before checking his rebreather, only to see it shine green. He pretended to fumble with his tools while taking a few steps closer to the Foreman, making sure to position himself behind him. Once the large guard was out, he would have to make his move.

After 30 more seconds, the large guard collapsed into the snow. The Foreman noticed and pulled out his radio.

Only to get a massive bicep and forearm wrapped around his neck.

Dax squeezed a chokehold, cutting off arteries in the Foreman's neck. He was out in three seconds. Dax let his body slump into the snow, ripping the rebreather tube out of his mouth and taking his rifle.

"Dax!" Gideon shouted, having already secured the large guard's rifle. "Gimme your rifle, and call the dropship now!"

Dax did as his captain said. He handed over the rifle, pulled out his phone, and saw the text from Noora. *I knew you'd make it!* he thought, but he didn't have time to text her back. He began queueing up the dropship to fly to their position.

Gideon took Dax's rifle and shoved it into the hands of a shocked Andreja. "Take this!" he said, making sure to breathe in through his tube.

Andreja took the rifle, in utter shock at what he'd just witnessed.

Gideon propped up the rifle he had taken from the large guard, and gave Andreja a quick lesson in firearms. "All right. Press the release there to let the magazine go."

Andreja did as he was told.

"Now, rack the slide right there to make sure it's clear."

Again, Andreja did as he was told.

"Good. Now pop the magazine back in, like this," Gideon said, sliding his own magazine in. "And then rack it once to make sure it's loaded."

Andreja followed his instructions.

"Finger off the trigger at all times, like this," Gideon demonstrated.

Andreja nodded.

"When you're ready to fire, you hold it up to your shoulder like this, look down the sights, aim at their torso, and pull the fucking trigger."

Andreja nodded again, then said, "But there's so many of them. There's not many of us."

Gideon sucked oxygen through his tube and said, "Let me tell you something. None of them know how to shoot. They carry their rifles wrong, they aim from the hip, they know less than you know. So you take that fucking rifle, follow me back in, and you shoot anyone who's a fucking Foreman, and you take their rifle, and you give it to someone else, and you tell them how to handle it, just like I told you!"

Andreja nodded spastically. "Okay, okay!"

Kiwi showed up on site. "Holy shit, you guys got them already?"

"Dax!" Gideon shouted. "You, Kiwi, and Noora take the

dropship to the *Skye*! I'm staying here for now!"

Dax scowled at first, but nodded. He didn't want to argue with his captain. The dropship flew into view, Dax controlling its descent on his phone. He knew Noora was already on board, and landed it quickly.

Gideon stood up, taking a pull through his tube. "All right, all of you!" he shouted to Andreja and the rest of the crew. "I've got a rifle, Andreja's got a rifle, we're going back into the colony, and we're going to shoot any goddamn Foreman we see!" He took another deep drag from his tube. "And let me tell you! I know how to shoot! Andreja knows how to shoot! But none of the Foremen know how to shoot! Every one of them we shoot, we're taking their rifle, and giving it to one of you!"

The mining crew was in shock.

"Or, if you like, I can leave with my own crew right now, and let you all deal with this on your own!" Gideon said. He could tell from the crew's body language that they were desperate for leadership.

"Right, then! Everyone follow me back into the colony!" Gideon said.

Dax and Kiwi stormed into the dropship. Dax found Noora passed out on the deck plate. He grabbed her and gently slapped her grease-covered cheek.

She snapped awake.

Dax was ready to cry in relief. "Hey," he said.

"Hey," Noora said, groggy.

Kiwi went straight for the pilot seat and lifted off. "Hey Dax, check your phone. Looks like we got a text from fuckboy."

Dax took a second to help Noora up and get her into a seat. Then he pulled out his phone and saw Jason's text. "Ahh, shit," he said. He went up to Kiwi. "He needs us to open a channel to their main ship! You do a better North American accent than I do!"

"Yeah, no shit, you East Texas hick," Kiwi said.

Dax sent a quick text to Jason.

Jason's phone chimed. It was a text from Dax.

Ascending now. Kiwi's gonna open up a channel. Listen in.

30 seconds later, he heard Kiwi's husky, confident voice over an open channel.

"*Morena, this is the dropship ascending from Lacaille. We understand you're having some communication issues. On our way to dock with the Isle of Skye right now.*"

"*Good to hear from you,*" a voice from the *Morena* said. "*How are you gonna dock with them? Docking bay was destroyed.*"

"*No worries, Morena,*" Kiwi said. "*This dropship has its own docking station. Will be in touch once we're on board.*"

Jason slowed the *Skye's* tumble, just enough to help the dropship dock. Once they were on board, they would have to destroy the *Morena* quickly.

"Let us in!" Andreja screamed into the radio. "The Foreman's rebreather is malfunctioning, and he's already passed out!"

The airlock started to cycle.

"Remember," Gideon said, readying his rifle. "Look down the sights, aim for center mass, and pull the trigger until they go down."

"But there's so many of them," a nervous voice said behind Gideon.

"There's a hell of a lot more of you," Gideon said. "Besides, none of them even know how to hold a rifle. Every Foreman we down, one of you grabs their weapon."

The airlock cycle was almost complete. Gideon pressed the rifle stock into his shoulder, aiming down the sights. Andreja did the same.

The door to the colony opened. He recognized Kiwi's

Foreman, who barely had time to be surprised before receiving seven rounds to the chest. He fell.

Andreja took a second to collect himself. This was the first time he had killed someone, but he knew it wouldn't be the last. He grabbed the Foreman's rifle and gave it to one of his crew, while Gideon shot the airlock operator and looked around for any other Foremen.

All he saw were stunned faces of technicians.

"Where do they store their munitions here?" he asked everyone.

One of the technicians pointed down a corridor.

"Wonderful," Gideon said. "Lead the way. The rest of you, follow me."

"*Dropship team, come in, any news on the original boarding party?*"

"Yeah, give us a minute, here," Kiwi said. "We just docked, internal comm is down, and we gotta find out where the hell they are. Will radio you again when we've made contact."

Kiwi, Dax, and Noora boarded the *Skye*, and were immediately greeted by Jason, who looked like a sleep-deprived mess.

"No Gideon?" he asked.

"No," Dax said. "He's too busy starting a revolution. They seriously don't know we have the ship back?"

"Well it's not gonna stay that way for long. All they have to do is hear from the surface that you guys escaped. How the hell don't they know already?"

"Gideon's keeping them busy," Kiwi said. "Why can't we just blow the *Morena* out of the fucking sky?"

"Because the Liminal's targeting system is still down," Jason said. "That and they'll fire on us the second they detect a target lock."

"Wait," Kiwi said. "Noora, you can do it."

"What?" Noora said.

"Like when you and I were outside on the *Skye's* hull that one time and took potshots at fuckboy's ship 1,000 kilometers away. The *Morena's* only a few clicks away. You can aim and shoot manually."

"Oh, yeah," Noora said, taking a deep breath. "Yeah, I could. I'll, uh, I'll get suited up."

"Are you okay on your own?" Dax asked.

"Yeah, I'll be fine."

Dax nodded. "I'm gonna get to engineering."

"I'll be on the bridge," Jason said.

A feline voice trilled.

"*Philly Cheesesteak you little fucker come here!*" Kiwi squealed.

The colony was finally on alert. It only took a dozen dead Foremen and Gideon raiding the munitions supply with his growing band of followers. They hadn't suffered a single casualty yet.

He had been right; the Foremen had just looked intimidating with their rifles. They didn't know the first thing about how to use them.

Gideon only had one mission before he contacted the *Isle of Skye* for a dropship.

He was going to find the leader and kill him.

He had already shown about 20 colonists how to handle and shoot the AK-style rifles, and those 20 had taught others who joined them.

Rifle fire echoed through the corridors, some at a distance, some close by, as squads of armed colonists took off on their own to find any Foremen they could.

It wasn't long before he found the leader's office. To his shock, the door was open. The arrogant asshole probably thought he was immune.

He heard someone from the office screaming into a radio. "No! It wasn't us! The colony's revolting! It's the *Isle of Skye* crew that was on that dropship! Fire on them now!"

Gideon popped a flashbang he had looted from the munitions stock, threw it into the office, and took cover in the corridor.

It went off.

He entered the office and grabbed the unconscious leader. As he dragged him to the nearest airlock, he opened his phone and called the *Skye* to warn them.

"Hey," he said. "I just heard them contact their ship! They're gonna fire on you!"

"*We know, Gideon,*" Kiwi responded. "*We're a little busy right now!*" She cut the call.

He didn't call them back. He would only be a distraction. He hoped he still had a ship after he was done with his business here.

Rifle fire still echoed through the corridors, but he didn't run into anyone on his way to the airlock.

The leader, being dragged by his collar, started to stir.

Gideon dropped him into the airlock and started the cycle. He still had his rebreather and bit down on the tube.

"I understand your favored form of execution was throwing people out in the cold," he said as the leader regained consciousness. "Shame you won't freeze to death before you asphyxiate." He grabbed the leader as the outer door opened and threw him out the airlock. Frigid cold stabbed at both of them.

The leader stood up, then turned around to face Gideon. He breathed in the frozen, oxygen-free atmosphere. He took deep, full breaths, not saying a word.

Gideon stared him down, rifle at the ready. He expected some flowery monologue, but the leader didn't say a word. He just kept taking deep breaths.

After about 90 seconds, his eyes started to flutter and he began to lose his balance. A few seconds more, and he fell into the snow.

Gideon waited, watching the whole time as the leader, now unconscious, gasped at air that didn't give him oxygen. His breathing slowed, and he started to turn blue. Gideon kept watching until his breathing stopped, and his eyelids slowly opened in a death stare.

He cycled the airlock and went back into the colony.

He wanted to call the *Skye*, but didn't want to distract them. Instead, he sent a group text, praying that he still had a ship and wouldn't be marooned on this ice planet for the rest of his life.

Please tell me you're alive and the ship's intact.

Dax was in engineering, trying to assess system status, and trying to fire up the engines.

Jason was on the bridge, monitoring everything he could.

Kiwi was with him, sitting at navigation. She was righting the ship, straightening it out from its drift, when the *Morena* chimed in.

"Hey, uh, just checking in, looks like you guys have restored power and navigation finally."

"That's correct, *Morena*," Kiwi responded.

"Who are you, by the way?" the voice from the Morena responded. *"I don't recognize your voice."*

"I'm Natalia," Kiwi said without missing a beat.

"Oh, from tech?" the voice said. *"I didn't know you were a pilot."*

Before Kiwi could give a smart-ass response, another signal pierced through.

"Morena, this is the surface! Fire on that dropship!"

"What!" the *Morena* responded. *"What do you mean? Natalia from tech is on it."*

"No! It wasn't us! The colony's revolting! It's the Isle of Skye crew that was on that dropship! Fire on them now!"

"Oh, fuck me," Kiwi said.

Noora, in a pressure suit, was on the aft fin of the *Isle of Skye*, where the Liminal rifle was in place. She could see the *Morena* through her scope, and at only a few kilometers away, it was an easy shot.

She knew the stakes. If they were found out, there would be no choice but to destroy it, killing almost everyone on board.

The thought made her nauseous, but she kept her focus through the scope.

She heard the chatter through the open radio comm. Kiwi was doing her banter with the *Morena*, still convincing in her act.

Then the radio from the surface cut through, and Noora felt her stomach drop.

They'd been found out. She would have to fire.

"*Oh, fuck me,*" she heard Kiwi say over the radio.

Jason chimed in. "*Noora, did you hear that? You need to fire on the Morena now. Aim for the bridge.*"

"I—I just, I—," Noora stuttered, starting to hyperventilate.

"*Noora,*" Dax said over the radio. "*We can't escape. You have to shoot.*"

"I just, I mean," she stuttered again. *I don't want to kill them,* she thought.

Kiwi's voice, husky, warm, and calm, came through the radio. "*Noora. They're locking onto us. If you don't fire now, we all die.*"

Noora got her breathing under control. She took a final deep breath, held it, then exhaled.

She targeted the bridge and pulled the trigger.

Several dozen .22-caliber bullets, each traveling at 5% the speed of light, ripped through the *Morena*. The bridge exploded in fire and decompression, and the ship started to drift. Noora saw through her scope at least half a dozen bodies fly out into space from the bridge.

"*Gottem!*" Jason said.

"*You did it, girl!*" Kiwi said.

But Noora went back to hyperventilating. Her nausea returned, and she felt mucus build up in her mouth.

"*Hey, Noora,*" Dax said, hearing her out-of-control breathing over the radio. "*You all right?*"

Noora didn't respond. As quickly as she could, she went to the nearest hatch, got inside the ship, ripped off her helmet, and vomited.

"*Noora,*" Dax said. "*Stay there. I'm coming to you.*"

She thought of everything she'd been through since coming to this system, and it put her panic attack into overdrive.

She'd been captured, sexually humiliated, in constant fear of being a prisoner for the rest of her life, was still filled with adrenaline from her escape, had killed one of the original boarding party members, and now had killed at least six people on the *Morena*.

Her breathing was rapid and out of control, and only stopped briefly to let her dry-heave. She stared at the deck plate, tears streaming down her contorted face.

She heard Dax come in, but couldn't look up at him.

"Hey, shhh," he said, crouching down and putting an arm on her back. "I'm right here."

Noora tried to say his name, tried to say anything, but her lungs wouldn't let her. She managed to sit up enough to look at him, only for her face to clench up. She cried loudly into his chest as he held her.

It took 20 minutes for her to breathe normally, and even then she still couldn't speak.

Kiwi chimed in over the intercom. "*Hey Dax, I'm taking the dropship to go pickup Gideon. You and Noora doing okay?*"

"Yeah, we're good," Dax said. "How's the ship? Anything you need me to do?"

"*Nothing that can't wait,*" Kiwi said. "*Hey Noora, love you, girl.*"

"I—I—," Noora tried to say before tearing up and hiding her face in Dax's chest.

"She loves you, too, Kiwi," Dax said.

"*What, no love from you, Dax?*" Kiwi jabbed.

"Fine," Dax said. "Love you, too, just don't tell anyone I said that."

Noora managed a brief laugh.

The *Isle of Skye* stayed in orbit around Lacaille 9352-C for several more days, making repairs and trading what they could with the colony's new de facto leader, Andreja.

They had parted with two tons of whey protein, a CNC machine, and three tons of welding rods and wire in exchange for processed aluminum, titanium, and digital currency. Noora had even given Gideon her entire Christmas bonus to buy them an industrial-grade 3D printer.

Kiwi, in all her generosity, uploaded the entire *Tenjou Rayden* series to the colony.

Gideon had asked the colony if they would be all right, as they were now stranded without the *Morena* and would be cut off from Earth for a long time, but Andreja had insisted they would be fine with their new equipment, and that they might even be able to restore the *Morena* enough to fly it again. The bridge had been destroyed, but its systems were intact.

The crew sat in the mess, exhausted, but enjoying a dinner of pork loin and roasted corn that Dax had put together.

"So," Kiwi said through a mouthful of pork. "When can we leave this fucking glacier and go somewhere else? And where are we going next?"

Noora, who could never finish half a beer before giving the rest to Dax, finished her first beer and cracked a second.

Philly Cheesesteak sat patiently on the floor, hoping for some pork loin.

"Well, it's back to Earth," Gideon said. "But given what we just went through, I want to know what the hell kind of a deal Lacaille's former leader made with Dmitry."

"So back to the solar system?" Dax asked.

Gideon nodded. "Back to the solar system."

"Hey, by the way," Kiwi said, raising her beer. "I can't believe I'm saying this, but, to fuckboy, for recapturing the ship."

"Hey, to fuckboy," Dax said.

"To Jason," Gideon said.

"To Jason," Noora echoed, raising her beer.

Jason raised his tea in appreciation. His eyes were half-closed and he was ready to sleep. "If, um, you guys don't mind," he said, "fuckboy is tired and wants to go to bed."

"Go ahead," Gideon said. "Leave your plate, we'll take care of it."

"Thank you."

Philly Cheesesteak rubbed up against Jason's leg, purring.

4. I NEVER THANKED YOU

Noora screams in her sleep, Kiwi has a shower scene, Gideon teaches the blade, Jason discovers a love of anime, and Dax doesn't get Tenjou Rayden.

Noora screamed for the fifth night in a row.

Her howling scared the hell out of Dax, who tried to shake her awake. "Hey," he said. "Hey hey hey, wake up."

Noora snapped awake, her lungs paralyzed for a few seconds as she came to her senses. She stammered a long exhale as if she were freezing cold, even though she was sweating profusely. She grabbed Dax's arms, trying to control her breathing.

"Shhhh," Dax said. "I've got you, I've got you." He didn't ask her what she had dreamt; he knew she couldn't speak. Instead, he let her have as long as she needed.

Her jaw jittered, and her breathing was a stuttering mess for a good 10 minutes before she finally got it under control.

Dax felt her body relax and heard her breathing normalize. He still didn't ask what she'd dreamed. He'd asked her when it first happened, but she hadn't been able to talk about it, so he didn't press her.

Noora finally took a deep, controlled breath, and said, "I'm sorry."

"No no no," Dax said. He kissed her temple. "Nothing to be sorry for."

Noora turned around, and Dax saw how swollen and red her eyes were. She slid on top of him and he slid his arms around her. She took another relaxed breath. "Thank you for holding me," she said.

"I'm just being selfish," he said.

Noora chortled, sniffing heavy snot back into her nose. She

listened to the gentle hum of the ship's vector drive for another minute before speaking again. "I don't know how to talk about it."

"You don't have to," Dax said, rubbing her back. "But if you ever want to, you know you can."

Noora teared up again, this time out of relief.

"What the fuck do you mean you don't understand!" Kiwi said. "We're halfway through the third season!"

Dax sat dumbfounded, staring at the wall screen. The crew were together in the mess hall watching Kiwi and Noora's favorite anime, *Tenjou Rayden*. Gideon was just as dumbfounded as Dax. Jason was enraptured with the show. Noora had already had two beers and was now sipping a mixed drink of whiskey and sour mix. Philly Cheesesteak was half-dozed on the floor.

"It's just," Dax said. "I mean, so, what just happened?"

"The *Rayden's* caught in the time-slip," Jason said.

"But the time-slip hasn't happened yet," Dax countered.

"No, the time-slip's been happening since the end of season two," Jason pointed out.

"Thank you!" Kiwi exclaimed. "See? Even fuckboy's been paying attention!"

"No no," Dax said. "Because they clearly established that season three is the prequel to season two, and that season one is, like, some in-between or something?"

"Yeah," Jason said. "That's because of the time-slip."

"Which hasn't happened yet!" Dax sparred. "Besides, where the hell's Dizzy? She didn't show up at all this episode."

"She'zz, umm," Noora slurred. "She'zzon that covert mission from Admiral Gossak."

"Yeah, and she was supposed to get the charge crystals to prevent the time-slip in the first place," Dax pointed out. "What am I missing here?"

Kiwi rolled her eyes. "Gideon, please tell me you're

following all this."

"I mean, I'm with Dax," he said. "I was hoping to see more Dizzy. She's the funniest character in the series, and she uses a katana. I mean, she doesn't wield it properly, but it's cool."

"That and she's just like Kiwi," Dax pointed out.

"Oh my god," Jason said. "You're right."

"Yeah, no, t-totally," Noora slurred again, pouring more whiskey into her glass. "Kiwi's not as goth as Dizzy, but she's got the right aesthetic."

"Plus, Dizzy drinks and swears all the time," Dax pointed out.

"And she hates authority," Gideon said.

"Jesus Christ, you guys are right," Jason said.

Philly Cheesesteak licked his mouth.

"Okay yes, she hates authority," Kiwi admitted. "But she's doing what Admiral Gossak said, just in the worst way possible with the best outcome."

"Yeah, just like you," Dax said.

"Just let me teach you how to use a katana one of these days, Kiwi," Gideon said. "Then you'll be exactly like Dizzy."

Noora blurted a drunken laugh. "Pffff." She pulled several long gulps from her drink, then stood up and said. "Hey, I gotta, um, I gotta go use the restroom, you guys can totally start the next episode without me." She stumbled out of the mess hall.

"Yeah, um," Dax said, standing up and following Noora. "Yeah, you guys go ahead."

Kiwi, Gideon, and Jason had all watched Noora stumble out and knew Dax was going to check on her.

"Guys, I'm worried about Noora," Kiwi said.

"Yeah, me too, love," Gideon said.

"What do you think's wrong with her?" Jason asked. "She never used to drink."

Gideon sighed. "I think she doesn't know how to deal with what we just went through at Lacaille."

"I thought she was a military sniper," Jason said. "She hasn't seen combat, or had to kill anyone before?"

"No, she hasn't," Kiwi said. She got up. On her way out of the mess, she said to Gideon, "Hey, do you think you actually could teach me how to use a katana?"

"Of course," Gideon said. "I mean, if you want to."

"Let's do it, maybe start tomorrow morning?" Kiwi said.

"Bright and early in the armory?" Gideon asked.

"You got it!" Kiwi said. "I'm gonna go check on Noora and Dax."

Dax didn't want to embarrass Noora, but he was too worried not to check on her. He opened the door to the bathroom nearest to the mess hall to see her emptying her stomach into the toilet.

"Oh, Jesus, hey hey hey, I gotcha," he said.

"Nnno," Noora fumbled. "Go away, Dax, I jus, I need to—"

"Not going anywhere," he said, trying to stabilize her. "Just let it out, it's all right."

Noora vomited again. A long string of spittle hung off her mouth. She spit it out and flushed the toilet.

Dax had left the door open. Kiwi came in. "Hey, guys, are you—ohhh, shit, lemme go get some water and a towel."

Noora tried catching her breath, only to start crying. "I'm so sorry, I'm just, I—"

"Shhhh," Dax said, rubbing her back.

Kiwi was already back with a towel and a canister of cold water. She gave Dax the towel while shaking the canister. "Here's a towel, it's already damp, and I put some electrolytes in the water."

Dax took the towel, helped Noora sit upright and gently wiped her face.

"Here ya go, girl," Kiwi said, handing Noora the canister.

Noora fumbled the top open and took a modest sip. Her eyes eventually found Kiwi, and she said, "Thank you, Kiwi," before tearing up again.

"Hey, hey," Kiwi said in her warm voice, kneeling on the floor with them. She put a hand on Noora's leg and another on her cheek. "We gotcha, girl. We gotcha."

"Here, have another sip," Dax said.

Noora sniffled and then sipped the water again.

"Think you can stand?" Kiwi asked.

Noora gave a sluggish nod. She stood up like a newborn fawn. Dax helped her up. "Sorry," she said again. "I'm so embarrassed. I've never drank that much before, I just—"

"Hey, stop apologizing," Kiwi said.

"She's right," Dax agreed. "Stop apologizing. We're here for you."

"Holy shit, Dax, did you just agree with me?" Kiwi said.

"Let's not make a habit of it, okay?" Dax said.

Noora managed a laugh, then her face contorted back into tears. "I love you guys," she said.

"Ohhh, hey," Kiwi said, hugging her. "We love you, too."

The three of them held each other for a moment.

"Now," Kiwi said. "Let's get you into the shower. Come on, I'll shower with you."

"You got her?" Dax asked, handing off his share of Noora's weight to Kiwi.

"I got her, don't worry," Kiwi said, escorting Noora out of the restroom. "And don't get your hopes up, Dax. You know I don't do girl-on-girl."

"Fuck you, Kiwi," Dax said. "I'll get you guys some dry clothes and leave them outside the showers."

Noora leaned her weight into the shower wall with both hands. The hot water was a relief, but the floor wouldn't stop spinning.

Kiwi was next to her, under her own shower head, lathering up, but keeping an eye on Noora to make sure she didn't slip.

"I keep having these—these nightmares," Noora said. "Like, and I wake up screaming and I can't move, and—but Dax is there and he holds me, and, like, I want to tell him, but I can't even talk, and—"

"I know, sweetie," Kiwi said, putting a hand on Noora's shoulder. "He's told me. He's really worried."

"I just—I just don't wanna dream anymore," Noora said.

"I know what you mean," Kiwi said.

Noora looked at her. "You do?"

Kiwi nodded.

"But, but you've been fine since we left Lacaille."

"It's not because of Lacaille," Kiwi said, rinsing her hair. "It's from, well," she hesitated. "Let's just say I know what you mean when you say you don't want to dream."

"Oh my god," Noora said. Her drunken mind heard an entire tragedy behind what Kiwi just said. "Oh my god, I'm so sorry, Kiwi. What happened to you?"

But Kiwi just smiled. "It's all right. I'll tell you one of these days. For now, finish up your shower, because I'm not soaping you up."

They both finished up, Kiwi making sure Noora didn't stumble. They dried off and got into the fresh clothes Dax had laid out for them. "Here, lemme walk you to Dax's room," Kiwi said. "And drink all of that water you can. You'll thank me in the morning."

"Thank you," Noora said. Her stomach still swam, but she drank the water.

They got to Dax's room, who opened the door and said, "Hey," to Noora.

"Hey," she said back.

"Here, wanna lay down?" he asked.

Noora nodded, giving Dax a hug.

He held her for a bit, made eye contact with Kiwi, mouthed the words, *Call you*, and brought Noora in.

"Goodnight, Kiwi," Noora said.

"Goodnight, girl."

"How is she?" Kiwi asked. She and Dax were back in the mess, pouring bourbon for each other.

"She passed out about three seconds after I got her into bed," Dax said, taking a gulp. "But I made sure she downed more of that water first."

"Good," Kiwi said, raising her glass, then downing it.

"How was she in the shower?"

Kiwi sighed. "She was a mess. Like, she was telling me how she doesn't wanna dream anymore, and that's why she drank so much tonight."

"Jesus," Dax said. He sighed himself, taking another sip of bourbon. "I mean, it's been bad, I'm not even complaining, it's just hearing her scream at night, I don't know what I can do."

"Just keep being yourself," Kiwi said. "She loves you, and you're doing exactly what she needs. All we can do is be here for her, and we're doing that."

Dax nodded, poured them both another bourbon, and raised his glass. "I never thanked you, by the way," he said. "So thanks."

"No problem, dude. Last one, bottom's up!" Kiwi said, draining her glass. "Whew!"

"Last one?" Dax asked. "You're not even warmed up."

Kiwi stood up. "Yeah, but Gideon said he'd start teaching me how to use a katana tomorrow. That shit's sharp! Can't be hungover!" She stepped over to Dax, gave him a peck on his head, and said, "Goodnight, you."

Dax poured himself another bourbon. "Night, Kiwi."

"Morning, Kiwi," Gideon said as his technician strolled into the armory.

"Morning, captain!" she greeted.

"My, you're in a good mood," Gideon said.

"Yeah," Kiwi said, lightly stretching out. "Enjoy it while it lasts!"

"Can I ask, how was Noora last night?"

"Oh, man," Kiwi said. "She'll be fine. It's just, she's a sweet, great person, and she's never been through anything like that before. I think she's just, she's still processing what happened."

"Yeah, I figured," Gideon said. "Think she'll be all right?"

Kiwi nodded. "It sounds corny, but she's got us, and we've got her. She works out like a motherfucker, and that's like 90% of mental health right there. The rest of it is just us being us and being here for her when she needs it."

Gideon nodded. "Thanks for that, Rosevine." He grabbed what looked to Kiwi like two wooden, katana-shaped sticks. "Right then, let's get started."

"Um, where's the katana?" Kiwi asked.

"We'll get there," Gideon said. "Right now, you start with a bokken."

"A bo—a bo-what?"

"A wooden katana."

Kiwi scoffed playfully. "Why do you tease me like this, Gideon? You know I wanna touch that lever-action katana of yours."

"And you will, love. You'll just learn to throw your first hundred thousand cuts or so with this before I give you a real blade." He handed her a bokken. "Right, now here's how you hold it."

Noora woke up, mildly dizzy and with a slight headache, but not nearly in as bad shape as she deserved. Kiwi and Dax had been right about making her chug that water.

She had enjoyed a dreamless sleep, but knew she couldn't drink herself into oblivion every night. She would need to find other ways to get a handle on things.

She looked at her phone. It was early morning. She turned

over to see Dax, still asleep, his mouth ajar, and his long, wavy hair draped over the pillow.

She nuzzled into him. He stirred and put his arms around her. "Morning," he said, waking up. "How you feeling?"

"A little out of it but I'm fine," Noora said, enjoying the feel of his arms. She slid an arm and a leg over him. "You know, I never thanked you for saving me at Lacaille."

"How do you mean?" Dax asked, stroking her back. "You got out of there and to the dropship on your own."

"I know, but, I mean, what you said to me just before they separated us. You told me to focus on escaping, whatever it took, because that's what the rest of you were doing. I was so scared and didn't know what to do, and I don't think I would've escaped if you hadn't said that to me."

Dax gently squeezed her. "It was genius what you did," he said.

Noora squeezed him back. "Have you ever had to kill anyone before?"

"No," Dax said. "Lacaille was the first time I've had to."

"Does it bother you at all?"

Dax thought for a moment. "No," he said. "They boarded us, kidnapped us, and tried to kill us. I would've killed 100 of them if that's what it took."

Noora wished she could have that mindset. "Do you ever dream about it?"

"A few times, yeah," Dax said. "I see the Foreman whose rebreather I sabotaged, and I see the Foreman I choked out, and I wish I could've made them both suffer more. I know that's not good of me, but when I've dreamed of them, that's the only thing I can think of."

Noora took a pensive moment.

"I'm sorry," Dax said. "That was dark of me."

"No, no, it's okay," Noora insisted. "I asked, and, I don't know, it helps to hear." She slid a hand up and down his chest, feeling safe and comforted. "You feel so good."

"So do you," Dax said. They lay together for a couple

minutes without saying anything, until Dax broke the silence. "What do you say? Get some coffee in the mess?"

Noora kissed his cheek. "Good idea."

"So how does a Scotsman get into katanas?" Kiwi asked, strolling with Gideon from the armory to the mess.

"Oh don't get me wrong," Gideon said. "I love a good claymore like any fellow highlander. Just something about the Japanese blade speaks to me. A refined, lethal work of art."

"Hey, I never thanked you, by the way," Kiwi said. "Thanks for the lesson."

"Of course," Gideon said, as they came up to the mess. "Same time tomorrow if you're up for it?"

"Let's do it!"

They strolled into the mess to see Dax, Noora, and Jason chit-chatting over coffee. They both noticed Noora seemed to be in good spirits.

"Morning, lovelies," Gideon said.

"Sup, gang," Kiwi said.

Dax and Jason raised their coffees in greeting.

"Good morning you guys," Noora said sweetly.

Gideon got himself a coffee, Kiwi a water, and both joined the rest of the crew.

"Right then," Gideon said. "Any hope of finally repairing the docking ring? We get to the solar system in about a week, so it's what I'd like to call 'a priority.'"

"Oh yeah, we're almost done," Kiwi said. "Can probably finish today or tomorrow."

"Dax, what do you think?" Gideon asked.

Dax shrugged. "Kiwi's been leading all the refitting, fabrication, and welding, so I defer to her."

"Speaking of getting back to the solar system," Jason said. "What's the plan once we get there."

"Actually, I wanted to talk to you about that," Gideon said.

"Don't worry, I'll fill all of you in eventually, but yeah, Jason, let's talk after coffee."

Philly Cheesesteak sauntered into the mess, yawning, stretching out his front legs, then his hind legs, and jumping up onto the table with everyone.

"Philly bear!" Kiwi said, rubbing him down.

"Hey, Philly Phil," Dax said.

"Hey, Philly Cheesesteak," Noora said.

"What's up, asshole?" Jason said.

"Don't talk to him that way," Kiwi chided.

"Hey," Jason said. "That little asshole and I saved each others' asses and took back the ship when all of you were stranded. He and I understand each other."

Philly Cheesesteak blinked in agreement.

While this went on, Gideon pulled out his phone, typed a few things, then put it away. He got up. "Well then. I'm going to head to the bridge. Jason, meet me up there when you get the chance. Dax, get to engineering when you can just to check on everything, and Kiwi, lemme know how the docking bay goes today."

"Yessir," Kiwi said, getting up. "Noora, wanna join me if you feel like it?"

"Oh, um, yeah, I'll be there soon, just gonna finish my coffee."

Gideon and Jason got up and headed for the bridge. Kiwi got up to go put on a pressure suit so she could work on the docking bay. Dax got up, nipped Noora on the head, and headed to engineering.

Leaving just Noora and Philly Cheesesteak together at the table.

Noora smiled. "Hey, Philly Phil."

Philly Cheesesteak came up to Noora and head-butted her.

"Oh my god, why are you so cute?"

He purred loudly.

"You really did save Jason and the rest of us, didn't you?"

Philly Phil blinked.

"How do you do it?"

Philly Cheesesteak trilled, wondering what Noora was asking.

"I mean, like, Jason told us what happened. You don't, like, have any qualms about leading that guy back to engineering and then Jason killing him?"

Philly Cheesesteak blinked proudly.

Noora chuckled. "Of course. You cats love murder."

Philly held his eyes closed, purring loudly.

Noora smiled. She scratched his face and head, saying, "You're such a cute, bad boy. Thank you, Philly Phil."

She got up, ready to put on her own pressure suit to help Kiwi finish out repairs to the docking bay. She reflexively checked her phone.

And found a text from Gideon.

Hey Noora. Check in with me sometime today. No rush, no worries. Anytime that works for you.

She put her phone away and made her way to the docking bay.

"So, what's up?" Jason asked, taking a seat on the bridge with Gideon.

"I just have one question for you," Gideon said. "Do you still have doses of that truthinol stuff?"

"Why yes, I do," Jason confirmed. "In fact I gave samples to the mender in the infirmary. It can produce the stuff on command."

"Excellent," Gideon said. "Once we get to the solar system, I'll brief everyone on what's going to happen. For now, suffice to say we might be doing some kidnapping and interrogation."

Jason raised an eyebrow. "Well, just so happens those are two strengths I have."

"Yeah, I know from experience," Gideon chuckled. "By the way, I never thanked you for what you did back at Lacaille."

"What do you mean?" Jason asked.

"I mean that even though the rest of us were kidnapped, you took it on yourself to hold the ship and prevent it from being captured. You didn't have to do that, but I'm fucking grateful for what you did, because we wouldn't be here if not for you."

Jason nodded. "Thanks, Gideon."

"Thank *you*," Gideon said. "Now, I know I've got the same access to the Ralston database that you have, but I'd like you to find out what you can about Dmitry Ivanoff. He's a contact of mine in Macedonia. I've already tried to look him up, but I have a feeling you'll find more than I have."

"He wouldn't be the one we might be kidnapping and interrogating, would he?"

Gideon winked. "Can't give away all my secrets."

Noora had been in a pressure suit for the last six hours, working with Kiwi on welding together the last bits of the docking bay so that it could hold an atmosphere.

"*You think we're good?*" she asked Kiwi over shortwave.

"*Yeah, I think we're good. Here, let's get back inside the ship and see if it can hold any pressure.*"

The two of them went through the nearest airlock, waited for the pressure to normalize, and took off their helmets. Noora could smell the buildup of sweat in her suit.

"All right," Kiwi said, tapping some commands into a local console. "Flooding the docking bay with some atmosphere. Not detecting any leaks. Looks like we're good."

"Nice," Noora said. "Do you, um, do you mind if I take off? Gideon wanted to see me when I had the chance."

"Oh, of course!" Kiwi said. "No problem. Go ahead. There's nothing left to do anyway. I'll keep the docking bay pressurized and see if there are any small leaks we're not seeing yet."

"Thank you," Noora said. She cycled the next airlock door, entered the ship, and got out of her pressure suit. She went to her room, grabbed some fresh clothes, then made her way to the showers. When she was done, she called Gideon over the intercom. "Hey captain, it's me. You free?"

"*Hey, Noora, yeah, come on up to the bridge.*"

She wasn't sure what he wanted to see her about, but Gideon wasn't the type to spring surprises on people one-on-one. He probably just wanted to check in with her.

She got to the bridge to see Gideon staring at his captain's viewscreen, flipping through various charts. "Hey, thanks for coming up," he greeted.

"Of course," Noora said, sitting down at her usual navigation console.

"How's the docking bay looking?"

"Yeah, it's looking good," Noora said. "We just pressurized it, and there are no obvious leaks. I think Kiwi's going to keep checking it to make sure there aren't any micro-leaks. We'll probably run a scanner over the whole thing tomorrow to double check."

"Hell of a number Jason did on it, eh?" Gideon said, smiling.

Noora smiled, too. It had taken her and Kiwi weeks to fix the docking bay. She hadn't even minded the work. "He did indeed. Can't say I blame him, though. I mean he did save the ship that way."

"That he did," Gideon said. "I wanted to ask, how've you been?"

"I, um, yeah," Noora said, pondering how to answer, when out of nowhere she teared up and started crying.

"Oh no!" Gideon said, pulling out a handkerchief. "Don't worry, Kiwi makes all of us cry from time to time."

Noora managed a laugh through her tears, accepting Gideon's handkerchief. "I'm sorry," she said, wiping her face. "It's just been, um, it's…"

"Take your time, love."

Noora took a few calming breaths and said, "It's like, I mean it's like right now. I'm fine, and I feel fine, and out of nowhere I start crying. And I keep having nightmares about, you know, what happened at Lacaille. And I can't believe I killed at least seven people, probably more, and I'm just, I just don't know."

Gideon nodded thoughtfully. "You know, I never thanked you for saving all of our lives."

Noora looked up at him, then sheepishly said, "Don't give me too much credit. If Jason hadn't held the ship, we'd still be there. If Kiwi hadn't gotten our phones, we'd still be there. If Dax hadn't done what he did, we'd never have escaped. If you hadn't distracted the whole colony for as long as you did, we wouldn't have made it back to the ship."

"And if you hadn't done what you did, we would've lost the ship, and you, Kiwi, Dax, Jason, and Philly Cheesesteak would all be dead," Gideon said.

Noora looked down and nodded. She understood.

"You're a good person, Noora, the most kind-hearted out of all of us. You've got an incredible sharpshooting talent, this is the first time you've used it to defend yourself, and it won't be the last. But in a way, someone like you is best-suited for violence. You don't want to use it, but when the situation comes up, you can, and you'll do what's right, even though you don't want to. And I don't know if any of what I'm saying helps, I just don't want you to think you're not a good person, because you're a great person. Don't let the harshness of space ever change your mind on that."

Noora nodded again. "Thanks, Gideon."

"Is there anything I can do? Anything you need?"

Noora shook her head. "No, it's okay, I think, um, I think I needed to hear that." She wiped her eyes.

"That's all I really wanted," Gideon said. "Just to see how you're doing, and remind you that you can bug any one of us anytime."

Noora stood up. "I know I can," she said. "You guys are great." She didn't know what to do with the handkerchief now that it was soaked with her tears and nose drippings.

"Keep it," Gideon said, as if reading her mind.

"Thanks, Gideon," Noora said, then left the bridge.

She was thirsty, realizing she hadn't had anything to drink since before she and Kiwi had started working on the docking bay. She made her way to the mess.

Along the way she thought about what Gideon had said. He had been right. Maybe reminding herself of that would eventually make things easier, but she still saw the face of the man she'd shot, and the bodies she saw fly out into space when she fired on the Morena.

She made it to the mess hall to find Kiwi and Jason. Kiwi was fresh out of the showers with a beer can popped open. Jason had his usual tea. The two were in deep conversation about *Tenjou Rayden.*

"No, see, that's the thing," Kiwi said. "It's heavily *implied* that Dizzy is way older than she looks because—oh hey Noora!"

"Hey guys."

"Hey, Noora," Jason said.

"Dude," Kiwi said to Noora. "Fuckboy here is totally into *Tenjou Rayden.* He even gets all the back lore!"

Noora poured herself some cold water and joined them.

"I've never even watched anime before," Jason said. "I don't know what it is, it's just addicting."

Kiwi could see Noora was down. "Hey, you all right?"

"Oh, um, yeah, it's just, I'm sorry," she said.

"Sorry for what?" Kiwi responded with playful enthusiasm.

Noora stared off at the wall. She wanted to talk, but didn't want to bring everyone's mood down.

"Hey," Kiwi said, rubbing her arm. "Really, what's on your mind?"

Noora exhaled, remembering what Gideon had said, that they're all there for her. "I'm sorry," she said. "I'm just thinking about that guy on the boarding party. I didn't mean to kill him. And I'm thinking about the *Morena* and what I did."

Jason chimed in. "You mean the guy you shot from the first boarding party?"

Noora nodded.

"You didn't kill him," Jason said.

Noora looked at him, confused. "But, when we were down there, their leader said we'd killed four of them. That includes the guy I shot."

Jason shook his head. "The only one killed was the guy Gideon shot. The other three did die, but you didn't kill the guy you shot."

"What are you talking about?" Kiwi asked. "How do you know all this?"

Jason held up his phone. "I, uh, I may have downloaded Lacaille's entire database while we were in orbit."

"What the fu—*how?*" Kiwi asked.

"It's easy," Jason said. "Their protocols are all a couple decades out of date, and they had no cybersecurity of any kind. Probably figured they didn't need it out here. Anyway, their records show the guy that was shot and the one that you smacked with your whip, Kiwi, both arrived alive to their infirmary, but the cold-hearted bastards in charge decided it wasn't worth fixing them up, so both were thrown out into the cold. But the guy that Dax punched, he died soon after they arrived. Brain swelling. He slammed his head pretty hard on the deck."

Noora was stunned, and almost felt guilty at her sudden relief. She had been careful not to kill him, and she had succeeded. The *Morena* had given her no choice, but this bit of knowledge would help her sleep easier.

"Thank you, Jason," she said. She got up to get herself more water.

"Noora, you good?" Kiwi asked.

"Yeah," she said. "Yeah, I feel a lot better. Thank you guys. I'm gonna go find Dax, hang out with him for a bit."

"See you later," Kiwi said.

"See you," Jason said.

On her way out of the mess, Noora heard Kiwi say to Jason, "Hey, do you think you can, like, show me how you downloaded that database and, like, how you do what you do in general?"

Noora queued up the intercom. "Hey Dax, you busy?"

"Not at all. In my room. Come on by."

She made her way to Dax's room to find him sitting on the floor, leaning against his bed, staring at the large viewscreen on the opposite wall. He was watching *Tenjou Rayden*, and had a focused scowl on his face, which Noora knew to mean that he was in deep concentration.

"Oh my god," she said, delighted. "You're watching *Tenjou*?"

"From the beginning again," Dax said. "Join me."

Noora sat down on the floor next to him. "I didn't think you were enjoying it."

"It's personal now," Dax said. "I don't care what it takes, I will understand this fucking plot if it kills me."

Noora giggled, then let out a deep, hearty laugh.

5. A CHAT WITH THE FAMILY

The crew arrives back in the solar system and plans a trip to Chicago to kidnap a mafia boss.

"*Coming out of vector space in 5 seconds,*" Dax said over the intercom. "*3...2...1.*"

The *Isle of Skye* did a gentle lurch, the hum of vector space disappeared, and the crew worked on getting their bearings.

"Noora, Jason," Gideon said. "How we looking?"

"We are," Noora said, tuning her navigation screen. "Damn, looks like about a 10-hour flight to Earth."

Jason whistled. "Yeah, confirmed. How the hell do you do that?" he asked Noora. "You basically just threaded a needle from 11 light years away."

"You know," Noora said, a touch of pride in her voice. "It's funny. When you put me on navigation, Gideon, I was like, 'what the hell, I've never done that before,' but it really just feels like shooting. I aim the ship and hit my targets."

"Well, again, a brilliant snipe," Gideon said. "Dax, Kiwi, how are things in engineering?"

"*We're good,*" Dax confirmed. "*Engines are powered up, so blast away.*"

"Well, then," Gideon said. "Noora, if you would kindly blast us towards Earth."

Noora keyed in a series of commands. "Gideon," she said. "When I'm done here, do you mind if I take off for a few minutes? Now that we're back in the solar system I wanna send a message to my family, you know, let them know I'm still alive."

"Of course," Gideon said. "And actually, I'm gonna have everyone meet up in the mess hall in an hour, so once you're done here, take your time with your message, and meet us in the mess."

Noora gave a cute salute.

Gideon smiled. It was good seeing Noora in better spirits.

"All right, my lovelies," Gideon said in the mess hall, with Dax, Kiwi, Noora, Jason, and Philly Cheesesteak giving him rapt attention. "How many of you thought that little ambush at Lacaille was maybe a wee bit too convenient?"

Everyone raised their hand. Philly Cheesesteak gave a feline trill.

"Yeah, me too," Gideon continued. "Now, I don't know if it was malice, incompetence, or maybe just an unhappy accident, but we're gonna find out."

Kiwi raised an eyebrow. "Aaaand, how are we gonna find out?"

"We're gonna kidnap and interrogate a Macedonian crime boss," Gideon said.

Kiwi threw her arms up to the ceiling. "Of course," she said sarcastically. "Why do I even ask such stupid questions?"

"I'm sorry," Dax said. "But wasn't it a Macedonian crime boss that got us the contract for Lacaille in the first place?"

"Why yes, it was," Gideon said.

Noora quietly raised a hand. "I'm, um, I'm sorry, what's a crime boss doing getting us interstellar contracts?"

"Give the mafia some credit, Noora," Gideon said. "Sure, they do shady dealings, but they've all got their hands in legitimate business ventures."

"He's in Chicago," Jason said out of nowhere.

"I'm sorry, what?" Gideon said.

"This is Dmitry you're talking about, right? The one you asked me to look up?"

Gideon nodded.

"Yeah," Jason said. "He's in Chicago."

"How the—"? Gideon asked.

"How in the—?" Dax inquired.

"What?" Noora asked.

"Oh great," Kiwi said. "My fucking psycho mom is in Chicago."

"*Mr-r-reh?*" Philly Cheesesteak asked.

"I mean, it's easy," Jason said. "I knew who we were looking for, tapped into Earth's data streams as soon as we dropped out of vector space an hour ago, found him referred to on social media even though he's not on social media. He's in Chicago. Gonna be there for the next week. He's at some convention with Braxton Keller and all his millionaire friends."

"Braxton Keller, huh?" Dax asked.

Kiwi and Noora were clueless.

"Australian. World champion light heavyweight kickboxer," Dax said. "Nickname is *The Thunder from Down Under*. Playboy, millionaire, braggart. Sells himself as a natural businessman when he's clearly into some shady shit."

"How do you know all that?" Gideon asked.

Dax shrugged. "Because I follow all that stuff. Boxing, MMA, even kickboxing. Keller's well-known for a kickboxer, and no one gives a shit about kickboxing. I mean, say what you want about him, but the sonofabitch can fight."

"I feel like there's a joke here," Kiwi said. "A Macedonian crime boss and an Australian kickboxer walk into a bar."

"More like a nightclub," Jason said. "Keller's constantly posting his lifestyle on social media. Always out clubbing, buying champagne by the case, picking up as many women as he can, all while dropping vague hints at the business he's doing."

Kiwi's interest spiked. She opened up her phone and started browsing social media for him.

Gideon nodded. "It makes sense that we'll find Dmitry with him. Majority of his business deals get done at a bar, restaurant, or nightclub."

"All right," Dax said. "So we're gonna kidnap and interrogate a crime boss who's hanging out with a world champion fighter and god-knows who else. I hate it already. What's the plan?"

Gideon looked to Jason. "You said he's gonna be there for the next week?"

Jason nodded. "Keller's promoting it as a private convention to his followers. Starts in a couple days. He's vague on where it's gonna be held, but I can find that out easily."

"Right then," Gideon said. "The plan is we get to Chicago, do some reconnaissance, make our move when it looks best, shoot up Dmitry with some truthinol, ask him our pressing questions, and go from there."

"Hey, um," Kiwi said. "Where are we staying?"

"Don't know yet," Gideon said. "Only just found out he's gonna be in Chicago."

"Why don't we crash my grandparents' farm? It's close enough, and Philly Phil likes playing around the barn."

Dax scowled. "You're from Wisconsin. Chicago's in Illinois."

"And you're from Texas and don't know any geography north of Oklahoma. The farm is like 70, maybe 80 miles from Chicago. Can get to downtown in like an hour."

Gideon liked the idea. "Out of the city, out of the way. Inconspicuous. I like it. Sure your grandparents will be okay with the lot of us staying there?"

"Oh, trust me, they'll love it," Kiwi said. "Besides, they'd disown me if they found out I was back in the solar system, in Chicago of all places, and didn't bother to see them. I'll call them once we're close enough to Earth. They'd love to meet all of you, anyway."

"Right, then," Gideon said. "It's a plan."

"Hey, I'm sorry, Gideon," Dax said. "But *what's* a plan? Like, what are we gonna ask him? What if he did betray us? What if he didn't? Either way, do you think he's gonna be happy that we kidnapped him and shot him up with truth serum? In what scenario does this work out well for us?"

"Here's the plan," Kiwi interjected. "We take the dropship to Chicago O'Hare Orbital. We head up to my grandparents' farm. We relax and drink and have a beautiful feast. Then we all head back down to Chicago so Noora and I can have a girl's day shopping and getting our hair done while the three of you do your reconnaissance. After that, we'll decide just what the hell we're doing."

Gideon raised his eyebrows and nodded. "What she said. In the meantime, we'll be close enough to Earth soon so you can do live calls with anyone there. We'll set in a parking orbit, take the dropship down, and make our way to Wisconsin. Make sure you're all packed and ready to go. That means you, too, Philly Cheesesteak."

"*Myeh, br-r-r-reh.*"

"Grandpa bear!" Kiwi squealed.

"*Holy fucking shit, Kiwi! Where are you!*"

"Well obviously I'm back in the solar system, dumbass. You didn't get my message?"

"*You coming down to Earth? You stopping by the farm?*"

"Yes! Of course! And actually, I'm bringing the whole crew with me. That gonna be okay?"

"*Shouldn't be a problem! How many are coming with you?*"

"You really didn't read my message, did you. I hope grandma did. Anyway there's me, Gideon, Dax, Noora, fuckboy, and Philly Cheesesteak, so me plus four and a cat, and honestly a couple of us will probably sleep in the barn."

"*It's the middle of goddamn February in Wisconsin, Kiwi! Who the hell wants to sleep out in the fucking barn!*"

"You know I love the barn! Besides, it's got that huge wood stove. Turns the place into a blast furnace."

"*Yeah for maybe a few hours.*"

"Jesus Christ, grandpa, I've slept out in the barn plenty of times in the winter, we'll be fine."

"*Hey, wait, you said Dax is coming, right?*"

"Yeah."

"*That the motherfucker you say is a better chef than me?*"

"Yeah."

"*All right,*" grandpa sighed. "*I'll deal with him when he gets here. So, I know Gideon is your captain, you've mentioned Noora before, I know Philly Cheesesteak, and who's this 'fuckboy' you're talking about?*"

"Oh, yeah, he's the asshole whose ship we shot up last year, and somehow he's now part of the crew."

"*And you trust this piece of shit?*"

"Yeah, just, trust me, he's cool."

"*I trust you, sweetie. When are you guys getting here?*"

"Oh, shit, I'm guessing, like, in about eight hours?"

"*Okay, we'll make sure everything's set up. Text or call us when you land.*"

"See you soon!"

"*Dax! Hey!*" Dax's mom said. "*It's so good to—HEY, EVERYONE, DAX IS ON THE LINE!*"

"Hey, mom, good to see you, too. What family gathering did I interrupt this time?"

"*Oh, you didn't interrupt anything! Just your brother and sister and their families. Your father is outside playing around in the garden. So you're back near Earth! Are you stopping by?*"

"Don't know if I'll have time," Dax said. "Just wanted to call and say hi."

"*You look different,*" Dax's mom said. "*Almost like you're happy.*"

Her observation caught Dax off guard. "I mean, um, heh heh," he stuttered.

"*Oh my god!*" his mom exclaimed in realization. "*Are you seeing someone? You're seeing someone aren't you!*"

"*Dax is seeing someone?*" his brother said off screen.

"*Wait, he's got a girlfriend now?*" his sister said off screen.

"*Uncle Dax has a girlfriend?*" he heard one of his nieces say.

"How the f—," Dax said before censoring himself in front of his nieces and nephews, all of whom were trying to cram into the camera's view. He put his forehead into his palm, realizing there was no point in deflecting. "Okay," he said. "I wasn't planning on talking about it, but yes, I'm seeing someone."

"*I knew it!*" his mother exclaimed.

"*How do you meet someone in space?*" his sister asked.

"*Is she pretty?*" a niece asked.

"*Is it that Kiwi that showed up at the barbeque this last Fall?*" his brother asked.

"*Oh I remember her. She was making everyone's head turn,*" his sister said.

"Everybody calm down," Dax interjected, feeling the cross-talk starting to get on his nerves. "No, it's not Kiwi. It's um, it's someone else."

"*Well who is she? What's she like?*" his mom demanded.

"*What's she look like?*"

"*Is she someone on your ship?*"

"*Can we meet her? We have to meet her!*"

Dax knew he had only two choices: give his family what they wanted, or get tortured by their interrogation. "Yeah," he sighed. "Gimme a sec, okay?" He chimed Noora on the intercom. "Hey, it's me, are you, uh, you free?"

"*Of course! Just packing. What's up?*"

"So, um," Dax said awkwardly. "I'm on the line with my family, and they found out about you, and they wanna meet you."

"*Oh! I'd love to! Gimme, like, 30 seconds I'll be right there!*"

Dax exhaled. "She's on her way," he said to his family, who collectively cheered. Dax couldn't help but smile. Their constant talking drove him crazy, but he knew they were happy for him.

Noora came into the room and sat down next to him in front of the viewscreen. She wore her usual, simple tank top that showed off her arms. "Hey! Is this your family? Hi everyone! I'm Noora," she waved.

"*Look at her arms, she's so strong!*"

"*Nice to meet you, Noora!*"

"*Hiii!*"

"*Oh my god, Dax!*" his mom exclaimed, charmed by Noora's look and her bright energy. "*It's Noora? I'm Stephanie, Dax's mom.*"

"Stephanie, hi," Noora said, kind, bright, and grateful. "I'm sorry, Dax literally just called me. I didn't know I'd be meeting all of you today."

Dax stayed silent, but his mom picked up on his subtle smile at Noora.

"*So, um, Noora,*" his mom continued. "*Tell us about yourself! Where are you from? How did you two meet?*"

"*Are you from Canada?*" Dax's sister asked.

"*No, her accent's from Minnesota,*" his brother said.

"*She's got muscles!*" one of Dax's nephews exclaimed.

"Oh, yeah," Noora said with a giggle. "No, I'm from Finland. I, um, Dax and I met, when was it?" she said, glancing at Dax. "Almost a year ago? It was on Titan station around Saturn. His crew hired me, and I've been along with them ever since."

"*What do you do?*"

"*Yeah, what do you do?*"

"Yeah, so, um, I—" Noora said awkwardly before Dax stepped in.

"She's a sharpshooter," he said. "She's clean, she's precise, and she's lethal. So I expect all of you to be on your best behavior when you meet her." Dax had hoped his sarcasm would betray some truth, but it only backfired.

"*Oh my god, when do we get to meet her!*"

"*When are you guys coming?*"

"*I mean we're talking to you live, so you're almost here, right?*"

"*So, like, you'll be here this week? We should plan something!*"

"*Can you flex for us?*"

Noora giggled, both embarrassed and charmed. "If I flex, you promise you won't tell anyone?"

Dax's family was also charmed, and collectively nodded.

Noora cocked her left eyebrow, smiled, and flexed both arms.

"*Oh my god!*"

"Just, holy, I mean wow."

"Did you see that?"

Noora giggled and leaned into Dax, who couldn't help a smile.

"Look, I don't know if I can get down there, but I'll try. But if I do, can we please keep it to no more than 800 people?" Dax pleaded.

"Oh no, now don't you worry, Dax," his mom said. *"It'll just be me, your dad, your brother, your sister, and all your nieces and nephews."*

Dax exhaled in relief. That was only 11 people, including him and Noora, and was within his social limit. "Okay, good. We've got some business in Chicago first, and if we can get down to Marshall, I'll let you know."

"Noora," Dax's mom said. *"Dax is not coming without you. I just want you to know that."*

"I can't wait," Noora said, delighted. "It was so nice meeting all of you! I'm excited to see you all in person!"

"Take care, Aunt Noora!"

"Can't wait to see you!"

"Can you flex again?"

"Dax, don't come here without her!"

"Yes, yes, yes," Dax said, moving to cut the communication. "I love you guys, I'll be in touch, okay?"

"Hey, everyone!" Noora said in her native Finnish.

"Noora!" her mom said.

"Hey, Noora!" her little sister said.

"Noora, you're back!" her dad said.

"Yeah!" Noora said. *"I'm back!"*

"We got your message! You went interstellar?" her dad asked.

"I, um, yeah," Noora hesitated.

"That's so exciting!" her sister said.

"I mean, in a way, yeah," Noora said. "Sorry I wasn't in

touch earlier. We just got back."

"*Where did you go?*" her sister asked.

"Oh, it was a colony out on Lacaille, it's like about 11 light years from here."

"*Oh yeah,*" her dad said. "*I remember hearing about that expedition 20 years ago or so. So what did you guys do? Did you trade with them?*"

"Yeah," Noora hesitated, not wanting to divulge what she went through. "We, um, we traded. It was good."

"*Noora,*" her mother said. "*You seem, I don't know, you just seem different. Like, older since we saw you a few months ago. And happier.*"

"*Yeah,*" her sister confirmed. "*You're, like, glowing.*"

Noora blushed. "Yeah, it's um," she hesitated, knowing she couldn't hide anything from them. "It's um, well, Dax and I are a couple!"

Her sister squealed with delight.

But her mom gave a confused scowl. "*Noora, he's—he's married.*"

"*Yeah, I thought he was married,*" her dad echoed.

"No no, he *was* married," Noora emphasized. "It's really sad. He was married for, like, 14 years, and then his wife died like four years ago, and that's when he quit his engineering job to fly around in space, and like, we got to know each other so well before we, you know, we started seeing each other, and like, he was so patient and held back a lot because at first because he hated the idea of trying to date someone again, but we just hit it off so well, and he's really great, like, he," Noora started crying, remembering Lacaille. "He's the reason I was able to escape, because we got captured at Lacaille, and like, we made it out, but I had to destroy a ship that was about to fire on us, and Dax has just been really great helping me since then, because like I wake up screaming sometimes and I can't move, and like he's just there for me and doesn't tell me I'm overreacting and he just holds me and he's so sweet about it and, it's just, he's the best."

Noora's family were all stunned and didn't know what to

say.

"I'm sorry, guys," Noora said, wiping her face and realizing everything she'd just spilled. "I don't want you to worry about me, it's just, I want you to know I'm really happy where I am, and —"

"*You got captured?*" her dad asked.

"*Noora, oh my god!*" her sister exclaimed.

"I'm fine, guys!" Noora insisted, still wiping her eyes.

"*But Noora,*" her mom chimed in. "*You understand, every time you go out, we're scared you'll never come back. We're scared you'll get killed. Or you could fly off to some star or colony and we'd never hear from you again, and it sounds like that's almost what happened.*"

"No, I know, it's just," Noora stuttered, unable to explain to her family how tied she was to the *Isle of Skye*, how they needed her, and she needed them.

"*How much longer are you planning on working with them?*" her dad asked.

Noora shrugged. "I don't know. I just know I need to be here with them, not just with Dax, but everyone, like I'd be letting them all down if I didn't stay," she said. "Anyway, would you like to say hi to Dax? I met his family earlier, and I know you guys met him a few months ago, but he's great and I love him and I don't know if I'll make it to Finland this time, so I just wanted to talk with you guys and I wanted you to see him and know that I'm actually really happy and this is where I want to be."

Her family nodded. "*Yes,*" her sister said. "*We'd love to see him.*"

Noora nodded, and started to call up Dax on the intercom.

"*Oh,*" her sister chimed in again. "*Can you get Kiwi, too! She's so much fun!*"

Noora gave a full-toothed smile and said, "Yeah, lemme see if I can get her." She chimed the ship's intercom. "Hey Dax and Kiwi, this is Noora. There's an emergency in my room. My family wants to say hi to both of you."

Kiwi was the first to answer. "*Ooo, fun! I'll be right there!*"

"*Oh for Chrissake,*" Dax chimed in. "*Kiwi can I not have like three seconds to politely introduce myself to her family?*"

"*They already know who you are, jackass!*"

Noora's family heard the whole exchange, and couldn't help but laugh.

6. A LOUD CRACK & A STEEL ECHO

Dax makes dinner, Kiwi closes a boutique fashion store, Noora is a Finnish Duchess, Gideon buys some deep dish pizza, and Jason goes down a back alley.

"Grandpa bear!" Kiwi shouted, climbing out of the crew's rental van.

"Kiwi!" grandpa shouted back, trudging through the Wisconsin snow. "Where's that motherfucker Dax!"

Dax stoically got out the opposite side of the van, brushing his long hair behind his head, trying to act like the Wisconsin cold didn't bother him.

"Is that him?" Kiwi's grandpa asked, pointing at Dax.

"Yes," Kiwi said. "That's him."

Grandpa, 5-foot-2 on a good day, stout and tough as nails, ignored everyone else getting out of the van, and walked up to Dax, offering a handshake. "My little Kiwi says you're a better chef than I am."

Dax, 6-foot-2 and shaking grandpa's hand, scoffed. "Not *my* fault she's a liar."

"Pff," grandpa blurted. "Ha-ha! HA-HA-HA-HA-HAAAA! Get your ass in here! You're cooking tonight!" He brought Dax towards the house, still ignoring everyone else. "Hey sweetie!" he shouted as they entered the house. "We might have an asshole who can cook better than me! Also, Kiwi's here!"

"Well, it's official," Kiwi's grandpa said at the dinner table. "I'm never cooking again."

"Really, now, Richard," grandma said. "I can't believe you made our guest do all the cooking."

"Are you kidding?" Dax said. "That's how I relax. Thanks for letting me take over your grill."

"What are you making tomorrow?" grandpa asked.

"No, Dax, you don't have to cook tomorrow, you've already done more than enough," grandma said before looking to Noora. "Noora, you sure I can't get you a beer or some wine?"

"Oh, no, that's all right, I really just want water, but thank you."

Dax looked to his crewmates. "Are we even gonna be around tomorrow? What's the plan?"

"Mm, here's the plan," Kiwi said, finishing off a beer and popping another can. "We take the van back down to Chicago tomorrow morning. Noora and I are gonna have a girls day together so we can get our hair done and go shopping, and you boys can go do your reconnaissance thing or whatever."

Gideon liked the idea. "Sounds good to me," he said, looking at Jason. "What do you think?"

Jason, who was always on his phone, responded while flipping through his phone. "Yeah, that'll be perfect. I got a list of all the really high end clubs Dmitry and Braxton are likely to be at. There's only a few. Can scope them out during the day when they're closed, get an idea for the entrances, exits, all of that."

"What exactly are you guys planning?" grandpa asked.

"We're gonna kidnap a Macedonian crime boss," Kiwi said.

Gideon slapped his own forehead and wiped his face. "Kiwi, please, have the good decency not to announce our plans like that to your lovely grandparents."

"Oh relax. They're not gonna tell anybody."

"Why do you have to kidnap him?" grandpa asked.

"Exactly, do you really need to kidnap him? That just sounds like so much work," grandma said.

"Thank you," Kiwi said. "I totally agree. Like, why do we have to kidnap him?"

Gideon shrugged. "How else do you propose we interrogate him?"

"Well why can't we just go up and ask him nicely?" Kiwi asked.

"I mean," Gideon said. "Because he may very well have betrayed us."

"Yeah," Kiwi said. "But what if he didn't?"

Gideon shrugged again. "I'm all ears, Rosevine."

"Dahhhh," Kiwi exclaimed, chugging a beer. "All right, hear me out. What if, we're like, just nice, and go up to him and ask him politely if he sold us out to a bunch of commies?"

"The whole point of kidnapping him is we need to shoot him up with truthinol," Gideon pointed out. "I don't like needing to do that, but what alternative do we have?"

Kiwi took a pensive chug of beer. "Good point," she said. "Lemme sleep on it. Which, by the way, who wants to sleep in the barn with me?"

"Fuck that shit," Dax said. "Sorry for my language, grandma, grandpa, but fuck that."

"No, you're right, fuck that shit," grandpa said.

"Yeah, no, I'm good," Jason said.

"I'll, erm, I'll sleep in the house, if that's all right," Gideon said.

"Oh of course, we've got plenty of room," grandma said.

"Bunch of fucking pussies," Kiwi said. "Noora, don't leave me hanging, girl. You'll be warmer out there than you will be here, because that wood stove pumps out more BTUs than the *Skye's* reactor. Plus Philly Phil's sleeping out there with me." She looked to the floor. "Aren't ya, buddy?"

"*Br-r-r-ryah*," Philly Cheesesteak confirmed, rubbing against Kiwi's leg.

"I, um, I mean yeah," Noora said, looking to Dax and touching his arm. "If that's okay?"

"Of course," Dax said. "I'll just sleep with Jason. Jason, you're the small spoon, just so you know."

Noora giggled, as did the rest of the crew.

"I mean," Jason said in a deadpan tone. "You did make me dinner. Seems only fair."

A loud crack and a steel echo snapped Noora awake. At first she thought it was a gunshot, but her sniper ears knew better.

Two more went off successively, and as the fog of sleep dissipated from her brain, Noora recognized the snap of a whip. Kiwi must've been outside the barn practicing.

Philly Cheesesteak came up to Noora and greeted her. "Hey, Philly Phil," she said, sitting up from her cot. She was warmer than she thought she'd be. Kiwi had been right about the wood stove. Still, she kept herself wrapped in the blanket as she got up and made her way outside.

More snaps, cracks, and rings went off as Noora exited the barn and walked around to find Kiwi on the west side, power whip in hand. Two steel targets were set up on opposite sides of her, as well as a steel pipe sticking up six feet out of the ground.

To Noora it looked like a ballet as Kiwi executed two more perfect strikes on both targets, wrapped the whip around the steel pipe, and sent a power surge through it.

"Hey, good morning!" Noora said.

"Oh hey!" Kiwi said. "You sleep okay?"

"Yeah. Your whip woke me up."

"Yeah, sorry," Kiwi said. "I just wanted to get some practice in, and, you know, maybe wake up everyone else. It's already eight!"

"I like your setup," Noora said.

"Oh thanks," Kiwi said. "That's my mom," she said, pointing to a steel target. "That's also my mom," she said, pointing to the other steel target. "And that's Randall," she said, pointing to the steel pipe.

"Oh," Noora said, confused and mildly disturbed. "Okay."

Grandpa was making his way through the snow to Noora and Kiwi, two hot coffees in his hands. "Hey, you two!" he greeted. "Heard Kiwi's whip, figured you were both up."

"Oh, thank you so much," Noora said, accepting her coffee.

"Thank you, grandpa!" Kiwi squealed, accepting hers.

"So, you're headed to Chicago this morning?" grandpa

asked.

Kiwi nodded, blowing on her coffee and sipping it.

"Are you, uh, you planning on visiting your mom? I mean, it's been a while."

Kiwi nodded again. "It won't accomplish anything, but I was thinking about it."

Noora kept to herself, feeling the gravity of Kiwi and grandpa's conversation. She went to find Philly Cheesesteak.

"Of course you don't have to," grandpa said. "Just asking."

"When was the last time you spoke to her?" Kiwi asked.

Grandpa shrugged. "Don't remember. Long before the last time you were here. How about you?"

Kiwi shook her head. "Not since before I joined the *Isle of Skye*, so it's been a few years."

"Well, look, like I said, you don't have to," grandpa said. "Just with her, I mean, you know. Your grandma and I expect to wake up one morning and find out she's dead."

Kiwi cocked a surly eyebrow. "Who knows. Maybe she's already dead and has saved us all the trouble."

Grandpa shook his head. "We keep our eye on the obituaries. She's still around."

"Still where she used to be?" Kiwi asked.

Grandpa shrugged.

"Well look, thanks for the coffee," Kiwi said, making her way to the house. "And don't worry. If I do see her, I won't do anything naughty."

"Meh, it's okay if you do," grandpa said. "I mean yeah, she's my daughter, but you know I'll never forgive her."

Kiwi put an arm around him. "I love you, grandpa."

"Love you, too."

"Ahh, here we are," Kiwi said as the van pulled over to the curb in downtown Chicago.

"How long are you two gonna be?" Gideon asked as Kiwi

grabbed an oversized bag and got out with Noora.

"Please," Kiwi scoffed. "Two girls going shopping and getting makeovers? All fucking day. We'll text you guys when we're done."

Gideon gave a mock salute, the doors shut, and the van pulled away.

Kiwi and Noora were on the corner of East Hubbard and North Michigan. The din of the Chicago downtown was jarring compared to the quiet farm of Wisconsin and the silence of space.

"All right!" Kiwi said. "You ready to have fun?"

Noora looked at the storefront they were facing and read the sign.

Skövde.

"Oh my gahd," she exclaimed. "Kiwi what the fuck! This place is super expensive!"

"Well, it's a good thing I'm fucking rich!"

"I can't afford anything here!"

"Don't worry! It's all on me!"

"I just, I mean it'll take me forever to pay you back!"

"Noora, Noora, calm down," Kiwi said. "You gave away your bonus to buy an industrial printer for that colony, and that's after you saved all of our asses. We've been locked away on a ship in space for months. Let me treat you to this. We're gonna buy expensive clothes, we're gonna get our hair done, we're gonna get our nails done, and we're gonna be drop dead gorgeous."

"I mean," Noora hesitated. "Okay?"

Kiwi smiled. "All right. Do you, uh, do you have your sunglasses with you?"

"Oh, um, yeah," Noora said, taking them out of her purse.

"Okay, put those on, and do this; when we enter the store, don't take them off, don't speak to anybody, and only speak to me in Finnish."

Noora was confused. "Um, okay? Why?"

"Trust me, it'll be fun!" Kiwi took Noora's hand and led the way. "Hey, also, what's the name of a big city in Finland? One that's not Helsinki?"

"A big city? I mean, there's Turku," Noora said, not sure what Kiwi was planning.

"Toor-ku," Kiwi pronounced. They got to the entrance, and Kiwi opened the door for Noora.

"Hello and welcome," an impeccably dressed young woman greeted Noora.

Noora kept her sunglasses on and looked at Kiwi. "Toivon että tietäisin mitä teet." [I wish I knew what you're doing]

"Hi," Kiwi greeted the Skövde employee, her tone slightly dismissive. "Sorry, I have a discreet favor to ask. Is there a manager available I can speak to?"

"Of course, I'm a manager," the employee said. "Right over here." The boutique shop was empty except for them and two other employees. The manager led them to the checkout table. "What can we do for you?"

Kiwi whispered in Noora's ear. "Start looking around, grab whatever you want and try it on." She turned to the manager and pulled out her phone. "I see there's no one else here. Do you think you can keep it that way for the next 45 minutes?"

The manager was confused. "You, you want me to close the store?"

Kiwi nodded, as if she were expecting the answer to be 'yes.' She queued her phone to transfer $20,000 and tapped it to the cashier tablet. "I know this is sudden, but like I said, we're trying to be discreet."

"Oh, *oh*," the manager started, seeing the sum. "I, um, of course." She tapped a few tablet commands to lock the front door.

"Thank you so much," Kiwi said. "Let me know if you need more, especially when we're ready to check out."

"May I, um, may I ask who we have the pleasure of serving today?"

"Yeah," Kiwi said, leaning in. "She's the Duchess of Turku, part of the Finnish royal family. I'm her assistant. She insisted on going out shopping, so here we are."

Noora overheard her. "Suomessa ei ole kuningasperhettä!" [Finland doesn't have a royal family!] she yelled at Kiwi.

"And as you can see," Kiwi continued. "She's quite insistent."

"Well, both of you take all the time you need, and let us know if we can help."

Dax let loose another bored sigh.

"You can at least pretend to pay attention," Gideon said.

"Pay attention to what?" Dax asked. The Chicago noise was getting to him. "I've got no idea where we are in this fucking city, all these clubs and streets and back alleys look the same to me, and it's goddamn freezing out."

"Well pay attention to everything, because you'll need to know where you are when we grab Dmitry."

Dax shook his head. "Kiwi's right. This whole kidnapping thing is stupid."

"I'm still waiting for a better idea," Gideon said, just as Jason emerged from an alley.

"There's an exit back there to this club, but it's one way. You can get out, but you can't get in," he said.

Gideon nodded. "Well that works. Just gotta figure a way inside, assuming they come here."

"Yeah, that's gonna be a problem," Jason said.

"Why?"

"All these places we've checked out, do you know how exclusive they are?" Jason asked.

Gideon shook his head. "I don't go clubbing."

"Well, guys like us can't just get in," Jason said. "I mean, if you're a hot woman you have a good chance, but men like us have to be somebody if they're gonna let us in."

Gideon sighed. He started thinking of other ways they could kidnap Dmitry, when Dax's phone rang. It was Kiwi.

"Hey, what do you want?"

"Hey, can Noora and I get the van for a bit? We need to dump all the clothes we just bought so we can go get our hair and nails done!"

"Do we need the van?" Dax asked Gideon and Jason.

Jason shook his head. "We can walk to the next place, won't take long."

"Yeah, no problem. We'll call you if we need it."

"Thank you, Dax!"

Dax hung up. "Well I'm hungry, and it's time for lunch," he said.

Gideon nodded. "Sounds good. What do my two American crewmen recommend for Chicago food?"

"Don't know," Jason said. "Never been here."

"We could try one of those deep-dish meat and cheese casseroles they call 'pizza,'" Dax suggested.

Gideon shrugged. "Sounds good. I'm buying."

"Kiwi, you're ridiculous," Noora said, holding several bags of clothes.

Kiwi's mischievous grin was back as she called the van to their location from her phone. It was less than a minute away. "I know you had fun," she said.

"Finland doesn't have a fucking royal family, Kiwi!"

"Oh, funny that."

The van pulled up, they unloaded their merchandise and got in.

"Hey," Kiwi said, her tone turning serious. "Before we go get our hair and nails done, would you mind helping me with something?"

"Of course," Noora said. "What is it?"

Kiwi plugged some map instructions into the van, which started driving to their new destination. "A little side quest," she said. "I, um, we're gonna stop by and see my mom."

"Oh! Okay."

"It's not gonna be fun," Kiwi said. The van crossed the DuSable bridge over the Chicago River, heading south. "Remember that night you got drunk?"

"Yeah," Noora said in shame. "Of course."

"Remember when I told you I knew what you meant when you said you don't wanna dream?"

Noora felt a chill, and pity. "Yeah."

"Yeah, well, I never talk about her, but my mom's a psycho cunt. I haven't seen her in years, and I don't wanna see her alone, and I thought, I dunno, I mean you're here and I just feel like I'll be able to handle her if you're with me."

"Oh, of course, Kiwi," Noora said, not quite understanding what Kiwi meant by 'handle.'

Kiwi checked her phone. "Looks like we're about 20 minutes away."

"Can I ask?" Noora said, remembering Kiwi's names for her steel targets back on the farm. "I mean, if it's too personal, just let me know, but, um, who's Randall?"

Kiwi cocked an eyebrow. "If we're lucky, you're about to find out."

The two of them exited the van and made their way to the subsidized high rise. Noora felt uneasy looking around. Vagrants were everywhere, drug use was open, and trash littered the sidewalks and streets.

But Kiwi walked with confidence.

Noora followed her into the building, not looking at anyone else they passed by. She got a number of uncomfortable looks. They made it to an elevator.

Kiwi tapped the 7th floor, and said. "Hey, whatever happens up there, just stay calm and don't do anything."

"Okay," Noora said. Kiwi was carrying her oversized bag. "What's in the bag?" Noora asked.

"My power whip," Kiwi said.

Noora felt a chill. Again, she didn't know what Kiwi had planned, and she didn't bother asking.

The elevator parked on the 7th floor and the doors opened. Kiwi led the way to an apartment and hit the buzzer.

"*Ye-um, yeah?*" a tweaked out voice answered.

"It's me," Kiwi said in her husky tone.

"*Who—um, ohmygod, KIWI! Oh, um, yeah, um, just, yeah, come on in!*"

The door unlocked and the two of them entered the apartment.

Beer cans were strewn everywhere, and a dank, musty smell permeated the drab interior.

"Jesus Christ," Kiwi said, kicking a can.

It was another 10 seconds before a short woman, barely 5-feet tall, gaunt and with a nervous twitch, appeared. She flashed a fake smile. "Kiwi!" she said.

"Mom."

"I, I just," the woman flashed paranoid glances at Noora. "I mean, it's so nice to see you."

"This is my friend, Noora," Kiwi said.

Kiwi's mom gave Noora a quick nod. Noora reciprocated.

"What, um, I mean, you know, what brings you here?" her mom asked.

Kiwi looked around. "Oh, you know, just wanted to make sure you're still a fucking loser."

"Oh, Kiwi, I'm just so happy to, um, you know, see you," her mom said, trying to approach her.

"Don't!" Kiwi said.

Her mom stopped in her tracks.

"Hey," a male voice said from around the corner. "Babe, who's here, who you talking to—"

As the man rounded the corner and Kiwi saw his face, her eyes widened.

"Oh," the man said. "Kiwi?"

"I don't fuckin' believe it," Kiwi said, yanking her power whip out of her bag.

"Whoah, whoah, wait, Kiwi—"

"Kiwi, no—!"

But Kiwi was too fast, and even in the cramped apartment, her power whip found its target around the man's neck.

Her mother tried to grab her, but Kiwi gave her a left hook to the jaw, and she fell.

The man crumpled to his knees, grabbing at the whip around his neck. He was still able to breathe, but barely.

"You asked me before who Randall is," Kiwi said to Noora. "Randall, don't be rude! Say 'hi' to Noora."

Randall couldn't undo the whip around his neck. His face was beet-red, and he gurgled, "G-g-k-kiwi."

"You know, I didn't think I'd see you here," Kiwi said. "But it figures that you are. My mom cycles through boyfriends faster than I do, but she always comes back to you, doesn't she."

Her mom started wailing. "Kiwi! Why are you doing this to us!"

"Not now, mom!" Kiwi shouted, before looking back to Randall. "Come heeeeere, Randallllll," she said, slowly pulling on the whip.

Randall had no choice but to do what he was told.

"Randall," Kiwi said. "Mom's asking me why I'm doing this. Do you want to remind her what you did to me when I was 8?"

Noora, wide-eyed and mouth agape, just watched.

"And mom, you want to tell Randall what you told me when I told you what he was doing to me?"

"Kiwi! Please, just, just stop!"

Randall suddenly shot up and charged Kiwi.

But Kiwi sent a power surge through the whip. Randall seized and collapsed.

"Now now, Randall," Kiwi said. "Hands off. You touched me plenty when I was younger."

"Kiwi, please—!"

"Mom, mom, shhhhhh, it's okay," Kiwi said. "You know, part of me hoped you'd changed, that maybe you got everything together, that maybe you weren't a sociopathic cunt anymore.

But that's my fault for thinking that. I should've known better."

"Kiwi, please, what do you want!"

"What do I want?" Kiwi asked. "I want to torture Randall here until he pisses himself, and then I want to leave and never see you again." She looked at Randall and said, "Are you ready, Randall?"

Randall, face red, veins popping, and spittle everywhere, barely managed to glance at her.

"All right, then," Kiwi said, sending another power surge through the whip.

Back in the elevator, Kiwi threw her arms around Noora. "Thank you," she said.

"Oh, of course," Noora said, returning the hug.

Kiwi pulled away, wiping a few tears. "I'm sorry, I um, I don't know, I really wondered if she had gotten any better, if she had changed at all, and I knew she hadn't, I just needed to see for myself. God, she's such a narcissistic bitch. Thanks for being there with me. I'm sorry you had to see all that."

"No, it's, it's okay, Kiwi," Noora said, rubbing Kiwi's arm, feeling sad for her.

Kiwi actually smiled. "You know, it's funny. After that, maybe I don't mind dreaming again."

They got to the ground floor, exited the elevator, exited the building, and got back into the van. Kiwi queued up the map and entered a new destination.

"All right," she said. "We're getting our hair done, and our nails done, and then we'll pick up the boys and head back to my grandparents' place."

"Okay," Noora said.

Kiwi stared out the window, unusually pensive.

Noora rubbed her arm. "Are you, um, are you okay?"

"Oh, yeah," Kiwi said. "Just thinking about Gideon's plan. I don't know, I just don't like the idea of kidnapping that guy.

There's gotta be a better way."

"All right, here me out!" Kiwi said. The entirety of the *Skye's* crew was back in the van, heading north on I-94 back towards Wisconsin. "So fuckboy, those clubs you looked into today, they're all impossible to get into?"

"I mean, yeah, for us," Jason said.

Kiwi laughed. "No, for *you*," she said. "Guys, remember back on Mars, well, fuckboy you weren't there, but you remember back on Mars how I got into that invite-only pre-race party?"

Gideon nodded.

Dax, suffering from indigestion, also nodded.

"Look, hot girls like me and Noora can get into these places, but guys like you can't. So here's what we do. We're back down to Chicago tomorrow night. Noora and I got some killer fucking outfits today. Plus we got our hair and nails done, and none of you have said anything! Anyway, so we go to whichever club Dmitry and Braxton are at, and Noora and I are the bait."

Everyone scowled. "How, what, I mean what do you mean the *bait*?" Gideon asked.

"No offense," Dax said. "But there's gonna be a ton of hot girls there. What makes you two the bait?"

"Easy," Kiwi said. "We play the Duchess of Turku game, and you, Gideon, and fuckboy are our security."

"I'm sorry," Gideon said. "The Duchess of what game?"

Noora laughed.

7. A NIGHTCLUB IN CHICAGO

Kiwi hatches a plan, Jason spikes some wine, Noora kisses Kiwi's neck, Gideon reveals himself to a mob boss, and Dax throws Noora around a hotel room.

Kiwi and Jason sat at her grandparents' dinner table, sipping their morning coffee, discussing the finer points of the unholy alliance between government and corporations.

"Are you serious?" Kiwi asked.

"Oh yeah," Jason confirmed. "When I was with Ralston, we had a direct line with all of those agencies. The SIC, the FCA, all of them. And not just with the U.S. Most of the European agencies were happy to work with us, too."

"And just like that, you could get anyone's info?"

Jason nodded, sipping his coffee. "Just contact Johnny-Whoever in the SIC or wherever, say, 'Hey, can you send me what you have on Braxton Keller?', and 10-seconds later we'd get it."

"How is that not illegal?" Kiwi asked.

"Oh it is illegal," Jason said. "But it goes on all the time, and they all get away with it."

Kiwi lifted an eyebrow, opened her phone, and called up the Ralston database Jason had downloaded and shared with the *Skye's* crew several months ago. She quickly found files on Braxton Keller. "Oooo, looks like you guys already had info on him."

"Yeah, governments have been investigating him for a while for tax fraud, money laundering, all kinds of wonderful stuff."

"Huh," Kiwi said, scrolling through the files. "Known phone numbers?"

"Yup, know how to track them?" Jason asked.

Kiwi shook her head. "I take it that's this morning's lesson?" she asked, referring to everything Jason had been showing her the past several weeks.

Jason nodded, tapping his phone. "More of an app than a lesson, but yeah."

Kiwi looked back at her phone and tapped the notification. "What's this?"

"Backdoor tracking app. Got it from one of my SIC contacts. Plug in any phone number, you can track where the phone is."

"Again, how is this not illegal?" Kiwi asked, opening up the app and trying Braxton's various phone numbers.

"Again, it's totally illegal," Jason said. "Besides, you're a mercenary. What are you so concerned about legality for?"

"I guess I'm just floored that it's that easy," Kiwi said. "Aaand, gottem."

"You find the number that's in Chicago?"

"Yup," Kiwi said. "By the way, where are you expecting him to show up?"

"Well he loves going to nightclubs," Jason said. "We narrowed it down to a few he's probably going to go to. The Mercury, The Stone, and Transparency."

"What are you two conspiring about?" Dax said, strolling

in, coffee in hand.

"Oh, just illegally tracking Braxton Keller's location," Kiwi said.

"Oh nice," Dax said, sitting down. "Where is he?"

"Looks like he's staying at the Mansion Resort," Kiwi said, looking at her phone.

"Hey everyone, good morning," Noora said sweetly, entering the dining room and sitting next to Dax.

"Morning."

"Good morning."

"Hey, girl."

"Morning, lovelies," Gideon said, coming in.

Grandma was right behind him with a fresh pot of coffee. "Morning everyone. You all have your coffees?"

"Oh, can I get some more!" Kiwi said, holding out her cup.

Grandma topped it off.

"Thank you!"

"Everyone else good?" Grandma asked. "Well this'll be in the kitchen. Just help yourselves."

"Well then, Rosevine," Gideon said, having a seat. "I'm curious to hear this plan of yours."

"Okay, okay!" an excited Kiwi said, putting her phone down. "So I've been following Braxton on all his socials, right? Flaunts how he's a millionaire, all the business deals he's doing, how smart he is, and more importantly all the girls he's getting. So I'm thinking me and Noora get decked out in all the new clothes we just got, doll ourselves up, and you, Jason, and Dax act as our 'security' when we go to whatever club he's at."

Dax rolled his eyes. "Is this like an ongoing theme?" he asked. "Where you go clubbing and I'm you're fucking chaperone?"

"No no!" Kiwi said. "Okay well maybe, but hear me out! So Noora, you're The Duchess of Turku again, and I'm your assistant. We roll up on whatever club Braxton and what's-his-name are at."

"Dmitry," Gideon said.

"Yes, Dmitry. So we roll up, and you three surround me and Noora. Noora, you only speak to me and only in Finnish. Let me do all the talking to everyone else. We bribe our way into the club if we need to, and Noora and I just sit at the bar and wait with the three of you acting as our security."

Dax slapped his forehead. "And, I'm sorry, what does this have to do with capturing Dmitry and interrogating him?"

"Yeah, I've got the same question," Gideon said.

Kiwi scowled. "I'm sorry, is it not obvious?"

"No," Jason said.

"No," Noora said.

"No," Dax and Gideon said together.

"Okay, look," Kiwi said. "This whole capture a mob boss and interrogate him thing, I mean come on, there's a better way. We get to Dmitry through Braxton. They're hanging out together, and Braxton's always looking to nail some new girl. But see, girls always come to him. The idea is we're mysterious. We make him come to *us*."

"How do you figure that?" Gideon asked.

"Guys, Jesus Christ," Kiwi said. "Think about it. You're in a club. Two hot girls stroll up, acting like they own the place, and they've got their own three-man security team with them. That doesn't make you curious? That doesn't make you want to know just who the hell they are?"

"And how does this get us to Dmitry?" Dax asked.

"Yeah, and in case you've forgotten, Dmitry knows my face," Gideon said.

"And how are we gonna hit him up with truthinol?" Jason asked.

"Yeah, and what's my role exactly? I'm a bit confused," Noora said.

"Guys, guys," Kiwi said. "Calm down. Drink your coffee. And let me explain."

West of North Michigan Ave, on East Walton Street in downtown Chicago, a 6-foot-2 world champion Australian kickboxer sat in the back of the Transparency nightclub. He wore a simple shirt, designer jeans, custom red leather shoes, a platinum chain, and a diamond-studded watch.

He scratched his thin, manicured beard and mustache, ran a hand through his short, sandy-blonde hair, and looked over at a group of young women nearby, dancing. Nothing but run-of-the-mill city girls with a bit of money, vying for his attention.

Braxton had his own troupe of six young women around him. His plan worked every time; the more girls he brought, the more at the club lined up to try to meet him.

But this game was distracting tonight. Even boring.

He looked across the table to his business contact from Macedonia. "Hey mate," he said in his Brisbane accent. "Got an ETA for when Thomas gets here?"

Dmitry tapped away at his phone. "I'm messaging him now, says he's about 30 minutes out."

Braxton nodded. He looked around the club. Bathed in sapphire lights, the local girls all looked the same to him. None of them stood out as worthy of his attention.

That and he found the local Chicago accent, hard and nasal, impossible to tolerate for more than a few minutes.

Resigning himself to not picking up anyone new tonight, he was about to scroll through his phone when a group of five people entering the club caught his attention.

Specifically, two women surrounded by their own three-man security team.

And the two women stuck out from the crowd.

The tiny one wore black leggings and a tailored one piece that was modestly gray, but showed off generous curves. Her thick, raven black hair was highlighted perfectly, and she had a confident sway in her hips.

But the other one also caught his eye. She was taller, maybe 5-4, short blonde hair, and a stiffer, more European gait to her stride. She wore designer sunglasses with pink lenses, accenting her natural beauty. When she took off her jacket, Braxton recognized her plain dress as a status symbol in itself; her tank top showed off a set of shoulders and arms carved from marble.

The three-man security team was an interesting mix. They all wore dark sunglasses. One was short, maybe 5-7. Another was above average height, 5-10 or 11, with a black beard and thick, black hair.

The third one was at least as tall as Braxton, and with bigger arms. He had wavy, Mediterranean hair that was tied back.

Braxton had money, and knew what he was looking at. Only the daughters of billionaires walked around with their own security team. That, or royalty.

Finally, something interesting.

The group strolled up to the bar, the security team clearing a spot for the two ladies by shooing some customers away. The ladies chit-chatted, acting oblivious to all the stares they were getting across the club, while their security made sure they were given enough space.

Braxton couldn't help himself. He stood up. "About half an hour, you said?" he asked Dmitry.

Dmitry nodded.

"Well then. I'll be at the bar for a bit."

He strolled to the bar, unconsciously straightening any wrinkles out of his shirt, making sure it showed off his physique. He adjusted his watch as he came up to the bar, as a subtle ploy to get their attention.

"Excuse me," he said to a bartender, getting immediate service. Management knew Braxton's money well. "Whoever those two lovely ladies are, tell them I'd like to buy their drinks."

"Oh, I'm so sorry, Mr. Keller," the bartender said. "They specifically told us not to let anyone buy them drinks."

Braxton Keller was stumped for a moment. He wasn't used to being told no. "They told you that?"

The bartender, a young woman, nodded. "Their big

security guy said so, and management told us to give them whatever they want."

Braxton openly looked at them, trying to get a read. "Who are they?" he asked.

The bartender shrugged. "No idea. Anyway, can I get you anything, Mr. Keller?"

Braxton kept staring at the two ladies, trying to catch their eye. The one with raven black hair was scrolling her phone while chatting with the blonde, who sipped her drink and chatted back while looking around, somehow not even noticing him.

He also wasn't used to being ignored.

"Yeah," he said to the bartender. "Vodka martini, splash of Kina Lillet, shaken over ice, garnish with a long lemon peel, and meet me over where they are."

The bartender nodded, and Braxton strolled over to the ladies, and up to the largest security member. He had sized him up correctly from across the club; he was Braxton's height, but with larger arms, and he stood like a fighter.

"She don't wanna talk to you, man," the security member said in a southern American accent. "Get lost."

"Who says I want to talk to either of them?" Braxton said. "I actually wanna talk to you, mate."

"I ain't your mate," the security member said. "Now scram."

The bartender handed Braxton his martini. She had a nervous look, not knowing what was about to happen.

"Cheers," Braxton said, accepting his martini and taking a sip while looking at the stoic security member. "Whereabouts in the South are you from?"

"No amount of talking to me will get you to talk to her," the security guard said. "Because she don't wanna talk to you."

"Oh, I don't believe that for a second," Braxton said with charm. "Come to a club like this just to *not* meet people?"

"Don't care what you believe," the security guard said.

"You keep saying *her*, by the way," Braxton said. "Yet I see two beautiful young women behind you. Which one of them is *her*?"

The large security guard was about to respond, when the black-haired woman touched his shoulder and whispered a few things into his ear.

Braxton leaned against the bar and sipped his martini with his left hand, showing off his watch.

The woman finished speaking to the security guard, who said to Braxton, "You got 30 seconds," before stepping back.

Finally, Braxton had his opening.

"And who are you?" the black-haired woman asked, not even looking up from her phone.

Braxton tried to catch the eye of the blonde woman, but was still out of luck. "I'm Braxton Keller," he said, expecting his name to be familiar to them.

The black-haired woman flicked her hair over to her left, exposing a seductive neckline. She still didn't look up from her phone. "And what do you want?"

Braxton wasn't used to this. Even if a woman didn't know his name, his Australian accent always did the trick, especially with Americans. "I need your help, actually," he said. "You see I'm sitting up in my private booth, surrounded by girls, and unimpressed with all of them, when I look up and see the two of you enter the club, and with your own security at that, and I think to myself 'well I have to at least buy them a drink and introduce myself.' But when I do, I learn that your wonderful head of security here won't allow it."

The blonde said something in a language Braxton didn't understand. It sounded Scandinavian. The black-haired woman giggled. Still, neither of them bothered to make eye-contact with him.

"And two lovely young women like yourselves shouldn't be buying their own drinks," Braxton said.

The large security guard got in front of him. "That was 30 seconds," he said. "Now leave."

Braxton nodded respectfully. "Private booth, right up there," he said past the guard. "Feel free to join us." He returned to his booth, not in the least bit dissuaded. His senses told him he had made an impression.

"That was a long trip to the bar," Dmitry said.

"Yeah it was," Braxton said. "Got side-tracked trying to flirt with a billionaire's daughter."

Dmitry looked up from his phone, then over towards the bar. He noticed the two women surrounded by their own security detail. One of the guards reminded him of his longtime contact Gideon, captain of the *Isle of Skye*. He wondered when they would be getting back from Lacaille.

"A billionaire, huh?" he said.

"Who else struts around with their own security?" Braxton asked. "Either that, or some kind of royalty."

Dmitry scoffed.

Braxton kept his eyes on them. He saw the black-haired woman order something, receive a bottle, and start making her way up to him. She approached the booth. Braxton's troupe all looked at her. As small as she was, her aura intimidated the rest of the women.

"Well, congratulations," the black-haired woman said, her tone a mix of disinterest and mild irritation. "You got her attention. She says no one's stood up to Dax like that."

"Dax?" Braxton asked. "I take it that's the gentleman I spoke with?"

She nodded. "And she'd like to apologize and offer you this '79 Chieti Nebbiolo."

Braxton smiled, his gratitude masking his cockiness. He knew that was a $2,000 bottle of wine. "So *she's* the special one," he said. "Well tell her I said thank you, that she has nothing to apologize for, and that I will only open this bottle if you and she share it with me."

The black-haired woman nodded curtly, placed the bottle on the table, and returned to her companion. Everyone at the booth watched her as she walked away.

"Thomas will be here soon," Dmitry said.

"Not for another 20 minutes," Braxton said. "All of you, out. Go dance or something," he said to his troupe of young women.

They all got up and left the booth, leaving just Braxton and Dmitry.

A minute later, flanked by their security detail, the two women at the bar approached the booth. The black-bearded guard stayed back to survey the rest of the club, while the tall one and the short one kept station by the booth.

"Hey," the black-haired woman said. "One of you get us a carafe."

The short guard returned to the bar while the two young women sat down together in the booth, opposite Braxton.

"So," Braxton said. "With whom do I have the pleasure of sharing this wonderful Italian vintage?"

"I'm Kiwi," the black-haired one said.

"Kiwi," Braxton smiled. "I love the name. And who's your lovely friend?"

The blonde leaned into Kiwi and whispered something. Kiwi giggled. Her smile was seductive.

"She's just a girl who wanted to enjoy some Chicago nightlife," Kiwi said.

"And are you enjoying it so far?" Braxton asked the blonde.

The blonde spoke to Kiwi, again in that Scandinavian language.

Kiwi nodded. "So far."

The small security guard returned with a carafe and some wine glasses. He opened the bottle of Nebbiolo and procured an eyedropper.

"There's no need to do that," Kiwi said, irritated.

"I have my orders," the small guard said.

Braxton and Dmitry didn't notice the clear liquid already in the eyedropper. They only noticed him pull a small sample of the wine, place a drop onto his phone, and do some sort of analysis.

Kiwi rolled her eyes in annoyance.

The security guard was apparently satisfied with the results his phone showed him. He poured the Nebbiolo into the carafe and swirled it.

"About time," Kiwi said.

"Quite the security measure," Braxton said. "I'm almost afraid to ask who you are."

"Don't be afraid to ask," Kiwi said, before raising an eyebrow. "But you might be afraid to find out." She reached for the carafe and poured out four measures of the Nebbiolo.

"We're gonna need more than that," Braxton said, looking towards the bar and snapping a finger. 10-seconds later a bartender was at the booth. "Bring us a case of this Nebbiolo."

The bartender nodded without hesitation and was off. The establishment knew Braxton could casually drop $24,000 on a case of wine. He was hoping the move would garner some interest from Kiwi and the blonde, but they didn't seem any more impressed than if he had ordered sparkling water. Whoever they were, he was enjoying the challenge.

He took his glass of wine, as did everyone else at the table. "To Kiwi, and our mystery princess," he said.

They all raised their glasses. Braxton drained half of his, Dmitry took a modest gulp, and neither of them noticed Kiwi and the blonde only pretending to sip.

Braxton decided to change his approach. Instead of going directly at the blonde, he would see what he could get from Kiwi. "So tell me," he said, already feeling the wine in his blood. "If she's our mystery royalty, what does that make you?"

"Me?" Kiwi asked with a coy smirk. "I'm her assistant."

"What exactly do you assist her with?"

The blonde leaned into Kiwi, brushing her hair aside, kissing her ear and neck.

Kiwi gave a sensual smile. "With whatever she needs."

Braxton took another sip of wine, trying to act unfazed. "Funny, I didn't take you two for lesbians," he heard himself say. The wine was getting to his head fast.

"Oh, we're not," Kiwi said, as the blonde leaned back and slid an arm up Kiwi's spine. "But come on, a little snack like me? Can you blame her?"

"I can't say that I do," Braxton said, taking another drink. "She has good taste."

"And she tastes good, too," Kiwi said, looking at the blonde. "Don't you?"

The blonde said something to Kiwi, who laughed and said, "Oh I don't think I should tell him *that*."

Then the blonde made her first eye contact with Braxton.

Finally, he thought. He swirled his wine and drained the rest of his glass.

Dmitry, still quiet, did the same.

Kiwi and the blonde pretended to take another sip.

The bartender returned with 12 bottles of the Nebbiolo on a linen-draped cart.

"There we are," he said, snatching a bottle and opening it himself. He poured himself and Dmitry another glass, then said to Kiwi, "Come on, you two have barely had two sips. You need to keep up!"

"It's a great vintage," Kiwi said. "Have to sip it to enjoy it."

Braxton shook his head. "The real flex isn't buying a $2,000 bottle of wine and sipping it delicately. It's buying a case of it, guzzling what you want, and throwing the rest away."

The blonde said something. Kiwi laughed.

"What'd she say?" Braxton asked.

"She says to flex away."

Braxton swirled his wine. "You know, I've been asking all the questions. You two aren't curious about me at all?"

The blonde said something to Kiwi.

"She says she knows who you are," Kiwi said. "She's wondering what brings you to Chicago."

"Easy," Braxton said. "Biggest interstellar business investment of all time. Isn't that right Dmitry?"

The quiet Dmitry nodded, and found himself spilling all sorts of details to the two strangers. "Braxton's the lead investor, got a number of others lined up. We're funding a major expedition to Gliese-892. A startup colony's already there. Ocean world, and they seeded it with whatever bacteria they use that spits out oxygen. We're going to turn it into a major port."

Kiwi pretended to be confused. "And why would you want

to throw a bunch of money out into space?"

"Because the possibilities are infinite," Braxton said with charisma. "Think about it. Space is infinite. The resources out there are infinite. Interstellar is barely a generation old, and people are still afraid of it. But they won't be afraid when there's a major space hub they can stop off at. Venture capital companies are too squeamish on interstellar because they're cowards. But there are enough private investors like myself who want to see it happen. And we're only going to see major returns on investment. It's also a perfect opportunity for me to get off-world since I got several governments investigating me for tax fraud and money-laundering." Braxton did a double-take. "Don't know why I'm telling you that, guess I just trust you two."

Dmitry continued on with the logistics. "We've already got two ships lined up. Well, one at the moment. The *Philadelphia*. Its captain is actually coming by in a few minutes. Guy named Thomas. Nice guy."

Kiwi kept her poker face. She knew Thomas. So did Gideon and Dax. "And the second ship?" she asked.

"Well, they're actually interstellar now," Dmitry said. "They're off at the Lacaille colony. Was hoping they'd be back by now, but I haven't heard from their captain yet. Ship is the *Isle of Skye*. Scottish captain named Gideon. Not as jovial as Thomas, but still a good man."

Kiwi made her move, knowing the truthinol was in effect. "Oh. So you didn't set them up to get captured at Lacaille."

Dmitry frowned. "Why would I do that? I've already got a ton of money invested in them, and I'm counting on them to run to Gliese with the *Philadelphia*." His brain was too fogged with the truthinol to wonder why Kiwi would even ask such a question. He thought nothing of the truth he was spilling.

Kiwi smiled. She had what she needed. She pulled out her phone, whispered a few words into it, and stood up. "Well, gentlemen. Thank you for your honesty, and thank you for the wine. If you don't mind, my princess and I have had our fill."

Braxton was stunned and didn't know what to say.

Noora, who had been paralyzed for the last minute, let loose a sharp exhale. She grabbed her glass of wine and downed it.

"No no, wait, Noora!" Kiwi tried to interject.

Noora stared wide-eyed at the wine glass, realizing what she'd just done. "Oh, fuck!" she blurted.

"So she *does* speak English," Braxton said. "You know I should be livid, but I'm still hopeful I have a chance at fucking both of you tonight."

Kiwi gave a salacious smile. "Not a chance, tough guy."

Noora got dizzy. She clenched her eyes and held her forehead.

"Wait," Dmitry said. "How do you know I was telling the truth?"

Kiwi winked. "Can't give away all my secrets."

The black bearded member of the ladies' security detail came up to the booth and took off his sunglasses.

Dmitry gawked. "Gideon!"

"The one and only," Gideon said.

Noora opened her eyes. She fixated on Dax and launched herself at him.

"Oh," Braxton said. "So she really does like guys."

Dax tried to catch Noora, but she was all over him.

"Heyyy," she said, trying to drown him with her mouth. The truthinol had soaked into her brain, and she lost all inhibition. She only spoke loud enough for him to hear. "I just I love being with you Dax and I feel so bad that you lost your wife but like it only shows me how great you are and I really wanna meet your family can we go see them in Texas because I've never been to Texas and I wanna meet them so bad and I just goddamnit I want you to throw me around the hotel room right now because you stood up to that asshole Australian and I know you can kick his ass and—"

Dax picked up Noora and hauled her away from the booth. She kept pawing at him.

Gideon sat down. "So, you've got something lined up for us

already?"

"You're back from Lacaille and you didn't contact me! And you're here?" Dmitry responded.

"I'm here."

"Wait," Braxton said. "This is seriously the captain of the other ship?"

"Gideon!" a voice shouted from 20-feet away.

Gideon, Kiwi, Dmitry, Braxton, and Jason all turned to see who the voice had come from.

A lanky, lean, bright-faced, clean-shaven man with charismatic eyes was approaching the booth.

"Thomas!" Gideon shouted back. He got up and gave his friend a hug.

"The hell you doing in Chicago?" Thomas asked in his New Jersey accent. "Thought you were all important now that you're flying around between the stars!"

"Just waiting for you to catch up," Gideon said.

"Sir Thomas Burnell," Kiwi said, slinking up to the captain of the *Philadelphia* and sliding an arm around him.

"Ms. Kiwi the Rosevine," Thomas said, returning her hug. "I forget, how many roses on that body tattoo of yours?"

"You'll just have to count them up again," Kiwi said.

"How ya been?"

"Just tell me your hotel and room number and I'll be fine," Kiwi said.

Thomas laughed, then leaned into her ear and told her.

Kiwi grinned from ear-to-ear and said, "I'll see ya later, then." She went to the cart of Nebbiolo and snatched a bottle. "Since you're gonna throw the rest away, you won't miss a bottle, will you?" she said to Braxton.

"No," Braxton said wink. "No I won't. You enjoy that, now."

"Take care, champ," Kiwi said.

"Oh you'll be seeing me again," Braxton said as Kiwi strolled off.

"Well this is perfect!" Dmitry declared, oblivious to the truthinol in his system. "Come on, everyone sit down. Here, get them some wine glasses. We've got a lot to discuss!"

Back in their hotel room, Noora, naked and catching her breath, had an arm and leg draped over Dax. The truthinol had worked most of its way out of her system, and she was starting to feel self-conscious of what it had made her spill earlier.

"Hey," she said. "I'm sorry about before, it's just, you know how that stuff makes you say things."

"It's all right," Dax laughed. "I mean if anything it was kind of cute."

Noora smiled. "I really would like to meet your family, but, you know, it can be whenever you're ready. I know I met them over video chat. They just seem so great and I'd love to see them in person, and see where you're from."

"Yeah, no," Dax said. "We should go. I like seeing them, I just, I can't handle groups larger than about 10 people."

"You seemed like you could handle that Australian. God, he's such a fucking asshole."

Dax scoffed. "He's also a professional fighter."

"I don't know," Noora said. "I just feel like you could beat him."

"I mean, I've got a good 20-pounds on him at least, who knows," Dax said.

Noora rubbed his arms. "Yeah, that's all in your arms, too."

Dax smiled.

"Hey, who is that Thomas they were talking about, by the way? Captain of the *Philadelphia*?"

"Oh, he's a friend of Gideon's."

"The *Philadelphia*," Noora echoed. "That's so funny. Kinda like Philly Cheesesteak."

Dax laughed. "Yeah, that's, uh, that's not a coincidence."

"What do you mean?"

"I mean that's where we got him," Dax said. "We were docked at Mars a few years ago, and Kiwi goes missing for like three or four days. We found out by accident that she'd been on the *Philadelphia* in the captain's cabin the whole time. Their ship had a few extra young cats, and Kiwi comes back with Philly Cheesesteak."

Noora took a sharp inhale. "Oh my god that's so fucking cute!"

"But yeah, Thomas is a good guy. You'll like him. From New Jersey."

Noora scowled. "New Jersey? I thought Philadelphia was in, like, Pennsylvania?"

"It is, but he's from a part of Jersey right next to Philadelphia," Dax said. "Besides, what city from Jersey is he gonna name his ship after? The Atlantic City? The Camden?"

Noora laughed.

Dax's phone chirped a notification. He picked it up and swiped it.

"What is it?" Noora asked.

"Just a text from Gideon. Wants to see us all in the morning. Says 'major fucking plans.'"

"Wonder what that means," Noora said. She yawned. "What time is it?"

"2am," Dax said.

Noora nuzzled into him and said, "You sure it's okay if we go to Texas and see your family?"

"Let's do it," Dax said. "We'll see what these 'big fucking plans' are in the morning, then I'll give them a call and tell them we're coming."

Noora gave him a gentle squeeze. "You know," she said. "Jason's taken it, Kiwi's taken it, and now I've taken it. I wonder what you'd be like on that truthinol stuff."

"Careful what you wish for," Dax said. "Jason becomes a drowsy, miserable mess. Kiwi turns chaotic. You get ridiculously sweet. Me, you'd probably just see a bunch of piss and vinegar."

Noora smiled. "I'm sweet, you're sour. Perfect combination."

8. A HOTEL CONFERENCE

Dax slaps Noora's butt (gently), Noora insists on a "follow through," Jason looks up information on his phone, Kiwi quietly expresses her hatred of Braxton, and new characters are introduced!

Dax could tell Noora was awake, and gently slapped her butt.

"Oooo," Noora said. "Good morning."

"Morning, you," Dax said, wrapping his arms around her and pulling her against him.

Noora breathed sensually and writhed her hips into him.

"Heh heh, look at you."

Dax kissed her cheek, then worried about the time. He reached back and checked his phone. "Ah, shit, we gotta get going."

"No, I'm sorry, excuse me, you can't wake me up like that and not follow through."

"You were already awake," Dax said with a smile. "Don't be lying to me like that."

Noora moaned, still writhing into him. She reached behind and touched his face. "Fine," she said. "I was awake. Now you gotta follow through." She reached down and grabbed his hip.

Dax bit her neck, then followed through.

Gideon, Kiwi, and Jason were mingling in a hotel conference room with Thomas and his crew from the *Philadelphia*. Except for Jason, they were all familiar and friendly with each other.

In one corner of the room, at a large, round table, sat Braxton Keller, Dmitry, and a number of presumed investors.

"So how do you and Gideon know each other?" Jason asked Thomas.

"Yeah, we served together for some years. Mostly ran shipments between Earth and Mars under another captain. We both wanted to eventually venture out on our own, and we did. Have stayed in touch since," Thomas said. "How about you? Last I knew it was just Gideon, Dax, and Kiwi. Now I find out he's brought on two extra people over this last year. Which is good, I mean running a ship like the *Skye* with just three people? Come on."

"Yeah, um," Jason said awkwardly. "He, uh, he didn't tell you?"

Thomas shook his head.

"So, um, how do I put this?" Jason said. "I was hired by Ralston last year—"

"Ralston, huh? Damn."

"Yeah. They, uh, let's just say they contracted me to find whoever committed a bit of corporate theft, turns out it was the *Isle of Skye*. I, um, well long-story-short I failed, got blacklisted, found Gideon, and for some reason he took me on when no one else would."

"Well, shit," Thomas said. "He speaks well of you. Said you saved their asses at, where was it, Lacaille?"

Jason nodded, then shrugged. "I mean, it wasn't just me. None of us would've made it out if we all hadn't done what we did."

"So how the bloody hell have you been, mate?" Gideon asked the *Philadelphia's* first mate, Jack.

Jack shrugged his shoulders and pursed his lips in his New York city style. "I've been great, man, you know? Still with Thomas, still with the gang, and Thomas has all this talk about how we might be going interstellar, I'm kinda excited, man, you know?"

"Tricia! Come here!" Kiwi screamed, launching herself at the *Philadelphia's* lead engineer.

With a wholesome smile and a warm voice, Tricia grabbed a hold of Kiwi. "Hey, Kiwi," she said, trying to pull some of her braided ebony locks out of the way. "How ya been?" she asked in her mild Alabama accent.

"Oh you know, been driving Dax crazy. How are you girl!"

Tricia looked around. "Where is Dax, by the way?" Her voice calm and soothing.

Kiwi gave a measured response, remembering Tricia had, or at least used to have, a thing for Dax. "I texted his ass, said he's running late."

Tricia raised an eyebrow. "Dax? Late?"

Kiwi shrugged. "Hey, first time for everything. Where're your techs?"

"Oh I told them to go have fun while we're in Chicago. I'll fill them in later once we see what this is all about."

Dax and Noora entered the conference room. They ignored

the investors table and went to the crew. Dax shook hands with the team from the *Philadelphia* while Noora waited to be introduced.

When they got to Tricia, she gave a warm smile and an even warmer, "Heyyyy, Dax," before giving him a hug.

Dax smiled. "Oh, we're giving each other hugs now?" he joked, returning the hug.

Noora picked up on Tricia's energy. She could tell she liked Dax.

"It's been a while, how ya been?" Tricia said.

"Would you believe me if I said I've been in a good mood?"

Tricia raised a skeptical eyebrow. "You?" she laughed. "We have to catch up. We should do lunch."

"Yeah, um, yeah," Dax said, unconsciously glancing at Noora.

"And who's this?" Tricia asked, looking at Noora.

"This is Noora," Dax introduced. "She joined us last year. She's our resident navigator and sniper."

"Noora, hi. I'm Tricia."

Noora shook her hand. "Tricia, it's so nice to meet you. My god, you're so beautiful."

"Well thank you," Tricia said. "You're radiant, yourself, and you've gotta tell me how you got those arms."

Noora blushed and smiled. "Oh, I just, you know, a lot of weights and a lot of beef."

Tricia leaned in, a cute eyebrow raised. "Dax spoils you with that cooking of his, doesn't he?"

Noora laughed. "He spoils all of us with his cooking." She touched Dax's arm and said, "I'm gonna get some coffee. Get you some?"

"Yeah, that'd be great."

"Tricia, can I get you anything?" Noora asked.

"Oh no thank you, dear."

As Noora went to grab coffee, Dax looked back to Tricia, who was watching Noora.

"So, you two, um…?" Tricia asked, looking back at Dax.

"Yeah," Dax said. "She's been with us for what, nine months now. We've been together for a few."

"That's great, that's, you know, that's really great."

Braxton Keller had made his way over to the crew. "Right then, everyone here?"

Gideon and Thomas both nodded. "Yup," Thomas said. "Everyone who's gonna be here is here."

"Excellent," Braxton said, clapping his hands once and rubbing them together. "Let's get started then."

The investors and the crew all gathered around four tables set up as a large rectangle and sat down.

"Gentlemen, ladies," Braxton began, putting his phone on the table and setting it to project a holographic presentation in the center of the area. "As some of you know, we are putting together an expedition to HD 219134, otherwise known as Gliese-892."

Jason pulled out his phone and started calling up what information he could find.

"More specifically, to the second planet in the system, Gliese-892-B," Braxton said. The hologram zoomed in on what seemed to be an Earth-like planet. "As you can see, an ocean world with a number of continents. It was lifeless until a colony set up there about 10 years ago. They seeded it with cyanobacteria, and already it's pumping out enough oxygen to maintain a breathable atmosphere."

Everyone leaned forward.

"Our expedition is simple," Braxton continued. "We're taking the *Isle of Skye* and the *Philadelphia*, loading them up as much as we can, and we're flying to Gliese to start the infrastructure for humanity's first extrasolar space port."

A few scoffs and whistles went through the conference room.

Dmitry took over for a moment. "As you all know, when the first vector drive was made a generation ago, the initial excitement around interstellar space travel died down quickly once everyone realized just how large and empty space is. There aren't that many colonies out there, and even the established ones need investment on a heavy scale to do what we're proposing."

"And investing in them is exactly what we're looking to do," Braxton said. "Gliese is the furthest successful colony so far, it's the only ocean world that's been colonized, and its potential is limitless. The colonists have plans to turn this place into a second Earth. Terraforming, introducing wildlife, all of that. They just need people willing to invest in them. And here we are."

"The furthest colony, you say?" Dax asked. "How far out?"

"Just over 20 light years," Braxton said.

"21.34," Jason said, looking up from his phone.

Dax raised his eyebrows. "Damn," he said.

"How long would it take to get there?" Gideon asked.

"At least 10 weeks," Dax said.

"Damn," Thomas said.

"Wow," said Noora.

"Well shit," said Kiwi.

"Oh my," Tricia said.

"Now that we've got investor money lined up," Braxton said, "we'll be fitting the *Philadelphia* with its own vector drive and loading it up. Then once we're ready, we'll be on our way to Gliese."

Kiwi spoke up. "I'm sorry, you keep saying 'we' and 'us'?"

"That's because I'm going with you," Braxton said.

This got a confused frown out of both crews.

"Think about it," he continued. "The world's still skittish about expanding out into the cosmos. You tell people there's a colony out there, they think 'oh, that's quaint.' There's no excitement. They need to see someone with skin in the game. They need to see what another world is like. They need to feel that excitement. I'm going with you, I'm documenting the experience, and when I get back, my socials are going to explode. People will want to ship out to Gliese. It'll draw even more investment, more opportunity. We're turning that planet into a second Earth, into a spaceport, into a commercial hub. You wanna venture out into the rest of the galaxy? This will be your jumping point. A fully independent colony and spaceport. Whatever supplies or materials you need, you can get. No need to fly all the way back to Earth. Resupply your ship, refit your ship, gather up anything you need to venture out into the galaxy. That's our vision."

"I mean, no need to convince us of your vision," Gideon said. "Just a matter of logistics, getting there, how long we need to stay there, and getting back."

"You say you've got funding to fit us with a vector drive?" Thomas asked.

Braxton nodded. "Yes we do."

Thomas looked to Gideon. "How long does that take to install?"

Gideon looked to Dax. "How long did that take? Remind me."

"About a week to install," Dax said, looking to Tricia. "Me, Kiwi and Noora can help you out, too. The company does the installation, but their techs don't know your ship like you do, plus you need an extra reactor just to power the thing, and that causes all sorts of problems on its own."

"Sounds like fun," Tricia said.

"All right then," Braxton said. "I understand they can do vector drive installation on the moon somewhere?"

"Yeah," Dax said. "I forget the name of the valley, but yeah, on the moon."

"Why all the way on the moon?" Jack asked with his New York skepticism.

"Interplanetary regulations," Dax said, then had a question himself. "By the way, does Gliese-89-whatever have any moons?"

"Um, I believe so," Braxton said, tapping his phone. The hologram of Gliese-892-B panned out to reveal two moons.

Dax's eyes widened and his jaw dropped. "Holy shit," he muttered.

"Holy shit," Tricia echoed. "Is this to scale?"

"Yeah, it's to scale," Braxton said. "What's the problem?"

Dax and Tricia, the two engineers in the room, didn't know where to start.

"I mean, Jesus," Dax said. "That first moon is what, 80-thousand kilometers from the planet?"

"79,300, on average," Jason quietly said to Dax.

"Um, yeah, about 80-thousand," Braxton confirmed. "Is that a problem?"

"I mean, it's several problems," Tricia said. "A moon that large and that close. I mean, the tides must wash in, like, hundreds of miles."

"Yeah, and how is the planet not ripping itself apart?" Dax said. "They've gotta have earthquakes all the time. And how many volcanoes are there?"

"I, um, I don't know," Braxton said.

"Yeah, no, there's lots," Tricia said to Dax, looking at the hologram. "Zoom in, you'll see tons of archipelagoes, all volcanic."

Braxton shrugged. "And how is this a problem?"

"I mean, it's just," Dax said. "This isn't exactly a second Earth. I'm trying to understand how a colony has survived here. Tidal forces just ripping into the planet, constant earthquakes. I mean, do they have the infrastructure to survive this already?"

"Yeah, they do," Braxton said. "They've survived there for a decade, and they're trying to expand."

Dax huffed. "Okay then."

"Right then," Braxton said. "Unless there are any questions or objections from the captains?"

Gideon shook his head.

Thomas shook his head.

"Then we shall proceed," Braxton said. "Take us a few days to gather all the money from our investors, after which we'll see to the *Philadelphia* getting fitted for a vector drive. Then once all is set, we'll be on our way."

Braxton stood up, as did the rest of the main investors, and he closed the holographic presentation.

Gideon and Thomas nodded and stood up themselves. "Well, we'll be in touch," Thomas said.

The rest of the *Philadelphia* and *Skye* crews also stood up.

"That we will," Braxton said. "We'll pool the investment money and be in touch with you within a few days."

Braxton and the main investors gathered everything and left the conference room.

The *Isle of Skye* and the *Philadelphia* crew got themselves some more coffee, and mingled.

"Gideon," Kiwi said, after Braxton and the investors had all left the room. "I don't like him."

"What's to like?" Gideon said. "They're funding this whole venture."

"No, I just," Kiwi said, moving in close to him to talk discreetly. "Look, I don't like him. I know a sex pest when I see one, and I don't trust this whole 'expedition' of his. I just, I don't know, I've been following his socials, and he looks more like a scam artist than anything."

"Kiwi, look," Gideon said. "Not that I don't value your opinion, but we've got a metric ton of money already guaranteed coming into this. It's a long trip, but the payoff in the long run is going to be incredible for us."

Kiwi nodded, not giving any lip back to her captain.

"So tell me, Dax," Tricia said. "What kind of trouble does an extra reactor and a vector drive do to a ship?"

"Oh, Christ, don't get me started," Dax said. "The problems it gave us almost got us killed at Lacaille. But that being said, we'll make sure you're set up right. Those techs install the new reactor and vector drive just fine, but they don't take into account anything else."

"Well, looking forward to having you help out," Tricia said.

"Dax," Noora said quietly. "Is it really 10 weeks just to get there?"

"Yeah," Dax said.

"Oh, wow," Noora said. "If we have time, can we also go see my family in Finland?"

"Of course," Dax said.

"Oh, so you're from Finland?" Tricia said.

"Oh, um, yeah, I'm from Finland."

"She's from Finland," Dax confirmed. "Hey, um, if you'll excuse me, I need to talk to Gideon."

"Of course," Tricia said.

Dax went to Gideon, who was talking with Thomas and Jack. "Hey, captain, got a question."

"Of course."

"Well, not so much a question," Dax said. "I'm gonna take off with Noora for a bit. Head back home to Texas. Maybe head off to Finland as well. I wanna help out with the *Philadelphia*, though, so lemme know when they're headed to the moon."

"Of course, Dax," Gideon said. "Don't know how long you'll have before I contact you, so pack in as much fun as you can."

"I will." Dax went back to Noora and Tricia, grabbing Noora's hand. "Tricia, we'll be in touch," he said. "Hey, Kiwi, go fuck yourself."

"Go fuck yourself, Dax," Kiwi replied.

Dax tried to hide his smile.

9. SHORE LEAVE

Gideon visits his hometown, Dax introduces Noora to his wife's headstone, Jason schedules himself to meet with his dad, and Kiwi plays a drinking game with grandpa.

It took two more days of talks, negotiations, and logistical planning with the investors before Gideon finally had some time to himself.

Dax and Noora were already down in East Texas. Kiwi had stayed an extra night with the *Philadelphia's* captain before heading back up to her grandparents' farm. Even Jason had taken off to Connecticut to "see someone," as he'd put it.

This left Gideon on his own, still in Chicago.

He thought about staying in the city, but the slushy, dirty snow, constant cold, and the local accent were starting to irritate him. He'd always enjoyed poking fun at Kiwi's accent, which resembled Chicago's, only to now understand that hers was milder. She'd probably lost a lot of it in her years in space.

Then he thought about Dax's accent, wondering how much of it he'd lost while in space. Thick, slow, and stereotypically Southern, he wondered what Dax sounded like back in his hometown.

He smiled, thinking of his own accent. A unique Scottish cadence, incomprehensible to most people in England, much less any other English speaker in the world, it had turned to a smoother, generalized, easy-to-understand version of Scottish over his 22 years in space.

And every time he visited his hometown of Portree, they made fun of him for how "American" he sounded.

He opened up his phone to check the *Isle of Skye*, safely parked in orbit. He ran through a standard systems diagnostic, seeing everything check green.

He felt strangely on edge, as there was nothing to do, nothing to plan, and all he had to do was wait.

He wondered what to do with himself. He didn't want to stay in Chicago, and Dmitry and his lot had said it could be up to a week to gather all the investor money they'd need.

He thought of his hometown again. A small place, barely 2,000 people, and a big tourist spot for the rest of the UK. He had grown apart from it over the years. Whenever he was back on Earth, he'd rarely felt the urge to visit.

But he started feeling the urge now. It would be easy enough to get there. Just take the dropship to the UK's one spaceport and charter private transportation from there.

First, he gave Dmitry a call.

"Hey, Gideon, what's up?"

"Hey, Dmitry, sure you don't need me for now? Was thinking of heading off to visit the motherland for a bit."

"Oh no, you're fine," Dmitry said. *"Braxton and I are just getting all the money together. All our major investors are here, but we've got a lot of mid-to-lower ranged investors ready to go. We're making a final pitch to all of them now that we got both you and the Philadelphia. Like I said, give us a week or so, we'll be in touch."*

"Right then, call me when you're ready."

Gideon hung up. He called up a taxi on his phone, grabbed his suitcase, and made his way to the hotel lobby. He texted the *Skye's* crew on his way.

Oi. I'm taking the dropship to the UK. Will be in touch when I hear from Dmitry.

"Who was that?" Braxton asked. They were in their own hotel restaurant, having a late breakfast and some coffee.

"That was Gideon," Dmitry said. "Just making sure he can go have a vacation."

Braxton smiled. "You know, I like Gideon. Well traveled, a bit stoic, but knows his ship, knows his business."

"That he does," Dmitry confirmed. "By the way, I wanted to ask you this in private, you sure you want to go with them to Gliese?"

"It's the best opportunity I've had," Braxton said, leaning back and spreading out his limbs. "I can get off-world while the feds are on my ass, I can document the whole journey, and when I get back, I'll post the whole thing, and I'll have single-handedly driven space travel into the next generation."

Dmitry nodded, motivated by Braxton's charisma. "By the way," he said. "Which ship you think you'll travel on?"

"Dunno," Braxton admitted. "I mean, the *Isle of Skye* has those two females, but I like that black one on the *Philadelphia*."

Dmitry scowled. "Oh, you mean the *Philadelphia's* engineer?"

"Yeah, she's gorgeous," Braxton said. "But I'll probably go with the *Skye*. Twice as much opportunity there. I mean none of my girls are going, so gotta try to get whatever pussy I can."

A 20-minute taxi ride, a 1-hour suborbital dropship flight, 3-hours of waiting, and a 2-hour charter flight later, Gideon stepped out onto the small landing strip just outside Portree on the Isle of Skye. The air had its dank flavor of the ocean, the hills, and the countryside. That alone made him feel like he'd been away for too long.

Luckily it wasn't tourist season yet, so it was easy enough

to call a car. While in flight from London spaceport, he had booked himself a bed & breakfast, and had the car take him there.

The route went along the A855, giving him a perfect view of Loch Portree and the harbor. Even though the sun was setting, the view was nostalgic; surrounded by hills, water, and the small shops of the town all still keeping their traditional architecture, and with the typical gray overcast, he felt both at home and out of place.

Nevertheless, he was here, and he would take a breather from being a captain.

The car dropped him off at his bed & breakfast. He entered, and was greeted by a plump woman at the front desk.

"Evening, love," she said. "Checking in?"

"Evening. Yes. Name's under Bruis," Gideon said, trying to say his family name in his Scottish Gaelic accent.

"Bruce, you say?" the pleasant lady said, checking her tablet. "Ah yes, just booked with us a few hours ago, looks like. Funny, we had a family of Bruce's who used to live here. Single mum, buncha kids. Haven't seen them in years. Anyway, where you coming from? You sound American. Don't get many Americans here. Mostly Brits what want some time away from the city."

"Erm, yeah," Gideon said, just going with it. "Coming in from Chicago," he said putting a touch of Chicago's nasal quality in his voice. "Saw my favorite distillery is in this very town, wanted to see it for myself."

"Oooo, well then you're in for a treat, love," the lady said, grabbing a key fob and coming out from behind the desk. "Follow me, I'll show you to your room. We got you in the royal suite upstairs."

Gideon followed. They got to the room, he put his duffle bag down, and the nice lady showed him around. "Got your lavatory right there, two queen size beds so spread out all you like, and these doors open up to the balcony where you've got a lovely view of the loch. We serve breakfast between 8am and

9am downstairs in the dining room. You need anything, just let us know."

"Thank you," Gideon said. He thought about asking for a pub recommendation, but he knew all of the local spots. The nice lady left, leaving Gideon wondering what to do next.

A pub sounded good. A couple pints and some whisky would help reset his internal clock from Chicago time.

He left his room, made his way downstairs, thanked the nice lady again, and enjoyed an early evening walk to the North Highlands Bar.

Gideon had been lucky enough to not be recognized. He tried to enjoy his pints and his local whisky, and his plate of greasy fish and chips, but still couldn't relax.

He checked his phone, tapping into the *Isle of Skye's* systems again. Everything was still in the green.

He put his phone away, wondering why he still couldn't relax.

He thought about what Kiwi had said to him about Braxton. He didn't know much about Kiwi's past, only that she'd had a tough upbringing, and that he'd suspected she'd been abused.

Something about her tone when she talked about Braxton made him worry. She hadn't been hyperbolic or flippant. She'd been serious.

Still, the money from Dmitry and Braxton was all but secured, and once it was, Gideon didn't right care about the character flaws of his investors, just so long as the money was procured.

Then again, Kiwi's warning stayed with him. He wondered which ship Braxton would be traveling on, and made a mental note to keep an eye on him if he ended up on the *Skye*.

He drained the rest of his whisky and paid his bill. On his way back to the bed & breakfast, he wondered how Dax and

Noora were fairing in East Texas.

Dax was turtle-shelling up at the grill, grateful, as always, to have something to do while everyone else socialized and screamed at each other. Noora was running around with his nieces and nephews, playing with them and having a great time.

It made him smile. His family had taken well to her.

He had warned her coming into Marshall, Texas, that whatever she thought of his Southern American accent was about to get 10-times worse once they entered the town, and while she initially struggled to understand everyone, her personality had charmed everyone, and she eventually caught onto the cadence of East Texas.

He flipped the steaks, chicken, and skewered vegetables on the grill, enjoying the activity, but feeling uneasy.

He'd visited Rochelle every day they'd been in Marshall, but he'd done so without Noora. He would say to her, "Hey, I need to go do something," and Noora would touch him and say, "Of course, take your time," and she would never ask what he was up to.

Of course Rochelle knew about Noora. He couldn't hide anything from her. She'd been insisting on meeting Noora, but Dax hesitated.

He scowled at himself. Of course there was no meeting possible between them. He just went to Rochelle's grave, talked to her as he always did, and kept it at that.

But he remembered his conversation with her the day before:

Dax, I really wanna meet her. She sounds great.

"I just, I don't know," he'd said, feeling guilty. "I mean I wanted her to meet the rest of the family, but, I just don't know."

I know you feel guilty. You don't have to. I've told you that you need to move on.

He'd wiped a few tears away. "Yeah, I know, it's just..."

It's okay, Dax.

"It's just, when I lost you, I didn't want to date again because I knew I'd never meet anyone like you, and besides, dating's a real pain in the ass."

[Laughs]

"And then, I don't know, I met her, and…"

I'm glad you met her. Please, I wanna meet her.

He'd nodded and poured some chardonnay over her headstone. "Okay," he'd said. "Okay, fine. I'll bring her by."

Dax turned the heat down on the grill to keep everything warm. He told his dad to monitor the grill, he went and grabbed Noora, apologizing to his nieces and nephews that he was borrowing her for a bit, grabbed a bottle of chardonnay from the fridge, and brought Noora with him on a walk.

"Where are we going?" Noora asked.

"There's uh, there's someone I want you to meet," Dax said awkwardly. Then he handed Noora the bottle of chardonnay. "Here, would you mind? It's just, it'll be better coming from you."

Confused, Noora accepted the bottle and said, "Oh, um, okay."

They entered St. Anthony's graveyard, and the observant Noora said, "Oh, is this Catholic?"

"Yeah. One thing the French and the Spaniards have in common," Dax said, referring to both sides of his family.

He led the way to Rochelle's gravestone, stopping in front of it, not saying a thing.

"Who are we—" Noora started to ask, before seeing the headstone. She took a sharp inhale. "Dax, oh my god, is this…?"

Dax nodded. "She, um, she wanted to meet you."

"Oh," Noora said, in a mild emotional shock, not sure how to interpret Dax's comment. "Um, hello?" she said to the headstone.

"She, um, she likes chardonnay," Dax said.

"Oh?"

"It's okay," Dax said. "Just pour some on her headstone."

Noora opened the chardonnay and held the bottle over the

headstone, hesitant on what to do.

"It's okay, really," Dax said.

Noora nodded, and dribbled some of the chardonnay over the headstone.

Dax laughed. "You can give her more than that."

"Oh, okay," she said, pouring more over the stone.

Dax laughed again, this time at the headstone, saying, "Yeah, yeah she is, isn't she."

Noora didn't understand. "Who, um, what was that?"

"Oh, nothing," Dax said. "She, uh, she likes you."

Noora noticed the dates on the headstone and said, "Oh my god, Dax. She was, she was so young."

"Yeah, she was," Dax said. He took the chardonnay from Noora and had a swig, then gave the bottle back to her. "Go ahead, have a sip."

"Oh, okay." Noora took a small sip.

Dax took the bottle back again and poured some over Rochelle's headstone. He nodded and said, "Yeah, I know."

Noora almost asked again who he was talking to, but held back. She'd never seen Dax act this way, and had a feeling it was an important moment for him. She slid an arm around him to let him know it was okay.

Dax scoffed and said to the headstone, "I mean, I know."

Noora kept silent.

"It's just," Dax said, tearing up and trying to wipe his eyes discreetly. "Anyway, yeah, I know." He poured another measure on Rochelle's headstone, took another sip himself, and offered Noora the bottle.

Noora accepted it and took a small sip. She gave the bottle back to Dax, who drained the rest of it on the headstone.

"Oh, stop complaining," he said to the headstone. "You love the stuff."

Noora smiled, realizing he was having a conversation with Rochelle. She suddenly felt self-conscious with her arm around him, but sensed it was okay.

Dax pulled her in, gave her a warm hug, and said, "Thanks

for coming. Sorry, it's just, thanks."

"Of course," Noora said, holding him.

Dax let go, moved to the headstone, knelt down, said a few silent words, and stood back up. He looked back at Noora and said, "We can head back."

Noora smiled, approached the headstone, and said, "Actually, may I?"

"Oh, um, of course," Dax said, giving her some space.

Noora knelt down to Rochelle's headstone. *"Minä pidän hänestä huolta. Lupaan,"* [I'll take care of him. I promise] she said. She stood up and joined Dax, who held her hand as they left the graveyard.

"Thanks for taking me with you," Noora said.

"Can I ask, what did you say to her?" Dax asked.

Noora smiled. "I told her I'd take care of you."

Dax smiled, too.

"And what did she say about me?" Noora asked.

"She said you're adorable, and that you balance me out perfectly."

Noora latched onto his arm as they walked. "You know," she said. "I never knew you were religious."

"I'm not," Dax said.

"Oh, oh really?"

"Yeah, it's just, I don't know."

Noora nodded and left it at that.

"Hey," Dax said. "Let's head to Helsinki soon, see your family. No telling when Gideon's gonna tell us we need to get back to the *Skye*."

Noora nodded. "Let's do it." As they left the cemetery, she said, "I wonder how Kiwi and Jason are doing?"

"Well, Kiwi's still up at her grandparents' farm," Dax said. "And Jason, who friggin knows."

Jason got off the elevator on the 40th floor of the tallest

high-rise in New Haven, Connecticut.

He found the correct suite, let himself in, and greeted the secretary. "Hello," he said. "I've got an appointment with Robert Dufresne."

The secretary keyed her tablet. "And your name?"

"Jason Dufresne."

"Oh," the secretary exclaimed. "Are you related?"

"Not by choice," Jason said.

The secretary touched a finger to her ear and said, "Hey, Bob, your 4pm is here to see you… okay, I'll send him in." She let go of her ear and said to Jason, "He's ready to see you now."

Jason nodded and entered the corner office, to see the executive behind the desk too involved with work to acknowledge him.

"Hello, dad," he said.

The executive looked up, startled to see his son standing in front of him.

"What?" Jason said. "You don't check your own schedule?"

"Why would I?" Robert Dufresne said. "My secretary handles all that. And what are you doing here? What do you want?"

Jason shrugged. "Who says I want anything? Was in the neighborhood. Just thought I'd stop by."

"In the neighborhood?" his dad mocked. "What, you're finally done prancing around in space? I heard what happened to you, by the way."

"Really?" Jason said. "What did you hear?"

"Lost your space commission or whatever, not working anymore, I'm actually surprised it took you this long to come crawling back."

Jason scoffed. "I've flown through the entire solar system, flew 10-light years out, saved my crewmates, killed men to save my own life, and flew 10-light years back, all for you to say that I'm crawling back?"

"Well why else would you be here?" Robert said. "It's obvious. You're out of work, your whole space adventure didn't pan out, I didn't even understand why you wanted to fly out into space anyway, and now you want a job with me."

Jason laughed. "No."

Robert, his dad, scoffed. "No?"

"No," Jason confirmed.

Robert threw his hands up in the air. "I don't get it. You know, I put you through private education, I put you through an Ivy-league business school, and instead of doing something sensible, you fly off into space."

"There's a lot of business out in space," Jason said.

"And look where it's gotten you."

"It's gotten me command of my own ship, it's gotten me out of the solar system, it's gotten me back into the solar system, and it's about to get me out of the solar system again."

"And are you in command of your own ship now?"

"No."

Robert scoffed. "Of course." He shrugged. "So what do you want?"

"Don't know," Jason said. "Maybe I just wanted to say hi."

Robert shrugged again. "Could've sent me an email saying hi."

"Would you have responded?"

"Eventually."

Jason nodded. "Good seeing you, dad," he said, making his way for the door.

"Wait, wait," Robert said.

Jason stopped and looked back.

"What is this, really?" Robert asked. "Why are you here?"

Jason shrugged. "Just to say hi."

Robert shook his head. "There's gotta be something more."

Jason took a stoic moment, then looked back at his father. "I'm going back out there," he said. "I'm going back out into space, and I don't know when I'll be back. In fact, maybe I'll never be back. But I know I'm gonna command more than you do sitting in this expensive fucking office 14-hours a day. So take care of yourself, dad. If I wanna see you again, I'll hack my way into your secretary's schedule again."

Jason left the office without hearing another word from his dad. He made his way to the elevator, and punched in the command for the bottom floor.

On the long way down, he smiled to himself. Here he was, serving on the *Isle of Skye*.

He thought back to last year, when he had captured Kiwi, and how that was the catalyst to him losing his commission with Ralston, which led to him being hired on the *Skye*, which led him to where he was now.

He wouldn't trade it for anything.

As he got to the bottom floor and exited the elevator, he wondered how Kiwi was doing.

Kiwi slammed the shot of bourbon down her gullet, then slammed the shot glass onto the table. "All right! That makes 14 to 12!"

Grandpa poured her another shot. "Okay," he said. "Okay okay okay, I can do this." He pulled another card from the deck, sticking it to his forehead without looking at it. Kiwi did the same. A jack stuck on her forehead. Having won the last round, he guessed at his own card first. "It is a 7?"

"Lower," Kiwi said. Now it was her turn to guess her own. "Is it an 8?"

"Higher," grandpa said. "Is it a 4?"

"Lower," Kiwi said. "Is it 10?"

"Higher," grandpa said. "Is it a 3?"

"Fuck!" Kiwi exclaimed. "Yes, it's a 3." She drained another shot of bourbon, smacking her gums. "That makes it 14 to 13."

Grandma came into the dining room with dinner. "Oh really, are you two still playing that silly game?"

"Yes," grandpa said.

"Well for heaven's sake, put that whiskey away for now and get some food in you. I don't wanna hear either of you complaining about your hangovers tomorrow morning."

Kiwi and grandpa started digging into a feast of ham and potatoes while grandma went back to the kitchen.

"So, I haven't asked," grandpa said. "But you planning on seeing her while you're here?"

"I already did," Kiwi said, knowing he was talking about her mother.

"Oh, you did? And, uh, how is she?"

Kiwi shrugged. "Hasn't changed. Randall's back with her, by the way."

"Oh Jesus, that fucking scumbag," grandpa said, his face a mix of anger and disgust. He took a sip of whiskey to cleanse his palate. "I regret not killing him."

Kiwi managed a smile. "Don't worry about it," she said. "Besides, I got to torture him for a bit while mom watched."

Grandpa's grim look turned into a smile. He held up his whiskey glass in salute. Kiwi followed suit.

Grandma returned with some water. "Oh now enough with the whiskey," she said. She served the water to Kiwi and grandpa and helped herself to some ham and potatoes. "So, it's gonna be a long trip this time?"

Kiwi nodded. "Longest one yet. Flying out to a place 21 light years away."

"Jesus," grandpa exclaimed. "Didn't realize there were colonies that far away."

"It's the furthest one out there," Kiwi said. "Goddamn, grandma, this ham and potatoes are delicious. But yeah, a group of investors are trying to turn it into a spaceport. They describe the place like a second Earth. Water planet, breathable atmosphere. Looks promising."

"Are you excited?" grandma asked.

Kiwi shrugged. "I mean, it's gonna take 10-weeks just to get there. Then who knows how long we'll be there setting everything up. Then another 10-weeks just to get back. I don't know."

Philly Cheesesteak jumped up on the table next to Kiwi.

"No, you little shit," Kiwi said, petting him. "Ham and potatoes are not for kitties."

"Well damn," grandpa said. "Five months to get there and back, and who knows how long you'll be there. Dare say we'll be lucky if we see you again this year."

"I know," Kiwi said in a dejected tone.

"You don't sound so excited this time," grandma said.

"I mean, I don't know, it's just," Kiwi said. "It's just, there's this new asshole who's coming with us. He's one of the main investors. And, I mean I don't know, he just gives me these pervy vibes."

This caught both her grandparents' attention. "As in?" grandpa asked.

"I mean, look, don't worry," Kiwi said, shoving more ham and potatoes in her mouth. "Goddamn, this is so good. I mean, it's like, he doesn't give me Randall vibes, he just, I don't know, I'm just gonna keep my eye on him."

Grandpa gave a huge sigh. "Well, look, Kiwi, just take care of yourself, okay?"

"Oh, come on," Kiwi said, her dejected manner having evaporated. "I'll be fine, grandpa bear. You know me."

"Yeah, I do," grandpa said, raising his whiskey glass.

"When do you ship out?" grandma asked.

"Sometime soon," Kiwi said. "Just waiting for Gideon to message us." She looked at Philly Cheesesteak. "Hey, Philly Phil, I didn't ask you yet, but you sure you wanna go? It's a long trip out there and back. Plus spring is almost here, and you can stay here with grandma and grandpa-bear, I mean, if you wanted to."

Philly Cheesesteak took a few steps to Kiwi and head-butted her.

"Ohhhh, you sweet little fucker, you sure?" Kiwi asked.

Philly Cheesesteak blinked his eyes to confirm.

Kiwi scratched his head. "I love you, little buddy."

"Well look, dear," grandma said. "Just, you know, let us know when you leave the solar system, and let us know when you get back, okay?"

"Of course, grandma, Jesus Christ." Kiwi's phone chimed a notification. She picked it up. "Oh damn," she said. "And there's the message from Gideon. He's flying back to Chicago to pick us up. Says he'll be here tomorrow morning."

Grandpa smiled, then snatched a card from the deck and held it to his forehead.

Kiwi did the same.

"7," Grandpa said.

"Higher," Kiwi said. "Jack."

"Lower," grandpa said. "8."

"Fuck!" Kiwi shouted before taking another shot of bourbon.

10. THE ISLE OF SKYE & THE PHILADELPHIA

Kiwi gets laid, Thomas gets laid, Dax gets laid, and Noora gets laid.

"I know what the manual says," Dax said to the technician. "And I'm telling you don't run it through the plasma junction without a regulator."

The technician nodded, and got to work.

"Look at you," Tricia said behind him. "Barking out orders in my engine room."

"Sorry," Dax said, self-conscious. "I don't mean to be captaining, it's just these guys installed the new reactor and vector drive on our ship, all according to their manual, and we had constant systems problems after. Just hoping to save you the headaches."

Tricia gave a wholesome smile. "I was kidding, Dax," she said. "I'm glad you're here helping out."

Dax softened up and smiled. "Have you seen Kiwi, by the way? Said she was gonna be here helping out."

Tricia nodded. "She's helping Sven and Becky. As soon as you told me to insulate all of our systems, I put them on it. Hope that was okay?"

"No, yeah, that's good, get a head start on it," Dax said. "Like I said, we found out the hard way you have to insulate everything. Yet another thing not in their fucking manual."

Tricia cocked an eyebrow. "With all the things they missed, you'd swear an engineer designed the thing."

Dax let out a proper laugh. "Takes one to know one, am I right?"

Noora had been making her way through the *Philadelphia*, eventually finding engineering, and finding Dax and Tricia having a laugh together near the new reactor. She felt like she was interrupting something; Tricia was warm and kind, but Noora picked up on how much she liked Dax.

"Hey, there you are," she said. "Hope I'm not interrupting!"

"No, not at all," Tricia said. "It's great to see you on board."

"Hey, there you are," Dax greeted her.

"I just got all my shit back on the *Skye*," Noora said. "Was wondering if there's anything I can do to help out here?"

"Well, um, I don't know, is there anything you can help out with?" Tricia asked. Her tone wasn't rude, just curious.

"Actually, yeah," Dax said. "You remember Jack? The first mate?"

"Yeah, of course," Noora said.

"Well he runs navigation here. Go find him and teach him how to lay in an interstellar course with the vector drive."

"Are, um, are you sure?" Noora asked, suddenly self conscious.

"Trust me," Dax said. "You nailed the shot to Lacaille, and you nailed the shot back here. No one else can do it that accurately."

Noora nodded, then smiled and touched Dax's arm. "Okay. I'll see you later?"

"Of course," Dax said. "We're all having dinner here on the *Philadelphia* later."

"Oh, we are? That's great."

"Check your phone, Gideon messaged us not long ago," Dax said.

"I will," Noora said, giving him a quick kiss. "Take care, Tricia."

"You, too, Noora. It's good seeing you again."

Tricia watched Noora leave engineering, then she looked back at Dax and giggled. "You two are adorable, you know that?"

"Pff," Dax scoffed. "*She's* adorable. Not me."

Tricia smiled. "Come on. Let's make sure these techs don't rig engineering to explode."

"Five-million for a freight shuttle?" Braxton asked, looking at the budget on his tablet.

"Yeah," Gideon said, slamming the side of his fist into the hull of the freight shuttle. "We call them cargo loaders, but I included it in the original estimate."

"You sure you need it?" Braxton asked. "I thought you already had a dropship."

"We do," Gideon confirmed. "And while we can fit most cargo on it, it's not exactly designed to do that, and with everything we're carting off to Gliese, we need something designed to run heavy freight back and forth. This will do the job. Besides, if our usual dropship breaks down, we'll definitely need this, especially 21 light years away with no support."

"And you sure you got space for this thing on the *Skye*?"

"Have you seen the landing pad on top of the engineering section? I could fit six of these things back there if I wanted to."

Braxton raised his eyebrows, signing off on the expenditure. "You got it then."

"By the way," Gideon said. "Which of us are you flying with? The *Skye*, or the *Philadelphia*?"

"Oh, good question," Braxton said, pretending to think about it for a moment. "Was thinking I'd fly with you. I mean you've flown interstellar before. *Philadelphia* hasn't. Not that I don't trust them, it's just, you know."

Gideon nodded. "Yeah, I mean, we got space for you, mate." He wasn't about to say no to his primary investor.

"Well," Braxton said. "It'll be a pleasure to fly with you."

"Hey, Sven!" Kiwi shouted from inside the navigation console on the bridge of the Philadelphia. "Can you grab me the insulation primer?"

"Oh, um, yeah," Sven said, reaching for the tool from his bag and handing it to Kiwi.

"Thanks," Kiwi said, grabbing the insulation primer and running it along the power cables. "All right, that should do it." She crawled out of the navigation console, wiping the sweat off her forehead and replacing it with a stain of grease.

"You sure you needed to insulate navigation that much?" Jack asked from the captain's chair.

"Trust me," Kiwi said. "With the extra reactor and the new vector drive, you'll get power surges in the worst places. We found out the hard way." She handed the insulation primer back to Sven. "By the way, you're not Scandinavian, are you?"

"Nah, man," Sven said. "I mean my name is, but I'm from Las Vegas."

"Oh, no shit," Kiwi said. "Only been to Vegas once, but holy hell I loved it."

Noora entered the bridge.

"And speaking of, there's my favorite Scandinavian!" Kiwi squealed, running to Noora.

"Oh my god, Kiwi!" Noora squealed back, giving her a hug. "So good to see you!"

"You, too!"

Jack and Sven just watched as the two girls hugged.

"Hey, um, I was looking for—oh hey, Jack!" Noora said.

Jack gave a quick salute.

"Yeah, um," Noora continued. "Dax said I should show you how to, like, lay in an interstellar trajectory?"

"Oh, yes," Jack said with relief. "Thank fucking god. He'd mentioned you basically sniping your way across 10 light years and back. Yes, please, show me everything you know."

Noora nodded, then looked back to Kiwi. "I'll see you later at dinner?"

"You got it!" Kiwi said. She turned to Sven and Jack. "You fuckers good for now? I'm gonna go check on Becky, then I'm done for the day because I need to start drinking."

Jack and Sven smiled at Kiwi's charm. "Go on, get outta here," Jack said. "You've helped out enough for today."

Kiwi left.

"All right then," Jack said, slapping the armrests of the captain's chair. "Show me how we fly to a place 21 light years away!"

"Yeah, um," Noora said, looking around the bridge. "Where's your weapons system?"

Jack cocked an eyebrow. "What do you need weapons for? You gonna shoot us there?"

Noora smiled. "More or less," she said. "The navigation systems we have are perfect for interplanetary flying, but they don't work for the vector drive, so I literally use the weapons' targeting system to plan a vector, point the ship in that direction, and off we go."

"Well then," Jack said, getting up. "Here, you can access both navigation and weapons from that station Kiwi was just working on. Let's have a look."

In the mess hall of the *Philadelphia*, Dax and Tricia were preparing dinner.

Kiwi was talking with Becky and Sven about the lore of

Tenjou Rayden.

Gideon, Jason, Thomas, and Braxton were at a table figuring out cargo logistics.

And Noora and Jack were just strolling in.

"Well, looks like everyone's here!" Thomas said, his manner jovial as always. "Shall we?"

"You guys don't wanna eat first?" Dax shouted from the kitchen. "I'm slicing the ribeyes now!"

"Yes! Food!" Kiwi declared.

Both crews went to the open kitchen and grabbed plates and silverware. Dax served up sliced ribeye and Tricia served up mixed greens and grilled corn.

After the hearty dinner, Thomas spoke up again. "All right, everyone. First, all of you from the *Skye*, thanks so much for helping out. Looks like installation will finish up tomorrow, am I right?"

Dax and Tricia nodded.

"Wonderful. At which point we're going to load up the *Philly* with our cargo share, and once that's done, we'll be ready to launch, do a test flight to make sure everything works, and then be underway to Gliese."

Kiwi held up her beer. "Cheers!"

Everyone else who had a drink held it up and joined the toast.

"So how does this work?" Kiwi asked.

Gideon scowled in confusion. "What do you mean?"

"I mean, like, are we flying together?" she asked. "Like, how do we fly together with the vector drives?"

"It's easy," Dax said through a mouthful of ribeye and grilled corn.

Everyone raised their eyebrows.

"Well, I mean, it's never been done before, but it should be easy enough. All we need to do is attach the *Skye* and the *Philly* together, a standard docking connection will do it, and we can fly through vector space together the whole time."

Gideon scowled again. "Forgive me if I don't understand the

subtleties of the vector drives, but how will we not fly apart if we do that?"

"Because it's all in how the vector drive works," Dax said, trying to cram in another bite of ribeye. "The surface area of whatever mass the vector drive is attached to is what it sends into vector space. To the vector drive, two ships attached together are just one big surface area. We'll fly seamlessly."

It was Braxton's turn to scowl. "If that's the case, why did we need to spend all this money outfitting the *Philadelphia*?"

"Because a vector drive is only rated for the surface area of the ship it's on," Dax answered. "Yes, we could technically fly both ships attached together with just one drive, but the drive would burn out before long. We fire up both drives together, we'll be good."

Now Kiwi scowled. "What happens if we don't turn on the vector drives at the exact same time?"

Dax shrugged. "Nothing. I mean, we'll make sure they're synchronized, but even if there's a small delay between the two, it'll be fine. Like I said, it's all one mass, it's all one surface area to the vector drive. We're not gonna fly apart or anything."

Kiwi nodded, masking her delight that she'd be able to shack up with Thomas for the whole trip.

"And you're sure about all this, Dax?" Gideon asked.

Dax nodded confidently. "Yeah, man, it's in the manual. And I was talking with the vector drive engineers. They all confirmed it can be done, just no one's done it yet. So far every ship that's flown out has gone solo. A couple expeditions have had two ships, but they've never linked up, didn't want to risk it, even though there's no more risk to it than turning the drive on in the first place."

Thomas also expressed his skepticism. "Dax, not to doubt you, but," he said, looking at his own engineer, "Tricia, can we get a second opinion?"

Tricia shrugged. "Not much for me to add. Both Dax and I talked with their engineers, they all say it'll work. They even described the math behind it all, and it makes sense. It really is just as simple as docking our two ships together and turning the drives on. Besides, Dax has been using vector drives. I haven't. He knows what they can do better than anyone."

Thomas and Gideon looked at each other. Thomas shrugged. "I'm willing to do it if you are. Make the next 10 weeks a lot less lonely for all of us."

Gideon nodded. "It would be nice," he admitted. "Besides, if we fly separately, even if right next to each other and just a few kilometers apart, we won't be able to communicate, and won't know if anything's happened to the other ship until we reach Gliese."

Dax chimed in. "We could set up scheduled stops where we both drop out of vector space at the same time, but that would get messy. If something goes wrong on one ship and it has to drop out before a scheduled stop, we'd never find each other. But if we're connected and fly as one ship, if something goes wrong and we need to drop back into normal space, we can drop out together and help each other out. Honestly, it'd be the safest way to fly."

Both captains seemed convinced. "Well," Thomas said. "After we take our own vector drive for a test run, like I said, if you're willing to, Gideon, I say we at least test a joint a flight, see how it goes."

Gideon nodded again, then looked towards Braxton. "If our chief investor is fine with it?"

"Yeah, all for it," Braxton said.

"Right then," Gideon said, not sure if Braxton was even paying attention. "In that case, everyone enjoy the rest of your dinner, and we'll see how things go tomorrow. By the way, Jason. How long do you figure to load the *Philadelphia* with all the planned cargo?"

Jason was staring at his phone, but Gideon knew he was being studious with it. "Not long. Already got the loading logistics figured out. Take three, maybe four hours."

Thomas lifted his eyebrows. "Damn. Dare say we can lift off tomorrow."

As people started gathering their own plates, Dax said, "There's more ribeye if anyone wants it. And you can leave the dishes. I'll clean up."

"Oh, lemme help you," Tricia said.

"I can help, too," Noora said, feeling paranoid at Dax and Tricia spending so much time together.

Kiwi came up to the table. "Hey, you guys heading back to the *Skye*?" she asked Dax and Noora.

"Oh yeah," Dax said. "Why, you're not?"

"Meh," Kiwi said. "I kinda just wanna crash after this. Gonna be here again tomorrow, anyway. Check on Philly Cheesesteak for me?"

Thomas Burnell entered his captain's cabin on the *Philly* and flicked on the lights.

Only to see Kiwi laid out on his bed, wearing a slinky set of lingerie, and playing on her phone. "I was wondering when you'd stop by," she said, putting her phone down, rolling onto her side and looking at him hypnotically.

Thomas scoffed a laugh, his eyes running the length of her rosevine tattoo. "Jesus Christ. I'd ask you how you got in here, but honestly it's just good to see you."

"And I'd ask you to explore my body with your tongue like you're so good at," Kiwi said, "but honestly, it's just good to see you, too."

Thomas raised an eyebrow. "You're not gonna dance for me first?"

"Oh I'm gonna dance," Kiwi said, slinking herself out of the bed. "Just waiting for you to get that tight ass into bed.

Thomas smiled, took off his shirt, and got into bed.

Kiwi linked her phone to the cabin's speakers and queued up a song. She spilled all of her raven-black hair over to her right side, waiting for the song to start.

"Whew," Noora said, getting into bed with Dax. "Hell of a day, huh?" She could tell he was exhausted, but she couldn't get Tricia out of her mind, and wanted to ask him about her.

"Definitely, but it's going quicker than when we installed our own vector drive. More smoothly, too," Dax said. He yawned. "How'd it go with Jack?"

"Oh, it went well," she said. "He was so funny, he couldn't believe that we use our weapons targeting system to project a course, but when I explained it all to him, it made sense."

"Mm, good," Dax said, his eyes heavy.

"How'd it go with Tricia?" Noora asked.

"Oh, great. She's more observant than I am. Smarter, too. Probably why everything is going so smoothly."

"She seems really sweet."

"She is," Dax confirmed. "She also runs a tight ship."

Noora hesitated for a moment before her next question. "She's really pretty, don't you think?"

This got a scowl out of Dax, who looked at Noora. "What are you asking?"

Noora felt like she'd been made, but she kept up with the small talk facade. "I mean, she is, don't you think so?"

"Okay," Dax said. "Tell me what's really on your mind."

Noora instantly felt bad, then started getting at the truth. "It's just, I mean, I can tell she likes you."

Dax shrugged. "Yeah, I mean, she and I have always gotten along the few times we've been around each other. We're two engineers who love complaining about other engineers. You've seen her. She's a great person."

"No, it's just, I mean, she *likes* you likes you," Noora said.

Dax scowled in disbelief. The thought had never occurred to him. "Come on," he said.

"No, Dax, I mean, like, really," Noora said, concerned. "I can tell. It's her body language, the way she looks at you. A woman can tell."

"What, you a mind reader?" Dax said, trying to make a joke.

"I'm serious," Noora said. "I can tell. She thinks about you. She's thought about a whole future with you."

Dax raised an eyebrow. "You sure you're not projecting?"

His delivery made Noora smile. "Okay, maybe a little, but, I don't know, I can just see it."

"You know what she said to me today?" Dax asked.

"What?"

"She said that you and I are adorable together."

Noora laughed. "She did not."

"She did," Dax said, giving a rare smile. "So maybe that door swings both ways. Maybe she can read you just like you read her. And maybe she has a good heart."

Noora nodded, feeling a bit ashamed.

Dax squeezed her and kissed her forehead. "Besides," he said. "Yeah, she is pretty, but I'd never tell you that."

Noora slapped his chest. "You fucking asshole, I knew it!"

"What!" Dax said, getting on top of Noora and running his fingers up and down her ribs.

"Dahh!" Noora squealed.

"What did you think you knew!" Dax teased, relenting his tickling.

Noora's face was ruddy and warm. She reached up and touched Dax. "I love you."

Dax gave her a deep kiss. "I love you, too. You know that," he said, ripping off her pjs.

11. HAYMAKER

Dax has sparring practice, Kiwi and Noora workout together, and Philly Cheesesteak doesn't get any pot roast.

"*Philadelphia,*" Gideon said on the bridge. "Confirming vector drive launch in 30 seconds, over?"

"*Confirmed,*" Captain Thomas said from 10 kilometers away. "*Activating vector drive in t-minus 26 seconds for a planned flight of 60 seconds, over.*"

Gideon tapped his communications to switch to the *Isle of Skye's* intercom. "Dax, you and Kiwi read that? Confirm we're ready to launch, too?"

"*Confirmed,*" Dax said from engineering. "*We're set to launch exactly when they do, same 60 second flight, and we'll see each other on the other side.*"

"Noora, just confirming that navigation is set?"

"Yup," Noora said. "We'll be flying a parallel vector."

"*Launching in 10 seconds,*" Dax said. "*5, 4, 3, 2, 1.*"

The *Isle of Skye* did its gentle lurch as the vector drive engaged and the low-key hum vibrated through the bulkheads.

"That's it?" Braxton asked. He was standing on the bridge, out of the way, just observing.

Gideon nodded. "That's it. We'll fly for 60 seconds, cut the drive, and make sure they made the test flight as well."

"And there's no communicating with them now?"

Gideon shook his head. "Impossible."

Braxton nodded. "I can see why we'd want to fly together. If something happens to either one of us, the other would never find out."

The 60 second flight came to an end with another gentle lurch. Gideon gave a silent, heavy exhale, then tapped his communications panel. "*Philadelphia*, this is the *Isle of Skye*, trusting you had a safe and pleasant trip, over?"

"*Isle of Skye this is the Philadelphia,*" Thomas's voice said over the radio. "*That we did. Tricia, everything in the green?*"

"*Yup,*" Tricia said. "*Everything looks good. How are things on the Skye?*"

"*Everything checks clear, we're looking good,*" Dax said.

"Right then," Gideon said. "*Philadelphia*, what say we dock together and get underway?"

"Meetcha half way, over," Thomas said.

Noora on the *Skye* and Jack on the *Philly* kept in touch as they gently piloted their respective ships to dock together.

"How's our direction and velocity, Noora?" Gideon asked.

"We're still on target for Gliese, and our velocity is good for when we enter their system," she said. "I know we're planning for a pit stop in 10 light years to double check our vector, but we're looking good."

Gideon nodded. "Well then, dock away." He chimed the intercom. "Hey Kiwi, head to the docking bay, make sure we link up securely."

"*Aye aye, captain,*" Kiwi acknowledged.

The two ships were soon lined up parallel to each other, less than 50 meters apart. Their docking rings extended, automatically linking up. Kiwi tapped the control panel from the Skye's docking bay, pressurizing the umbilical connection. She opened the airlock and felt a gentle wind as the pressure in the ship and the pressure in the umbilical equalized.

The airlock on the other end of the umbilical also opened.

"Hey Becky, that you?" Kiwi shouted.

"Hey!" the red-headed, freckled Becky shouted from the *Philly*. "Yeah, it's me!"

"We watching *Tenjou Rayden* tonight?" Kiwi shouted back.

"Isn't there anything else you watch?" Becky shouted.

Kiwi thought for a second. "Not really!"

"*Kiwi,*" Gideon chimed in over the intercom. "*How's the connection?*"

"We're good, boss," Kiwi said. "Connection's secure, pressure is good, and Becky says hi."

"*Excellent. We're gonna launch into vector space in a few.*"

"Roger that," Kiwi said, closing the channel. "See ya later, girl!"

Becky waved back.

Back on the bridge, Braxton had a question. "And it's just that easy? Like, we just hook up and fly together like this? We're not gonna rip apart?"

Jason took the initiative to explain. "No. Like Dax was explaining before, now that we share one surface area, that's all that matters to the vector drives. With both of them on at the same time, we'll fly just as smoothly as if we were separate."

Braxton raised his eyebrows and exhaled.

Gideon raised the intercom again. Now that the ships were linked, they could share one intercom. "Well, now that we're linked up and everything is secure, are we ready to launch our first leg of this journey?"

"*We're good over here,*" Thomas said. "*Tricia, you and Dax on the comm?"*

"*We definitely are,*" Tricia said. "*Dax, we can set a timer whenever you're ready.*"

"*How's our vector looking?*" Dax asked. "*I know our first leg is about 10 light years out.*"

Noora chimed in. "Oh yeah, we're good, Dax and Tricia. Our first leg just puts us in empty space, still on track for Gliese."

"*Yeah, what Noora just said,*" Jack said from the *Philadelphia.*

"*Well, if everyone's ready,*" Thomas said. "*Shall we?*"

"Surely," Gideon said. "Dax, Tricia, set a 1-minute countdown with each other. We'll initiate the countdown whenever you're ready."

"*Roger that,*" Dax said.

"*Got it,*" Tricia said. "*Dax, just checking that we've got our timers synched.*"

"*That we do,*" Dax confirmed. "*Captain Gideon, Captain Thomas, we're good to launch.*"

"Right then, Captain Thomas," Gideon said. "Please, do us the honors."

Thomas took an audible breath and exhaled. "*Tricia and Dax, initiate countdown in 3, 2, 1, mark.*"

"*Countdown initiated,*" Dax and Tricia said together over the radio.

"You sure this is gonna work?" Braxton asked quietly, not realizing it was being picked up on the audio.

"*Yeah, we're good,*" Tricia said. "*Like we said before, one surface area, one ship, one launch. We'll be fine.*"

Braxton took a deep breath, as did everyone else.

"*Tricia,*" Dax said. "*Reading t-minus 30 seconds on my mark, in 3, 2, 1, mark.*"

"*Read you, Dax, we are synched,*" Tricia said.

Another anxious pause filled the bridges of both ships as their vector drives were about to switch on.

"*T-minus 10 seconds,*" Dax said.

A few more seconds went by before Dax and Tricia spoke in unison.

"*And 3, 2, 1, launch.*"

The *Isle of Skye* and the *Philadelphia* shared a gentle lurch, then launched together at 112-times the speed of light.

Gideon took a sharp inhale, and when nothing happened, he said into the intercom, "Well, Thomas, I take it you're still there?"

"*As I take it you're still there, too,*" Thomas replied.

Gideon smiled in relief. "Dax, Tricia, how are we looking?"

"*We're looking great just as I predicted,*" Dax said. "*You know, you can trust your engineers every now and then.*"

This got a relieved laugh out of everyone.

"*So,*" Thomas said over the intercom. "*You treating us to Dax's cooking tonight or what?*"

"*Your place or mine, Captain Thomas?*" Dax jested.

"Hey, Kiwi," Gideon chimed in. "How's the docking ring looking?"

"*Just fine,*" Kiwi responded. "*Pressure's stable, no changes at all. We're looking good.*"

Braxton raised an eyebrow. "So, that's it? We're flying faster than light now?"

Gideon nodded. "We're flying faster than light."

It'd been two weeks in vector space, and Braxton Keller was bored.

The *Skye* crew had their daily routines, involving a lot more checks and maintenance than he would've thought. Then again, this was his first venture into space, and he didn't understand what they were doing.

That, and space was turning out to be a lot bigger and emptier than he'd imagined.

Braxton worked out, trained, and ran laps around the ship, but everything else was lacking. He had no business to conduct, and no social media to promote himself and his business ventures.

And more importantly, no girls to fuck.

He had his eye on both the women of the *Skye*: one a cut, tomboyish blonde, the other a tiny, fit seductress with raven-black hair and a rosevine tattoo that extended over her entire body. Both fuckable in their own right. He vaguely remembered the first time he met them in Chicago, but he barely remembered anything from that night.

Neither had shown him any interest since he'd been on board, but that was okay. He was used to playing the long game with women.

He had noticed their engineer, Dax, was a proper boxer, seeing him work the heavy bag in the workout room. Besides his obvious power, he had a subtlety and finesse in movement that made Braxton wonder if he'd had a professional career before.

Maybe that could be his inroad: get along with the engineer to get in with the girls.

He didn't mind if he made the girls hate him, because even if they hated him, they were at least thinking about him, and from there, they'd be easy enough to manipulate.

He timed his next visit to the workout room to coincide with the engineer. "Hey, Dax," he said. "You ever box professionally?"

"Me? Oh, no," Dax said.

Braxton could tell he took the flattery well even though he tried to dismiss it. "Don't meet many engineers who've got your kind of fighting skill."

Dax scoffed. "Doubt you meet many engineers," he said. "But you're not wrong."

"Let's go a few rounds, if you feel like it."

"I'd love to," Dax said. "But I'm not a kickboxer."

Braxton shrugged. "Let's just keep it at boxing," he said, grabbing a pair of gloves. "Light sparring, keep it at 30%?"

Dax nodded. It wasn't often one got to train with a world champion. "Let's do it. I'll set the timer."

"So what are we working today?" Kiwi asked Noora, on their way to the workout room.

"Today is deadlifts, Bulgarian squats, more deadlifts, calves, leg presses, and abs," Noora said.

"Jesus fuck me, we gonna be able to walk after that?" Kiwi asked.

Noora shrugged. "More or less."

They strolled into the workout room to see Dax and Braxton by the heavy bag. Dax was going through a slow feint-into-left-hook motion, asking Braxton about some detail of positioning. Kiwi had a brief, reflexive sneer; Braxton hadn't interacted with her or Noora past the occasional "good morning" or "good evening" in the mess hall, but he still gave her the vibes of a sex pest.

"You okay? You seem distracted?" Noora asked as they got to the squat rack.

"Oh, yeah, no, I'm fine," Kiwi said, recentering her focus.

The two of them ran through their routine, taking close to an hour. Dax eventually left, saying a quick "see ya later" to them. Braxton stayed for a bit to do some heavy bag work, leaving only a few minutes before they wrapped up. When he was finally gone, Kiwi said to Noora, "What do you think of him?"

Noora wiped some sweat off her forehead. "What, of Braxton? I don't know. He's kinda kept to himself. Nice to see him and Dax hitting it off well. Dax is so anti-social, you know."

Kiwi nodded. "I don't know," she said. "He creeps me out."

"Really? Why?"

Kiwi shook her head. "Just, I don't know, call it intuition."

They racked everything back into place and made their way to the showers.

"Christ, I can never walk right after leg day," Kiwi said.

Noora laughed. "Feel like you're gonna collapse, yeah?"

Kiwi nodded.

"I know I said it before, but you're looking great, by the

way," Noora said. "Not that you didn't look great before, it's just you can see it in your arms, legs, everywhere."

Kiwi smiled, happy at her progress. She leaned closer to Noora and said, "Thomas has been saying the same thing. He's all like, 'Jesus Christ, you been working out since I last saw you?'"

Noora smiled. She could tell how happy Kiwi was to be seeing Thomas again. They got to the locker room and stripped down. "Speaking of, aren't the Philly crew having dinner with us tonight?"

"Oh yeah, that's right," Kiwi said. "I'm so glad we're able to fly together. Not that I don't love you guys, but I don't know…"

"Makes it less lonely," Noora said.

"It really does," Kiwi said. They entered the showers. Kiwi pointed at Noora's stomach. "I'm gonna have abs like that one of these days."

"Hey, leg day *is* ab day. You'll get there."

They turned their showers up to as hot as they could stand.

Just as Braxton casually strolled in, just as naked as they were. "Oh, hey," he said, moving to his own shower head.

"Dude! What the fuck!" Kiwi shouted. "Get the fuck outta here!"

Braxton barely glanced at her. "What. Just came for a shower just like you."

Noora had frozen. She tried in vain to cover herself with her arms and stay hidden behind Kiwi.

Kiwi didn't care to cover herself. She only cared about her anger. "I said get your pervy ass out! *Now!*"

"Jesus, calm down," Braxton said, not even looking at them. "I'll just be a minute."

Noora stayed frozen, and started to hyperventilate.

Kiwi, naked and unafraid, went right up to Braxton, used both hands to grab his arm and spin him around, and screamed, *"OUT! NOW!"*

Braxton looked her up and down, his expression dismissive. Kiwi knew he was trying to intimidate her. "All right," he said, holding his hands up. "No harm no foul." He took a slow stroll towards the exit, making sure to look Noora up and down as well.

Noora shuddered, hugging herself tighter at Braxton's look, her breathing going out of control.

Kiwi kept her eyes locked on Braxton the whole time. Once he was out, she went back to Noora, and could tell she was having a panic attack. "Oh noooo, heyyy, sh-sh-shhhh, it's okay," she said.

Noora crumpled down to the tiles, still gripping herself, her face contorted, her lungs spastic, crying uncontrollably.

"Shhhhh," Kiwi said, putting her arms around her. "Shhhhh, it's okay. Let it out. It's okay."

"I—I—I'm—I'm sor—I'm sorr—"

"No no no no no," Kiwi said. "Don't be sorry, girl. I gotcha." She held onto Noora for the next 15 minutes.

Kiwi knew she'd been right about Braxton; a creepy pest who played off at being charming, he was the kind of asshole who could piss off a woman then gaslight her into sleeping with him.

Her anger swelled, but she kept holding her friend. Noora had been so much better recently; she hadn't had a panic attack in weeks, and she hadn't been having her nightmares.

And now this asshole had triggered her.

Kiwi's jaw clenched as she thought of shoving a knife in Braxton's throat, when she felt Noora's quivering hand touch her arm.

"Th-thank you, Kiwi," she stuttered. Her breathing was still heavy, but was mostly under control.

"Of course, of course," Kiwi said. "Think you can stand? It's okay if you can't."

Noora gave a nervous nod. Kiwi helped her up and they went back to the locker room.

After grabbing some towels and sitting Noora down, Kiwi raised the intercom.

"Dax, Gideon, can you both get to the lockers? It's urgent."

"*Urgent?*" Gideon's voice chimed through. "*What's going*

on?"

"It's just simpler if you come down here now," Kiwi said.

"Right then, be there in a few."

"On my way, too," Dax said.

"Just promise me you won't do anything, Dax," Gideon said.

"Fine," Dax said, sitting with Noora in the locker room. "I won't do anything. I also agree with Kiwi. I want him off the ship."

Gideon nodded. He agreed, but needed to think about how to go about it. If Braxton was some regular person, he would have him off the ship already, but he was their chief investor, and Gideon knew he needed to approach this with some finesse.

"Noora, you sure you're all right?" he asked.

"Yeah," she said quietly. "Sorry, I'm probably overreacting, I mean, like we said, he didn't touch us or anything—"

"No, don't apologize," Kiwi said. "He knew what he was doing, and Gideon I fucking promise you, when you talk to him, he's gonna say, 'bro, whatever, it's not like I touched them or anything, they wanted to be alone, so I left them alone, what's the big deal,' I *fucking* promise you."

Gideon sighed. "Well look, it's almost dinner, and the Philly's crew are mostly here. I'll talk to him after we've eaten. I also gotta talk to Thomas, see if he's okay with it."

The rest of the crew weren't happy with the timing, but they understood.

"I'm gonna head to the mess now," Gideon said. "Say hi to everyone, ask them how their day went, yadda yadda. See you all there."

"Sure you're okay?" Dax quietly asked Noora.

Noora nodded. "I'm fine, now, really. I'm gonna change. I'll meet you in the mess."

"Why don't I bring dinner to your room?" Dax offered.

Noora shook her head. "It's fine, um, no, it's all right."

Dax nodded and kissed the top of her head. He stood up and held out his left fist to Kiwi. "Good job handling Braxton."

Kiwi fist-bumped him. "See ya in the mess, asshole. Try not to punch him with that hand."

Dax smiled and left.

Noora put her face in her hands and started crying again.

"Oh, nooooo, it's okay, girl," Kiwi said, sitting down next to Noora and hugging her.

"I just, I don't know why I overreacted like that!" Noora said through her crying.

"Hey," Kiwi said warmly. "You didn't overreact. Please don't blame yourself for anything." She held Noora for a bit longer, then said. "Hey, you sure you can go to the mess? Braxton's probably gonna be there."

Noora wiped her tears. She nodded.

"Good," Kiwi said. "Because we need to show him he didn't get to us. We stroll in, we chit chat with each other, we grab dinner, we don't look at him, and if he talks to us, I'll tell him to fuck off. You don't need to say anything to him."

Noora nodded again, more confident this time.

Kiwi smiled. "Come on, let's get changed."

The crew of the *Philadelphia* were hanging out in the mess hall of the *Isle of Skye*. All save Tricia, their engineer. Someone had to stay behind to monitor the *Philly*. Gideon, Jason and Dax were there, as was Philly Cheesesteak. So was Braxton.

The two crews had made it a point to have dinner together every night. The added company was necessary on a long flight like this. Often some would socialize after dinner, either over games or a movie or a series.

Tonight it was the *Skye's* turn to host. Dax had thrown a couple pot roasts with an array of vegetables and some wine into the oven several hours before, and was taking it all out now.

"Goddamn," Thomas said. "Dax, if you ever need a job, I'll

hire you as our chef."

"Just wait for Gideon to fire me first, then I'm all yours," Dax jested back.

Kiwi and Noora strolled in as the crews started to help themselves.

Braxton let the two of them ahead of him. "Please after you, and sorry again about before."

Kiwi gave him a skeptical look and a cocked eyebrow. She held up a middle finger, and brought Noora with her to the spread.

Dax was the last to serve himself. He saw Braxton sit down at the same table as Kiwi and Noora. Dax cracked a beer, chugged most of it, took his food, and sat down to Braxton's immediate left.

Philly Cheesesteak trotted over and rubbed against Dax's legs.

"Hey, Dax, good sparring with you today," Braxton said.

"Same."

"No really, mate. I had no idea you were so good. Most sparring partners don't amount to much, but you fight like it's a game of chess."

"It's nice to be a few steps ahead," Dax said, his tone deadpan.

Philly Cheesesteak rubbed against Dax again, then looked for a spot on the table to jump up to.

"Tell me about your training," Braxton said. "Seriously, I can't believe you weren't pro—"

Philly Cheesesteak jumped up to the table, right between Dax and Braxton.

"Fucking cat!" Braxton shouted, giving Philly Cheesesteak a hard slap. The *Isle of Skye's* cat yelped and flew several feet away.

"*YOU FUCKING COCKSUCKER!!*" Kiwi screamed, grabbed a knife, climbed onto the table, and charged Braxton.

But Dax's left haymaker got to Braxton before Kiwi did.

Braxton flew out of his chair, his head slamming the metal floor.

The entire mess hall was frozen in shock.

Dax stood up and approached Braxton, who was too stunned to know what was happening.

Dax knelt down, and with a full windup, pounded Braxton's face with three more blows.

"Dax," Gideon pleaded, still frozen.

Dax stopped and turned around, but not to face Gideon.

Kiwi was still on the table, knife in hand, mouth trembling, head trembling, eyes a murderous frenzy, staring at the limp Braxton.

"Look at me," Dax said.

Kiwi still stared at Braxton.

"*Look* at me!"

Kiwi looked at Dax.

Dax held out a hand for the knife and helped Kiwi down. "Go grab Philly Phil, then get outta here."

Kiwi handed Dax the knife, walked a beeline to Philly Cheesesteak, now hiding under another table, picked him up, and left.

The room was still frozen.

"Jesus Christ!" Gideon exclaimed. "Someone get him to the fucking infirmary! Make sure he doesn't have a goddamn brain hemorrhage!"

Jason got up, as did Jack, the *Philadelphia's* first mate. Jason went to the first aid station and grabbed a foldout stretcher. They eased Braxton onto it and carted him off.

"Everyone else out, now! Dax, you stay!" Gideon said. He gave Thomas a look.

The captain of the *Philadelphia* nodded.

Noora ran off to find Kiwi.

Sven and Becky left their plates at the table and went back to the *Philadelphia*.

Dax, Gideon, and Thomas were left in the mess.

"You have any idea what you've just done!" Gideon shouted.

Dax rubbed the knuckles on his left hand. "Yeah," he said calmly. "I just beat the shit out of a sex pest, an animal abuser, and a former kickboxing world champion."

"An animal abus—the fucking cat is fine, Dax!"

"That fucking cat has literally saved our lives! Or have you forgotten!"

Thomas stayed quiet, understanding he was missing some context. It also wasn't his ship.

"What were you gonna do, Gideon?" Dax continued. "Have a *talk* with him about it!"

Gideon flared his teeth and gave a hard sigh. "That man you just put in the infirmary is our primary investor. He's the reason we're on this venture. He's the reason we're being financed. He's the reason both us and the *Philadelphia* are making so much money on this!"

"He creeps on the girls and triggers Noora's PTSD, and you're all, 'oh I'll have a talk with him,' he hits our fucking cat and you don't give a shit. If you're the captain, *then act like a fucking captain!*"

Gideon was seething. "If we weren't in vector space, I'd fire you on the spot."

Dax didn't back down. "But we *are* in vector space, and we're not turning back. So what are you gonna do, captain?"

"I'm starting to see why you were fired from your last job," Gideon said. "You have a habit of pissing off your bosses, don't you?"

Dax stayed quiet.

"You know," Gideon said. "When Kiwi fucked up last year and you gave me lip, I held back, because I thought maybe you were right. When we brought Jason on board, and you said you were gonna throw him out of an airlock if he didn't pass our little interview, I held back, because he had a history of kidnapping all of us, and I thought maybe you were right. I swear I'm seeing a pattern here. Maybe your last boss was right to fire you."

Dax pointed a finger at his captain. "That's your one free pass," he said. "You know what happened between me and my last boss. You ever bring up my dead wife again, I'll do twice to you what I just did to Braxton."

Gideon was done. "Go to your fucking room and don't come out," he said. "If I catch you anywhere else in the ship, I'll fucking tase you, throw you back in, and weld the door shut."

Dax gave a mock salute. "Aye aye, sir."

12. A FLASHBACK AND A GLASS OF BOURBON

Dax goes to his room, Thomas gives some advice, Braxton has a broken face, Noora visits Dax, Kiwi visits Dax, Philly Cheesesteak visits Dax, and Gideon visits Dax.

"Go to your fucking room and don't come out," Gideon said. "If I catch you anywhere else in the ship, I'll fucking tase you, throw you back in, and weld the door shut."

Dax gave a mock salute. "Aye aye, sir," he said, and left the mess.

Gideon took a deep breath and exhaled.

Thomas let a few seconds pass before he spoke. "I take it there's some context I'm missing?"

"Yeah," Gideon said, still riled up and unsure what to do with his engineer.

"Well," Thomas said, holding up a hand in Gideon's direction. "Tell me."

"It's um, there's not much," Gideon said. "Basically, Braxton tried to take a shower with the girls today."

Thomas scowled. "Goddamn, really?"

"Yeah, I mean he didn't touch them or anything, it's just, they were both creeped out by it."

Thomas nodded. "Is that what Dax meant when he said Braxton triggered Noora's PTSD?"

"Yeah."

Thomas scoffed. "Christ, didn't even know that about her. Can't say I blame him, then."

Gideon looked at his counterpart. "You understand what he just did?"

"I mean, Braxton creeps on the girls and then slaps Philly Cheesesteak, yeah, I do understand what Dax just did."

Gideon slammed a fist into the table.

"Also," Thomas added. "You saw what Kiwi was about to do."

Gideon nodded. "Yeah, I did."

"What's better?" Thomas asked. "Our chief investor takes a few punches to the face, or he takes a knife to the throat?"

"Neither of those are better!" Gideon shouted. "Besides, Kiwi weighs 95-pounds at her biggest! You think she would've had a chance at a 6-foot-2 kickboxing champion?"

Thomas raised an eyebrow. "She would've found a way to shank him, and you know it."

Gideon let loose a huge sigh. He knew Thomas was right. "If you were me, what would you do?"

Thomas took a contemplative moment. "From what I now know, yeah, Braxton had it coming to him. But he's also our chief investor."

Gideon listened.

"He can't stay on the *Skye* after what he did to the girls, and after what Dax did to him," Thomas said. "Let's check on him in the infirmary, then get him and his stuff over to the *Philly* once he's ready."

Gideon nodded. "Yeah, good call," he said. "But also, what would you do with Dax in my position?"

Thomas took a deep breath and a heavy exhale. "You understand why he did what he did. You also can't condone it. I can tell you that Kiwi and Noora are both on his side, not yours. Jason, I don't know, but he didn't seem happy with Braxton there. Dax also gave you lip, but at least he didn't do that in front of everyone else. And I don't know what that threat was over his dead wife, Christ I didn't even know he'd been married, but I can tell you he meant what he said. Whatever that business is, you mention it again, he will fuck you up."

Gideon took a heavy sigh himself.

"He's also your engineer," Thomas continued. "He knows more about vector drives than any one of us, and he's fucking brilliant at what he does. You need him running checks and maintenance, and yet you need to discipline him."

Gideon nodded. "Thanks, Tom. Let's go check on Braxton."

Jason knew enough about first aid to see that Braxton, while awake, would likely not remember anything when he woke up tomorrow.

Braxton squirmed and tried to focus, but his limbs were wet noodles. "What am–where, where am I?" he said.

"Calm down, man," Jason said. "You've got a broken jaw, a broken nose, and a broken occipital bone." He held a mender to Braxton's face, trying to patch his wounds.

"Am I, I mean, I slap a cat off a table and I get hit?" Braxton said.

"Look," Jason said. "I don't like cats myself, but that cat literally saved my life. Fuck, he saved all of our lives back on Lacaille. You need to understand that he's a member of the crew. When you slapped him off the table, the *Skye's* crew sees it as worse than you slapping any one of them."

Braxton, still dazed and confused, said, "Over a cat?"

"You saw what Kiwi was about to do to you," Jason said.

"Heh heh," Braxton said. "That half pint? Like she could do anything to me."

"Trust me, and this is from personal experience, do *not* underestimate her."

Braxton still squirmed, making it difficult to mend him.

"I'm gonna give him a sedative," Jack said, reaching for a jet injector.

"I—I—I'm fine," Braxton insisted.

But Jason gave Jack a nod, and Jack put the jet injector to Braxton's neck and pushed the button.

Braxton was out in two seconds.

Jason kept the mender on Braxton's face, making sure his bones and tissue were at least somewhat stitched together.

Gideon and Thomas entered the infirmary. "How is he?" Gideon asked.

"Broken nose, broken jaw, broken face, but we're fixing that up now," Jason said.

"He gonna live?" Gideon asked.

Jason nodded. "He's definitely got a concussion, but he'll live. Doubt he'll remember much from tonight. Dax landed some nasty shots."

"How much longer to fix him up?" Thomas asked.

"Not sure," Jason said. "Say an hour? We gotta let the mender do its thing. Still gonna take weeks to fully heal after this."

Thomas nodded. "Best if we get him to the *Philadelphia* while he's still unconscious."

"That's a good idea," Gideon said. "Whenever you guys are ready, cart him over to the *Philly's* infirmary. We can worry about his stuff later. I think he's got like 50 cases of liquor and wine onboard, and I'm not carting that over anytime soon." Gideon left the infirmary.

"You good?" Thomas asked.

"No," Gideon said. "I gotta go decide what to do with my

engineer."

Dax was in his room, on the floor, leaning against his bed, with his knuckles in a bucket of ice water. He'd put on reruns of *Tenjou Rayden* as a distraction, but he was too riled up from the mess hall to pay attention.

His door chimed.

"Hey, it's me," Noora said.

"Yeah, come in."

Noora came in. "Heyyyy," she said, going right to Dax and sitting on the floor with him. "Are you okay? Oh my god, I can't believe what happened. What did Gideon say to you after we left?"

His door chimed again.

"Hey, it's me," Kiwi said.

"Yeah, come in," Dax said again.

Kiwi entered, holding Philly Cheesesteak tightly.

"Oh my god, Philly Phil, is he okay?" Noora asked.

"You sure you're good?" Kiwi asked the cat.

"Mrrrrreh," Philly Phil confirmed, as Kiwi plopped down on Dax's bed and laid down sideways. Philly Phil squirmed his way out of Kiwi's grip, walked up to Dax, sniffed his head, and gave him a lick. A mess of Dax's hair got caught in his mouth.

"Dah!" Dax said, gently removing his hair from Philly's mouth and then petting him. "I'm glad you're okay, buddy," he said.

"How's your hand?" Noora asked Dax, seeing his hand in a bucket of ice water.

"It's fine," Dax said.

Noora gave him a skeptical squint. "Let me have a look."

Dax rolled his eyes and pulled his hand out of the bucket.

"You watching *Tenjou*?" Kiwi asked.

"Yeah," Dax said. "Not even paying attention. Too distracted."

"Doesn't look too bad," Noora said. "Just sore? You can still flex it?"

"Yeah, just fine," Dax said, flexing his fingers.

"So what did Gideon say to you?" Kiwi asked.

Dax sighed. "He said that I'm to stay in my room, and if he sees me anywhere else on the ship, he's gonna tase me, throw me back in here, and weld the door shut."

"Fuck," Kiwi said.

"Oh my god, did he really?" Noora said.

Dax nodded.

"Surprised he didn't say the same to me," Kiwi said.

"No shit," Dax said. "You're goddamn lucky I got to Braxton before you did."

Kiwi's eyes started trembling. In a few seconds she was curled up in a ball, hiccupping her cries, trying to keep quiet.

"Kiwi, oh no, what's wrong?" Noora asked, putting a hand on her head.

Kiwi kept crying, unable to answer.

"Hey," Dax said, tapping Kiwi's shoulder. "Come here."

Kiwi unlocked from her fetal position, crawled off the bed, and latched onto Dax with both arms. Dax wrapped an arm around her, and she cried into his shoulder. She managed to reach one arm out to Noora, who came in and joined the hug.

Dax's door chimed again.

"It's me," Gideon said.

"Come in," Dax said.

The anger Gideon carried quickly evaporated when he walked in to see the three of them wrapped in a hug with Kiwi crying into Dax's shoulder. He remembered what Thomas had said; the girls were on Dax's side, not his. He would need to be careful. "Sorry, I can come back later."

"No," Kiwi said, her sadness sobering up. She sniffled and wiped her face, but didn't leave Dax. "No, it's fine."

"So you wanna join the group hug, or…?" Dax asked.

This broke some tension. Even Gideon managed a short laugh. "Okay if I sit?"

Dax nodded. Gideon took a chair. Noora let go, but stayed seated on the floor. Kiwi let go and got back up on the bed.

"Braxton's been taken to the *Philadelphia*," Gideon said. "He's got a concussion, a broken jaw, broken eye socket, and broken nose. Jason and Jack are patching him up. He'll be fine eventually. But he'll be staying on the *Philly* for the rest of the trip."

Dax nodded. "Makes sense."

Noora just listened. Kiwi stared at the screen, watching *Tenjou Rayden* but not paying attention to it. Philly Cheesesteak cuddled up to Kiwi.

"And I probably don't need to say this, but the three of you are to stay off the *Philadelphia*. No going over there for any reason."

He gave it a second before he continued.

"Kiwi, Noora," he said. "I'm sorry I didn't have my talk with Braxton right away. I wanted to give myself time to think how to go about it. Never had a major investor on board before, much less one that creeped on my crewmen. But again, I'm sorry I didn't do it right away."

Noora kept silent, as did Kiwi.

"And I'm sorry to ask, but can the two of you give Dax and me some privacy for a bit?"

"I'm not fucking leaving," Kiwi said, quietly.

Noora put a hand on Kiwi's head. Kiwi took her hand and held it.

"Whatever you want to do to me, I'd rather they both hear it from you," Dax said.

Gideon gave a hesitant nod. He decided pushing back on this was not a good idea, and started wondering if there was anything he *could* do to discipline Dax. He got to the point. "But that's the thing, Dax," he said. "What exactly do I do with you?"

Dax shook his head. "I don't know."

"You promised me you weren't gonna do anything, and then you go off and almost beat him to death."

"And I kept that promise," Dax said. "I mean, considering

he creeped on the girls, I was ready to grab my kinetic fists and tenderize him on the spot. But I kept my cool and didn't do anything. And then he smashed Philly Cheesesteak clear off the table, so I decided a creep psychopath like him won't learn anything from a talking to, but *will* learn something if he gets the shit kicked out of him."

"You think you taught him anything?" Gideon asked. "Christ, he'll be lucky if he remembers what happened, but even then, he's gonna find out real soon. And then what?"

Dax shook his head. "Don't know."

"What if he wants revenge?" Gideon asked. "What if he wants to scrap this whole mission? What if he wants to pull all his funding? What if he wants to blacklist all of us when we get back to Earth?"

Dax shook his head again. "Don't know."

Gideon loosed a frustrated sigh. "All back to the question of what do I do with *you*? And don't fucking say 'don't know' again." Gideon kept thinking, then decided to think out loud. "I can't exactly keep you locked in your room, because we need you in engineering. I could tell you to stay here when you're not in engineering or not working out or not in the mess, but that's what you do already. I could promise to fire you when we're back in the solar system, or at least dock your pay, but I need you at your best for all of this mission, and you won't be at your best if I threaten either of those."

Dax nodded. "I don't envy the decision you have to make," he said. "But know this, I will stay off the *Philadelphia*, and I won't do anything else to Braxton. Just make sure he stays the hell off the *Skye*. I can keep my cool if I see him, but he so much as looks at Noora or Kiwi, I'll pulverize his face again and throw him out an airlock, and then you and Thomas will have to make up some 'he was in an accident' story when we get back to Earth."

Gideon took another frustrated breath. He knew Dax was right, and he knew he would keep his word. He decided the only thing he could really do was let them know how dire the situation could be, which he'd already done.

He also understood that if he did punish Dax, it would all but be an endorsement of what Braxton had done.

He nodded, stood up and said, "We'll see what happens when Braxton's finally up and moving," he said. "In the meantime, goodnight all of you."

"Goodnight, Gideon," Noora said.

"Night, Gideon," Kiwi said.

Once he was gone, Noora sat on the bed and said to Kiwi, "Hey, you okay?"

Dax turned around to look at Kiwi.

Kiwi nodded. "I know I yelled at Braxton in the shower and threw him out, it's just, I don't know why I just had this flashback now, it just felt like when I was a kid again when I didn't know how to protect myself from—from the fucking creep that—"

Kiwi balled up again and cried. Noora leaned down and put her arms around her. Dax gave her his hand, which she grabbed with both of hers.

A few deep breaths later, Kiwi relaxed and sat up. She wiped her face with her sleeve. "Thanks guys, I'm sorry."

"No no no, you don't get to be sorry," Noora said, rubbing Kiwi's arm.

Dax propped himself up, grabbed a bottle of bourbon from his liquor shelf, ripped off the cap and handed the bottle to Kiwi.

She took it and gulped down several ounces. "Dahh," she said, smacking her lips and tongue after pulling the bottle away. "I would've killed him."

"I know," Dax said, taking the bottle back, taking a pull himself, and grabbing a couple of glasses. He poured out hefty measures for himself and Kiwi, knowing Noora wasn't going to have any.

Kiwi's face relaxed as the bourbon made its way into her blood. "Thanks for saving me from myself, Dax."

Dax handed Kiwi a full glass.

"More importantly, thanks for the liquor," she said, taking

the glass and drinking a measure.

"And thanks for beating the shit out of Braxton, Dax," Noora said. "I knew you could."

Dax raised his glass and took a sip. He sat back down on the floor, leaning against the bed.

Kiwi swallowed another mouthful of bourbon. A wave of sadness washed over her face, but was over as soon as it came. "Hey, uh, do you guys mind if I stay with you tonight?"

"Oh, of course not!" Noora said.

"I'll grab a cot after this episode," Dax said, sipping his bourbon and watching *Tenjou Rayden*.

Kiwi took another deep breath, letting out some stress. "What is it, three more weeks until we hit our checkpoint? Then another five after that?"

"Yup," Dax said. "Two more months till we get there."

"Goddamn," Kiwi said. "It's gonna be a long two months."

13. THE APOLOGIST

Braxton goes for a run, Noora flies a gunship, Kiwi falls in love, Jason looks up something in a database, Gideon calls a conference in the kitchen, and Philly Cheesesteak flicks his tail.

Braxton Keller ran the corridors of the *Philadelphia*, as he did everyday for the past three weeks.

Space travel hadn't been what he'd thought. It was long, claustrophobic, and boring.

That, and the *Philadelphia's* crew had been cold to him since he came aboard.

He'd tried his wiles on the gorgeous engineer, Tricia, only to receive one look from her that shut down any possibility.

He'd even tried a few lines on the homely redhead, Becky, only to get a sneer in return.

All that in spite of the warnings captain Thomas had given him; don't creep on the women, and don't touch the cats.

He had the good sense to stay away from the cats. There were two of them on this ship, and they wanted nothing to do with him.

The coldness of space and the coldness of the *Philadelphia* crew had been getting to him.

Then again, he wouldn't have been better off on the *Isle of Skye*.

He remembered what had happened there, even though his memory of that evening was in patches.

And he had come to realize that the people he was flying with were of a different stock than he was used to.

He was used to convincing people to invest in his schemes. He was used to getting what he wanted through charm and charisma.

None of that worked on anyone out here.

He stopped his run and threw a series of shadow boxing punches, wondering how he could make some human connection during this trip. They were almost five weeks out, with another five to go, then who knew how much time they would take at Gliese-892 before another 10-week trip back to Earth.

Braxton reassessed himself. Too much money was riding on this expedition, most of it not even his money. He needed to rely on these people to make the expedition successful, and he couldn't rely on them if they treated him this way.

That and he needed to not feel so isolated.

He had a sudden brainwave of what to do.

He'd learned humility as a kickboxer. Maybe now was a good time to show some.

He pulled out his phone and sent a message to captain Thomas.

Hey, when you have a few minutes, would like to talk. No rush.

Kiwi had been spending almost all of her free time over the past few weeks in the flight simulator. The *Skye* had a new cargo loader dropship, and she wanted to get as much time in the simulator as possible before flying it for real when they got to Gliese.

She had talked Noora into learning to fly it, too, and was

giving her a lesson.

"Aaand, lift off," she said.

Noora lifted the loader off the back platform of the simulated *Skye*.

"And spin the wheel," Kiwi said.

Noora turned the loader around to face aft.

"And light the tires," Kiwi said.

Noora lit the engines up. The loader began a slow, lazy descent to the simulated planet.

Kiwi yawned.

"I'm sorry if this is boring," Noora said. "Thanks for teaching me. This is so different from piloting the *Skye*."

"Oh no, no worries, girl," Kiwi said. "Sorry, didn't mean to yawn. Besides, you've got this down."

"Thanks to you."

The boredom was getting to Kiwi, she just didn't want to admit it. She opened up her phone as Noora piloted through the simulated planet's atmosphere. The loader was so slow and pokey. She wanted to fly something fun.

On a hunch she checked the Ralston database Jason had shared with them, looking up any ship she could find.

She found their list of interplanetary ships, but didn't want to pilot something so clunky.

She also found a list of terrestrial airships. One of them caught her eye.

"Holy shit," she said.

"What?" Noora said, still descending through the simulated atmosphere.

"Oh my god, who are *you?*" Kiwi asked flirtatiously.

"Who, what are you looking at?" Noora asked.

"Jesus tits, look at those hips and ass," Kiwi said.

Noora giggled. "Kiwi, what are you looking at?"

Kiwi found full schematics and flight simulator compatibility for her new obsession. "Hey," she said to Noora. "Can we switch to something else?"

"Of course," Noora said.

Kiwi tapped her phone to the flight simulator console, loading up the new program.

"What the—," Noora started. "What the hell is this?"

Kiwi read from her phone. "The Peregrine DC-130 gunship. Room for one pilot and one gunner. Has its own reactor, can you believe that? Engineered for both terrestrial flight and space flight, how the fuck did they do that! Oh my god, this is brilliant, the vertical jet rotors act as gyros in space, don't even need thrusters. And *look* at this! Wings are fixed, but it has an active, dynamic tail feather! Can handle 20-g maneuvers and has its own gravity system to counteract all the g-forces. And holy shit it's loaded with every goddamn gun you can think of. Two mini-guns chambered in .30-06. Two 120-millimeter cannons. Two 40-millimeter grenade launchers. Two 57-millimeter rocket launchers. Two 50-cal bmgs with Gauss acceleration attachments. Can carry up to six javelin missiles. And as if all that weren't enough, it's packing a 30-megawatt plasma lance as its main front-facing weapon. Noora, I think I'm in love."

"This thing is insane," Noora said. "Never saw anything like this in the military."

Kiwi, in the gunner's seat, queued up her controls. "This has been sitting in the Ralston database this whole time. I'm gonna give fuckboy shit later for not telling me."

Noora went through her own pre-flight checks. "Well then," she said, giddy. "Shall we?"

Kiwi's smile went from ear to ear. "Spin the wheel and light the tires!"

Dax was enjoying time alone in the mess. Apron on, he was making a fresh coleslaw while six racks of ribs slow-roasted in the oven. The *Philadelphia* crew was coming over for dinner soon.

All except for Braxton.

It had been interesting the past few weeks. The crew of the

Philly would come for dinner every other night, but only Gideon and Jason could go to the Philly for dinner on opposing nights.

This didn't bother Dax. He got to cook all he wanted for himself and the girls, though he had to endure more *Tenjou Rayden* when it was just the three of them.

Gideon came into the mess and found Dax in the kitchen. "Hey," he said. His tone had been friendly lately, which felt strange to Dax, but was welcome. "Goddamn, smells great. What are you making tonight?"

"Well, last week Jack was telling me how great the barbeque is in Brooklyn."

"Not his fault," Gideon said. "Everyone from New York thinks they're superior in every way."

Dax laughed. "Anyway, told him what he calls Brooklyn barbeque we call pig slop, then Tricia overheard us and was like, 'Well, Dax, now you need to show us how it's done in East Texas.'"

"You spoil us, you know," Gideon said. "They mostly just defrost packaged dinners on the *Philly*. Jason and I have started giving them shit for it. Need some help, by the way?"

"Uh, yeah, you wanna toss this coleslaw? I'm gonna take the ribs out."

Kiwi, Jason, and Noora all came into the mess, with Philly Cheesesteak trotting behind them. Noora joined Dax and Gideon in the kitchen, while Kiwi and Jason were deep in conversation.

"How could you not tell me about it! Noora and I spent the last hour and a half flying it around and shooting shit up in the simulator! It's so much fun!"

"Because I didn't know about it," Jason said. "Reminder, that's Ralston's entire database. It'd take months, probably years to go through everything in there." The two of them sat down. Jason called up info on the Peregrine gunship.

"I didn't know they made stuff like that," Kiwi said. "I thought they were just a mercenary group."

"Yeah," Jason said. "I mean, they're a defense contractor first, but what defense contractor doesn't employ an army of mercenaries?" He finally had the Peregrine pulled up on his phone. He whistled. "Goddamn."

"Isn't she sexy?" Kiwi said.

"Refractive armor, has its own reactor, can fly in atmosphere and in space, and Jesus look at that armament." He kept scrolling through the info. "Huh, looks like they've had production problems. They've only made two. And *Christ* it's expensive."

"I want one."

Jason laughed. "Maybe if you're a good girl this year Santa will get you one."

"Gideon!" Kiwi shouted towards the kitchen. "Can I get a gunship for Christmas! I promise I'll be good!"

"Well you can start being good now and let the *Philly* know they can come over anytime!"

Kiwi tapped a text to Thomas.

Looks like dinner's ready. You guys can come over. Stop by my room later if you have time?

"And actually," Gideon said, peeking out from the kitchen, "oh good, everyone's here. Both of you, come to the kitchen."

Jason and Kiwi joined the rest of them in the kitchen.

"So," Gideon said, mixing the coleslaw in a massive bowl. "I had an interesting talk with Thomas earlier."

Dax, Noora, Kiwi, and Jason all had their interest piqued.

"He's telling me," Gideon continued, "that Braxton would like to apologize. In person."

Dax didn't miss an opportunity for a dry joke. "To whom, to Philly Cheesesteak?"

Philly Cheesesteak jumped up on the kitchen counter.

Gideon chuckled. "Yeah, actually. And to you, Kiwi, and Noora."

Noora was stunned. Kiwi raised a skeptical eyebrow. Dax kept a straight face. Jason waited to see what everyone else said.

"So," Gideon said. "What do all of you think?"

"I mean, like," Noora spoke up. "Is he serious?"

"He can't be serious, he's a fucking pervy scam artist," Kiwi said.

Dax gave a shrewd look. He could tell Gideon wouldn't make a decision until he heard from everyone.

Gideon, as if sensing what Dax was thinking, looked at him.

"Well," Dax said. "What makes you think he's serious?"

"Because Thomas seems convinced," Gideon said. "And, Braxton is our main investor who made this expedition possible. And he's willing to apologize in person." Gideon looked to Jason next.

Jason shrugged. "I mean, I get the need to appease investors, but it only matters what you guys think," he said, looking at Dax, Kiwi, Noora, and Philly Cheesesteak.

Kiwi, Noora, and Philly Cheesesteak looked at Dax.

Dax shrugged. "I'll hear him out," he said.

Gideon nodded. "Promise not to do anything?"

Dax scoffed. "You mean like last time?"

Even Gideon managed a laugh. "Let's assume he doesn't assault anyone."

Dax looked to Kiwi and Noora. "I'm fine with it if you two are."

"Yeah, it's fine," Noora said, rubbing his arm.

"I'm keeping an eye on him," Kiwi said.

Philly Cheesesteak flicked his tail, but blinked his eyes in acceptance.

Gideon looked at Jason.

"Yeah, I'll keep an eye on him, too."

Gideon nodded. "So, you're all okay with it, then? Let's do it after dinner."

"How are ya, mate?" Braxton greeted from the opposite side of the table.

"Fine," Dax answered. "How's the face?"

Braxton touched his eye, nose, and jaw, then he nodded. "Just about back to normal."

Dax stayed silent. Kiwi and Noora were on both sides of him, pretending to play with their phones, as if uninterested. Philly Cheesesteak was laid out on the table, tail flicking, claiming his territory.

Gideon and Thomas were stationed at the middle of the long table, as were Jason and the rest of the *Philadelphia* crew, just in case anything were to happen.

Dax just held eye contact with Braxton, waiting for him to make his move.

Braxton, hands in front of him, fingers laced, said, "I just wanted to thank you all for agreeing to meet with me, and I wanted to apologize."

Dax kept his thousand-yard stare. Kiwi looked up from her phone and gave a dead-pan gaze. Noora kept to her phone.

Given the silence, Braxton felt compelled to say more. He looked at Philly Cheesesteak. "I want to apologize to you for smacking you," he said, then looked to Kiwi and Noora. "And I want to apologize to both of you for any misunderstanding."

Kiwi rolled her eyes to Gideon. "That doesn't cut it," she said to her captain.

Braxton nodded. "You're right," he said. "I apologize for creeping on you two. I'll admit, I'm used to getting what I want without question, but I understand I'm not on Earth, and I understand that you guys just function differently, more directly than who I'm used to working with. So again, my apologies."

Noora refused to look up from her phone.

Kiwi squinted a skeptical look at Braxton.

Dax held a plain face.

Gideon went to the kitchen.

"So, um, are we good, mate?" Braxton asked Dax.

"No, we're not good, *mate*," Dax mocked.

Braxton waited patiently for more. Everyone else sat on needles.

"Lead investor or not," Dax said. "World champion kickboxer or not. You creeped on girlfriend, and you creeped on my best friend. I'll let you figure out who's who. So here's how we're good from now on. Don't ever talk to them again, don't so much as look at them again."

Braxton nodded. "And let me say to both of them directly and for the last time," he said to Kiwi and Noora, "I apologize."

Gideon returned from the kitchen with a bottle of single malt and two glasses.

"You touch the cat again," Dax continued, "and, well, just don't touch the cat again."

Braxton nodded without hesitation, his fingers still laced.

Gideon poured two measures of single malt, setting one in front of Dax, another in front of Braxton.

Both Dax and Braxton grabbed their measures.

"I'll tell you honestly that I still don't trust you," Dax said. He raised his measure. "But I appreciate you coming here and apologizing."

Braxton raised his measure and said, "And I appreciate you listening." He downed his Scotch, as did Dax. Braxton stood up. "Come over to the *Philadelphia* sometime. I'd love to spar with you again."

"I'll think about it," Dax said.

Kiwi was a sweaty, ruddy mess. Her arm, leg, and rosevine tattoo were draped over the lanky Thomas. "You probably have to head back soon, don't you?" she said.

"Yeah, I do," Thomas said, brushing her raven-black hair aside.

"You think Braxton's telling the truth?" Kiwi asked.

"Strangely enough, I do," Thomas said. "He's a fucking arrogant prick, but yeah, he seemed authentic tonight."

"Yeah, it's weird," Kiwi said. "I believed him, too."

"Well," Thomas said. "You get a better read on people than anyone I know."

Kiwi scoffed a laugh. "I wish I could read that you're staying all night and fucking me a couple more times, but, you know."

"Yeah," Thomas laughed. "Sorry. You know I'd stay if I could."

"Hey, you don't gotta apologize to me," Kiwi said. "Thanks for stopping by when you can."

"You really believe Braxton?" Noora asked. She was in her pjs, snuggled into Dax.

"Kind of, I don't know," Dax said, giving her a gentle squeeze. "Remember what I told you about how guys can be rivals one day and friends the next?"

"Yeah, of course."

"Well, guys can also beat the shit out of each other and still be friends. In fact, they'll thank each other for doing so."

"Really?" Noora asked.

"Yeah," Dax said. "Have you never seen boxing or MMA? All they do is hype it up, insult each other, fight, and then thank each other for beating each other up."

Noora smiled. "But I don't take it you and Braxton are friends."

"No, far from it," Dax said. "But, I don't know. Maybe he actually means it. Maybe he'll actually be useful when we get to Gliese."

"Really? You think so?"

"Maybe," Dax repeated. He squeezed Noora. "I love you," he said.

"I love you, too, Dax."

14. THE FREQUENT SEAS I

Kiwi does some crowd control, Noora flies a dropship, Dax also flies a dropship, and a 9-year-old doesn't understand Gideon.

Teddy was having a bad day.

Breakfast hadn't been enough. It never was.

That and the sadness of having lost his dad a few months ago came in waves. Today it was hitting hard. His regular bullies never failed to mention it, even when they tried to steal his lunch.

"Hey, Ted! Gimme that!" It was always Steven to yell at him first.

"No," Teddy had protested meekly. He was already small and scrawny for a 9-year-old. He needed to eat all he could.

Mike smacked the back of Teddy's head. "Hey, what did he just tell you!"

Knowing he was going to lose it, he tried to cram as much of his protein biscuit into his mouth as he could, only for Steven to grab his face and squeeze his cheeks. "You spit that out now!"

Of course he couldn't in Steven's grip. He managed to slip out of it, only to get a blindsided slap from Bill.

"Spit! It! Out! Pussy!" Bill shouted.

Teddy just wanted it to stop. He spit out the chewed up biscuit. It plopped on the floor.

"Now get down on your hands and knees and eat it," Steven commanded.

Teddy could feel tears coming up. He knew crying in front of them would only make things worse. He tried to walk away.

"Hey! Where you think you're going?" Bill said, pushing Teddy from behind.

Teddy fell into the wall but remained standing. He tried to keep going, but Mike grabbed him and threw him back to the biscuit.

"Eat it you pussy bitch," Steven said.

Teddy couldn't keep the tears back anymore.

"Jesus, such a cry baby," Bill said.

"No wonder his dad killed himself," Mike added. "Couldn't stand being around a cry baby bitch like him."

On rare occasions there would be an adult who would kill themselves by staying outside on purpose when a massive tsunami came. Their bodies were never found, of course.

But Teddy's dad hadn't done that. He had been outside repairing the suspension struts that kept the colony outpost in place. Several people had been swept away that day.

Teddy sniffled and wiped his eyes with his sleeve. "He didn't kill himself! He saved the colo—"

This got him another hard smack to the back of the head.

Steven knelt down. "Your pussy dad killed himself because he was a pussy bitch, just like you're a pussy bitch. Just go outside. Wait for the next wave to come. That way you can join him."

At that point the trio had decided they'd had their fun and had left him alone.

After that, Teddy hadn't wanted to go back to class. He

was too sad, too tired, and too hungry to concentrate. He went back to his family's apartment, which only consisted of him and his mom now. She wouldn't be back until late. She and all the other adults were too busy trying to keep everything repaired, pretending like the colony wouldn't eventually be washed away into the seas.

Teddy was young, but smart enough to see the signs; the constant repairs were never enough, resources were always getting tighter, and the colony's ship in orbit had a busted vector drive, so there was no way to fly to Earth's system to get what they needed.

Not that they could even get to their own ship. The two dropships the colony had were also broken.

He thought about Earth, and how it was distant and foreign to him. He had been born here on Gliese. All he knew about Earth's system was photos he'd seen and the histories he'd read. It sounded better than what they had here, but he knew he'd never make it to Earth. None of them would.

Steven's idea was starting to sound appealing. All Teddy had to do was wander outside and wait for the next series of waves. It would probably be quick. The tides always came in like a battering ram. He'd get slammed into rocks before he even had time to drown.

But he knew he didn't have the guts to do it. Besides, his mom was already sad enough after his dad had been killed.

Teddy didn't know what a good day looked like anymore. He only knew this one had been horrible, and he had no hope that things would get better.

Then the tsunami klaxon went off. He headed for the bunker below the colony.

Carved deep into the ground that the colony sat on, the bunker was a hollowed-out cylinder of reinforced basalt. The colony could handle the frequent earthquakes, but the tides were a different story. Teddy remembered back when he was 6, an entire wing of the colony had been swept away because the suspension struts had failed. That's when the excavation of the bunker began.

You had to go outside in the wind and rain to get to it, but it was safe, secure, and it never failed.

It was barely big enough to fit all 300 people. It was also immune to the earthquakes and the tides. Teddy didn't understand why they didn't just excavate more and live underground permanently, but he never understood why adults made the decisions they made.

The main entrance on the ground, an 18-inch thick retractable stainless steel door, was open, and he descended in-line down 70-feet of spiral stairs lining the basalt walls. There was an elevator, of course, but it was reserved for the injured and infirm. Teddy always noted how many more people claimed injury when the heavy tsunamis came.

He made it to the bottom and went through the other 18-inch stainless steel door into the bunker. It was already crowded. He would have to look for his mom. He wandered around looking for her, but didn't see her.

Eventually, he heard the bunker door seal. That meant everyone from the colony had made it down.

He kept looking for his mom, and found her near the main door.

"Hey, Teddy-bear," she said, relieved. She grabbed him and held on tightly. "My god, I was so worried. You all right?"

"Yeah, I'm fine," Teddy said. His mom's face was gaunt, but happy. The only time he ever saw her happy was when she saw him at the end of the day.

"Are you hungry?" she asked, as if she already knew.

Teddy nodded.

"Here, I'm gonna go get us some rations," his mom said. "Stay right here by the door, okay?"

Teddy nodded again, and his mom went off to the ration station.

Just as the tsunami waves started cascading on the surface.

They always sounded ominous, even in the bunker. Their deep resonance echoed through the basalt, even 70-feet down. All they had to do was wait it out. It typically only lasted several hours before the tides receded and they could come back up to the surface.

His mom returned and gave him a packaged ration meal. He snapped it open. It was bland, but it was nourishing. He ate it up quickly. Finally there were adults around to protect him and his food. Usually the adults were too busy trying to repair everything to pay him any mind.

"Hey," his mom said. "Can you finish this cornbread for me?" she asked, offering up her own ration.

Teddy hesitated. He knew his mom needed to eat, too.

"It's okay, it's a bit much for me," she said.

He took the cornbread and packed it into his mouth.

His mom smiled, slowly eating the rest of her ration.

---

15 hours had passed. Teddy had tried to sleep against a wall, but had barely managed a few minutes here and there.

The tides were long gone, but the adults in charge couldn't get the main door to the stairwell and elevator open.

This was typical. Everything was always breaking down.

Teddy's mom was trying to help. She was a civil engineer. He had an idea of what she did, but all it really meant to him was that she was always busy.

Everyone around him was irritable. They were all tired and wanted to get back to the surface.

And yet the adults couldn't open the door.

Teddy kept quiet and stayed close to the main door, where his mom was.

He could tell they were upset. They didn't know how to repair the door or even how to force it open. He started wondering if this was where they would all die.

That's when three knocks came from the other side.

Everyone froze. All of the colonists were accounted for. No one else was outside.

Three more knocks came.

Teddy's mom went up to the stainless steel door and knocked it three times with a wrench.

This time five more knocks came from the other side, with a different rhythm.

Everyone at the door stood back.

A curved blade with a white-hot edge popped through the main lock. It wrapped its way around, carving out the lock completely. Someone started to pull the door open from the other side.

Teddy saw a woman come through, a woman he didn't recognize.

She was small, beautiful, her raven black hair was matted wet, and she had a stern look on her face. She held the blade that had cut through the lock, and sheathed it on seeing everyone in the bunker.

"Hey," she said, to no one in particular. "You guys all right?"

Everyone was too stunned to know what to say. This woman wasn't from the colony. She could only be from off-world. Had someone come all the way from Earth?

Something on her chirped, and she pulled out a rectangular device. "Hey, yeah, it's me," she said.

Some voice in an accent Teddy didn't understand came through.

"I mean, yeah, we're in, and by the way, I was right to bring your katana," the woman said.

One person appeared behind her. He was tall, had long, wavy black hair, a thin, black beard, and thick arms. Teddy wished this guy was around when he got bullied.

"Hey," the woman said. "Are you guys okay? You speak English?"

"Ye-yeah," one of the adults said. "Who, where are—who are you?"

"I'm Kiwi," the woman said.

"And I'm Dax," the large man said in a strange accent. "How many of you are there?"

"About 300," Teddy's mom said. "I'm sorry, but who are you? Where'd you come from? Are you from Earth?"

Kiwi nodded. "Yeah. We got to this system like 10 hours ago. We hijacked all the frequencies, no response."

Teddy smiled. He knew she meant the radio frequencies, but the way she said it sounded like the 'frequent seas' to him. That summed up his home.

"We've been down here for the last 15 hours," another adult said. "We couldn't respond."

Kiwi spoke back into her thin, rectangular device. "Hey, Gideon, there's about 300 of them here," she said, waiting for a response. A response came through, again in an accent Teddy didn't understand. "Yeah, I mean no, the colony's intact on the surface, they were just hunkered down here, I assume because of the oceans. This place is soaking wet."

"So the colony's safe?" an adult asked.

"Yeah," Dax said in his strange accent. "Looked fine to us when we came down. Don't know how it's still standing, though. The tides coming this far in, this place was under water when we first got to orbit."

Teddy looked at his mom, and saw her eyes go wide in horror. "Oh god," she said, looking at Kiwi. "Did you have to cut through the bunker door up top as well?"

"Yeah, of course," Kiwi said as if it were nothing.

"We need to get out of here, now!" Teddy's mom said. "We're all dead if we don't!"

Panic started to spread in the bunker, as the colonists realized that the people who had just saved them had likely just killed them all.

"What do you mean? You're safe down h—oh shit," Dax said, realizing what was going to happen.

"This whole place is gonna flood when the next tides hit!" Teddy's mom said.

"When's that?" Dax asked.

"We–we don't know," another adult said.

Dax scowled. "You can't predict your own tides?"

"We used to, but, anyway we can't anymore," the same adult said.

"We have to get out of here *now!*" Teddy's mom shouted. She grabbed his hand and went to the door.

The panic built in crescendo, and people started pushing their way forward.

"Hey!" Kiwi shouted. When that didn't work, she snapped her blade out from its sheath and carved a gash into the basalt, sending sparks everywhere. The entire crowd stopped and stared while Kiwi racked a lever on the handle. A cartridge popped out.

"Now *listen*," she announced to the colony, all of whom listened. "You're gonna be *calm*, you're gonna be *cool*, and for the love of Christ you're not gonna trample each other, *got it!*"

Everyone got it. Teddy wished he could have Kiwi's attitude whenever he got bullied.

"Come on, Teddy," his mom said. "I know it's a lot, but we're taking the stairs."

Kiwi led the way up. She talked into her device again. "Gideon, we need to evacuate them."

Whoever Gideon was, his response didn't sound pleasant.

"I mean, I don't know, all of them?" Kiwi said. She looked to his mom, who nodded.

Gideon's response sounded hesitant.

"I'll explain later," Kiwi continued. "Have Noora pilot the cargo loader down, and tell Thomas to send his dropships down, too."

Gideon said something.

"Yes, Jesus Christ, I've spent a ton of time with her in the flight sim. She can do it on her own."

"Hey," Teddy's mom said to Kiwi. "Can you ask whoever you're talking to if the tides are coming in?"

Kiwi nodded. "Captain, sorry to interrupt, but can you see if the ocean is about to pummel us or not?"

Teddy started to get the hang of Gideon's accent. He made out a few words like "from orbit," "coming in," and "visible."

"Does that sound like enough time?" Kiwi asked Teddy's mom.

She shook her head and said, "I don't know. Maybe? Once everyone's out, we need to repair the top door. We can't afford to have the bunker flooded."

"You don't have pumps down here?" Kiwi asked.

"None that work anymore," Teddy's mom said.

Gideon said something. Teddy made out the words "anything else?"

"Yeah, tell Noora to bring a MIG welder with her."

"Because we couldn't repair it when it was open, that's why!" Dax shouted into his phone.

Most of the colony had been evacuated up to space. Teddy, his mom, and about six others were still on the surface. Except for Teddy, they were all working on repairing the top bunker door.

Gideon said something from his end, but it was too windy for Teddy to hear anything. It was always windy.

"Hey, *you* try welding stainless steel in the rain!" Dax said back into the phone. "Yes, we know the tides are almost here! Give us, like, two minutes!"

The blonde woman who had flown the larger cargo loader came up to Dax. Teddy had learned her name was Noora. As crazy as things were with the evacuation, she had a bright personality and seemed fun. "Got the last of them on the cargo loader!" she shouted over the wind and rain.

"Go on ahead!" Dax said. "We'll see you up there!"

Noora nodded, touched Dax's arm, and left.

Teddy had learned a bit just listening to the adults' conversations. Two ships had come from Earth. One was called the *Philly*, the other the *Sky*. He didn't know what *Philly* meant, but he thought *Sky* was a good name for a spaceship.

They called their rectangular devices "phones," though he'd never heard the term.

Gideon, the person they had been talking to, was their captain. He was up on the *Sky*. He'd heard Kiwi mention "Thomas" a number of times, and from all of the context, Teddy figured he was captain of the *Philly*.

"We're almost there!" Kiwi shouted. She had a welding helmet on and was trying to keep the area dry while a couple of the colony technicians welded the bunker door.

Dax looked towards the horizon as the cargo dropship lifted off. "Ah, shit," he said. "Guys, you need to finish up, now!"

Teddy looked towards the horizon, too, and saw the white churn of the tides rushing in. It wasn't a tsunami like before, but it would kill anyone left on the surface.

"If this isn't fixed right then there's no colony to come back to!" Teddy's mom shouted.

"The hell you talking about! The colony's up here on the surface!" Dax shouted back. He looked back to the horizon. "I'm gonna start up the dropship! Finish up and get over there now!" He ran to the dropship, about 100-feet away.

"Almost there!" Kiwi shouted.

"Teddy! Go to the dropship!" his mom shouted.

Teddy hesitated. He didn't want to lose her to the tides, too.

"Teddy! NOW!"

He started to cry. His bullies had made sure he hated being yelled at, and now his mom was yelling at him.

"And got it!" Kiwi exclaimed.

"Is that good enough?" Teddy's mom asked.

"It'll hold! Let's go!" Kiwi shouted. She threw her welding helmet to the ground and ran for the dropship.

"What about the MIG welder!" a technician yelled.

"Leave it!" Kiwi answered.

Everyone ran to the dropship. Dax came to the airlock, saw everyone running towards him, and disappeared back inside, probably headed to the pilot's seat.

This dropship was smaller than the cargo loader, but still large enough for everyone. Teddy strapped himself into a seat.

"Kiwi! Everyone on board?" Dax asked from the pilot's chair.

"We're all here!" Kiwi confirmed. "Light those tires, baby!"

Teddy smiled. As small as she was, Kiwi cracked like a whip and had a funny way with words.

The dropship started to lift off before the airlock had even sealed.

Thirty seconds later, the tides washed over the colony.

15. THE FREQUENT SEAS II

Gideon asks why he had to evacuate an entire colony, Dax meets another engineer, Kiwi belches, Jason sips some tea, Noora cleans up, and Teddy learns how to fly.

Teddy had barely managed a few minutes of sleep over the past 24 hours, but he had too much adrenaline in his system to care.

Their dropship had docked with the *Sky*, which he had learned was actually the *Isle of Skye*. He had seen the name in large letters stenciled on the hull. He didn't know if there was a difference between Sky and Skye. He'd ask his mom later, if he had the chance. She was always busy.

He was with her and a number of other adults on what they called the "bridge." It reminded him of the command center on the colony.

He recognized Kiwi and Dax. He finally saw Gideon; bigger than most guys on the colony, but still smaller than Dax, with black hair and a black beard. Teddy was getting used to the way he talked. It sounded like English, but at times it didn't. Kiwi and Dax understood him fine, but even his mom and the other colony adults had to ask him to repeat himself at times.

Noora wasn't there. She was roaming the corridors and the "mess hall," which sounded like a cafeteria, trying to keep everyone under control, and letting them know where the bathrooms were, and where they could and couldn't go.

Teddy had also heard the name "Jason," but hadn't seen him yet. It sounded like he was part of the *Isle of Skye* and that he was helping Noora.

Besides his mom, a few other people from the colony were there, too. One in particular Teddy didn't like.

He was Mr. Timothy Caldwell, or Director Caldwell, rather.

His look and the way he talked was condescending. Teddy's mom always complained about him, how he wouldn't listen to her because she told him how the colony needed to go underground in order to survive, and he didn't want to hear it.

"I'm sorry," Gideon said. "Why exactly did everyone need to be evacuated when the colony is still standing there on the surface?"

"Because," Teddy's mom said. "We lost integrity to the bunker when you came to save us. Not that we're not grateful, it's just—"

"But what does the bunker have to do with the colony?" Gideon asked. "The colony survived that tsunami, why wouldn't it survive that smaller wave that came in?"

"Because we can't trust any of the tides," Director Caldwell said. "A few years ago we lost an entire wing of the colony to the waves, and that wasn't the first time. So anytime the waves come in, we have to take shelter in the bunker."

"But the colony's still standing," Gideon said.

"But there's always repairs," Teddy's mom said. "We can't fix everything fast enough. We're always repairing leaks, the suspension struts need constant maintenance, as do the breakwaters, and half of our machinery has been washed away into the oceans. That's why we need to relocate the colony undergrou—"

"That's enough, Marie," Director Caldwell cut her off.

"Shut up," Kiwi said. She was sitting on a console. "Let her finish."

"I'm sorry, who are you?" Caldwell asked.

"I'm sorry," Kiwi said. "I'm the one that just saved your entire fucking colony. Now shut the fuck up and let her finish."

Teddy tried to hide his smile.

Caldwell looked to Gideon for help, but Gideon was looking at Teddy's mom.

She took a breath and said, "Okay, look, the only way to save the colony, the only way we can survive is if we go underground. We've already excavated out the bunker. It's safe every time we use it. It's immune to the earthquakes, to the tides, we just don't have the equipment or the time to both expand underground and keep up with repairing the colony."

Gideon looked to Dax.

"I mean, it makes sense to me," Dax said in his strange accent. "Tunnels underground are the safest place to be for an earthquake. Doesn't sound intuitive, but it's true. You've got the tides constantly rolling on the surface. And by the way," Dax asked, looking at Director Caldwell. "Why'd you set up the colony right in the path of the oceans? They come in hundreds of miles every day."

"Because they didn't at first," a colony member spoke up. Teddy only knew him as a meteorologist. He didn't know his name, but he was one of the older members of the colony. "We watched this planet for three months years ago when we first got here, and this was a great spot. The oceans never came this far in. Then, what was it, six or seven years ago, there was a massive cataclysmic event thousands of miles east, in the middle of the ocean. We think it was an underwater volcano that blew. The oceans contained all the ash and magma, but whatever it was it shifted the continents and the axis of the planet. We don't fully understand it, but that's when the waves started coming in."

Gideon nodded. "And you've been slowly losing the colony ever since, I take it."

"Yes," Teddy's mom said. "But if we just move the colony underground, that solves all of our—"

"We're not moving the colony underground," Caldwell interrupted.

"Goddamnit, Tim, if you'd just listen—"

"You two can argue about it later," Gideon said. "Right now, between the *Philly* and us, we've got 300 people on board that we're not exactly designed to handle."

"That and we can't stay here long," Teddy's mom said. "Like I said, we're constantly trying to repair everything. We need to get back down there as soon as the tides recede and get to work, otherwise there'll be no colony to return to."

"By the way," Gideon said. "We noticed your ship in orbit. Why haven't you sent some people to Earth to pick up what you need?"

"The vector drive hasn't worked for years," Caldwell said.

"Can't repair it?" Dax asked.

"One, we can't get to it because both of our dropships are out of service, and two, we don't even know what's wrong with it in the first place," Caldwell said.

Gideon looked to Dax. "Think you and Kiwi could fix it?"

Dax shrugged. "I mean, we can take a look."

"Speaking of, we should probably link up the ships again," Gideon said, pulling out his phone. "Would make it easier on everyone." He held the phone to his ear. "Hey, Thomas, how are things over there?…yeah, same, look, what do you think about hooking the ships together again? I'll bet a bunch of families are separated and worried…nice, yeah, let's do it soon, also, how are you on packaged meals?…Dax, how are we on packaged meals?"

"We have thousands," Dax said. "We never use them, but they're frozen and take all of 30 seconds to heat up."

Gideon nodded. "Yeah, same here," he said into his phone. "Nice, well listen, I've been talking to some of the colony people, and they need to get back down there once the tides recede…oh I don't know how many, we'll figure that out later, anyway I'm thinking we get them all a hot meal, sleep on it, then head back down when ready…oh *is* he now, well tell Braxton we'll keep him up to date…"

Dax leaned in towards Teddy's mom while Gideon kept his conversation going. "It's incredible how you guys set up the colony. From the breakwaters to the angle of the buildings to those suspension struts. Genius stuff."

"Thank you, yeah, I designed a lot of that, I mean it wasn't only me, but, you know," she said.

"What kind of engineering you study?" Dax asked.

"Civil. You?"

"Mechanical."

Gideon got off the phone. "All right," he said, before tapping the intercom. "Hey Noora, Jason, you guys hear me?"

"*Yes, Gideon, I'm here,*" Noora said over a background of noisy conversations.

"*I'm here, too,*" another voice came through. Teddy assumed it was Jason.

"Listen," Gideon continued. "We're linking up with the *Philly* in a few minutes and we're gonna let the colonists find each others' families, then we're gonna feed them all. I wanna make sure we cordon off any sensitive areas."

"*I've already password-protected engineering and the armory,*" Jason said.

"Oh, fuckboy, can you do the same to the rec-room? I don't want anyone messing with our weights," Kiwi said.

Teddy tried to hide his smile again. Kiwi had a bad mouth, but it was funny.

"*On it,*" Jason responded. "*And Gideon, I'll do the same for the bridge.*"

"Thank you both, will be in touch," Gideon said. "Right then, Dax, Kiwi, pull what you need out of the freezer, figure about 150 portions for our share, Thomas says he can handle his side no problem."

"Ugh, I fucking hate those packaged meals," Kiwi said.

"That's because I've spoiled you with my cooking," Dax said.

Kiwi hopped off the console she'd been sitting on. "It's Teddy, right?" she asked him.

Teddy was startled. He wasn't used to someone casually coming up to him and being friendly. "Oh, um, yes."

"Well, Teddy, Dax and I could use some help getting food ready, wanna come along?" she asked, before looking to his mom. "If that's okay? We're just gonna be in the mess."

"Yeah, of course," she said. She rubbed Teddy's arm and said, "Go ahead, I'm gonna stay and talk with Gideon and Mr. Caldwell a bit more."

Teddy didn't understand what Kiwi had been complaining about. These packaged meals were more lavish than anything they had down at the colony. He didn't know what half of them were, but he could tell they all contained meat and vegetables, neither of which he'd had in a long time.

Some were labeled "Ground Beef, Mac & Cheese, Peas," others were, "Pork Sausage, Sweet Potato, Green Beans," and there were a lot more.

Teddy pulled them from the walk-in freezer, Dax heated them up, and Kiwi handed them out.

The two of them were funny. Dax was large and stern and intimidating, but he was super nice to Teddy and talked to him like he was an adult. Kiwi couldn't say a sentence without the f-word, but she was really sweet to him.

Teddy finally felt useful, like two adults were treating him with respect, and that he was contributing to something. Before long, they had fed everyone on the *Skye*.

"Here you go," Dax said, handing him a packaged meal. "Barbeque beef, mashed potato, and carrots and peas."

"Thank you," Teddy said.

"Hey, thanks for helping out," Dax said back.

"Thanks, Teddy," Kiwi said. "I gave your mom a meal, I think she's somewhere here in the mess? Anyway, you can join us, too, if you want."

"Thank you, Ms. Kiwi," Teddy said.

Kiwi smiled. "It's just 'Kiwi'," she said.

Teddy smiled back.

He took his packaged meal, but the mess was loud. He wanted to go someplace quiet. He went to the corridors, which were also packed with people, but he found a quiet corner behind some cargo pallets.

And 10-seconds later found himself cornered by Steven, Mike, and Bill.

"Hey," Steven said. "What, you think you don't owe me your meal now?"

Teddy turtle-shelled up. "I need to eat," he said.

That got him a slap to the head from Mike. "We don't care what you need!"

"Give us your meal, pussy," Bill said.

"No!" Teddy said back, his stomach growling.

Steven grabbed Teddy by the throat. His meal splattered to the floor. "Look what you fucking did, now you have to get me a new—"

"*HaNYAH!*"

Steven got a work boot to the side of his head.

It took Teddy a couple seconds to shake the blood back into his head. When he came to, he saw Kiwi pinning Steven to the floor, her knee on his stomach, one hand on his throat, and another on his right thumb, twisting it back.

"*Dah! C—can't breathe—*"

"That sounds like a personal problem, you fucking retard," Kiwi said. She twisted his thumb back even more. Steven squealed like a pig. Kiwi looked up to Bill and Mike, both of whom were frozen. She looked back to Steven. "Looks like your girlfriends are fucking pussies themselves."

Steven gargled, gasping for air.

"I'm gonna make this easy for you," Kiwi said. "If you touch Teddy again, if you *breathe* on him again, if you *think* about him again, I'm gonna find you, all three of you, and I'm gonna fucking hurt you for real. You don't *fuck* with me on my ship. Do you understand, you stupid bitch?"

Steven struggled to nod.

"I didn't hear you," Kiwi said.

"Ye—yes," Steven gurgled.

Kiwi squeezed a bit more just to make her point, then she let go, got her knee off of Steven's stomach and stood up. She looked at Bill. "Do *you* understand?"

Bill nodded.

She looked at Mike. "How about *you*?"

Mike nodded, too.

Steven had finally climbed up from the floor, still gasping for air. He scrambled off along the corridor, with Bill and Mike following him.

Kiwi leaned down to Teddy, who was still holding his own throat. "Hey," she said warmly. "You okay?"

Teddy nodded, then a flood of tears spilled out.

"Oh, no, it's okay," Kiwi said, giving him a hug. "Shhh, shhh, it's okay."

Teddy was crying more out of relief than anything. His bullies were gone, and someone was accepting him and his sadness. Whenever he cried at home, his mom always wanted to know what was wrong, but he never knew how to express himself.

Kiwi just held him and demanded nothing.

When he finally stopped crying, Kiwi said, "Hey, here's what we're gonna do. We're gonna head back to the mess, we're gonna get you a new meal, and you're gonna hang out with me and Dax, okay?"

Teddy wiped his eyes and nodded.

Kiwi stood up, helping Teddy up. "I'm glad I followed you," she said. "Dax was like, 'where'd Teddy go, I thought he was gonna eat with us,' and I'm all like, 'I saw him leave, lemme go check.'" She took his hand and led him back to the mess. "Don't worry," she said. "I know Dax looks huge and intimidating, but he's secretly a teddy bear."

Teddy couldn't help a smile.

"Hey, where you been?" Dax greeted them in the mess.

"Oh, we were just beating the shit out of some bullies," Kiwi said casually.

"Oh no, are, are you guys okay?" Noora asked.

"We're fine."

"Well I saved you a couple spots," Dax said.

"Have a seat," Kiwi said to Teddy. He sat down next to Dax. "I'm gonna grab us a couple dinners, be right back."

"Thank you," Teddy said.

Gideon was also at the table, as was Noora, and someone else Teddy hadn't seen before. He wondered if it was Jason.

"I had an interesting talk with Marie and Tim," Gideon said. "I'll wait till Kiwi gets back, wanna see what all of you think."

Everyone nodded.

"And by the way, Braxton wants to have a word with everyone. Thomas is saying he's worried, wants to know the plan to save the colony. Now that the ships are linked up again, you uh, any of you mind if he has access to the *Skye*?"

Dax shrugged. "I mean, does it even matter anymore with what's going on?" he said, waving his fork in a circle, indicating the full mess hall. "He knows to keep his hands to himself."

"Yeah, it's fine," Noora said. "I think he'll behave."

Kiwi came back. "There's your barbeque beef, good sir," she said, sliding a meal in front of Teddy.

"Thank you," Teddy said. It smelled incredible. He was about to dig in when an animal leapt up onto the table, startling him.

"Philly Phil, there you are!" Kiwi said.

Philly Cheesesteak sniffed Teddy, then sniffed his food. Teddy didn't know what to do.

"He's trying to be your friend so he can take some of your food," Kiwi said. "Don't let him, though."

"Right then," Gideon said. "We're all here. So, this colony

that we're supposed to turn into a spaceport is slowly getting washed away."

Kiwi snapped open a can of something. It read 'Two-Stroke Lager'. Teddy didn't know what it was. She chugged it while Gideon kept talking.

"Tim is their current director and he says the colony needs to stay on the surface. Marie is their chief civil engineer, and says the colony is gone unless they relocate underground. In the meantime, they need to make daily repairs or else they lose the whole place, and they've got a ship in orbit that they can't use. So, what do we prioritize?"

Kiwi belched. Teddy tried not to laugh.

"I can fly over to their ship with Kiwi, see what's wrong with their vector drive, see if we can fix it out here," Dax said. "Shouldn't take long."

Gideon nodded. "While Tim and Marie disagree on a lot, the one thing they do agree on is that we need to get back down there once the tides have receded to make repairs."

"Do they know when that's gonna happen?" Noora asked.

Gideon shrugged. "They're telling me they can't really predict it anymore. They say it could be six-to-twelve hours."

"Well I can fly whoever they need to make repairs back down when it's time," Noora said. "We can fill up the loader with any equipment they need."

Gideon nodded. "I like that. I'll check in with Tim and Marie, see who and what they need to do all that." He looked to the man that Teddy didn't know, and said, "Jason, what do you think?"

Jason had been sipping tea, listening the whole time. "I know they're in a load of shit, but they're also poorly managed. Between us and the *Philly*, we've got more than enough cargo and equipment to set them up right, expand, do anything they want, but it's not gonna last if it all gets washed away. For now, we can stick to trying to fix their ship in orbit and their dropships, and make sure all the daily maintenance happens, but we're gonna need a permanent solution, and we're gonna need it fast."

Gideon nodded again.

"And one more thing," Jason said. "Braxton's gonna want a say in what happens. I know he's not popular, but he is the main investor. Might actually be good for someone like him to just straight up tell the colony what they need to do."

Gideon then looked to Teddy. "And what do you think, Teddy?"

Teddy froze. No one ever asked his opinion on anything.

Kiwi leaned into him. "What do you think? Above ground, or below?"

"Um, well, we're always safe underground," he said. "I know people don't like it, but the waves can't get us and the earthquakes don't hurt us."

"Smartest thing I've heard yet, today," Gideon said.

Teddy smiled.

People were finishing up their dinners. Teddy loved his meal, and kept eating. It felt like he was finally getting the nutrients he needed.

"Hey Teddy, there you are, you doing okay?" His mom had found him sitting with the crew of the *Skye*.

He looked up and nodded.

"Actually," Gideon said, standing up. "This is good timing. I wanted to talk to you and Tim about who and what you need for your next round of repairs."

"Oh, yeah, um, of course. Teddy, are you okay by yourself for a bit?"

Teddy nodded.

Jason got up and joined Gideon and Teddy's mom.

"Dax, whaddaya think?" Kiwi said. "Wanna check out their ship while I'm still in the mood?"

"You mean before you get too drunk?" Dax asked.

"Yeah, that's what I meant," Kiwi said.

"Let's do it," Dax said, getting up. "We should probably find someone from the colony to come with us." He went to Noora. "You gonna be good?" he asked her, touching her back.

"Yeah, of course," she smiled, holding Dax's other hand. Teddy realized they were probably married, or at least a couple. "There's not much to clean up. We'll probably just throw everything in the compactor, then I'll see about getting blankets for everyone."

"Take it easy, Teddy," Kiwi said. "If that trio fucks with you while I'm gone, just let me know and I'll ruin their lives."

Teddy smiled. He'd never felt protected before.

As Kiwi and Dax left, Noora said, "And Teddy, I could use some help if you're up for it."

He nodded. He liked feeling useful.

"Well, that didn't take long," Noora said. "The mess is clean, we got blankets for everyone, I think we're good. Thanks for helping!"

"Thanks for taking care of us," Teddy said.

Noora gave a lovely smile. She looked to the other side of the mess. Gideon, Mr. Caldwell, Teddy's mom, Jason, and several others were still talking.

"Looks like your mom is still busy," Noora said. "I'm gonna head to the armory, wanna join me?"

Teddy nodded. He didn't know what an armory was, but there was nothing else to do. That, and he didn't want to be alone while protector Kiwi was off the ship.

He walked with Noora through the corridors.

Along the way, he saw Steven, Mike, and Bill, who sneered at him, but kept their distance.

They arrived at a door with ARMORY stenciled above it. Noora entered a passcode, and they strolled in.

"I was hoping to get more time in the flight simulator," Noora said, leading the way to a piece of machinery that looked like a cockpit. "And I could use a co-pilot. Interested?"

Teddy nodded in excitement.

Noora saw his enthusiasm and smiled. "Come on, hop in.

And actually, you take the pilot's seat. I'll co-pilot for you."

"But, I've never flown before," Teddy said.

"Well, I'll just have to teach you."

Teddy didn't know how much time had passed, he just knew he was having too much fun.

Noora seemed to be having fun, too, even though he was doing all the flying.

"And ease up a bit," she said as they came in for a simulated landing.

Teddy slowed his rate of descent.

"Nice," Noora said. She was always encouraging. "And don't forget to lower the landing gear."

Teddy lowered the landing gear.

"And just be gentle as we touch down."

Teddy landed with finesse.

"Excellent!" Noora said. "You're really good at this! Landing's the hardest part. If you can do that, you can do anything."

Teddy's smile was beaming.

"Hey, Noora," Gideon's voice chimed in from somewhere. *"Is Teddy with you?"*

"Yeah," Noora said. "We're in the armory. Teaching him to fly, and he's a natural, by the way."

"Oh nice," Gideon said. *"Well look, we just finished up in the mess. Took longer than it should've. Teddy's mom is asking about him."*

"Okay," Noora said. "Well tell her we're on our way, and tell her she and Teddy can sleep in my room tonight if they'd like."

"I will," Gideon said. *"But actually, meet us in the cargo bay. I want to get the loader ready with all the equipment they'll need, that way we can head back down as soon as the tides recede."*

"Got it, see ya there," Noora said, looking to Teddy. "Well then, great job. Let's go meet everyone at the cargo bay."

Teddy couldn't do much in the cargo bay except stay out of everyone's way. His mom was busy helping everyone out, just like she always was down on the colony.

He started to feel himself fade, and wanted to go to bed.

"Hey, sweetie, you tired?" His mom had come up to him when his eyes were closed.

He nodded.

"It's okay, you can go to bed," she said, rubbing a hand through his hair. "Did Noora show you where her room is?"

Teddy nodded again. He slid off the shelf he'd been sitting on and rubbed his eyes.

"Well go on ahead, sweetie," his mom said. "I don't know how much longer we're gonna be here."

"Good night, mom."

Teddy left the cargo bay and headed towards Noora's room. He was too tired to notice he was being followed.

In a quiet section of the corridor, two people grabbed his arms and dragged him in between two cargo pallets.

Steven stood in front of him, with Bill and Mike each holding an arm. "Not so tough when there's no one to protect you, huh, pussy?"

Teddy had never seen him this angry. He knew that whatever was about to happen would be worse than anything they'd done to him before. "Help! HELP!" he bellowed, before Steven shoved a hand over his mouth.

"You shut up!" Steven said.

"Hey," Mike said. "Make him puke up his food."

An evil smile spread itself on Steven's face. He threw a punch into Teddy's stomach.

Teddy winced through the pain, unable to breath.

"Oh, you like that, huh?" Steven said before landing two more shots.

Teddy felt like his stomach was going to rip open. Steven

winded up for a heavy punch, but someone behind him grabbed his arm and threw him into the opposite wall.

Bill and Mike both let go of Teddy and tried to escape, but the large figure made sure that didn't happen. Faster than Teddy could see, Bill got a punch to the head, and Mike got a kick to the ribs.

Teddy couldn't stand, and keeled over, gasping for air, holding his stomach as if it were ready to spill out on the deck.

"Hey, you all right?" the stranger asked. He was just as tall as Dax, and he also spoke with a funny accent.

Teddy tried to speak, but couldn't. He just shook his head.

"Here, I gotcha," the stranger said, picking him up and carrying him off. He left Steven, Bill, and Mike to squirm on the deck plates. "These bullies of yours?" he asked.

Teddy managed a nod.

"What's your name, by the way?" he asked.

"T—t-teddy," he whimpered.

"Well, Teddy, my name's Braxton."

Teddy recognized the name.

"Here's what we're gonna do," Braxton said. "I'm taking you to the infirmary, and we're gonna make sure you're okay. Then tomorrow morning, I'm gonna teach you how to throw a punch."

Teddy couldn't respond. The pain was so bad.

Braxton pulled out his phone. "Hey Gideon, it's me. I just got on board, but I need to head to the infirmary. Can you or someone else meet me there? I don't know how to work the equipment."

"Infirmary?" Gideon's voice came through. *"Everything all right?"*

"I'm fine. Kid just got beat up badly. Gonna make sure he's okay."

16. THE FREQUENT SEAS III

Teddy learns how to throw a punch, Gideon smashes a coffee mug, Jason makes a deal with Braxton, Noora remote-pilots a ship, Dax hands out a six-pack of beer, and Kiwi gets a new scar.

Teddy was aware of Gideon and Jason when they entered the infirmary, but he was in too much pain to say anything. That and he could hardly breathe.

"Jesus, the hell happened?" Gideon asked.

"A few other kids were bullying this one," Braxton said. "Mender says he's got a torn diaphragm. Gonna need surgery."

"Here, let me," Jason said. He tapped a few things on the mender.

"I'll go let his mom know. Can you tell if he's gonna be all right?" Gideon said.

"He should be fine," Jason said. He looked at Teddy. "Teddy, I know it hurts. We're gonna have to put you under for a bit of surgery, okay?"

Teddy could only manage a nod.

"And hey," Braxton said, pointing a finger at him. "I was serious. Tomorrow morning I'm gonna teach you to throw a punch."

Teddy didn't remember anything else after that.

After a black, dreamless sleep, he woke up in the infirmary, squirming a bit from the stitching in his stomach, but not in so much pain as before.

"Heyyy," he heard his mom say before feeling her hand on his head. "Hey, shhhh, don't move, it's okay."

"He awake?" Jason said from a far corner. He came up to the bed. "Hey, you had a nasty tear in the muscle that controls your lungs, but it's fixed up now. Also had a bad stomach bleed that we didn't see at first, but that's also fixed. It's gonna be tender for a few days, so just take it easy, okay?"

Teddy nodded.

"What happened?" his mom insisted.

But Teddy didn't want to talk about it. He just held his head low in shame.

"Teddy, come on, if I don't know then I can't help," she said.

Kiwi entered the infirmary.

"Oh hey, you and Dax back?" Jason asked.

"Yeah, got back last night, you been here the whole time?" she asked. It sounded to Teddy like he had been asleep all night. She looked at him. "I go to have my morning coffee and Gideon mentions you're in the infirmary. What happened? Was it those same three as before?"

Teddy hesitated, but nodded.

Kiwi's face twitched in anger.

"What? Who?" his mom asked.

Without a word, Kiwi turned around for the exit.

"Hey, whatever you're gonna do, I don't want anyone else in the infirmary," Jason said.

"Don't worry, Gideon's already pre-approved what I'm about to do," Kiwi said. "Also, Gideon, Thomas, and Braxton are holding a conference in the mess. Dax and everyone else from the *Philly* are there, too, and a bunch of the colonist higher ups are gonna be there, including that one stuck up prick." At the door, she turned around and looked to Teddy's mom. "You should be there, too. You're about the only one who's talking any sense. And you should be there, too, fuckboy. No offense, Marie, but you guys really need someone who knows logistics."

Kiwi took off.

Marie looked to her son. "Do you wanna stay here? Do you wanna come with?"

"I'll come with you," Teddy said. He didn't want to be alone, and in spite of the ache, his stomach was telling him he needed to eat.

Marie looked to Jason, who said, "He'll be fine."

His breakfast ration was so tasty that Teddy was mostly distracted from what the adults were talking about. Eggs, sausage, bacon, and hash browns. He had never had any of it before. As with his dinner last night, he felt like he was finally getting nutrients his body lacked. The adults talked as he ate.

"So," Braxton said, taking a commanding stance while most everyone else was sitting. "We show up to turn this place into humanity's first proper extra-solar spaceport, and turns out you're on the verge of getting washed away into the ocean."

Director Caldwell scowled. "A—a spaceport?"

Braxton gave a confident nod. "Not just a spaceport," he said, using practiced body language. "A new jumping point to expand humanity even further into the cosmos. Think about it. Of the few colonies out there, this one included, they all rely on Earth for steady trade. This is the one colony so far that has set up a breathable atmosphere. It's already on its way to becoming a second Earth, and with that, it's going to become self-reliant, just like Earth. It'll be more than a spaceport. It'll be a destination. A resort. People will be *begging* to fly here."

His charisma drew a lot of the colonists in.

But not Teddy's mom. "I'm sorry, you're talking about building resorts when you said yourself we're getting washed away into the oceans?" she said. "I mean, just, like who are you?"

"I'm Braxton Keller," he said, as if his name was supposed to mean something to them. "I'm the main investor behind this expedition, I'm the reason we're here, and assuming Teddy there is your son, I'm the one who saved him last night."

As if on cue, Kiwi entered the mess, with Steven leading the way. She gripped him by his hair and his collar. His top lip was split and bleeding. The room, filled with colonists, were all too stunned to say anything.

Kiwi dragged him over to their table and put him on his knees while maintaining her grip. "You know!" she shouted to the whole room. "We rescue you from the surface! We give you a place to stay! We even give you hot meals! And I'm starting to think that some of you are ungrateful!"

"I have to object!" Caldwell exclaimed, standing up. "What happened? Gideon, can you not control your crew?"

"Not control them?" Gideon mocked. "I told her to find him and bring him here."

"What's this about!" Caldwell demanded, as a pair of people, presumably Steven's parents, made their way to Gideon's table. The captain of the *Skye* gave one glance to Dax, who got up and prevented anyone from approaching Kiwi's captive.

"What's your name?" Gideon asked.

"His—his name is Ste—!" the father pleaded.

"I didn't ask you," Gideon said, without looking away from the kid. "What's your name?" he repeated.

The kid kept his eyes between the floor and Gideon, unable to look him in the eye.

Gideon glanced at Kiwi, who smacked the kid upside the head.

"Hey!" the mother exclaimed.

"I've asked you twice," Gideon said. "I'm not asking a third time."

"S—Steven," he said.

"Steven, I'm Gideon, and in case you didn't know, I'm the captain of this ship. I understand that two of your girlfriends held Teddy last night while you pummeled him in the stomach. That true?"

"Oh my god, he would neve—" the mother exclaimed.

"SHUT UP!" Gideon bellowed with command. He looked back at Steven. "Is that true?"

Steven did a few awkward glances between Gideon and the floor, before shrugging his shoulders and saying, "Just messing around."

Kiwi grabbed his hair and squeezed his face together like she had seen them do to Teddy yesterday. Caldwell, along with Steven's parents, wanted to do something, but Dax was an impervious wall.

"Yes or no," Kiwi said. "Did you and your fucking girlfriends hold him and punch him in the fucking stomach!" She slapped his head again.

"Y-yes," Steven said meekly.

"Braxton," Gideon said, keeping his eyes locked on Steven. "You witnessed this right?"

"Oh yeah," Braxton said, arms crossed.

"And how about his compatriots?" Gideon asked. "You see them here in the mess?"

Braxton looked around. "I do, indeed."

"Jason, what were Teddy's injuries like?"

"His diaphragm was torn, and during the surgery we also

saw he had a stomach bleed. If they'd left him in the corridor last night, he would've died."

Teddy had been hypnotized by what was happening, but Jason's words sent a freezing jolt through his spine. He hadn't realized he could've died. What he'd always felt as shame and fear was turning into anger.

"So!" Gideon announced to the entire mess. He stood up to project his voice. "When you're a guest on my ship, I have certain manners that I expect from you! Casually trying to kill a 9-year-old is not one of them! Kiwi!"

"Yessir!"

"I understand you caught those three bullying Teddy yesterday before this happened!"

"That's right!"

"And you warned them to stop, didn't you!"

"Boy did I!"

Gideon allowed for a pregnant pause before continuing. "Now when you're on my ship, an order from my crew is the same as an order from me. You disobey that, and you're out! So on the next flight down, Steven, his girlfriends, and their families, are all going back to the surface, and they're staying there for good!"

"He's just a boy!" the mother objected. "Boys screw up all the time!"

"Your boy's a psycho, you dumb bitch," Kiwi said.

"Don't call my wife a—"

"Shut the fuck up, you dumb bitch," Dax said to the father.

Director Caldwell didn't like this one bit. "You can't just arbitrarily do that! You're putting them and everyone else in—"

Without a word, Gideon carefully took his coffee mug from the table, raised it up, and smashed it to the floor. It exploded like a grenade.

Everyone froze. Kiwi smiled.

Gideon rubbed his fingers with his thumb, as if to brush any ceramic residue away. When no one said anything, he said, "Kiwi, Dax, round up the three perpetrators and lock them in the spare room. Their families can join them if they want. We'll round all of them up when we're ready to head back to the surface."

Kiwi pointed out Bill and Mike, and Dax went to collect them. With Dax out of the way, Steven's mother tried to go to him, but Kiwi slapped her hand away.

"Like I said, you can join him if you want, but Kiwi's throwing him in our spare room for now. Don't worry, there's a sink, a bathroom, and running water."

Kiwi hauled Steven off.

"Now," Gideon said, sitting back down. "Braxton, I believe we were talking about your vision for the colony."

Caldwell, not liking the situation, but realizing there was nothing he could do, also sat back down.

Teddy was too shocked to listen to the rest of their conversation. The adults of the colony never punished any kid; they were always too busy to notice, and at the end of the day too tired to do anything about it.

But the adults on the *Isle of Skye* were quick to intervene and even faster to punish. Just as important, they were fair. Teddy never felt like he was treated fairly, until now. If only he could make people treat him fairly, like Kiwi, and Gideon, and Dax did.

But just as a kernel of confidence took shape, so did a chill of fear. He knew that as soon as he was back on the colony without anyone to protect him, Steven and his goons would do worse to him than they had done last night.

He wasn't hungry anymore, and couldn't focus well on the conversation around him. Braxton and Gideon argued for what they thought they should do, while everyone from the colony, even his mom, told them how it was impossible.

The conversation peaked when Braxton said, "Look, we can set you up with all the resources and equipment you need and you can do it my way, or we can leave you with nothing and you can keep doing things your way!"

This caused the conversation to stop, in time for the

intercom to ring.

"Hey guys, it's Noora on the bridge. Looks like the tides have receded. If we're gonna head back down, we should do so now."

"Thanks, Noora," Gideon said. "Meet us at the cargo loader." He then called Kiwi and Dax, and had them escort Teddy's bullies and their families there as well. Most everyone got up and left. His mom, too. She was headed back down to the surface and told Teddy to stay here.

Braxton stayed as well.

"Hey, Teddy, you didn't forget my promise did you?" he said.

Teddy smiled. "No, I didn't forget."

"Well then, I know you gotta take it easy, but come with me to the exercise room. I'm gonna show you how to throw a punch."

"Let's see," Braxton said. "Small hands like yours, I'll bet one of the girls' gloves will fit. Here ya go."

"Do you all know how to fight?" Teddy asked, accepting the gloves.

"Oh yeah," Braxton said. "I'm a five-time kickboxing world champion back on Earth, but everyone else here knows how to fight, too. Gideon's a mean shot and knows how to scrap. Noora's a trained military sniper. Dax throws a harder punch than I do. And Kiwi, well, Kiwi's the most dangerous of them all."

Teddy smiled, knowing what Braxton meant, but doubt suddenly creeped through him. "I don't know," he said. "I mean, the other kids are so much bigger than me."

"So?" Braxton asked. "That Steven is bigger than Kiwi. That didn't stop her from beating the shit out of him, just like it won't stop you when the time comes."

Teddy felt like Braxton was referring to what he'd thought about earlier, how Steven, Bill, and Mike were going to make things even worse.

"Look, you're safe for now," Braxton said, kneeling down. "But we both know that once we're gone, and you're back on the surface, you'll have to defend yourself."

Just then, the cat that Teddy had met last night strolled in through an air vent. He kept close to the wall.

"You see that cat?" Braxton asked.

"Yeah."

"Steven's a lot bigger than that cat, isn't he?"

Teddy nodded. "Yeah."

"Lemme ask you this. You let Steven hold that cat, then you dump a bucket of ice water on him, is he still gonna be able to hold onto that cat?"

Teddy shook his head.

"But why not?" Braxton asked. "He's bigger than the cat. Stronger. Why can't he hold onto it?"

"Because," Teddy thought. "Because the cat won't stop until it's free."

"*Exactly*," Braxton said. "That cat is gonna use all its muscle, all its claws, and all its fangs to get the hell outta there, and there's nothing Steven can do to stop it. I'm gonna teach you to be a cat with ice water on it. If you work hard enough, maybe I'll even teach you to be a Kiwi."

Teddy laughed.

Braxton laughed too, stood up, and said to the cat, "Hey, Philly Cheesesteak, I know you don't like me, but take care of Teddy here when I'm not around, all right?"

Philly Cheesesteak blinked his eyes, looked away, and flicked his tail.

"All right, got those gloves on? Okay, first, you're gonna stand like this."

Teddy was exhausted.

It had started simple. Braxton had taught him how to throw a jab, jab-cross. He'd even taught him a left hook to the body.

Then he'd taught him some basic footwork, which was tricky.

When Teddy had wanted a break, Braxton had him do push ups. When he could only manage three, Braxton encouraged him, saying that by tomorrow it would be four, the next day five, and before he knew it, it would be 20 pushups a day. Then 50. Then 100.

Then Braxton made him do jump ropes, which he could only manage a few at a time before tripping up.

But the encouragement didn't stop.

Today it's 5 or 10 reps. Tomorrow you'll get to 40 or 50. The day after you'll get to 100.

When that was done, it was sit-ups.

Only 10 today? No problem. Tomorrow it'll be 20. The next 50. Then 100.

He had showered off, but only had the clothes he had come up to the *Skye* with. He was used to this. The most anyone in the colony had was two sets of clothes.

He headed back to the exercise room, which Braxton had given him the passcode to.

Braxton had also given him a phone.

"Here," he'd said before, pulling out his own phone. "Got plenty of footwork and boxing videos you can watch. Got a phone?"

Teddy had shaken his head.

Braxton had scowled. "Oh, well then we'll have to change that." He rang up Dax over the intercom. "Hey, Dax, sorry to bother you, but I'm trying to get a phone for Teddy. You guys have any extras?"

"Of course. Can get him one in a few minutes."

And a few minutes later Dax had shown up, given him his new phone, and Braxton had shown him a few basics on how to use it. Then he'd uploaded an entire library of boxing videos to it.

Teddy was about to pull out his phone to watch some, when he noticed Philly Cheesesteak was still in the exercise room, napping in a corner. He noticed Teddy, got up, took a luxurious stretch, and strolled over, tail high.

Teddy squatted down to greet him. Philly Cheesesteak rubbed up against his knee.

"Hi," Teddy said.

Philly Cheesesteak rubbed against his other knee, back arched high. Teddy gave him a couple of pets. He knew what cats were, but this was the first one he'd met.

"I've never met a cat before. Well, I mean, I guess we met yesterday, but still, you're the first."

Philly Cheesesteak butted his head against the same knee.

Teddy laughed and gave him a couple more pets.

Philly Cheesesteak looked at him and chirped. "*Mr-reh.*"

Teddy shook his head. "*Mr-reh?*" he echoed.

Philly Cheesesteak trotted towards the vent, then looked back at Teddy and said, "*Meh-br-r-r-reh.*"

"You want me to follow you?"

"*Myeh, br-r-rh,*" Philly Cheesesteak said, heading into the vent.

Teddy went up to the vent, realizing he'd have no trouble getting in. But he hesitated. What if he got stuck?

But Philly Cheesesteak was insistent. He stared at Teddy from inside the vent and said, "*Mryah,*" as if to ask what Teddy's holdup was.

Teddy smiled. He could always trace back and find the exercise room if needed. He got into the vent and followed Philly Cheesesteak.

Despite the maze of vents the cat was leading him through, he felt confident about navigating all of it. That, and Teddy had tapped the "Library" icon on his phone, and had quickly found a map of the ventilation system, which was even kind enough to note his current position.

He followed Philly Cheesesteak for a while, who was always

ahead of him, always looking back, always meowing around corners to guide him.

When he eventually stopped in front of a vent to a different room. Teddy checked his phone, which told him he was at the bridge.

Philly Cheesesteak just stood like a statue in front of the vent.

Teddy heard voices from the bridge.

"Sure you can repair it?" Gideon's voice said.

"Oh yeah," Dax's voice said. "Turns out their vector drive is fine. Just a couple plasma conduits need some resealing, and their main reactor needs some new shielding."

Teddy heard a sigh from Gideon. "They didn't even know their vector drive was fine? They just said 'oh it's broken and we don't know why' and couldn't be bothered to check anything else?"

"Look," Dax said. "Not to defend their incompetence, but they don't even have a functioning dropship to manually double check."

"How about their dropships? Can those be repaired?"

"Oh yeah," Kiwi's voice said. "Already been talking with Tricia, Sven, and Becky. Dax and I are gonna fix their ship. The three of them are gonna fix their dropships."

"Good, good," Gideon said. "Tell me. How did that go in the mess, do you think?"

"You kidding?" Kiwi said. "They deserved it. Also I don't get why these people can't police their own."

"Yeah, no shit," Dax said. "Makes you wonder what else they're up to."

"I don't know," Gideon said. "Kids bully each other all the time."

"Not like that," Kiwi said. "I slapped Steven's mom, by the way." She giggled. "Out in the corridor, she tried to grab him away from me, and I slapped her so fucking hard. Dumb cunt. Dad didn't even do a thing."

Teddy covered his mouth, trying not to laugh.

"Thank you both, by the way," Gideon said. "I learned my lesson. Should've done that with Braxton at first, but maybe I owe you a thanks for putting him in his place, Dax."

"Don't mention it."

Teddy didn't know what they were referring to. Sounded like some previous conflict between them and Braxton.

"How long to repair their ship?" Gideon asked.

"Not long," Dax said. "Give us a day, maybe two."

"Damn, that fast?" Gideon said. "Tell me what do you think of their predicament. Braxton's got a clear idea, but tell me what you think this colony can do?"

Teddy heard Jason's voice next.

"Between us and the *Philly*, we have everything they need to expand, build, hell even become a spaceport. I think Braxton had a point. We can give them all this cargo and equipment, but are they gonna use it the right way?"

"What are you thinking?" Gideon asked.

"I'm thinking," Jason said. "That leaving all this stuff here with no supervision is a bad idea. That fucking idiot, Caldwell, would let everything wash into the ocean before he makes a good decision. But if you had someone here to oversee it all, someone who makes sure they do what we want, and that who can threaten to withdraw it at any time, I think that's the only way to make this work."

"Hm," Gideon said, interested. "Who would you suggest should stay behind to do this?"

"Me," Jason said.

There was a pregnant pause from the bridge, then Gideon said, "What makes you say that?"

Teddy heard a sigh from Jason.

"I don't know, it's a lot of things. I see a lot of potential here. As fucked as they are, I think this can work. Also, I know logistics, hell it was my specialty, and I miss ordering people around, and I can't do that while I'm part of this ship."

Teddy heard a couple of laughs.

"Besides," Jason said. "Sure, Braxton's an asshole, sure the feds are after him for money laundering and tax evasion, but, I don't know, I think he's right about this place. I think it can work. With the right direction, I think his vision can happen. And I think I can make something of this place."

"You sound confident, fuckboy," Kiwi said. "Where's that coming from?"

"Well," Jason said. "On top of all the cargo and equipment we can give them, have you noticed anything about this planet?"

"Other than the oceans?" Dax asked.

"Yeah," Jason said. "Funny, Dax, I thought you would've noticed this. Anyway, the diameter of this planet, it's 15% smaller than Earth, but has almost the same gravity."

"Oh, oh yeah, I hadn't thought of that," Dax said, realizing something.

"What does that mean?" Gideon asked.

"It means, um, I'm sorry, you tell him," Dax said.

"It means this planet is *dense*," Jason said. "They're sitting on massive deposits of gold, uranium, you name it. They can mine whatever the hell they want, make whatever the hell they want, export whatever the hell they want, and they can make good money on it."

"Jesus," Gideon said. "So they really can be an extrasolar spaceport."

"Just gonna take the right kinda leader," Jason said.

"And you're the man for it, huh?" Gideon asked.

"Yeah, yeah I am," Jason said.

Another pregnant pause from the bridge.

"I mean," Kiwi said. "Never thought I'd say this, but hate to see you go, fuckboy."

"You sure, Jason?" Dax asked.

"I'm sure. If you guys can repair their ship, and if I stay and oversee everything, I know it can work."

Another pause.

"Well then," Gideon said. "I agree, I hate to see you go, but I have a feeling you're right. Run this by Braxton. See what he thinks. He's the main investor, after all."

"I will," Jason said.

Over the next few weeks, Teddy found a daily rhythm that had made his life easier.

He got nourishing food everyday. He got daily boxing lessons from Braxton. He did his jump ropes, his pushups, his crunches, he even ran the corridors, which were gradually depleting as everyone was slowly relocated back down to the colony.

Braxton was tough, but inspiring. "Come on! Same combo, now!" he had screamed, and when he detected a hint of anger in Teddy's face, he'd said, "Oh, what! You're angry? Good! Use that! Anger's a gift! I was poor, and my anger made me rich! I was a bad fighter, and my anger made me a world champion!"

"But, my mom doesn't like anger," Teddy had said.

"That's because she's a woman," Braxton had said. "I've seen your mom, she's a good person, she works hard, but she's a woman. They think they can talk their way out of everything. They don't understand what you have to do as a *man*. *You* are a *man*. When those bullies come at you again when you're back in the colony, do you think you can talk your way out of it?"

Teddy had shaken his head.

"Exactly! Talk is for the weak! Talk is for women! Your problem, Teddy, is that you're a good person! But psychopaths like Steven know that! They prey on it! But the next time you see them, you're gonna show them! You're not gonna talk, you're gonna *show* them! Your anger is going to save your life! It doesn't mean you're a bad person! It means you're a good person who can defend himself from bad people! Now gimme that same combo again!"

During his downtime, Teddy slid into the vents, hung out by the bridge, and watched the boxing videos Braxton had given him.

While he silently watched the videos, picking up their

nuances and learning how to incorporate that into what Braxton was teaching him, he overheard some interesting conversations on the bridge.

He found out Kiwi and the captain of the *Philadelphia* were seeing each other.

"Heyyy," Kiwi said.

"Heyyy," Thomas returned, followed by a bunch of kissing sounds.

"You know, I could lock the bridge down and you could fuck me right here on the console."

Thomas laughed and said, "You're such a vixen, aren't you. You know I want to but can't."

"I know," Kiwi said sweetly. "But come on, it would be fun, wouldn't it."

He would hear Gideon communicate with lots of other people, mostly those down on the colony.

"Yes, goddamnit," Gideon said. "Tell them they're excavating now while the tides are out! I don't care about the debris! It'll wash away when the next tide comes in!"

He occasionally heard Noora on the bridge, when she wasn't busy flying teams back and forth between the ships and the surface. She mostly communicated with Kiwi, Dax, and whomever was flying dropships.

One day, he heard an interesting conversation between Braxton and Jason.

"So, tell me, what are you thinking, mate?" Braxton said.

"Look," Jason said. "They agreed to take everything and do what we're telling them, but what makes you think they're going to stick with that once we're all gone?"

"Hm!" Braxton scoffed. "Good point. How do you think we keep them in check?"

"Well, I've run this by Gideon and everyone else, and they all think it's a good idea, but you're the main investor, so I wanted to run it by you."

"I'm listening."

"I stay behind, I oversee everything, I make sure they're

doing what they need to be doing, and I threaten to pull everything if they don't," Jason said.

There was a pause, then Braxton said, "Huh, you're willing to do that?"

"Let's be honest, there's no other way to protect the investment," Jason said.

"I mean look, bro, it's 10 weeks out here, 10 weeks back, no telling how long you'd be here on your own."

"I don't think it'll be that long," Jason said.

"What makes you say that?"

"Because the mining prospects here are endless," Jason said. "I can get this colony's shit together, get them safely underground, and get them mining. We'll be able to fabricate whatever we need and then take their repaired vector drive ship back to the solar system loaded with materials, trade what we need, maybe even hire a team of welders and geological surveyors, and head back."

"Jesus Christ, mate," Braxton said. "You sure you can do all that?"

"Trust me, I got a background in logistics, also computers. I was a contractor for Ralston for several years for their space division."

"No kidding," Braxton said. "Didn't take you for a mercenary."

"Eh, I mean most mercenary work is logistics as it is. Anyway, I stay back, protect the investment, what do you think?"

"What do you want in return?" Braxton asked.

"Well, you're taking the investment risk, I'm taking the staying-behind risk," Jason said. "Rather than a direct payment, how about an equity stake?"

Teddy didn't know what "equity" meant, but it sounded important.

"What are you thinking?" Braxton asked.

"Say 5% of returns," Jason said.

Teddy swore he could hear Braxton nod.

"Not bad, not bad. I have to run it by the other investors, but it shouldn't be a problem." Braxton said.

Teddy heard a hand smack, indicating a handshake.

That's when a klaxon went off.

"Hey! Anyone on the bridge! This is Gideon in engineering!"

"Yeah, Gideon, I'm here with Braxton," Jason said.

"We got a tsunami warning from the surface! Noora's already shuttling some people up! Just make sure we're in position to receive them! I'm gonna send Kiwi down to grab any stragglers on the surface!"

"You got it, Gideon," Jason said.

Teddy, knowing the ventilation system, scrambled towards the dropship.

"Hey, how'd you get in here?" Kiwi asked, running some pre-flight checks on the outside of the dropship.

"Philly Cheesesteak's been showing me the vents."

Kiwi smiled. "He's good like that, isn't he? I'm headed down to the surface. Tsunami's coming in. Gonna pick up any stragglers still doing repairs. Wanna come?"

"Yeah, can I?"

"Of course! Hop in!"

Kiwi finished up and the two of them hopped in. As she fired up the dropship, she said into the intercom, "Hey, Gideon, about to take off. Teddy's with me."

"*Good. Double-time it. The first wave is only 20 minutes away.*"

"You got it, boss."

Teddy recognized Kiwi's motions as she flipped the levers and switches to release the dropship and start their descent. Noora had taught him all of that.

As if she were reading his mind, Kiwi said, "Noora tells me she's been teaching you to fly, and that you're a natural."

Teddy felt proud, but found the praise made him shy. "She's

really nice," he said. "We even fly this gunship after she lets me practice with the dropship and cargo loader."

"Oh my god, isn't that thing fun!" Kiwi said.

Teddy smiled.

"I told Gideon I want one for Christmas. Probably won't get one, but never hurts to ask."

Teddy laughed. Kiwi was always so funny.

They burned their way through the upper atmosphere. When the plasma outside faded, Kiwi raised the radio.

"Gliese, this is the dropship from the *Isle of Skye*, coming down to pick up any stragglers, over?"

The radio stayed silent.

"Goddamnit," Kiwi said. She repeated the hail, and when there was still no response, said, "Fuckin aye, we told them to have someone on their radio at all times."

"Everyone's always too busy repairing stuff," Teddy said.

"And we're here to hopefully change that." Kiwi did a quick circle of the colony, then pointed in the direction of the tsunami, which they could see. "About 10 minutes, plenty of time. I'm gonna set down closer than usual."

The dropship made its slow, powered descent, splashing air everywhere. They landed, and Kiwi opened the airlock to a steady rain.

"Teddy, hang out here, I'm gonna head outside, try to let people know we're here."

"Okay."

Kiwi left.

Teddy stayed by the airlock, peeking outside every now and then. Kiwi seemed to be impatient with one of the colonists. He looked around and found the door to the bunker. People were still filing in. He looked away, and didn't see that he'd been noticed by Steven, Bill, and Mike.

He found Kiwi again. She was running to different buildings and structures of the colony, letting the repair teams know she could lift them all to safety. After just a few minutes, she was back at the dropship.

"Jesus Christ, does it ever *not* rain here!" she asked.

Teddy smiled, then shook his head.

"I got word to the repair teams! They're on their—"

Teddy cut her off when three figures appeared behind her. "Kiwi, look out!"

As she spun around, Steven smashed a rock into Kiwi's face. She went down.

"Revenge, bitch!" Steven taunted.

"AhhHHHH!" Teddy screamed, launching himself at Steven and connecting a right hook into his jaw. Steven dropped faster than Kiwi.

Bill and Mike were stunned. Bill took an unguarded punch to the liver and keeled over. Mike tried to grab Teddy, but a quick dodge and a left cross sent Mike to the ground.

Teddy grabbed the rock Steven had dropped. As he tried to get back up, Teddy smashed him in the face, and back down he went.

Teddy checked on Kiwi. She was still on the ground. The skin above and below her left eye was split and bleeding badly. "Kiwi, Kiwi, you all right?"

But all she could manage to do was squirm and moan. Her eyes were open, but unable to focus on anything.

One of the repair teams finally made it to the dropship. Teddy's mom was with them. "Oh my god! What happened!"

"We need to hurry! Tsunami's almost here!" another voice yelled.

"Can't we just go to the bunker?"

"No! They already sealed it and there's still no way to communicate with them down there!"

Teddy grabbed Kiwi and started pulling her into the dropship. "Everyone into the dropship, now!" he screamed.

"Teddy, what happened!" his mom insisted.

"Inside! Now!" he bellowed. "Grab Steven, Bill, and Mike, too, and someone get the rest of the repair teams!"

He pulled Kiwi up to the main console and propped her in one of the co-pilot seats. "Kiwi, can you fly?" he asked.

Kiwi winced and held the left side of her head. She reached a hand out to the console, but couldn't focus on it.

"Teddy, none of us can fly!" his mom said.

"Not true," he said, strapping himself into the other co-pilot seat. "Let me know when everyone's on board!" he shouted at her, skipping the normal pre-flight checks to start up the engine.

"Teddy, you're not going to—you can't fly!" his mom said.

Teddy, remembering how quick and direct the *Isle of Skye* crew were, snapped around and glared at her. "Get back there and tell me when everyone's on board!"

His mom was stunned for a moment, but went to take a headcount.

He looked out the cockpit towards the horizon. The tsunami was rushing in. They had maybe a minute.

"Everyone's here, Teddy!" his mom called out.

He queued the airlock to close while lifting off. "Gently, gently," he said to himself. As the airlock sealed shut, he pointed the dropship up and pushed towards the sky.

Teddy felt disembodied. He'd never hit anyone before, and he had just knocked out all three of his bullies. He'd never thought of yelling at his mom, and he'd just yelled at her twice. He'd never thought he could be brave, yet here he was.

He realized he should probably contact the ship and let them know what was going on.

"*Isle of Skye*, this is, um, this is Teddy. Can you guys hear me?"

Gideon's voice came through. "*Teddy! What's happening, is everything okay?*"

"Kiwi's hurt," he said. "I've got the repair teams with me, and I'm flying the dropship back to the *Skye*, but I don't know how to dock."

"*Teddy, it's Noora, can you hear me?*"

"Hi, Noora. Yes, I can hear you."

"*Great, once you get within 10 kilometers just let go of the controls and I can remote-pilot you guys in.*"

"Okay, thank you, Noora."

"*What happened to Kiwi, is she all right?*"

"I'm here," Kiwi said, her eyes squeezed shut in pain and her hand trying to stanch the bleeding. "I just, just get the mender ready. My fucking face is split open."

"I should've executed all three of those little shits," Kiwi said while the mender stitched her face up.

"I agree," Gideon said, "but murdering children is generally frowned upon."

"They almost got the rest of us killed," Teddy said.

"And thanks to you," Kiwi said, "we're still here."

Teddy smiled, unable to hide his pride.

"I'm proud of you, Teddy," his mom said. "I didn't know you could fly!"

"Noora's been teaching me," he said. "Where is she, by the way?"

"She's on her way," Gideon said.

The door to the infirmary opened, and in strolled Dax and Noora. Dax was carrying six cans of that lager Kiwi always drank.

"Oh thank fucking Christ, about time," Kiwi said as Dax handed her a can. He also handed one to Gideon, one to Noora, and offered one to Teddy's mom, who hesitated at first, but accepted it.

"Jesus Christ, Kiwi, what happened?" Noora asked.

Kiwi, who was already chugging her lager, said, "Oh, it's my own fault, really. Should've at least maimed that cocksucker when I had the chance."

Dax snapped open his own lager. "Goddamn, that's gonna leave a scar," he said to Kiwi.

"It's fine," she said. "Adds to my character."

"The last thing you need is more character," Dax said.

Kiwi laughed. She held up her lager. "Hey, to character."

Everyone, Teddy's mom included, held up their lagers and took a sip.

"Hey, no fair, Teddy, you too," Kiwi said, handing him her lager.

"He's nine!" his mom objected.

"And he did a lot of growing up today," Kiwi said. "Just a sip. You deserve it more than anyone."

Teddy accepted the lager. Kiwi grabbed another one from Dax and snapped it open.

"Fine," his mom conceded. "But really, just a sip, Teddy."

Kiwi held up her new lager. Teddy tapped his can to hers, took a sip, forced it down his throat, and started coughing.

"There ya go!" Kiwi exclaimed, holding out a fist.

Teddy laughed, and gave her a fist bump.

17. JASON'S FAREWELL

Kiwi drinks and flies, Gideon laughs, Dax laughs, Noora has coffee, and Jason has a moment with Philly Cheesesteak.

On the one hand, Jason was regretting his decision to stay behind at Gliese; the colonists were competent and smart people, but their constant bickering and infighting kept them gridlocked on what to do. He had to spend most of his energy making decisions for them, and then had to be stern with anyone who disagreed.

On the other hand, he enjoyed having command again.

His instincts had been right. This colony could work, and could eventually become a spaceport, but not without a person in charge, and someone with major leverage at that.

Braxton, in his charismatic, persuasive way, had put the fear of god into the colonists with a fiery speech that basically went, "Jason is staying behind. You will do what he tells you, and if you don't, we pull all equipment and supplies we've given you so far, pull all future funding, and you can have your fun getting washed away into the ocean. Don't fuck with me. We will be back, and we will know."

Some, especially Director Caldwell, had given limp-wristed responses about the dignity of the colony and being told what to do, but even he had seen the wisdom in doing what they were told for the sake of surviving.

Jason was spending most of his days on the colony's vector drive ship. It was a converted cruise ship, meant to house hundreds of tourists for a few weeks at a time as it swam by the solar system's gas giants.

When it was about to be decommissioned, a colony collective had bought it, fitted it with a vector drive, and made their way to Gliese. Since then, the ship had sat in a stable orbit around the very unstable planet.

The colonists had even kept the original name of the ship. The *Saturnalia*.

Now that Dax and Kiwi had repaired it, Jason enjoyed its full functionality, and had been using it as a command center. He didn't need to be on board while the *Skye* and the *Philly* were still here, but he thought it better to get used to the ship before they left.

And they wouldn't be around for long. The *Philly*, relieved of its cargo already, was set to take off soon. The *Skye* would have to stick around for a bit more.

His communications chimed.

"*Hey, Jason,*" Gideon said from the *Skye*. "*You're coming for dinner tonight, right? The Philly's taking off tomorrow, so we're spoiling them with Dax's cooking.*"

"Definitely. I'm pretty much wrapped up here for today, anyway. Have someone come pick me up when they're free."

"*Hey Kiwi,*" Gideon said, keeping the comm open. "*You free?*"

"*Was about to crack open my first beer of the day,*" she said. "*What do you need, captain?*"

"*Go pick up Jason. He's coming for dinner.*"

"*No problem, let him know I'm coming.*"

"*He's on the channel,*" Gideon said.

"*Be right there, fuckboy!*" Kiwi said.

"Thanks, Kiwi," Jason said, laughing. "Meet ya at the docking bay."

"You're really staying behind, huh?" Kiwi asked in between chugs of her beer as she piloted the dropship away from the *Saturnalia*.

"I am indeed," Jason said. "And, uh, I thought drinking and flying were frowned upon."

"Oh no don't tell Gideon," Kiwi said with sarcasm.

"So, uh, yeah, I'm staying behind. Only way to make sure the colony does what they need to."

"You really believe all of Braxton's bullshit about turning this place into a spaceport?"

"Yeah, I do," Jason said. "Don't get me wrong. He's an arrogant scumbag, but who else is gonna raise that kind of money? Besides, you need a charismatic asshole to have that kind of vision in the first place."

"Don't even know when we'll be back, *if* we'll be back," Kiwi said.

Jason nodded. "Yeah, but that comes with space travel."

Kiwi took a long pull from her beer as they came up to the *Isle of Skye*. "Well, I'll miss ya, fuckboy."

Jason laughed. "Never thought I'd hear you say that."

Kiwi laughed as well. "Well look, before we leave you here, any last few tricks you can teach me with those database-hacking skills you have?"

Jason shook his head. "I mean, you know more about coding and programming than most people, and all that stuff I showed you is just simple, backdoor IT stuff."

"That reminds me," Kiwi said. "I gotta find someone to sell Ralston's database to when we get back to the solar system. Who should I sell it to?"

"I mean, anyone will pay for it, but their next biggest competitor is Aegis Dynamics. Trick is to be clandestine about it. Can't just walk up to someone at Aegis and say 'hey here's Ralston's entire database!'"

"I'll find a way," Kiwi said, docking the dropship to the *Skye*.

Jason smiled, knowing she would. "Save a cut for me if you

actually pull that off."

Kiwi held out a fist. "Hey, you have my promise."

Jason bumped her fist.

As they got up to exit the dropship, Kiwi said, "By the way, if you need to get laid out here, Teddy's mom has her eyes on you."

Jason scowled. "Marie? How could you tell?"

"Oh I saw the way she was looking at you, especially when you were helping Teddy in the infirmary," Kiwi said.

"She's gotta have, what, 10 years on me. What is she, early 40s? And she's a bit type-A for me."

"Hey, type-A girls in their 40s need to fuck, too," Kiwi said.

Jason made his rounds with the crew of the *Philadelphia*, all of whom expressed the same sentiment.

"Can't believe you're staying behind," Captain Thomas had said. "But then again, how else you gonna make sure they do what they're told?"

"I know, right? I'm the father figure this colony needs."

Thomas laughed. "Look, don't know if or when we'll be back, but happy to take you on if you ever need a job."

"I appreciate that. A lot."

"Hey, Jason," Tricia had said. "I heard you're staying behind. That true?"

"Yeah. Made a deal with Braxton. He needs someone to keep these colonists in check with all the cargo and equipment."

"Well, I mean good luck with everything. Hope we see you again."

"Same."

"You're really staying here, man?" Jack, first mate of the *Philadelphia*, had asked.

"Yup. But don't worry. I'll keep them in line."

"These fucking colonists need it, am I right?"

"Hey, man, good luck with everything," Sven had said.

"Yeah, take care, Jason," Becky had said.

"You guys, too. Hope the flight back to Earth is boring."

Even Braxton was at dinner.

"Hey, Jason," he said in his Australian tone. "Now that their ship is fully functional, what's gonna stop them from just, like, taking it over and flying back to Earth?"

"Don't worry," Jason said. "They can't fly that thing without me."

"What do you mean?"

"I mean I've got all of their ship's systems under a 16-trillion digit cypher, and a different cypher for each system at that. So let them come up to the ship, and let them see what happens when they try to fly it. I doubt any of them even remember how to fly a ship like that."

Braxton gave him an affirmative nod.

"Hey," Gideon had said when he had a chance to isolate Jason. "You got a minute?"

"Of course."

Gideon took him aside to the kitchen. "Just wanted to say thank you."

When Gideon didn't say anything else, Jason said, "I mean, thanks for taking me on in the first place."

Gideon smiled. "You know, if I hadn't taken you on, the rest of us would still be trapped at Lacaille."

"And I'd still be out of a job," Jason said.

The two of them had a laugh.

Jason slept in his room on the *Skye* that night. He'd already moved all of his stuff out of it.

He woke up, went to the mess hall, and found Dax and Noora having their morning coffee together.

"Hey, join us," Dax said. "Don't be a stranger."

Jason smiled and poured himself some coffee. "That's the second time you've said that to me, you know."

"I know."

He sat down with them.

"So, you're really staying here, Jason?" Noora asked.

Her tone was always so sweet that Jason could hardly believe she was a trained military sniper. "Yeah," he said. "Yeah, I'm really staying here."

"I'm sorry to see you go," Noora said.

"Same," Dax said. "Sorry to see you go. Hope we get to see you again."

Jason laughed. "You know, as someone who captured you and had you beaten up, that means a lot to me."

Dax gave a rare laugh. "Hey, never any hard feelings. Besides, you saved us at Lacaille." He held up his coffee as a toast.

Jason did the same.

Then Philly Cheesesteak jumped up on the table.

"Oh hey, Philly Phil!" Noora said.

The cat went right up to Jason and bashed his cheek against Jason's arm.

"Hey," Jason said. "What do you want?"

Philly Cheesesteak looked at Jason, as if expecting something.

Jason shrugged his shoulders. "Well?"

"*Myeh-br-r-eh*," Philly Cheesesteak said, jumping off the table.

"I think he wants you to follow him," Dax said.

"Can I finish my coffee first?" Jason asked.

"*Br-r-ryeh!*"

"I think that's a 'no'," Noora said.

Jason sighed. "Fine," he said, getting up. "Where are we going?"

Philly Cheesesteak led the way to the corridor.

"Come on, where are we going?" Jason asked.

"*Myah-br-r-reh*," Philly Cheesesteak said, sauntering down the corridor, his tail held high.

"Christ," Jason said, trying to balance his coffee while he followed the cat.

Philly Cheesesteak led him all the way to the entrance to engineering, where he finally circled up and sat down.

"What, something you want in engineering? I know you can get in there through the vents."

Philly Cheesesteak looked to a spot on the floor, then looked back up to Jason.

"What, you want me to sit down?"

"*M-r-r-reh.*"

"Fine, fine." Jason sat down.

Philly Cheesesteak walked up and rubbed his cheek on Jason's leg.

Jason laughed, giving him some pets. "I know you know that I've never liked cats."

Philly Cheesesteak purred.

"But thanks for tolerating me."

Philly Cheesesteak put his front paws on Jason.

Jason gave an endearing smile. "You know, I never thanked you for saving my ass at Lacaille. Then again, I feel like that's unspoken between us."

Philly Cheesesteak jumped onto Jason, purring loudly.

"I'm not staying here for long, you asshole," Jason laughed.

Philly Cheesesteak curled up and laid down on Jason.

"Fine," Jason said. "Fine." He took a sip of his coffee. "Look, just take care of everyone, okay? I do actually want to see all of you again."

Philly Cheesesteak purred, extending a paw up Jason's chest.

18. THE PRISONER OF GLIESE

The Philadelphia says goodbye, Gideon pulls out his revolver, Kiwi kicks someone in the crotch, Dax shares a laugh with his captain, Teddy flies the dropship again, and Jason gives some foreshadowing.

"Sure you guys don't wanna stick around for another week and wait for us to wrap up?" Gideon asked into the radio.

"*Trust me,*" Thomas said from aboard the *Philadelphia.* "*We'd love to, but you've heard Braxton. Wants to get a head start, get back to the solar system, update his investors, see if we can recruit a survey team and as many welders and miners as are willing to come out here for a tour.*"

"I know," Gideon said. "Just my way of saying I'll miss you guys."

"*Anyone else on board with you, or are they all down on the surface arguing with His Prissiness Mr. Caldwell?*"

"Oh no, got Dax and Noora here, too."

"Hey, Thomas," Noora said, on the bridge with Gideon. "You guys have a good trip. When will we see you again?"

"*Well, 10 weeks to get there, you guys figure you got another week here, so we should see you in about 11 weeks around Saturn,*" Thomas said.

"*In plenty of time for Christmas,*" Dax said from engineering. "*Sure you're still gonna be there by the time we arrive?*"

"*Oh yeah,*" Thomas said. "*We'll snap out of vector space, take us a day or two under normal thrust to get to Saturn, then there's restocking supplies, recruiting people, all that. Besides, Braxton says his investors already know we'll be there. Should be a couple of them waiting for us at Titan station.*"

"Right then," Gideon said. "Don't let us interrupt your countdown."

"*Oh we're already counting down,*" Thomas said. "*How long, Tricia?*"

"*About 90 seconds,*" Tricia said from the *Philly's* engineering section. "*Dax, Noora, Gideon, you all take care.*"

"You too, Tricia!" Noora said.

"*Take care. See you guys in December,*" Dax said.

"Godspeed," Gideon said.

The Philadelphia left their comm link open as they counted down, confirmed their trajectory, and disappeared into vector space.

After a few empty moments, Noora said, "Damn, feels a lot more lonely all of a sudden."

"*I don't know,*" Dax said. "*I was getting sick of cooking every night for that many people.*"

Gideon and Noora laughed.

"Dax, how'd their launch look on your end? Trajectory, all that good?"

"*They'll be fine, captain,*" Dax said, knowing what Gideon was really asking. "*Tricia knows what she's doing, and Sven and Becky are almost as good as Kiwi. We'll see them again.*"

The comm link chimed. It was Jason from the surface. "*Hey, uh, Gideon, Dax, Noora, any of you there?*" His tone didn't sound good.

"Yeah, we're here, mate," Gideon said. "What's going on?"

"The colonists have, um, well they've taken Kiwi prisoner."

Gideon looked up, slapped a hand to his face, and sighed.

When he didn't say anything, Noora said, "Wh—what happened, Jason? Is she okay? Are you okay?"

"I'm fine," Jason said. "They won't let me see her, but those three kids from before? They're all in the infirmary, and they're all hurt bad."

"Oh, those little shits. The same ones that beat up Teddy and almost got that whole repair team killed?" Gideon asked.

"Same ones."

"I take it Kiwi's not injured? I hope? Since she's not in the infirmary, too?"

"They've locked her in a room, but I don't think she's injured," Jason said. *"Also, those kids aren't the only ones in the infirmary. She injured about four or five others when they tried to restrain her. It doesn't sound pretty. I didn't see any of this, by the way. I heard a huge ruckus, and by the time I got there they'd taken her away."*

"All right. Stay put, and don't do anything. I'm on my way down. Call you when I get there."

"You got it," Jason said, closing the channel.

Gideon took a moment before talking to Dax and Noora. He was worried about Kiwi. He thought of the colony, how they had no idea how to take someone prisoner, had no justice system to speak of, and had a hunch they hadn't even thought to search her, much less confiscate her phone. He called her up on the comm.

"Okay," she answered. *"First of all, this is not my fault,"* she said.

Gideon tried to hide a chortle. "Rosevine, just tell me, are you injured? Are you all right?"

"I'm fine," she said. *"Just some bruises. One of those fuckers grabbed my tits when they tried to restrain me."*

"What happened?" Gideon asked.

"I ran into Teddy, he was showing me a new area they've

excavated. Got cornered by that Steven and his two little cocksuckers. They had wrenches and pipes for weapons, but they swung them around like wet noodles. Teddy knocked one of them out, then I knocked one out and choked out another. Then I may have kicked them all while they were down, and maybe I heard a few cracked ribs and saw some teeth flying, but those fuckers deserved it!"

Gideon nodded to himself. She was right. That was the same trio that had almost killed her, Teddy, his mom Marie, and an entire repair team, and the colony had done nothing to discipline them. If it took Kiwi to issue that justice, all the better.

Then again, they had her, and short of blasting their way through the colony, ruining everything they'd worked for, Gideon knew he needed to handle this diplomatically.

"All right, here's what's gonna happen," he said. "Stay in that room they have you in, but see what you can do about escaping, just in case."

"Oh, I can escape. This isn't even a cell, it's just a random room, and this lock on the door is basically a pair of tin cans and a string."

"Okay, good. Stay there for now and don't do anything. I'm flying down in a minute. I'll call you when we get there. We'll keep a channel open so you can hear everything."

"Gotcha. By the way, would you check on Teddy? I told him to go hide so he wouldn't get in trouble."

Gideon remembered that they'd given Teddy his own phone. "Yeah, I will, and remember, stay in your room for now. If I tell you to do anything, you'll know it."

"You got it, boss."

Gideon closed the channel, then said, "Dax, you get all that?"

"Yes, I did," Dax said from engineering. *"What are you thinking?"*

"I'm thinking meet me at the dropship. You and I are going down together."

"Think I should pick something up from the armory on the way? You thinking of busting Kiwi outta there?"

"Not directly," Gideon said. "Actually, bring your fists with you, but nothing else. Think of them as an insurance policy."

"*Got it, see ya at the dropship.*"

"And Noora," Gideon said. "Stay here on the bridge. I'm gonna handle this diplomatically, but I also don't trust the colony. Need someone up here piloting the *Skye*."

"Of course, Gideon," Noora said.

"Like with Kiwi, when we get to the surface I'll call you and keep an open channel so you can hear what's going on."

Noora nodded. "You got it, captain."

While Dax piloted the dropship to the surface, Gideon called Teddy.

"*Hey, Gideon?*" Teddy answered.

"Hey, Teddy! Listen, I heard what happened. How are you doing, all right?"

"*I'm fine, just, I don't know, just scared. I mean, they came at me and Kiwi with, like, pipes and wrenches, and—*"

"It's all right, mate, it's all right," Gideon said. "Look, I talked to Kiwi, she says she told you to hide. Are you hiding right now?"

"*Yes.*"

"Well look, Dax and I are about to land in a few minutes. Do you think you can get to the surface and come on out? I'm thinking you can hide here on the dropship."

"*Oh, um, yeah, I think I can,*" Teddy said, excitement in his voice.

"Excellent," Gideon said. "You know where we usually land. We'll be there in about five minutes."

After Gideon hung up, Dax said, "Feel like you got something big planned. Wanna let me in on it?"

Gideon smiled. "Nothing planned, exactly, just planning for the worst."

As Dax found the landing site and made a powered descent,

Gideon spotted a small figure darting from the underground bunker towards the landing zone. "Ha! And there he is," he said.

Dax landed, opened the main airlock, and shut the ship down.

Teddy was at the airlock as it opened. It was a rare day where it hadn't been raining on Gliese, and he was dry. "Hi, Gideon!" he shouted. "Oh, hey Dax!"

"Hey!" Gideon shouted.

"Hey," Dax said, holding out a fist and bumping it with Teddy's. "Good to see ya, man."

"So Teddy, you got your phone, right?" Gideon asked.

Teddy pulled it out. "Yup."

"Good, now here's what we're gonna do," Gideon said. "Dax and I need to head inside, so you stay here. I know you know how to fly this thing just in case it comes to that. What I'm gonna do in a moment is I'm gonna link up Noora, Kiwi, and you on my phone so all of you can hear what's going on. I'm gonna mute all of you so you don't come in on my end, so I won't be able to hear you guys. Now, I'll be talking to the colony, right? So, if I need to tell you to do anything, I'll have to do that in code, does that make sense?"

Teddy gave a confused nod.

Gideon smiled. "So here's what I'm thinking. I'm thinking that if I need you to do anything, I'm going to refer to you as 'Pilot.' For example, if I'm talking to the colony people, and I say, 'I could tell my Pilot to start the dropship engines,' that means you start dropship engines. That make sense?"

Teddy nodded with excitement. "Yeah, that makes sense!"

"Excellent," Gideon said. "Go hang out in the pilot's seat."

"Thanks for letting me hide here!" Teddy said.

Gideon and Dax left the dropship and made their way for the colony, which was now, for the most part, located in the slowly expanding underground bunker.

He called Noora. "Hey, Noora, you there?"

"*I'm here, Gideon.*"

He called Kiwi. "Rosevine, you there?"

"*I'm here, captain.*"

He called Teddy. "Hey Teddy, you there?"

"*I'm here, Gideon.*"

Finally, he called Jason.

"*Hey, Gideon.*"

"Excellent." Gideon keyed a few commands into his phone, then said, "All right, you're all muted on my end, but you'll be able to talk to each other. Jason, I know you're there already, just wanted all of you on the line for a moment. Dax and I are about to enter the colony. Noora, Kiwi, and Teddy, you'll all be able to hear us the whole time. We'll see how it goes, but we're gonna keep things calm, we're gonna keep things civil."

Inaudible to Gideon and Dax, Noora screamed, "Kiwi oh my god are you okay!"

"Girl, I'm fine! Christ, weren't you listening before? And Teddy, you're there, too?" Kiwi said.

"I'm here," Teddy said. "I'm on the dropship outside the colony. Gideon told me I could hide here for now."

"Yeah, good idea," Kiwi said. "Once Steven and those fuckers wake up, they'll start lying about what happened."

"What *did* happen?" Noora asked.

Over her phone, Kiwi heard Gideon and Dax enter the colony. "Well, we're about to find out what the colony *thinks* happened."

Gideon and Dax descended through the 18-inch steel door, down the elevator, and into the colony bunker. They were greeted by a nervous Director Caldwell.

"Ah, Gideon, and um, um, Dax," he said nervously. "You're here. I trust you've heard—"

"Where's Kiwi?" Gideon asked calmly.

"I, um, I think you don't quite understand the situation here, it's just, it's—"

"Director Caldwell, Tim," Gideon said, his voice calm and

soothing. "Please, I'm only asking where is Kiwi? Is she all right? Is she injured?"

"But, you, you have to understand," Director Caldwell said. "She's assaulted a number of people, and—"

Gideon pulled out his Remy-Larsson twin-cylinder revolver.

Caldwell, and a number of the colonists gathered around, all took a step back. They didn't have guns on the colony, but they recognized one.

Gideon's left hand reached into his pocket, pulling out a number of the large-caliber .457 rounds. He started loading the first barrel round-by-round. He looked up to Caldwell and said, "Oh no, please continue. You were saying she's allegedly assaulted a number of people?"

"Y—yes," Caldwell said, giving nervous glances to Gideon's revolver. "It's that, she, um, she appears to have attacked three of our children, and then when we tried to arrest her, she injured five other people."

Gideon finished loading the first cylinder, snapped it into place, and started loading the second cylinder. When Caldwell didn't say anything, Gideon casually said, "Please, continue."

"So, um, yes, anyway, when we tried to arrest her, she resisted, and injured five other people. All in all, she's assaulted eight people."

"Allegedly," Gideon said.

"I mean," Caldwell said nervously, "it's pretty clear that she —"

Gideon snapped the second cylinder into place, hefted the weapon, then holstered it back in his shoulder harness. When Caldwell didn't say anything, Gideon said, "So, Director Caldwell, if you would be so kind, please show me where Kiwi is. I understand you've taken her prisoner, and quite frankly, I'm irritated by the fact that you didn't contact me to tell me what you had done. You are holding my crewman, I do not know if she's safe, I don't know if she's injured, I don't know about these allegations against her, hell I don't even know if she's alive. So you will take me to her. You can keep her in her cell for the time being, but you will let me see her *now*."

Caldwell, a bundle of nerves, nodded, and led the way. "Just, uh, just don't try anything."

"I'm only trying to see my crewman," Gideon said to Caldwell. "After I've seen her, she can stay where you're holding her, and you and I can have a talk."

Dax followed, noting the large escort of colonists around them. He knew Gideon was too smart to try anything crazy.

The bunker-turned-colony was a large, hollowed-out tube, excavated deep into the basalt. New additions had been made recently with all the equipment and machinery from the *Isle of Skye* and the *Philadelphia*.

They went down a side corridor that led to several rooms. One of them was guarded by two nervous colonists who had never guarded anything in their lives. When they saw Caldwell, Gideon, Dax, and the entire entourage, they weren't sure what to do.

Caldwell turned to Gideon and Dax and said, "You can see her, but that's it."

"Caldwell, that's not how this is gonna work," Gideon said. "I assume you're gonna want some facsimile of a trial after this, and if that's the case, I'm gonna speak with her alone, and neither you nor anyone else from the colony is going to listen in on us."

Caldwell crossed his arms, and tension rose among the colonists around them. Gideon kept his look stern, but knew he'd have to be careful. "I'm, I'm afraid that's not possible. You can verify that she's not injured, but, I'm sorry we just can't trust you alone with her."

Gideon stayed silent, letting Caldwell know with a look that he was disappointed. Nevertheless, he conceded just to relieve the tension. "Well?" he said. "Open the goddamn door so I can see."

Caldwell gave a weak nod to one of the guards, who used an old-fashioned key to unlock the door.

A heavy work boot came flying out, landing right in the guard's crotch.

"That's for grabbing my tits, you fucking perv!" Kiwi screamed.

Commotion erupted. Caldwell and several others tried to intervene without really knowing how, but Gideon and Dax were faster.

"Back in the room, Kiwi, now!" Gideon commanded. Kiwi did as she was told.

"My god, is he all right?" Caldwell asked. "This is why we couldn't trust you!"

"Hey!" Gideon shouted. "I just ordered my own crewman back into the cell, so have a little fucking respect!" Gideon kept himself in the door jam, preventing anyone else from coming in. He looked at Kiwi. No one but her could see the smirk on his face. "Looks like you're not injured?" he said, though he already knew the answer.

"That's right," she said, a sly smirk on her face, too.

"And I, uh, I take it you've been…?" Gideon said, tapping his trench coat where he kept his phone. He knew Caldwell was right over his shoulder, listening.

Kiwi tapped the pocket on her overalls where her own phone was. "Oh yeah."

Gideon nodded. "Good. Keep it up. In the meantime, stay here and lay low. If anything changes, I'll make sure to let you know."

Kiwi gave a smile and a wink. He winked at her too, then closed the door. "Well go ahead, lock her up again."

The remaining guard locked the door, while a number of colonists were slowly dragging the other guard to the infirmary.

"You can add an assault charge to her for that," Caldwell said.

Gideon scoffed. "Caldwell, now's not a time to be keeping score. Let's just go have a seat and figure out how we're going to handle this. Jason tells me you have a new mess hall you've carved out? Let's head there."

Over the closed, encrypted channel, inaudible to Gideon and Dax as they strolled towards the bunker's new mess, Noora, Kiwi, and Teddy had a quick conversation.

"Kiwi, Jesus Christ, what just happened!" Noora asked.

"Meh, no big deal," Kiwi said. "Just kicked a guy in the balls for grabbing my tits earlier. Hey Teddy, you still there?"

"Yeah! I'm here!"

"Awesome. So, if, uh, if I needed to escape from here, you think you could help me get to the main bunker door quietly?"

"Oh, yeah, it's easy," Teddy said from the dropship. "You're small so you can fit in the vents like me. Why, are you gonna escape?"

"I don't know yet," Kiwi said. "Depends on how Gideon's conversation with Caldwell goes, and sounds like we're about to find out."

The newly carved mess hall in the bunker only had rudimentary benches and tables, and was poorly lit with its incomplete wiring, but it served its purpose. Gideon noticed that most of the colony was present, and made sure to say so loudly and clearly.

"My goodness! Is the whole colony here? Main corridors must be empty!"

Kiwi, locked away in her cell, smiled.

"Can we please just, she nearly killed those three boys," Caldwell said, frustrated.

Gideon scowled at Caldwell. "Director, calm down, have a seat. Offer me and Dax something. I know you've got a metric ton of freeze-dried coffee sitting in dry storage. You got it from us."

Caldwell scoffed. "Your crewman nearly kills three kids and then assaults half a dozen other colonists, and you want coffee?" He was still standing up, trying to put on a show for the colony, trying to take back some of the agency he'd lost since the *Isle of*

Skye had first arrived.

Gideon leaned back in his seat, calm, relaxed, and a pleasant smile on his face. "Director," he said. "Caldwell, your lack of manners is starting to irritate me, but this is your colony, so let's do business your way. You keep telling me that Kiwi assaulted those kids. Okay. Who witnessed this?"

Caldwell was caught off guard. He looked around awkwardly. "Well, I mean, a few of us arrived after it had happened—"

"Who *witnessed* the assault?" Gideon repeated.

"You don't understand, I'm telling you we got there and saw what had happened—"

"So no one, then," Gideon said.

Caldwell sighed as if Gideon were the idiot. "I'm telling you, we saw what happened after the fact, and—"

"You see, Director, this is exactly why I needed to speak with Kiwi. Her testimony has not been heard, and I get the feeling that you don't want to allow it, that you already have a guilty verdict written for her, and even though we're at the ass-end of space, 21 light years from Earth, I still have certain expectations of due process out here."

Caldwell didn't know how to handle the comment, so Gideon continued.

"From your perspective, Kiwi assaulted three kids. From my perspective, those were the same three kids that almost killed Teddy, and you did nothing to punish them. The same kids almost caused the deaths of Kiwi and an entire repair crew team, and you still did nothing. Then those same kids get in a scuffle with her and end up in the infirmary. Sounds to me like Kiwi was defending herself, all while dishing out the punishment you've been avoiding."

At the mention of Teddy, his mom, Marie, went up to Jason and whispered something in his ear. Jason took his eyes off his phone and whispered something back. No one noticed the brief shock on Marie's face, or Jason's hand motion to keep her new knowledge under wraps.

"But as eccentric as Kiwi is, she's also obedient," Gideon continued. "You'll remember a few minutes ago with what happened at her cell, how I told her to get back in and stay there, and how that's exactly what she did, right?"

Caldwell nodded.

"If I told her, 'Kiwi, this is your captain speaking to you right now, and I'm ordering you to escape this colony as quietly as possible,' she would do it, and she wouldn't hesitate," Gideon said. "Likewise if I had a pilot on the dropship, and if I told that pilot to start up the ship's engines because me and Dax are flying back up in a few minutes, they would do that." He stood up, glancing at Dax, who was hiding a smirk, for he knew what Gideon was doing.

Caldwell scoffed. "Just like that? You're leaving?"

Gideon gave a calming hand gesture. "Director, tensions are high right now. Let's wait until we're all calm and ready to go about this like adults."

Caldwell looked around awkwardly, but nodded, seeing the wisdom.

Gideon was about to leave, but decided to stall. "Personally, I think you just need to go through the painful process of setting up your own justice system, though how you do that when you're only 300-people big and you all know and rely on each other because you have to when you're this far out is beyond me. Still, it's something you need to figure out. In the meantime, Dax and I are heading back up, and you've got Kiwi as collateral. Give us a call when you're ready to talk."

Even Caldwell knew he shouldn't prevent them from leaving. They hadn't done anything wrong. He and a few others accompanied Gideon and Dax.

After they left the mess and made a slow walk for the bunker entrance, Gideon decided to stall for more time. "Actually," he said, turning back to the mess. "There's something I'd like to talk to Jason about." He didn't bother to wait for Caldwell, who was momentarily frustrated. "You can come if you like," Gideon said on his way back to the mess.

They were all too curious to let Gideon and Dax alone with Jason, and they weren't trustworthy, given that Jason had come from the *Isle of Skye*.

When they re-entered the mess, Jason and Marie had both been listening to something on Jason's phone, which he quickly put away on seeing Gideon and Dax, and the entourage return. He greeted his former captain with a handshake.

"Don't forget, send us a manifest of what you need delivered next," Gideon said.

"Of course, though you could probably just throw all that's left onto the cargo loader and send that down when you're ready. There's almost nothing left in the *Skye's* hold," Jason said.

"It'll be nice flying light for the first time in almost a year," Gideon said. "Can I ask, what do you think of the Kiwi situation?"

"Well," Jason said, one of his eyebrows in a subtle, coy raise. "Kiwi's *definitely* their prisoner."

Gideon hid his smile. "Definitely."

"Definitely," Jason repeated. "Look, I did tell them it was a bad idea to hold her, but their colony, their rules. Besides," he waved his phone. "I'm too busy trying to keep this place functioning."

Gideon nodded. He looked to Marie and said, "Marie, good to see you. Hope Teddy's doing well."

Marie nodded with nervous excitement. He could tell she knew what was happening, and he took that as his cue to leave the colony.

He and Dax walked back towards the bunker's entrance, with Caldwell and the others following them. They got to the entrance that led to the elevator that led to the surface. "Again, call us when you're ready," Gideon said.

Caldwell nodded.

Gideon, Dax, and a couple techs got in the elevator and ascended to the surface.

"Huh, that's weird," one of the techs said, punching away at a monitor on the elevator.

"What's wrong?" Gideon asked.

"The main bunker door is open."

Gideon pretended to be irritated. "Of course it is," he said, just loud enough for the techs to hear.

"I swear I closed it after you guys arrived," the tech said.

They got to the bunker door, got out of the elevator, and saw it was open.

"Well, just don't forget to close it behind us, this time, all right gentlemen?" Gideon said as he and Dax strolled out to the surface and headed for the dropship.

They heard the bunker door close behind them, kept their casual stroll towards the dropship, looked at each other, and laughed.

The dropship's airlock door opened, and they saw Kiwi peeking out. "Well take your fucking time, guys! Jesus, can we get outta here before they realize I'm gone!"

Gideon and Dax boarded the dropship, each giving Kiwi a quick hug.

"Teddy!" Gideon shouted towards the pilot seat. "Care to do the honors?"

Teddy flicked on the internal comm so everyone could hear him. "Strap in, everyone, because we're taking off."

Gideon, Kiwi, Dax, Noora, Teddy, and Philly Cheesesteak were all in the mess hall of the *Isle of Skye*, enjoying a light dinner.

Gideon was on the comm line with Director Caldwell. The rest of them were trying to not laugh at the conversation.

"You mean to tell me that my crewman, whom I let you keep as your prisoner and whose safety and well-being I entrusted to you, is fucking missing? You didn't think to call me sooner?"

"*We only just found out!*" Caldwell pleaded.

"Dax and I left the colony seven hours ago, and you're just now finding out?"

Dax and Noora covered their mouths, desperate to stop their laughing.

Kiwi held a fist to her mouth while slapping her knee.

Teddy quietly giggled to himself.

Even Gideon's face was breaking character, but he kept his tone serious.

"Her door's been locked the whole time! We don't know how, but she broke out, subdued the guard, threw him in the cell, relocked the door, and now she's gone!"

"Well, she's your problem now, Caldwell, so have fun," Gideon said. "I know Jason warned you about her, and well, you're about to find out."

"Wait! What are we supposed to do!" Caldwell screamed.

"If you find her, offer her a beer, and she might forgive you."

"We're not equipped to handle her! Can't you patch through to our intercom and tell her to stand down? Wherever she is!"

"You know what, Caldwell, that's a good idea. I'll tell her right now. Hey, Kiwi!"

Kiwi managed to stop laughing and said, "Yes, captain!"

"Stand down."

Kiwi gave a salute. "Can I have a beer for my efforts?"

"Help yourself."

"Wait, wait WHAT! She's already there? On your ship?"

"YOU'RE GODDAMN RIGHT SHE'S ON MY SHIP!" Gideon shouted. "I told her to escape, and that's exactly what she did! You think you can outsmart me, you sniveling little shit!"

"But how did—no, I can't allow this!"

"Caldwell, you're in no position to tell me what you can and can't allow."

"We've still got Jason down here."

"So?" Gideon asked, and when he didn't get an answer, continued. "Jason's not a member of my crew anymore, and I know you know that. He's your defacto overlord, he's your master, he's your fucking God Emperor, so I know you're not gonna do anything to him, you know how I know that?"

After a long silence, Caldwell finally asked, *"How?"*

"Because when we get back here, if we find out that Jason 'had an accident' or that he was 'swept away in the tides,' hell if we find out that there's so much as a scratch on that pretty little face of his, you lose everything! Funding, equipment, all of it! And most of all, you'll lose all contact with Earth! Investors will know you can't be trusted, and they'll leave all of you out here to be forgotten as just another sad, failed colony!"

Gideon gave a few moments of pause before continuing. "So here's what's gonna happen, Caldwell. I'm off-loading the last of your equipment and supplies onto the cargo loader, and I'm leaving all of it, cargo loader included, with the *Saturnalia*. I've got Kiwi back, I'm done talking to you, and I'm done with this fucking place."

He cut the comm without waiting for a response.

Kiwi, Dax, and Noora all started clapping, applauding their captain's performance. Teddy laughed and joined in the applause.

"Sorry," Gideon said, a little self-conscious. "I wasn't joking, I really am tired of this place."

"We all are," Kiwi said before winking at Teddy. "Sorry about that, Teddy bear."

Teddy smiled. "It's okay. I understand."

With a long exhale, Gideon said. "So, Jason, you hear all of that?"

Jason, still on Gliese and connected through another comm line, said, *"You kidding? Kept myself muted because I was laughing so hard."*

"How do you like that idea?" Gideon asked. "We throw everything on the cargo loader, then park that onto the *Saturnalia*?"

"Yeah, that's best," Jason said. *"Will take more time on our end to sort out, but it's a good idea."*

"Noora," Gideon said. "How long do you think to load everything up?"

Noora thought for a moment. "I mean, how fast do you want it done?"

"Five minutes ago."

"Well, we could load the rest of everything tonight then send the cargo loader over," Noora said, immediately regretting her honesty.

"Really?"

"*Oh yeah, she's right,*" Jason said. "*We wanted you on for another week so we could take our time finding storage space for everything, but if it stays on the cargo loader in orbit then it's not going anywhere, and we can take our time ferrying the last of it down here.*"

"Right then," Gideon said. "Everyone finish up here, you too, Teddy, and let's get to work. I want that loader heavy and pregnant and I want it gone tonight. Tomorrow morning, we're outta here."

"Oh, thank god," Kiwi said.

"Amen," Dax said.

"Teddy," Noora said. "I'll fly you back down to the surface when we're done."

Teddy nodded. "I'll miss you guys."

"Awww, we'll miss you, buddy!" Kiwi said.

"*And believe it or not, I'll miss you guys, too,*" Jason said over the comm.

"We'll talk to you again before we leave, Jason," Dax said.

"Get fucked, Jason!" Kiwi said.

Teddy laughed at Kiwi.

"Talk to you later, Jason," Noora said.

"*Don't worry. You guys'll see me again.*"

19. OVER-UNDER

The Philadelphia drops out of vector space, Braxton thinks he gets in touch with his investors, and Captain Thomas raises a glass.

Lt. Winston Marshall loaded two fresh shells into his over-under Benassi shotgun, snapped it shut, propped the stock into his shoulder, aimed down the sights, and shouted, "*Pull!*" into his helmet's radio.

Two clay targets launched, and two quick trigger pulls turned them to dust.

Marshall slapped open his shotgun, popping out both shells. In the low gravity and vacuum, they took a long, lazy arc before bouncing on the frozen surface. He snapped in two more shells, held up the shotgun to his shoulder, and yelled, "*Pull!*"

Two more targets launched. He hit one, and missed the other.

"*Dammit,*" he said, snapping open his shotgun. The white glare of the Saturn moon made honing in on targets difficult. His ebony skin helped mitigate the glare in his eyes, but it was still a harsh field of view. He loaded two fresh shells, and held the shotgun up to his shoulder again.

Just as someone chimed in over the shortwave.

"*Hey, uh, sir, we've got a communication coming in from Titan station. Chief wants to talk to you. Says it's urgent.*"

"*Got it,*" Marshall said, slapping his shotgun open and retrieving the unspent shells, then turning around to head back to base. "*Patch him through to me.*"

"*Lieutenant,*" Chief of Operations Egan said. "*How's the weather there on Enceladus?*"

"*Frozen as always, sir,*" Marshall replied in his London cadence. "*How that's cushy office on Titan station?*"

"*Well, I think if I look out my window I can see you guys from here.*"

Marshall feigned a laugh, even though his small-talking Chief, with his American twang and his general incompetence, had a penchant for irritating him. "*My staff said it was urgent, sir?*"

"*Important, yes, but not immediately urgent,*" Chief Egan said. "*Just got an interesting communique from headquarters on Earth. Ever heard of Braxton Keller?*"

"*Can't say that I have, sir.*"

"*Well turns out he's an accomplished kickboxer, wanted for tax evasion and money laundering.*"

Marshall wondered what this had to do with him and his supply outpost on Enceladus. "*And is he somewhere here around Saturn, sir?*"

"*No, or rather just as the feds were about to charge him, he suddenly disappeared. Looks like he went to an interstellar colony.*"

Marshall scowled. "*And what's our role in this, sir?*"

"*Our role is to capture two ships, the Philadelphia and the Isle of Skye, and most importantly Braxton Keller. The feds want him, and his investors want him. The feds are convinced he fled to avoid charges, and his investors are convinced he bilked them out of all of their money."*

"If we just need one man, why do we need to capture two ships?" Marshall asked.

"Because the investors want as much of their money back as they can get, and two ships fitted with vector drives will fetch quite a bit."

"And how do we know they're coming to Saturn's system, sir?" Marshall asked. *"Why wouldn't they just head straight to Earth?"*

"Because two of Braxton's main investors have told us the Philadelphia and the Isle of Skye are stopping off here. Makes sense, actually. Anything they need they can pick up here: food, supplies, equipment, anything. No need to deal with the bureaucratic mess around Earth, and a nice way to stay out of reach of the feds."

Marshall was slowly nearing his base on Enceladus. He looked up and saw Saturn and its rings, large and prominent in the sky. *"So do we have an ETA on when they might arrive, and do we have a plan on how to capture them, sir?"*

"ETA is we don't know, but we're guessing sometime in the next few weeks. Can never tell with interstellar flights. In terms of how to capture them? Also don't know. Any ideas?"

Marshall hid a frustrated sigh. Of *course* his superior didn't have any idea. Apparently no one in the Ralston corporation did. "Well, sir," he said. *"Assuming they're indeed stopping off here, what ships do we have in the area that could capture them?"*

"Won't work," Chief Egan said. *"If we have an active battle out here, people will notice. We need to do it quietly. That and our closest ships are between Mars and Earth right now, and Mars is on the other side of the sun at the moment."*

"Well, then, sir," Marshall said, trying not to lose patience. *"Why not you contact them when they arrive, tell them you've been in touch with their investors, and send them here to Enceladus? Make up some facade about how we're holding all the equipment they need for their next trip?"*

"You know, that's a great idea," Chief Egan said.

Marshall rolled his eyes. *"Thank you, sir. And may I say, sir, we mostly run supply and logistics out here, less so on clandestine capture and kidnap operations."*

"You guys got those four defense towers, though."

"To deter piracy, sir," Marshall said. *"Have no idea the last time they were fired. Besides, I assume we're to take both crews alive? Firing at them with these cannons would make that rather difficult, wouldn't you say, sir?"*

"Oh yeah, about that you're right, we need to take them alive," Chief Egan said.

Marshall bared his teeth. He hated having to guess his orders from his Chief. *"Well in that case, sir, let's lure them here as suggested, under the pretense of we have everything they need. We're a supply post, after all. Just direct them to us, we'll take over, talk them into coming down, and then we have them."*

"You know, there's something about you, Winston," Chief Egan said. *"I knew you'd make your way up through Ralston quickly."*

"Thank you, sir," Marshall said, ready to blow a fuse, not knowing how he'd pull off capturing two ships and their crews.

Captain Thomas Burnell sat on the bridge of the *Philadelphia*, scratching his beardless chin. After 10 long, boring weeks from Gliese, they were minutes away from dropping out of vector space into the solar system, ideally as close to Saturn as possible. Given their 21-light year jump, they could come out within a few hours or a few weeks of Saturn.

He was hoping for within a few hours. Everyone was getting claustrophobic of the ship, and they were all desperate for a change of scenery.

"Jack, Tricia, how are we looking?" he asked in his southern New Jersey accent.

"Looking good, captain," Jack said. "Dropping out in about two minutes. That sound right to you, Tricia?"

"Yup, lookin' good," Tricia said from engineering. *"Got Sven and Becky with me, ready to shut down the vector drive as planned."*

Thomas looked over his left shoulder towards the back corner of the bridge, where Braxton Keller quietly stood. He'd behaved himself the entire two-and-a-half months back. Apparently he'd learned his lesson from the *Isle of Skye* crew.

"Guess we'll see how well Noora aimed us," Thomas said to Jack and Tricia.

"Noora's insanely good," Jack said. "She got the *Skye* to within a few hours of Lacaille, and she got us to within 10-hours of Gliese."

"And cutting the vector drive in 30-seconds," Tricia said from engineering. *"Jack's right, by the way, Noora's probably the best interstellar navigator alive. When we drop out of vector space, we should be on a clear course for Saturn."*

"Well then," Thomas said. "Tricia, if you'll do us the honors."

"Cutting vector drive in 5, 4, 3, 2, 1—"

The *Philadelphia* made a gentle lurch, and normal space surrounded them.

"Lemme know when you get a fix on our position," Thomas said.

"Let's see, quick check," Jack said, punching away at his console. "Picking up navigational buoy signals, we're definitely in our system."

Thomas looked back over his shoulder to Braxton, who was unusually quiet. He seemed especially antsy to get off the ship, more so than the rest of them.

"And confirmed, we're on course for Saturn, just eight hours away. Goddamn," Jack said.

"That good?" Thomas asked.

"That's incredible," Tricia answered. *"Noora basically hit us on a bullseye from 21 light years away."*

"Yeah," Jack confirmed. "It's amazing. It's easy to overshoot or undershoot the solar system as is. But here we are."

Thomas breathed a sigh of relief. "All right, Tricia, Jack, set us on a burn towards Saturn. And Jack, send a message to Titan station traffic control letting them know we're on our way."

Braxton let out his own sigh of relief.

Thomas turned towards him. "Well, we're back."

Braxton gave him a nod. "That we are. No offense, but glad to be back. Need a break from this endless interstellar travel."

"We all do," Thomas said.

"Message sent to Titan air traffic control, captain," Jack said.

Braxton nodded. "I'm gonna message my investors, if that's all right?"

"Of course. Just patch into communications with your phone. Can message them anywhere in the solar system."

Braxton pulled out his phone. "Well they're supposed to be at Titan station, so I should hear back from them soon."

Thomas nodded. He let loose a silent, heavy sigh. His brain was still processing that they'd jumped 21-light years out and 21-light years back. He looked out the viewport. Saturn was perfectly visible to the naked eye. It wasn't Earth, but the ringed icon of the solar system made him feel safe.

Before long they received a confirmation from Titan traffic control with instructions on a concourse and gate to park at.

And not long after that, Braxton also received a reply. "Huh, got a response already."

"From your investors?" Thomas asked.

"No, it's someone from a company named Ralston? He knows my investors, though. Says they've already secured more funding, supplies, equipment. Says it was too much for them to hold on Titan station, so it's waiting for us at a supply outpost on Enceladus. What's Enceladus?"

"Saturn's closest moon," Thomas said. "And Ralston, huh? They're a defense contractor, mostly run logistics, especially out here. Makes sense your people went through them, but you're sure it's them?"

"Yeah," Braxton confirmed. "He's got their names, their electronic signatures, everything. My investors definitely contracted with them. Message says we're to communicate directly with the commander on Enceladus when we get within range."

Thomas considered it. Everyone desperately needed some shore leave. Even a change of scenery to a frozen supply outpost would help them all out psychologically. They could get any resupplying done, then head to Titan station and enjoy themselves there while they waited for the *Isle of Skye*.

"Let's do it," he said. "Jack, let Titan station know we're heading to Enceladus instead, and set in the appropriate course."

"You got it, sir."

Lt. Winston Marshall ran the pipe-cleaner through his shotgun one last time, then grabbed some fresh cloth wipes and smoothed them through the action. He was meticulous about cleaning his gun after every use, to the point where he would lose track of time.

But his meditative cleansing was interrupted with a communication notice. This was the second time today. First when he was out shooting, now this.

"What?" he answered tersely.

"Hey, uh, sir, we've got another communication coming in from Titan station. Chief wants to talk to you again, sir."

"Patch him through."

"Hey, Marshall."

"Chief. Twice in one day. What can I do for you, sir?"

"You're not gonna believe this, but I just got a message from Braxton himself. He's on the Philadelphia, and they just arrived in-system."

Marshall flashed angry teeth, grateful this was audio-only and that his Chief couldn't see his face. Apparently sometime in the next few weeks meant right now.

"How far away are they, sir?"

"Looks like about eight hours from us. I've already been in touch with Braxton. Told him his investors secured more equipment and supplies and that we're holding it on Enceladus for him, and they're headed your way."

"Right, then," Marshall said, his mind racing.

"Know what you're gonna do?" Chief Egan asked.

"Only thing I can do, sir. I'll need to bait them into coming down to the outpost. If I can get all of them to come down together, I'll have them."

"Sorry we can't give you more support at the moment, Marshall."

"No worries, Chief," Marshall said, snapping his shotgun closed and mounting it on the wall in his quarters.

"What's your over-under on how many of them you'll capture?" the Chief asked.

"'Over-under', sir?" Marshall asked. Probably another American turn of phrase he wasn't used to.

"Oh, it's a gambling term. Just asking if you think you'll be able to get all of them."

"I think so, sir," Marshall lied.

"Good luck, and keep me posted."

They closed the channel.

Marshall made his way to the command center. He had no ships of his own, he had weapon towers he couldn't use, and he needed to capture the *Philadelphia* intact with everyone alive. The only thing to do was what he told his Chief.

But how to bait all of them to come down in one dropship?

He'd never flown interstellar himself, but he knew that 21-light years meant months on a claustrophobic ship. The crew were probably looking for any excuse to get off-board, even if it meant some frozen supply outpost.

That and Braxton and the *Philadelphia* crew already trusted what was going on; they were already on their way to him.

The ruse that all their new equipment was here made sense, but he didn't know what kind of gear and supplies they were expecting. Maybe he could play that up. He'd throw in his own frustration with Ralston. Best to hide the ruse with a bit of honesty. I don't know what they delivered. I even asked them for a manifest but they didn't bother giving me one. It's just all marked for you.

That and his proper British English was already disarming to people.

He thought of what he could say to try and convince everyone on the ship to come down together. Ships could easily stay in orbit on autopilot.

He got to the command center and opened up the intercom. "Attention, all staff on the station. Report to the command center now."

The *Philadelphia* had to tighten their burn around Saturn when they entered orbit. Enceladus was close to Saturn, orbiting it in only one day, whereas Titan station was much further out, orbiting Saturn once every 16 days. Right now, they were on opposite sides of the gas giant.

Enceladus, with its frozen surface, shined brightly ahead of them. When they were close enough to communicate without any radio delay, Thomas opened up a line.

"This is Captain Thomas of the *Philadelphia*, contacting Enceladus supply outpost, over?"

"*Philadelphia*," a proper English accent greeted them. "*This is Lt. Marshall, commander at Ralston's supply outpost here on Enceladus. You gentlemen have a video option?*"

"Yeah, of course," Thomas said, opening up a visual channel with Enceladus.

Lt. Marshall's face was dark, chiseled, and charming. He had an inviting smile. "*Captain Thomas I presume?*" he said. "*Sorry, good to see another face. As close as we are to Titan we don't get too many visitors out here. I understand you're here to pick up some cargo?*"

"That we are," Thomas said, charmed by his demeanor and his accent. "We only just arrived in-system, and Chief Egan was it?, sent us here. We weren't expecting to come here, to be honest."

Lt. Marshall scoffed. "*To be honest, neither was I!*" he said.

"*Last week they drop off a huge shipment, don't tell me who it's for, won't even give me a manifest, they just say 'wait for the Chief to be in touch,' and well, may I ask, is this a secure channel?*"

Thomas smiled. "It is."

Lt. Marshall brought his tone to a whisper, as if telling a secret. "*And eight hours ago the Chief contacts me and says the Philadelphia is coming for their pickup, and I ask 'what pick up, sir,' and he says, 'you know, that shipment you received last week,' and I tell him, 'this is the first I've heard who this shipment is for, sir, and let me just say that it, um, that it's marvelous to be working with such talent out here.'*"

Thomas laughed, catching Marshall's British knack for sarcasm and understatement. He could tell Marshall was intelligent, hyper-competent, and tired of having to correct for other peoples' laziness. "Well listen, we're not that far away, probably hit a parking orbit in less than an hour. All right if we come down and see what kind of shipment we're dealing with?"

"*No, please. The whole crew's welcome. We can see what's in your shipment, and you and the crew can have dinner with me and my staff.*"

"Well thank you," Thomas said. He thought about leaving someone behind to watch over the *Philadelphia*, but they were all eager to get off the ship, whomever had to stay behind would be resentful, and he needed all of them to take stock of their cargo as quickly as possible. "I take it my ship will be okay by itself in a parking orbit?"

"*It'll be fine, captain,*" Marshall assured him.

"Well thanks again, lieutenant. Contact you once we're in orbit."

Jack landed the dropship in the northwest hangar bay of the outpost on Enceladus. Captain Thomas, Tricia, Sven, Becky, and Braxton were all together with him. They waited for the hangar bay to pressurize before opening the airlock and entering the hangar themselves, just in time to see Lt. Marshal stroll out from a pressurized door to greet them.

"Captain Thomas!" he said, jovial and in good spirits. He extended a hand, and they shook firmly. He took his time shaking hands with everyone else, making sure to memorize their names. "And I take it this is everyone?"

"This is everyone!" Thomas confirmed.

"Wonderful. Please, follow me," Marshall said, leading them out of the hangar bay. "I hadn't realized it was already past 19:00-hours. Why not have dinner first? You can relax, unwind. Can get to the cargo tomorrow morning?"

Thomas looked over his shoulder to Braxton and his crew, all of whom gave him a variety of nods and thumbs-up.

"That would be great," Thomas said. "Don't know if the Chief told you, but we just jumped back from Gliese. Been in vector space for the last two and a half months."

"Wow," Marshall said. "You must have been itching for a change of scenery. Here, come on in, this is the mess hall."

The crew of the *Philadelphia* followed him into the mess hall of the supply outpost. It was empty of people.

Marshall let loose a frustrated sigh. "I do apologize, I told my staff in charge of the mess to have dinner ready, and obviously, well, the level of incompetence I have to deal with here is beyond reason. Please, we have a full bar, help yourself, have a seat, make yourself at home. I'll be right back."

The crew hesitated at first, but Marshall had been so welcoming, and they were so relieved to finally be someplace other than the *Philadelphia*, that they helped themselves to the bar. Thomas, Becky, and Sven all poured themselves a lager. Jack couldn't believe he found a cabernet, and poured himself a glass. Tricia, who barely drank, found a chardonnay to try. Braxton looked for the most expensive liquor he could find and poured himself a measure.

They all sat down, raising their glasses in celebration. "Well, to all of your hard work, endurance, and patience." He nodded to Braxton. "Even you, Braxton."

As they all smiled and enjoyed their drinks, they noticed the mess hall door open and a number of men casually file in, but failed to notice they were all armed. The men kept their distance, and took positions around the crew of the Philadelphia.

Finally the crew noticed, scowled, and put their drinks down.

Lt. Winston Marshall was the last one in the mess. He held an over-under shotgun, stock propped into his right shoulder, barrels pointed down and away from the *Philadelphia* crew.

"Now that you have honored us with your presence," he said. "I mean to fulfill that promise of dinner, but I'm afraid it will have to be as my prisoners."

Thomas sized up the situation, knowing they had no chance against 16 armed men. "Well?" he said. "Don't keep us waiting. What's for dinner?"

20. RALSTON

Dax teases Noora, Noora teases Dax, Gideon drinks, Kiwi doesn't drink, and Winston Marshall attempts a cockney accent.

Noora always fell asleep soon after screaming her lungs out with Dax, but tonight she was wide awake and attentive. She put her elbow down on the bed and propped her head up, still catching her breath. Her face was a happy, ruddy mess as she looked at Dax and they both had a giggle.

"Look at you," Dax teased. "You usually pass out after I've had my way with you."

Noora smiled and slowly shook her head. "Guess you'll just have to have your way with me again."

"Can you give me, like, 10 minutes? I ain't in my 20s anymore."

"Tell you what," Noora said. "I'll give you 15 minutes."

Dax smiled, put a hand on her hip and slid it up her side. "Excited about tomorrow?" he asked.

"Oh my god, yes!" she said. "I think that's why I'm still awake. Excited to get back home. Well, not *home* home but just knowing we'll be back in the solar system. I don't know, I used to think Saturn was so far away, now it feels like it's next door."

Dax laughed. "It does, doesn't it?"

"Think we'll get some shore leave on Earth?" Noora asked.

"Dear god, I hope so."

"I was thinking," Noora said. "If we're able to get to Earth in time, would you like to come to my place for Christmas?"

"Christmas in Finland, huh?" Dax said. "Sounds cold."

"I mean, yeah, we have like two days of summer there. The rest is all winter. But we love our saunas, so we'll keep you warm."

"I'd love to," Dax said.

"I wouldn't want to steal you from *your* family, though," Noora said.

"No, it's okay. Christmas with them is, well it's intense. Maybe do Christmas at your place then fly to Texas for New Year's?"

Noora smiled. "That would be great."

Dax smiled back. He pulled her in and held tightly. "I love you."

"I love you, Dax," she said, feeling safe in his arms. "Has it been 15 minutes yet?"

"Oh fuck off, it hasn't even been five!" Dax teased.

Noora laughed. "Hey, I'm thirsty. You thirsty? Wanna head to the mess?"

"Let's do it."

Gideon strolled into the mess hall. He saw Kiwi pouring herself some coffee.

"What are you doing up?" he asked. "Figured you'd be passed out with a bottle in your room by now."

"I'll have you know I've barely been drinking since we left Gliese," Kiwi said. "Been going to bed sober, waking up sober, did you know you could do that? Because no one told me."

"Well no wonder you're still awake, pounding down coffee like that," Gideon said. He found a bottle of blended Scotch and poured himself a measure. He offered some to Kiwi.

She shook her head. "No thanks," she said, and found a seat at a table.

Gideon sat down with her.

"Think they'll be surprised to see us so soon?" Kiwi asked. "We're only like a day behind them. They'll probably just have docked at Titan by the time we show up."

"Yeah, it'll be good. We'll give Jack shit about his inferior navigation skills. It'll be nice to see them."

"It'll be nice to see anybody," Kiwi said, sipping her coffee. "Not that I don't love you guys, but Jesus, 10-plus-weeks on this boat and I'm feeling a little claustrophobic."

"You and all of us, love. Cheers."

"Cheers!"

They clinked cups.

"So, we getting any shore leave?" Kiwi asked.

Gideon nodded. "We'll see what Braxton's investors want us to pick up at Titan, then I'll make a point to them that between flying out to Gliese, unloading everything and setting the colony up, and then flying back, we've been out for over half-a-fucking-year."

"We should be able to get to Earth in time for Christmas!" Kiwi said.

"Yeah, we should."

"You gonna spend time with family?" Kiwi asked.

"Erm," Gideon hesitated. "Doubt it. I made it back to my hometown for some shore leave before we left, and I don't know, still a beautiful place but I think my heart left it behind a while ago."

Kiwi smiled. "Look at you, Mr. Irony. Leave the Isle of Skye just to fly a ship you named the *Isle of Skye*."

Gideon smiled and took another sip.

"No family you wanna see?" Kiwi asked.

Gideon shook his head. "Nah, fuck'em," he said, to Kiwi's surprise. "Bunch of money grabbers. I lettem take everything they wanted from our inheritance, then I buggered off."

Kiwi's eyes widened. "Well shit," she said, raising her coffee mug. "To not having dysfunctional family in your life anymore. Goddamn, I know what that means."

Gideon had a laugh, raised his glass, and touched Kiwi's mug again.

"But seriously," Kiwi said. "Come with me to Wisconsin. My grandparents love you already, they'd be happy to have you, you can head to Chicago if you want some city life, it'll be great."

Gideon smiled and felt warmed by Kiwi's offer. "You know, I'm gonna take you up on that. Though don't know if I wanna revisit Chicago. That fucking casserole they call a pizza would give an elephant indigestion."

"Well you can ignore what they call pizza down there," Kiwi said. "We can focus on getting you laid."

"No shit," Gideon admitted, the Scotch having loosened his tongue. "I could go for a good shag. Been too long."

"Same," Kiwi said. "I'm ready to grab the first two welders I see on Titan and tell them to spit roast me."

Gideon spit some Scotch back into his glass.

"What!"

"For the love of Christ," Gideon said. "I don't wanna think about you getting spit roasted!"

"Well I'm sorry if we're both horny in our own way, okay?"

Gideon sighed. "Well at least Dax and Noora have each other."

"Yeah no shit," Kiwi said. "Happy for them, though. They're probably fucking like rabbits right now."

Gideon held up his Scotch for another salute. "To shagging like rabbits. May we both find that sometime soon."

"Amen," Kiwi said, clanking his glass yet again. "Don't worry, American girls love a Scottish accent. I can drop you off at the first bar we see in Chicago and you'll be knee-deep in the puss in like three seconds."

Gideon spit out another sip of Scotch, blurting out a laugh.

Dax and Noora entered the mess, both loosely clad in their pjs, both still euphoric. They smiled and waved at Gideon and

Kiwi.

"Oh hey," Noora said, still a giddy, ruddy mess. "You guys are still up, too?"

"Hey," Dax said, keeping it short, but unable to hide an uncharacteristic smile.

"Hey you two," Kiwi said, before whispering to Gideon, "Yeah, like I said, they're fucking like rabbits."

Gideon hid a laugh.

Dax poured himself some ice water. Noora made herself some herbal tea. When they were done, they joined their crewmates.

Philly Cheesesteak sauntered in from an open vent and jumped up on the table, taking a long stretch and yawn.

"What, you can't sleep either, Philly boo?" Kiwi asked.

Philly Cheesesteak blinked his eyes.

"You guys excited for tomorrow?" Noora asked.

"Relieved, excited, relieved," Gideon said. "Did I say relieved?"

"Be relieved if we get some shore leave on Earth," Dax said.

Kiwi scowled. "Huh. Dax actually wanting to be around people? Never thought I'd see the day."

"We all have our faults," Dax said.

"By the way," Gideon said. "Was just telling Kiwi that as soon as we're done on Titan I'm telling Braxton and his investors that we're headed to Earth."

"I hope they're gonna be okay with that," Noora said.

"We're going to Earth," Gideon said bluntly. "Right now we're the only two ships they've got, and I'll bet the Philly's crew were even more eager for a change of scenery than we are."

"No shit," Kiwi agreed. "Christ, any change of scenery would be great."

"No kidding," Dax said. "I'm even ready to go clubbing with you on Titan, Kiwi."

Kiwi scowled again. "Who are you and what've you done with Dax?"

That got a giggle out of everyone.

Noora yawned, triggering a yawn from everyone else. "Well," she said, getting up. "I'm gonna head to bed. See you guys in the morning, then?"

"I'm right behind you," Dax said.

"Sleep well, guys," Kiwi said.

"Set your alarms," Gideon said. "We're due to drop out of vector space nice and early."

Philly Cheesesteak licked his chops.

Lt. Marshall had been up most of the night making sure his capture of the Philadelphia and its crew was complete.

His outpost didn't exactly have a brig to throw all of them into, so they rigged an unused, airlocked safety bunker and threw all of them in there.

But not before interrogating Thomas.

Marshall had been civil with the *Philadelphia's* captain, and had even apologized before injecting him with truthinol before asking his questions.

"Please understand," Marshall had said in his proper English. "I know things are contentious between us at the moment, but my orders were to capture you alive, and I need to know you're telling me the truth so that I can keep you alive."

He got access to the *Philadelphia's* systems. He got the nature of their mission. And he got the names of the *Isle of Skye* crew. Gideon the captain, Dax the engineer, Kiwi the technician, and Noora the sniper/navigator.

He even learned in Thomas's truthinol trance that he had a fondness for Kiwi, and got more details about their liaisons than he wanted to hear. Still, the information could come in handy.

He also got the *Isle of Skye's* defensive capabilities and knew to be careful. Apparently they had some powerful, converted auto-cannon that fired rounds at impossible relativistic speeds, and could hit targets thousands of kilometers away.

He would need to be much more careful this time.

He also learned they were about a week behind the *Philadelphia*. At least he'd have a chance to plan ahead this time.

Despite his lack of sleep, he was up at 05:30, his normal time. He retrieved his coffee, sat down in his chair in the command center, and reviewed yesterday's reports.

At 06:07, he got a communication from Titan station.

"Chief," Marshall said. "Bright and early. To what do I owe the pleasure?"

"*Marshall,*" a groggy Chief Egan greeted. "*You're not gonna believe this, but we just got a ping from the Isle of Skye. They're already in-system and on their way here. Only a few hours away.*"

Marshall wanted to scream a series of expletives, but he never lost his English composure. Knowing his commanding officer wouldn't have a solution, he offered one immediately. "Well, that's faster than anticipated, isn't it sir? Why not proceed with what's already worked? Tell them their next shipment is here on Enceladus, have them come straight here, and I'll try what we did yesterday. Shouldn't be a problem, sir."

"*I like it, Marshall,*" the Chief said. "*Will be in touch.*"

Marshall closed the line, flaring his teeth. They were supposed to be a week away, not a day. He thought about interrogating Thomas again, but knew he didn't have time.

On a hunch, he called up what he could about the *Isle of Skye* in Ralston's database.

After about ten seconds he spotted something. His eyes widened, and he immediately rang the Chief back.

"*Marshall, what's up? I was just about to contact the Isle of Skye.*"

"Sir! Whatever you do, do *not* tell them we're from Ralston! Have you looked them up in our own database, sir?"

"*Well no, haven't gotten around to it. Why, what'd ya find?*"

Marshall was ready to destroy his console. Of *course* his Chief hadn't bothered with something so basic. The incompetence out here around Saturn, hell in the entire company, was unparalleled. "Sir, if you check the database, you'll see Ralston had a contract out on them last year, looks like a year and a half ago, or so. And erm, sorry still reading through the file, looks like we were hired to capture them, but they damn near destroyed the *Sentinel* in the process, then Ralston decided it was too much trouble, and canceled the contract."

"*You think the Isle of Skye crew would even notice?*" Chief Egan said.

Marshall could feel his brain cells committing suicide just listening to his boss. "We simply can't take the chance, sir," he said. "They probably did their homework on the *Sentinel* and know to stay the hell away from us. Just, I don't know, make up something about being an independent contractor. Use the same story as before, just don't mention the name Ralston."

"*Got it, Marshall. And good catch.*"

Winston Marshall leaned back, took a deep breath, and let his stress out slowly. Time was not a luxury, and he needed a plan now.

He took a gulp of coffee, hoping the caffeine would provide the inspiration he needed.

He would have to do the same with the *Isle of Skye* that he'd done with the *Philadelphia*. There just wasn't time for another plan; be friendly, charming, subtly admit his frustration with his own boss to show some honesty, let them know he'd be excited to see them as they don't get much company out here, just like he lured the *Philadelphia* down.

And he knew the captain of the *Isle of Skye* was Scottish. Good chance for an endearing English vs. Scottish joke.

He immediately thought of his own accent. It was too proper, too refined, and it would sound too posh for an independent outpost. Americans had no idea, but a Scotsman could tell the difference. He'd have to add some cockney twang to cover up his King's English.

He would also have to change some details. No mention of Ralston, and no mention of his Lieutenant rank. He was just Winston, working the supply outpost for an independent contractor.

But there was still the *Philadelphia*. It was in a parking

orbit around Enceladus, and the *Isle of Skye* would notice it immediately. They would try to contact it first, and the lack of response would seem suspicious.

But he had access to the *Philadelphia's* systems, including their communications. He'd be able to tell once the *Isle of Skye* tried to contact them, and could ring them up soon after.

Still, they would want to talk to the *Philadelphia* crew, so Marshall would have to think of something.

He hit the intercom, summoning his staff to the command center. The incompetent lot, most of them wouldn't be awake yet, but too bad for them. This was an emergency.

"Fucking Enceladus?" Kiwi said over the intercom. *"We're going to the goddamn snowball closest to Saturn?"*

"That's what the slack-jawed American from Titan said," Gideon said from the bridge.

"Hey, watch your language," Dax said in his East Texas accent. *"I'm also a slack-jawed American."*

"Yeah but you're smart, Dax," Gideon said. "This guy, Chief Egan, just sounds clueless and, well, goddamn stupid."

"So we're just going to Enceladus?" Kiwi asked to confirm. *"Well shit, there goes my clubbing, goddamnit."*

"Yes we are," Gideon said. "Apparently that's where the *Philly* is, where Braxton is, and where our next cargo shipment is. Trust me, I'd rather be on Titan, but to Enceladus we go."

"You contacted the Philly yet?" Kiwi asked.

"Not yet, but about to," Gideon said.

"Let us know when you hear from them," Kiwi said.

"You know I will, love."

"'Ello there," a working-class but vaguely London accent greeted Gideon over the communication channel. *"You wouldn't be the Isle of Skye, now, would you?"*

"Now that we would, my mate," Gideon said, pleased at hearing an almost-countryman's voice. "I'm Gideon, captain of the *Skye*."

"*Gideon, great to meetcha, mate. Love the ship's name, by the name. Figured you'd be a Scotsman. You 'ave a, uh, video option, do ya?*"

"Of course," Gideon said, switching on the video call.

"*Ay, there you are. I'm Winston,*" a dark, chiseled, handsome face greeted them. "*Trust you've 'ad a long trip. Understand you've been out, like, 20-light years or so, that right?*"

Gideon was already charmed. "That we have. I, erm, I saw the *Philadelphia* is parked around you. I tried contacting them but didn't get a response. They with you on the surface?"

"*Why yes they are,*" Winston confirmed. "*Sorry, as you can probably tell, don't get too many visitors. Invited them down, and they're all 'ere. Guess they needed a change of scenery. God knows I would if I'da spent that much time on a ship.*"

"Any chance you can patch us through to Thomas?" Gideon asked.

"*Oh of course, 'ang on, they're all down in cargo. By the way, there's a shitload of equipment down 'ere for all of you. They just delivered it, didn't even tell us what is was for. Hell, Thomas thought you wouldn't be 'ere for another week! Anyway, 'ang on, lemme get 'im on the comm.*"

Gideon laughed to himself, waiting for Winston to patch him through to Thomas.

"*Ehhh, shit,*" Winston said. "*Of fucking course, intercom problems again. You know, I'm sorry, can I ask, is this channel secure?*"

"Yes, it's secure," Gideon said.

Winston lowered his voice to a whisper, as if that mattered over a secure channel. "*Can I just give you some advice? Don't get hired by an independent contractor. That Chief from Titan sticks me 'ere with facilities that don't work and barely have any staff. Anyway, our intercom is down, AGAIN.*"

Gideon laughed again. "That's all right. Thomas has his

phone with him, I'm sure. We can call him directly."

"Oh, of course!" Winston said. *"Can't believe I didn't think of that. I know they're all quite busy down there, taking stock of everything, so don't be surprised if he doesn't pick up. By the way, are you planning on flying down 'ere? Like I said, we don't get much company. The whole crew's welcome, by the way."*

Gideon didn't hesitate. "That sounds lovely," he said. "We're only about 15 minutes from a parking orbit."

"Roger that," Winston said. *"Fly on down when you're ready. Again, everyone's invited. I'll pick up Thomas on the way to the hangar. He and I will meet you when you land. In the meantime, I'll put you in touch with my flight tower."*

"Roger that, and thank you, Winston," Gideon said. "Looking forward to it."

As soon as they hung up the line, Kiwi chimed in from engineering. She had been listening the whole time.

"That's odd, don't you think, Gideon?"

Gideon rolled his eyes. He wasn't in the mood for Kiwi's attitude, and just wanted to get the hell off his own ship. Even a frozen outpost would do. "What's odd, Kiwi?"

"Everyone from the Philly is down there and we can't get in touch with them."

Gideon sighed. "Yeah, we talked about this last night. They were probably more antsy to get off the ship than we are. Besides, if there's a ton of cargo down there that's unlabeled, Winston's right that they're too busy to pick up."

There was silence from Kiwi's end.

"So, I take it you're coming with the rest of us?" Gideon asked.

"Yeah, sorry," Kiwi said. *"You're right. Meet you guys at the dropship?"*

"Be there in 20 minutes."

Kiwi cut the intercom with Gideon.

"You all right?" Dax asked.

"Yeah, sorry, it was nothing, just being paranoid," Kiwi said. "Look, I'm gonna head to the dropship. You good here?"

"Yeah," Dax said. "Just gonna make sure the engines do their thing for a parking orbit. Meet ya there."

Kiwi left engineering. She still felt off about the situation, even though everyone seemed calm. They were probably right.

Still, she stopped by the armory, grabbed a large duffle bag, and stuffed in a few semi-auto pistols, an auto-shotgun, an AK-style rifle they had picked up from Lacaille earlier in the year, and all the correct shells, clips, magazines, and round types needed. She also grabbed her power whip.

She made her way to the dropship, entered the airlock, opened the duffle bag, loaded each weapon to capacity, and stored all of it in the weapons locker.

She stuffed the duffle bag away and got to her preflight checks just as Gideon, Dax, and Noora came to the dropship bay.

"What've you been doing this whole time?" Dax asked. "Thought you'd have this thing fired up by now."

"Calm down, Dax," Kiwi said. "I'm excited to get off the ship, too. Anyone mind if I drive? I feel like stretching this girl's legs."

"Please, do us the honors, Commander Kiwi," Gideon.

"Oo! Am I promoted? Does that mean I can boss Dax around?"

"You already boss me around," Dax said, strapping in.

Kiwi giggled. "Noora, sit shotgun with me."

Gideon strapped in next to Dax. "I feel guilty saying this, but it'll be good to get off the ship for a bit." He looked up, as if talking to the *Isle of Skye*. "Don't worry, girl. We won't be long."

Kiwi finalized her checks. She was about to open communications to the outpost, but turned her neck towards Gideon and said, "And captain, you have that sexy revolver of yours on you?"

"Always do when we drop down anywhere," he said. "Why?"

"No reason," she said, opening communications.

"Enceladus outpost, this is the dropship from the *Isle of Skye*, requesting coordinates for landing, over."

"Oh, uh, yes, *Isle of Skye*, um—dropship, this is Ral—I mean, Enceladus outpost," the air traffic controller said with Lt. Marshall breathing down his neck. "S—sending you coordinates now, we're gonna have you land in our northwest hangar bay, over."

Marshall smacked the back of the traffic controller's head. "Southwest, *southwest* hangar you fucking idiot!" he scream-whispered. "Southwest hangar is empty!"

"Oh, um sorry, *Isle of Skye* dropship, our mistake, changing coordinates to our southwest hangar bay. More room for you to land there."

"*Roger that, Enceladus outpost,*" a young, husky-but-feminine voice answered. "*New coordinates received, estimating 15 minutes travel time. Will be in touch as we approach, over.*"

Lt. Marshall waited 30 seconds before flipping on communications himself and saying in his faux-cockney accent, "'Ey there, *Isle of Skye* dropship, Winston 'ere again, my traffic controller says he's gotten your landing coordinates to you? Sorry for his confusion, tough dealin' with incompetent staff, innit?"

"*Wouldn't know,*" the same woman's voice responded. "*No one's incompetent on the Isle of Skye.*"

Saucy bitch, Lt. Marshall thought. He needed a good riposte. "Heh!" he exclaimed. "You wouldn't be hiring now, would you?"

"*You guys get your intercom fixed?*" the voice asked. "*Captain Thomas or anyone from the Philly there?*"

"Oh yeah, but no, the intercom is still down. About to get down to cargo and grab Thomas to meet you at the hangar." Marshall searched his mind for a detail that might resonate with them. It quickly came to him. "Oh and by the way, Thomas mentioned over drinks last night that he was looking forward to seeing someone named Kiwi? So if she's on board there, let her know."

"*Oh,*" the voice responded with delight. "*Well you can tell Thomas that Kiwi is looking forward to him slapping her ass again.*"

Marshall smiled. This had to be Kiwi he was talking to. "And before I head to cargo, how many of you are coming down?"

"*Four total,*" the voice said.

Marshall clenched a fist in victory. Gideon, Dax, Noora, and Kiwi. All four were aboard the dropship. He had them.

"Thank you for that, dropship," Marshall said. "I'm heading down to cargo. I'll see if I can get Tricia and Braxton to come as well. My traffic controller will be in touch with you on the way, over."

Lt. Marshall closed communications and breathed a huge sigh of relief. He couldn't believe it. He was about to capture two ships in as many days. He looked to his controller and said, "Tell the gun towers to keep their eyes on the dropship as it approaches, but for Chrissake, tell them *not* to lock on to them. Do you understand me! Do NOT lock onto them!"

"Yeah, I—I understand," the traffic controller said.

"And do you understand *why* I'm telling you that!"

"It's, um, I mean yeah, because they'll detect the lock and know something's up."

"Amazing!" Marshall exclaimed, frustrated at how closely his traffic controller had come to giving them away. "Well then, explain to all four towers in painful detail that they are not to lock onto that dropship, and if they see anything amiss, they are only as a last resort to manually fire a disabling EMP shot. Do you understand?"

"I—I understand, sir."

"Manually, with no lock on!" Marshall emphasized. "Do you *still* understand!"

"Y—yes, sir!"

"Bloody amazing!" Marshal exclaimed, storming off. He knew he was rough on the man, but he needed to put the fear of God in him to make sure his orders were clear. He made his way to the southwest hangar. He couldn't bring Thomas nor anyone else with him, so he would go alone, wait to make sure they landed in the hangar bay, introduce himself in person, lead them to "cargo" where "Thomas was," and capture them there, where 15 armed men were already waiting.

As confident as he was in his second capture, there was one detail he had forgotten.

Having been stationed here for long enough, he hadn't remembered the massive RALSTON logo painted on the outside of all the hangar bays.

"Enceladus outpost, this is the *Isle of Skye* dropship," Kiwi said. "Approaching southwest hangar bay, requesting clearance to land, over."

"*Oh, um, yes Isle of Skye dropship, we're just finishing depressurizing the hangar before we open the bay doors. Please standby, over.*"

"Man," Kiwi said, after the channel closed. "Why does that asshole sound so nervous?"

"Well, you *can* be kind of intimidating, Kiwi," Noora jested.

Kiwi smiled at her friend. She hovered the dropship 100 meters above the hangar bay door, and switched her keel side cameras on. This side of Enceladus was facing the sun, and the hangar bay door reflected back clearly.

Kiwi saw the door, and her stomach dropped. The same logo she'd seen hundreds of times after logging into the database Jason had given them reflected onto the cameras.

RALSTON

"Fuck! Fuck *fuck FUCK!*" she screamed, trying to pull the dropship up as the hangar bay doors opened.

"What!" shouted Noora.

"What!" shouted Dax.

"What!" screamed Gideon.

Kiwi ignored all of them, desperate to escape. She screamed

at the dropship instead. "Come on, *faster* you little bitch!"

"Kiwi what the fuck are you doing!" Gideon demanded.

"*PULL UP FASTER YOU FUCKING CUNT!*" Kiwi screamed at the dropship, desperate for altitude.

Just as a focused EMP shot hit them.

"The hell was that!" Noora exclaimed.

"I *knew* it!" Kiwi screamed. "I *fucking* knew it! Hang on, everyone! This isn't gonna be a soft landing!" Her navigation system was shot, and there was only one way down: into the hangar bay.

She skipped the fly-by-wire system and went for the mechanical backups, which felt like wearing boxing gloves while trying to navigate. She aimed the dropship manually, and popped the thrusters at the right time to make their landing into the hangar bay as soft as possible.

It was still rough.

"God*DAMMIT!*" Kiwi exclaimed.

"What happened? Why did they shoot us down?" Gideon asked, unstrapping himself.

"It's Ralston!" Kiwi said. "Fucking *RALSTON!* Their goddamn logo was on that fucking hangar bay door! Those fuckers tried to capture us last year, and now they've finally fucking done it!"

Gideon, Dax, and Noora all dropped their jaws, remembering the name.

"Oh, Jesus," Dax said.

"Oh, shit," Gideon said.

"Oh, fuck," Noora said.

The hangar bay doors closed above them. They were trapped, but they still had time for the bay to re-pressurize.

"All right," Noora said, getting out of her seat. "What do we do?"

"I stashed a bunch of weapons in the locker," Kiwi said, getting out of her seat and scrambling under the console. She got to unscrewing the panels to see what she could repair. "Go help yourselves."

"Kiwi, need any help?" Dax asked.

"I'm good," she said. "Just go grab a shotgun or something."

Dax went to the weapons locker and grabbed the auto-shotgun.

Noora joined him, grabbing the AK-style rifle.

Kiwi got the panel off and started rooting around the guts of the console to see if she could repair it. "Go," she said. "Shoot anything that comes at us. I'll see what I can fix."

Gideon cycled his twin-cylinder revolver and snapped it shut. "Ready, gang?"

Dax switched the safety off of his auto-shotgun. "Ready, captain."

Noora racked the slide on her AK rifle. "Ready, captain."

They opened the dropship's airlock and stormed the bay.

"*Give'em hell, boys!!*" Kiwi screamed.

About the Author's Cat

Josh's sketch of Philly Cheesesteak on the back of this book, and on the back of the first *Isle of Skye* book, is based on his cat Harley. She enjoys sleeping on his shoulder and chasing bottle caps.

Voyage of the Skye is his second novel. He's currently writing book three in the *Isle of Skye* series.

Book three will be titled *Gunship of the Skye*.